SHAMKA FOR THE CITY

To Carlos,
With the very
best of well wishes
James 10/1/05

SHAMKA FOR THE CITY

J. C. APPIAH, Jr

JANUS PUBLISHING COMPANY
London, England

First Published in Great Britain in 2002 by
Janus Publishing Company Ltd,
76 Great Titchfield Street,
London W1P 7AF

www.januspublishing.co.uk

**British Library Cataloguing-in-Publication Data
A catalogue record for this book
is available from the British Library**

ISBN 1 85756 507 X

Typeset in 10.5pt Baskerville
By Chris Cowlin

Cover Design Ray Fraser (Acidtest Design)

Printed and bound in Great Britain

I would like to express my sincere thanks to my daughter Dinah and her husband Alex, for their moral and material support during the course of this work. I am also grateful to James McCreadie, Jane Williams and Janet Larke for reading the original manuscript and for their encouragement along the way.

*For my American mother, Betty Anderson
and in memory of my American father, John Anderson.*

CHAPTER ONE

He sat in his car outside his own front door, unwilling to leave the warmth and face the relentless rain outside. Inside the house his wife and family were waiting, but tonight, unlike other nights, he was afraid. How was he going to explain what had happened. Doctor Simon Carter was afraid and he was not used to feeling this way.

Flinging open the door he ran the short distance from the car to the front door. The rain, which was now coming down in sheets, seemed to have found its own rhythm and played a staccato against the large glass windows and the roof of the house. As always, his mind was separating tomorrow's activities into slots. All through medical school, he had followed this extraordinary habit of organizing things in his head, before crosschecking them against his diary and then making sure that allowances were made for eventualities. Tonight, however, he could not get his mind off the terrible embarrassment he had felt when the two men had come to see him at the hospital. He would have to tell his wife. But how? And most importantly, when? He could hear the chatter between the two children and his wife in the kitchen and cringed at the prospect of facing them across the dining table this evening. Simon Carter loved his family. He strode into the kitchen with false confidence, smiled at his wife and ruffled the hair of his son while at the same time bending over to kiss his daughter, Katherine, on the cheek.

'What a rotten day', he said as he pulled a chair to sit next to his wife.

'Darling, you are soaking wet. You'd better get out of those clothes before you catch cold', said Maureen Carter, rising to switch on the coffee pot. Maureen Carter adored her husband. They had been married for eighteen years, having met at the hospital where both Simon and Maureen worked; he, as a newly qualified surgeon and she, as a senior nurse. In between their hectic working schedules, they had managed to plan their family and were now very content with their two children, Katherine and John. The children had been born in the Carter's second and fourth years of marriage and, at their ages of almost sixteen and fourteen, they were more like friends than children to the doctor and his wife.

'Go on,' said Maureen, 'get out of those wet clothes. Your coffee will be ready when you come down. And by the way, there is a note for you by the bedroom phone.' Carter followed his wife's instructions, giving her a friendly pat on the backside as he walked past her. The children giggled and exchanged mischievous looks with their mother and watched their father disappear out of the kitchen. Prior to the doctor's arrival, they had been discussing Katherine's impending birthday on Saturday, two days from now, and resumed their conspiratorial discussion when they were sure he was safely upstairs in the bedroom and out of earshot.

'The gypsy at the farm said we could have the horse for next to nothing, Mum. I tell you she is the most beautiful horse you've ever seen', whispered Katherine to the other two conspirators. 'She is a two-year-old chestnut with a white face. Oh, she is so beautiful', continued Katherine. 'John and I stopped by after school to look at her.' Turning to her brother, she rolled her eyes and asked, 'John, is she gorgeous or what?'

'Now, now!' replied Mrs Carter. 'We'll have to hear what your father has to say about it before we make any promises. But if it'll make you feel any better, I am on your side.' With that olive branch, Maureen Carter turned her attention to the evening's supper preparations and sent the two children to continue with their homework.

At the age of sixteen, Katherine Carter was already seriously considering her future as a veterinarian. She was looking forward to the next two years of her life, because in her view those two years would determine which university she would choose and Katherine wanted nothing but the best. Unlike his sister, John at the age of fourteen was quite happy to enjoy himself with his friends and let life take its course. He was intelligent and conscientious and, although his grades always put him in the top five per cent of his class, he never felt the need to study any more than was required.

In the privacy of his bedroom, Simon Carter contemplated his family's future while changing into dry clothes and suddenly remembered the note Maureen had mentioned in the kitchen. He pulled on a warm, expensive sweater and reached for the note by the telephone. The message in Maureen's immaculate handwriting was concise. It read, simply, *Jack Dawson called at three this afternoon. Please telephone him at ten tonight. Urgent.*

For the first time in a long while Simon Carter experienced fear. He knew he would have to return the call. But what could he say? He had been a winner all his life and he could not fathom losing. In fact he had no idea how it felt to lose, because he had no concept of losing. He stared at the note again and found himself thinking about the two men who had visited him at the hospital earlier during the day.

* * *

The windscreen wipers swished ferociously in a serious contest with the driving rain as the large gray Buick turned on Carvel Avenue and pulled up in front of the dilapidated three-storey building. In the front seat of the car, the two occupants sat silently and puffed on the huge cigars. The driver switched off the engine. The sudden cancellation of power from the engine seemed to sap the energy out of the windscreen wipers. Like the arms of a flailing boxer, they swished for the last time and submitted to the rain. Victory celebration was spontaneous as water cascaded over the vehicle, shutting the two occupants of the Buick from the outside world. The dim, luminous clock on the dashboard read 20:57.

'Do you think he can come up with the money?' asked the driver.

'I sure hope he can't', replied his partner, feeling the deep scar in his cheek.

'I sort of feel sorry for the guy, Stump,' said the driver, 'you know, doctor and all.'

'When are you gonna learn that greed drives us all?' replied Stumpy. I hope we stitch him up good', he continued, filling the car with smoke from his cigar. 'The longer he takes to find the money, the more he has to pay,' Stumpy chuckled, 'and the more he has to pay, the more me and you make.' He cast a sneering look at the driver and added, 'Who says Stump ain't smart?'

Stumpy Lazarus was well known as one of the city's most notorious muscle men. He had grown up on the tough east side where drugs, prostitution and gangland-style killings were normal day-to-day activities. He could neither read nor write but, as far as he was concerned, that was a minor handicap so long as he could count the money he was

3

paid. Stumpy was a natural when it came to goons. Mickey Steiner, Stumpy's associate and the driver of the car this evening, was rather a different proposition. He was a good-looking, mild-mannered man of twenty-seven who had fallen on hard times when his parents had died in a car accident four years ago. Having had difficulty securing jobs, he had met Stumpy in a bar one evening and had been convinced that there was easy money to be made if he was not afraid to show a bit of brute force when necessary.

The two men finally decided that the heavy rain was unlikely to abate and stepped out of the Buick to feel the full weight of the heavy downpour. Stumpy led the way up the creaking stairs, shaking the water from his coat and hat. When they entered Jack Dawson's office at the top floor of the crumbling building, he looked up from the plate of spaghetti he was having for supper and spoke with his mouth full of food. 'That guy better call before ten tonight. Did you deliver my message to him at the hospital?'

'Yes mister Dawson', replied Stumpy. 'I think he was kinda shook up though.'

'That's the idea, that's the whole idea', repeated Dawson.

'Okay, boys, help yourselves to some spaghetti', he said.

The three men ate in silence. Dawson stared at the phone on his desk and mumbled, 'That son of a bitch better call before ten or he is a dead man.' While he spoke, Mickey Steiner glanced at the cheap ornamental clock on the wall. It registered 9.14.

* * *

Simon Carter sat uncomfortably at the dining table opposite his lovely wife and fiddled with his fork. Although he was hungry, he couldn't bring himself to enjoy the food on his plate. He felt irritated by the children's animated conversation and, for the third time this evening, looked at his watch. Maureen Carter ate her supper heartily and laughed and joked with her children, fully aware of her husband's unusual behaviour. Her instincts told her that there was something seriously wrong, but she was determined not to discuss her suspicions with her husband in front of the two children. Whatever it was, she was sure it could be discussed after the children had gone to bed.

Katherine Carter's only concern this evening was the chestnut filly.

All through supper, she was wondering when her mother would bring up the subject. She hoped her father would say yes when the time came. Katherine looked at her mother quizzically and all of a sudden stumbled on the name. 'Shamka!' Katherine shouted. 'I beg your pardon', replied Maureen. 'What was that again?' she asked. 'Shamka!' repeated Katherine. 'That's what I shall call the filly', she added.

Simon Carter had no idea what the other two were talking about but he maintained his silence and waited for the conversation to unfold further. 'You know how all the wonderful Arab racehorses have names like that', Katherine said to her mother. 'That's what I'll call her', she concluded.

'Call what?' asked the doctor finally, still unsure of the conversation.

'Oh! that's the name of Katherine's horse', replied Maureen.

'What horse?' the doctor retorted, feeling more agitated than before.

It was time for Maureen to support her daughter, and for Maureen that was not difficult despite the foul mood the doctor was in. 'Haven't you forgotten something?' asked Maureen smoothly.

'What are you talking about?' the doctor shot back, by now quite confused. 'How many children do you have?' Maureen asked her husband.

'Nonsense!' came the reply from the Doctor.

'No! No! Answer the question. How many children do you have?'

'Okay, two, at least as far as I know', Simon Carter replied.

'Ooooooh!' cooed Maureen and the children. 'Now, what's the date on Saturday?' asked Maureen.

'Good God!' exclaimed Simon, 'I had almost forgotten.'

Maureen knew she had won. She smiled sweetly at her husband and squeezed his hand. She felt sure that Katherine would get her birthday wish. 'You are forgiven', said Maureen. 'Now about the horse, it's going for a song, so you and I can discuss it later. Who's for some dessert?' she asked, moving deftly away from the table to signify the end of the horse episode.

* * *

It was exactly ten thirteen when the sharp ring of the telephone shattered the peaceful world of doctor Simon Carter. He knew instantly that the call was for him, realizing that ten o'clock had come and gone. He could feel an explosion in his head and almost choked on the cake he had just put in his mouth. By the third ring, he was already out of his chair and heading towards the telephone. He changed his mind in mid-stride and asked his wife to take the call and pass it to his private study. When he finally took the call he was trembling.

'Hello', said the doctor meekly into the mouthpiece.

'Doc! You were supposed to call at ten', said Dawson roughly. 'You wanna play games huh?' Carter found himself listening to the rain and waiting for the man at the other end of the line to continue.

'When I say ten I mean ten, not two minutes after. And you figure I gotta call you to chase you for my dough?' The rough voice of Dawson growled into the phone. 'Now, do you have the money?' he asked.

Stumpy Lazarus was enjoying himself. He shifted his weight onto his left leg, leaned against the wall and pretended to clean his nails with the long, shiny blade of the knife he carried as an accessory. This was going to be interesting. He knew the doctor was scared. And frightened men always found a way to pay up or they killed themselves. This doctor had a family and it was likely he would pay. He tried with some difficulty to work out his percentage of commission on the debt to be collected and concluded that he would settle for anything between two and three thousand. Not bad, just for roughing up a frightened man.

'I gave you thirty days Doc,' Dawson was saying into the telephone, 'and you assured me that was fine. You promised my boys this morning you were gonna call me at ten and now I am the one who's got to call you.' He shifted the phone from one ear to the other, 'Now, where is the money?'

Simon Carter had been listening to Jack Dawson's uncultured voice for the last few minutes without saying a word. He knew he would have to give the man a positive answer or do something desperate. He suddenly realized that his palms were wet and reached for a handkerchief from his hip pocket. He cradled the receiver between his left ear and shoulder and wiped both hands. His mind was racing as he searched for the right answer for Dawson. Finally, the words came involuntarily.

'Dawson', said the doctor, 'I know I gave you my word when I arranged for the thirty days.' He seemed to have regained some confidence and this was reflected in his voice. 'Obviously, it has not been possible, so I'd like to renegotiate terms.' His final words were drowned by Jack Dawson's infuriated screaming.

'You go to hell!' Dawson screamed. 'My boys will be at the hospital early tomorrow morning to collect and you'd better have the money, And I mean all of it. No checks, understand, no checks. And one more thing...'

Simon Carter did not hear the final words as the door of the study was flung open.

'Simon! You've got to come quickly', shouted Maureen. 'There has been an accident.' She had turned and disappeared from the room when she added, 'and please bring your bag.'

When Simon Carter reached the bottom of the stairs, his brilliant mind instantly assessed the situation. He could see the boy was traumatized. How old would he be? No more than thirteen, he guessed. The manner in which he cradled his right arm gave Carter the impression that the arm was broken. The blood on the boy's face seemed to be coming from a cut somewhere on his head. His eyes looked glazed as he stood in the doorway dripping. Just as Carter reached him, the boy buckled at the knees, collapsed in a heap, and fell forward into the doctor's arms.

The heavy rain had relented but was now falling as a steady drizzle. The porch lamps cast eerie shadows of the trees; shadows that seemed to dance in the puddles of water that had gathered in various areas in front of the house. Maureen Carter shut the door with the vision of the dancing shadows imprinted in her mind. John Carter rushed to his father's side while Maureen disappeared into the bathroom for warm water and towels.

'I know him dad', said John quietly to his father. 'He is the gypsy's son from the farm. His name is Kazeem.'

Doctor Carter worked in silence. He examined the injured boy's wounds, ensured his breathing was steady and proceeded to stop the flow of blood from his head. Within minutes of the boy being brought into the house, Maureen Carter had set up a 'mini hospital' next to her husband - bandages, syringes, antiseptic, splints, bowls of clear water, plastic tapes, scissors and other medical paraphernalia. They worked in silence, under the watchful gaze of their two children.

Outside, the rain continued to fall in a steady drizzle, cleansing all and inflating rivers and ponds. God knows Gulver City needed cleansing.

* * *

Shamon Kazi squeezed the frail hand of his wife reassuringly and hoped the trailer would not slide any more into the soft mud. He looked up through the gaping hole into the inky blackness and felt the cool drops of rain on his face. The large oak tree which had fallen on the trailer seemed to have settled itself after the initial upheaval and now looked like a gigantic magic octopus with tentacles encircling the teetering trailer. He wondered how the boy had managed to save his mother from being crushed by the huge branch that now pinned her securely against the wall of the trailer. Shamon Kazi said a quiet prayer and thanked his gypsy ancestors for saving the lives of his wife and his son. He was afraid to move for fear of unsettling the precarious balance of the trailer, but, at the same time, he knew his wife could not remain in her present position for long. If the boy could move, he would get help. Kazi bit his lip and prayed some more.

* * *

On Carvel Avenue, Jack Dawson stood in the middle of his shabby office, red faced and angry. His words were for no one in particular. He held the phone in his hand and for the third time repeated himself, 'Can you believe this guy? He hung up on me.' He could not believe the doctor had the guts. There was no goodbye, no shouting, no sound. The guy just hung up. What irritated him most was the fact that he was still speaking when the doctor hung up. Just like that. In the twinkle of an eye the phone had gone dead while he, Dawson, was trying to collect his money. His left eyebrow began to twitch violently. There would be hell to pay.

Stumpy Lazarus was not very bright but he was calculating and devious. He watched Dawson's twitching eyebrow and realized that the doctor had gone too far. He figured he could speed things up if he could manage to impress his boss. He had to be careful how he handled this. Stumpy carefully sheathed his knife and slid it up his right arm, inside the sleeve of his jacket. He moved slowly from his leaning position against the wall and approached Dawson. The twitch was now more pronounced as he got closer to Dawson. Calmly, he took the receiver from Dawson's hand and replaced it on the cradle.

'Boss,' he said nonchalantly, 'you want we pay him a visit tonight?'

Dawson looked at him angrily.

'Nobody hangs the phone up on the boss, but nobody!' sneered Stumpy. 'You been good to the guy, Boss,' he said, spreading his arms, 'and the guy goes and hangs up on the boss like it was nothing.' Stumpy had a habit of speaking to Dawson as if he were addressing someone else.

For the first time since entering Dawson's office, Mickey Steiner spoke. He chose his words carefully, directing his attention to Dawson and deliberately ignoring Stumpy's presence in the room.

'Jack, the doctor is truly worried', Steiner said calmly. 'I am sure he is doing everything possible to come up with the money. I know, because I saw him this morning. Maybe what he needs is a little more time.' He had not moved from his sitting position at the edge of Dawson's desk. His arms still folded, he continued, 'He will be expecting us at the hospital in the morning and be scared to death, but he probably still won't have the money because he may not have had time to raise it. Sixty-seven grand is a lot to find in a short time. I say we let him stew for a couple more days and see what he does.'

Dawson looked at Steiner questioningly and rubbed his chin. He was thinking of his own position. He would have to explain to his superiors why the money had not been delivered. But he could also see the sense in Steiner's argument. Why scare the doctor any more than was necessary? A few more days would not make any difference. He would explain the situation to his superiors in the morning. But for now he needed to relax and get the anger out of his system. He collected his coat and hat, stood for a moment in front of the cracked glass window and cursed the rain.

Mickey Steiner knew Stumpy Lazarus was fuming. He waited for the door to slam shut after Dawson and raised his left hand to silence Stumpy before he could utter his first angry words.

'Look Stump, I know you were trying to impress the boss and I don't blame you', he smiled. 'But think. It's Thursday night and there are better things to do than to go chasing money in the rain - money we ain't going to get tonight anyhow.' He picked up his hat and straightened the brim. 'I figure we'll have more fun at the Hood. Are you coming?' Steiner winked at his partner, not failing to notice the smile on the hoodlum's face that seemed to accentuate the ugly scar in his cheek.

The Hood Acre sat imperiously at the outskirts of the city, bathed in bright lights. On this particular evening it shimmered like Aladdin's Palace. Using the pools of water created by the rain for special effect, it gleamed gloriously in its seclusion. The building had been designed for one purpose only. To provide entertainment for those to whom money meant little other than the name. It was the place to which Mickey Steiner directed the car this wet evening.

* * *

Seventy miles away to the north, Ben Swinton sat shirtless on the single bed in room 202 in the Claxton Motel. He drank the whiskey straight from the bottle and screwed up his face as he felt the liquid burning through him. How long had he been here? Two, maybe three days. He had lost track of time since he had checked in that night and left instructions at the desk not to be disturbed. He had paid cash immediately for a full week's stay and had tipped the desk clerk handsomely for his cooperation. He needed to think. In a couple of days, when his mind was clearer, he would telephone Simon Carter and try to figure some way to explain his difficulties. Simon would understand. Indeed he would, because that's the way Simon was. Swinton took another swig from the whiskey bottle and lit a cigarette, wiping the perspiration from his forehead with the back of his left hand. *What is the worst that could happen? They might have contacted Simon by now. Surely they wouldn't press him too hard. He needed time. Time to correct the mistakes, to straighten things out, to breathe.* He was feeling woozy from drinking all day. His eyes had difficulty focusing on the ashtray when he tried to extinguish the cigarette. Was it rain he could hear? He tilted his head back with the bottle and fell backwards onto the pillow and once again felt himself sliding silently through the dark tunnel.

* * *

Maureen Carter pulled the blanket higher to cover the boy's shoulders and realized that his eyes were open and staring at her.

'How are you feeling?' she asked.

The white bandage around the boy's head made him appear even darker than he was. Maureen had managed to tidy him up considerably and his eyes now had a gleam to them. He was a good-looking boy, although somewhat skinny.

'My mother', said the boy.

Maureen was not sure if the boy had understood her question and repeated it. 'How are you feeling?'

Before the boy could answer Maureen's question, Simon Carter was bending over him. He held his hand and felt his pulse, peeled back his eyelid and examined his eyes. First the left, and then the right. 'He'll live', he said simply.

Within minutes the children had gathered around the injured boy and John Carter was in communion with the gypsy. 'Kaaz. It's John, how are you?'

'My mother is in trouble, can you help her?'

Maureen Carter looked towards her husband, her eyes wide open with concern.

'What happened?' asked John.

'The rain', panted the injured boy. 'A tree fell on the trailer.'

'Where is your dad?' asked John.

'With my mother. I think she is hurt.'

Simon Carter did not need to hear any more. He was on the telephone within seconds. 'Yes, an ambulance and the fire department', he said calmly into the telephone. 'Number one Maple Drive. Yes, yes, Doctor Simon Carter', he said with some urgency. 'No there is no fire. Yes! The fire department, emergency! Mud slide. A tree, yes! Yes! Please hurry. Right, cutting tools. Yes, yes, good, thank you. Okay, we are waiting, thank you.' He replaced the receiver, looked at his watch and remembered his unfinished conversation with Jack Dawson.

* * *

Mickey Steiner eased the gray Buick into the large car park in front of the Hood Acre and surveyed the surroundings. He could recognize many of the cars and tried to put names and faces to the familiar vehicles. He manoeuvred the Buick past several cars, reeling the

11

names of the owners in his mind - *Joe Lazlo, Sam Templeton, Jack Maldini, Jake Watson and - Good God, this was a bad idea*. Why, of all the places they could have gone this evening, did he suggest the Hood Acre? He stole a glance at Stumpy Lazarus as he slid into the parking space between the green Cadillac and the shiny black Desoto and wondered if Stumpy had noticed. At the far side of the parking area away from most of the cars, almost in isolation, was the light blue Volkswagen.

She sat alone at a small table in the dimly lit corner of the immaculately decorated Blue Room. She had chosen her place with care, placing her expensive coat and handbag on the empty chair in a deliberate attempt to ward off any unwelcome 'intruders'. On the table in front of her was a glass of white wine and next to that a shining silver cigarette case. Her position allowed her a panoramic view of the roulette tables below her and the two entrances that opened into the club. She could see clearly through the light blue, curved, reinforced glass, while she herself remained almost obscure. There was no question about her beauty as she sat statuesque and confident in her powers to control and to choose. Rosalynn Brando knew that she was regaining control of her life once again.

On the ground floor of the Hood Acre, most of the customers were gathered around the four roulette tables which were arranged in the shape of a square in the center of the floor, with a gap of twelve feet between each table. On the outer fringes of the roulette tables, in a semicircular arrangement, were the black jack tables, three on either side of the plush carpeted spiral staircase which led to the second floor. The second floor housed the four coloured rooms, which were essentially very expensively decorated bars, each room decorated to complement its designated colour. At the top of the spiral staircase, starting from the right, in an anticlockwise arrangement was the Yellow Room, followed by the Green Room, Mauve Room and the Blue Room. It was from the Blue Room that Rosalynn Brando observed Jack Maldini. Above her on the third floor, the music was soothing as couples danced in the Fantasia. She knew that surrounding the Fantasia were the four soundproof Red Rooms, within which large amounts of money were lost and won every night of the week, except Sundays, on the Poker tables. She picked up the silver cigarette case, fished out a cigarette and lit it, wondering how there could be a fire on a rainy night like this.

12

Chapter One

* * *

The two fire engines announced themselves loudly as they sped past the opulent night club, followed by the shrill sirens of the ambulance moments later. The emergency vehicles negotiated the open country road with ease and were soon turning onto Maple Drive. Simon Carter and his son were already outside the house, both holding flashlights and wearing raincoats and plastic boots. Carter ushered his son into the lead fire engine and joined the ambulance. He instructed the driver to follow the fire engines. They sped towards the farm approximately two miles from the house. Within minutes, the bright lights of the lead fire engine illuminated the horrible scenes ahead. The driver gasped and took in the catastrophic display of what appeared to be an opening to hell.

'My God!' he exclaimed in amazement, at the same time pressing hard on the brakes to bring the huge rig scrunching to a halt in the mud. The second fire engine screamed to a halt next to the lead engine, followed immediately by the ambulance. The headlights of all three vehicles illuminated the gaping hole ahead. The firemen and ambulance personnel scrambled out of the vehicles, quickly followed by Doctor Carter and his son. Carter thought to himself, there are times in life when experts get so shaken when confronted by nature's activities that the human mind finds it difficult to engage the moment and make sense of it. This night and the scenes confronting the onlookers was one of those horrible moments.

Shamon Kazi heard the sirens long before he saw the lights. His fingers were intertwined within his wife's as he continued to reassure her that help was on its way. Her breathing had been getting shallower and shallower as time had dragged on, but Kazi was determined to save her life, even if he had to breathe for her. He had kept chanting throughout the evening, chants of prayer only he could understand. On occasion, he had made an attempt to move in the vain hope of freeing his wife but had been reminded immediately with a creak or crunch and a slight sway of the trailer; such reminders always persuaded him to remain still. His chants of prayer seemed to intensify with the reminders. He lay beside his wife, hand in hand, heart to heart, wet with a mixture of sweat and rain. He had never lost faith that the boy would make it and that help would eventually come.

13

Now, here he lay beside his wife, bathed in the bright lights of the vehicles outside and listening to sounds of people's voices, strong engines and the incessant patter of drizzle on the roof of the trailer. Help had come at last.

Outside the trailer, it was as if time had stood still. The engines of the two fire trucks droned and vibrated through the silence of the drizzle. The emergency specialists stood mesmerized by the extraordinary scenes confronting them. Simon Carter wondered how the trailer had managed to remain balanced, suspended as it was over the deep trench below. The large oak tree seemed to embrace the feeble trailer, a broken branch piercing through a window like a dagger. The tree on its side exposed its twisted mud-coated roots as if revealing long-held secrets and bared its soul to the world on this illuminated stage. Occasionally, gravel and mud-softened by the rain, shifted and slid deeper into the trench. Beyond the trailer, what used to be cultivated farmland was strewn with broken, twisted trees and branches like matchsticks.

'Okay, let's go to work.'

The booming voice of Chief Fire Officer Johnson jolted everyone back to reality. They had been on the scene for less than a minute, a minute that seemed like an eternity.

'Sam, turn the rig around', Johnson began issuing instructions.

'Pappy, use the emergency lamps on number two engine to give us more light. And start slinging cable.' He ran over to Carter.

'Doc, I don't know if anybody is alive in that thing or in fact if anybody is in it,' he pointed at the trailer, 'but I aim to bring it down in one piece.' As he spoke, he watched Sam turning the lead engine and trying to manoeuvre it into position.

'How do you plan to bring it down safely from that position?' asked Carter.

'That's easy', replied Johnson. 'Watch.'

'Pappy,' Johnson shouted, 'now bring number two engine round the other side. You'll have to drive way to the right, then swing it left past the tip of the trench and position the engine, backing in towards the trailer. Now be careful. It's soft all around back there.'

Little John Carter watched in silence. Next to him the two ambulance attendants were engaged in a whispering conversation. The firemen worked almost mechanically, confident in their ability, honed in practice and experience. It wasn't long before Pappy had the second engine positioned exactly at the spot where Johnson had instructed. He was already unwinding cable from the spool when he jumped from the cab of the rig to inspect his position. In between the two fire engines, which were now positioned approximately fifteen meters either side of the gaping hole, was the fallen tree and the trailer. The top of the tree, which in better days used to be its crown, now dangled in an array of broken, twisted branches within which was perched Shamon Kazi's trailer.

'Now, extend the ladders, thirty-five degree angles from both trucks', instructed Johnson.

The engines whined, gears clicked and engaged and eventually the extension ladders met above the trench and formed a shallow upside down V-shape over the broken branch that impaled the trailer.

Chief Fire Officer Johnson knew exactly what he wanted to do. He was sure it would work provided there were no sudden shifts of the mud. He gathered his men around him and issued specific instructions to each and every one of them as to how they should approach this delicate task. Over the years, experience had taught him that in situations of crisis, a leader's confidence could often decide the ultimate positive outcome or, alternatively, indecisiveness could lead to catastrophe. Johnson had always got the best out of his men. He knew they believed in him. He would never consciously put his men in danger or, for that matter, let them do anything he himself wouldn't be willing to do. With a final wish of good luck, he sent them off to bring the trailer down out of the tree.

CHAPTER TWO

Stumpy Lazarus stepped out of the Buick and rubbed his hands together. He was glad that Mickey Steiner had suggested the Hood Acre tonight. He walked around the car and waited for Steiner to lock the door on the driver's side and put his right arm around his partner.

'This is going to be a wonderful night', he said gleefully.

Steiner gently removed Stumpy's arm from around his shoulder and said jokingly, 'Hey! What are people going to think when you and I walk in there like this?' The two men laughed and sauntered side by side into the Hood Acre. Their entrance was virtually unnoticed as most people in the club were either too busy chatting or gambling.

From her vantage position in the Blue Room, Rosalynn Brando shook momentarily as she observed the two newcomers. She smiled to herself, lit another cigarette and picked up the half-empty glass of wine. She sipped the wine slowly, keeping her eyes on the two men. Suddenly her past came flooding through her mind.

Rosalynn Brando, formerly Rosalynn Sprice, had left university six years ago with an excellent degree in textile and fashion design at the age of twenty-two. She had been sought after by many top clothing companies and fashion houses, including the large department stores which recognized her potential and were willing to pay her extraordinarily high wages to help improve the image of their clothing and fashion accessory departments.

She had finally chosen Stein and Cramer, the world-renowned clothing designers, on an annual salary of $52,000 plus fringe benefits. Fringe benefits translated into a sumptuous two bedroom, fully furnished flat in the fashionable part of the city and a late model top of the range Jeep Cruiser. Life was as she wanted it - hard work, travel, interesting, influential people, money in her savings account and peace of mind. She had met and married Charles Brando at the age of twenty-five and was divorced two years later. The divorce had caused her work to suffer. Eventually, she had left the West Coast and settled in the city of her birth, lonely and confused, but determined to take a grip on her life and make a fresh start. It was here that she had first met Mickey Steiner six months ago and, once again, fallen in love. She was sure that Steiner liked her but she wanted more than that. She would make him love her as she loved him.

Down on the ground floor, Stumpy Lazarus was feeling on top of the world. He cupped the fifty-dollar chip pieces in his left hand and rattled them from time to time, trying to make monumental decisions like which number to place his bet on. He decided he would be patient tonight, which in Stumpy's case was like asking a pregnant saturated cloud not to unleash rain. He watched the little white ball bouncing around. Eventually the roulette lost momentum and slowed.

Twelve, twelve, he thought, watching the little white ball. After bouncing around a few times, the white ball finally rattled and settled comfortably on eighteen.

'Shit', Stumpy shouted, oblivious to the other people around him. He was getting excited although he had not placed a bet so far. He rattled the chips in his hand and watched the roulette spin again after others had placed their bets. Round and round it spun and, as it slowed, Stumpy once more wished for his favorite twelve. The white ball went through its usual routine and finally, as if to spit in Stumpy's face, bounced softly on twelve and hopped on to twenty-two where it rested.

'I'll be upstairs with Rosalynn', said Mickey Steiner, tapping Stumpy on the shoulder.

'What?' asked Stumpy, showing surprise.

'I knew she was here before we entered the building', added Steiner.

Stumpy turned in excitement when the wheel was spun again and placed ten fifty dollar chips on twelve. He had been distracted by his conversation with Steiner and placed the bet without thought. It was more mechanical than deliberate, instinctive even. He returned to his conversation with Steiner while the roulette spun round and round.

'Are you sure you wanna go up there?' asked Stumpy, 'knowing how you feel about her.'

'Yes', Steiner said simply.

He was about to turn away from his partner when a woman's shrill voice uttered the single word - *twelve.* Stumpy Lazarus returned his attention to the roulette table and stared at the white ball in its comfortable cradle. The number above it seemed to pulsate - twelve-twelve-twelve. His eyes shifted from the little white ball to the pile of fifty-dollar chips stacked neatly one on top of the other. The number below the stack of chips was mostly covered by the chips but he could see the top edge of the one and the curved top portion of the two. All eyes were on Stumpy Lazarus when Steiner leaned over his shoulder, tapped him on the arm and whispered to his partner.

'That'll be seventeen thousand to you.'

Stumpy Lazarus was incredulous and was still staring at the stack of chips when Steiner walked off to meet Rosalynn Brando in the Blue Room. Around the roulette table somebody whooped, bringing laughter and shouts of Stumpy, Stumpy, reverberating through the room.

* * *

Maureen Carter sat next to the injured boy who was now fast asleep. Beside her, Katherine Carter was quietly reading.

'Do you know him as well?' asked Maureen.

The suddenness of the question and the surprise of her mother's voice caused Katherine to look up from the book she was reading. She peered at the injured boy and nodded her head.

'Tell me about the gypsies at the farm', said Maureen.

Katherine thought for a moment and replied, 'What do you want to know?'

'Who does he live with?' Maureen asked, nodding in the direction of the sleeping boy.

'His father and mother', replied Katherine. 'Well,' she pondered, 'I am not sure exactly but I think they are his parents. His father's name is...' she thought for a moment and continued. 'His father's name is Shamon Kazi, but I don't know his mother's name.'

'How long have you known them?' asked Maureen.

'They have been there for over a year', Katherine replied, adding, 'I don't really know them that well, but I know John likes the boy and rides his bike over to play with him sometimes.'

'Isn't that where you saw the horse?' asked Maureen.

Maureen detected a fleeting sign of worry in her daughter's face when she mentioned the horse and quickly added, 'I hope all is well at the farm.' Katherine Carter sighed. When she lifted her head, tears were rolling down her cheeks. Maureen Carter looked at her

18

daughter lovingly and motioned her to come forward by holding up her hand and gently flexing her forefinger. In a moment, mother and daughter were in a tight embrace. Maureen consoled her daughter and whispered, 'Katy, because you believe in God, nothing can go wrong.' She stroked her daughter's hair and wiped away her tears.

'Your daddy and brother will be fine and so will this boy and his parents and the horse. I can promise you that.' They held their embrace, exchanging the love and emotion and strength-giving feeling that emanates from true love in moments of stress and difficulty.

* * *

Mickey Steiner strolled casually into the Blue Room, which was now filling up with couples who were settling down for an evening's relaxation. He removed Rosalynn Brando's coat and handbag from the chair next to her. He carefully hung the coat on a peg against the wall and handed her the handbag. Rosalynn eyed him coolly, thanked him for the bag and placed it on the back of her chair, letting it dangle loosely behind her. Steiner pulled the now empty chair directly opposite to Rosalynn and sat down across the table from her.

'What will it be sir?' asked the waiter, pen and pad in hand.

'Scotch and soda,' Mickey replied, 'and a glass of white wine for the lady.'

Steiner watched the waiter as he walked away to prepare their drinks and Rosalynn watched Steiner with her right elbow on the table and her chin resting in her palm.

'It's been a while', she said quietly.

'Yep', replied Steiner, turning his attention towards her.

'Your friend did well down there', said Rosalynn, referring to Stumpy's success at the roulette table.

'Yeah, pretty good', he replied.

The waiter returned with the prescribed drinks and a shining silver bowl containing salted nuts.

'Thank you', Mickey said and placed the ten-dollar tip in the man's hand.

'Thank you, sir', said the waiter, backing away from the table, tray in hand.

'So, what have you been up to?' asked Rosalynn.

'Just busy,' he replied, 'and you?'

'Not as busy as I'd like to be', she said. 'I've been putting some sketches together for a new project. I may have to take a trip to the Coast when it's all finished in about two weeks. Other than that,' she sighed, 'I am here.' Mickey Steiner looked directly at her while she spoke and thought how beautiful she looked, sitting there in the simple but tasteful black dress. Her medium length, dark brown hair was tied together in a bunch at the back with a simple black bow. Her earrings were tiny silver sea horses with a matching silver necklace which was daintily highlighted by the beautiful black dress. The dress itself was cut in such a way as to accentuate her well-shaped breasts. Her skin was tanned and healthy looking and on this evening she wore pale red, almost pink lipstick and very little make-up. Her overall demeanour seemed to reflect a lady of high quality and great intelligence. Mickey Steiner looked at her admiringly and appreciated her beauty. As he listened to her, he thought how much fun it would be to be in her company far away from here and wondered why he had tried to avoid her all this time.

'I may want to go with you,' he said suddenly, 'that is, if you wouldn't mind', he added as an afterthought. Rosalynn picked up her wine glass, held it up high over the table and waited until Mickey Steiner realized she wanted a toast and clicked her glass against his.

'Shall we drive or fly?'

'Drive', Steiner replied.

'Good', she was looking past him. Stumpy Lazarus was entering the Blue Room, a bottle of champagne in one hand and a 'plumpish' looking blonde girl on the other arm. They stood briefly at the entrance to the Blue Room while Stumpy searched the room for his partner.

'I think your friend is looking for you...' Rosalynn nodded her head in the direction of the door. Steiner turned just as Stumpy found him and watched Stumpy, champagne in hand and the girl in tow, approach the table. He would have preferred a quiet evening alone with Rosalynn. Instead, he stood up when the other two arrived and introduced the newcomers to Rosalynn.

'I'll pull up a couple more chairs, Mickey. We've got to celebrate.'

Stumpy Lazarus placed the bottle of champagne on the table and returned momentarily with two chairs. He arranged the chairs in such a way that Steiner had to shift his position around the table closer to Rosalynn, while he sat to the left of Rosalynn with the plump blonde further to Stumpy's left between Steiner and himself.

'Meet Jacqueline', introduced Stumpy, slapping the blonde on the thigh. He raised his hand to attract the waiter's attention and asked for four champagne glasses when the waiter arrived.

'How did you know I had seventeen grand coming?' Stumpy leaned forward on the table and wagged his finger at Steiner.

'I hope they paid you all of it?' said Steiner, winking at Rosalynn.

'Sure they did,' Stumpy replied, holding up a large wad of bills, 'but I want to know how you knew.'

Rosalynn Brando slid her right hand under the table and held the left hand of Mickey Steiner's in hers. She squeezed his hand gently and, with a pleasant smile on her face, she watched Mickey Steiner talking to Stumpy 'scarface' Lazarus.

'You had ten fifty-dollar chips on twelve, right?'

'Right', replied Stump.

'There are numbers from one to thirty-two, alternate red and black, right?'

'Right.'

'Add the zero and double zero, and you've got a total of thirty-four, right?'

'Okay', said Stump.

'So, you've got half a grand sitting on twelve. If it hits, they pay you thirty-four to one.' Steiner paused for effect and added, 'It hit so they paid you. Because they paid you, the champagne is on you.' They all laughed.

'Mind you, not all places pay thirty-four to one'. Mickey continued. 'Some will only pay thirty-two to one. The zero and double zero are there to keep you honest, you know, the house has got to always have some kind of an edge.' There was a loud pop as the waiter uncorked the bottle of champagne. He filled the four glasses and placed the bottle in the silver ice bucket half filled with ice and draped the white cloth napkin around the bottle and the top of the ice bucket. The evening was going well.

* * *

Chief Fire Officer Johnson stood next to Simon Carter with his arms folded.

They watched in silence as two firemen climbed the extended ladders, a fireman on each ladder. They climbed, dragging behind them the long cables which were being unwound slowly from both fire engines. When the fireman from the lead engine on the near side of the trench reached three-quarters of the way up the ladder, exactly in line with the top edge of the tilted trailer, he hooked the cable that he had been carrying to a rung on the ladder. He then belted himself to the ladder in such a way that he dangled free over the edge of the trailer without actually touching it. From the bulging haversack he wore behind him, he produced a power drill and with one hand gently holding the top edge of the trailer, he began to drill a hole. By the time he'd finished, he had drilled two holes in the roof of the trailer, approximately four feet apart, and two corresponding holes in the side. Two grappling hooks were passed to him from below to which he attached the cable, before attaching the hooks to the trailer, by inserting them in the drilled holes. He tested the hooks and cable for strength and signalled his opposite number on ladder number two to proceed. When the cables on both sides of the trailer were secure, the first fireman climbed to the top where the two ladders met over the broken branch and signalled Johnson.

'Okay, Sam, pick up the slack on one', shouted Johnson. Winches were in action again as Sam slowly reeled in the cable with Johnson's constant 'slowly now, slowly now' in his ear.

'That's enough One! Hold your position Sam', instructed Johnson. 'Pappy, take up your slack', Johnson instructed, conducting the activity by dropping his hands and slowly bringing them up, palms skyward and repeating the performance, all the while repeating 'slowly now, slowly now'. Finally, came the loud 'Stop!' After the cacophony of noise, the silence was palpable. The Chief gave his men a brief spell and thought out his next move.

Johnson knew that the broken branch that was impaled in the trailer was the main support that prevented the trailer from slipping into the trench. If that branch was removed, the weight of the trailer would shift to the connecting cables. He braced himself and issued his instruction to the men on top of the ladders to cut the branch.

The sound was faint at first, then it came again, slightly louder this time. It sounded like, 'we are here, we are here'.

The fireman held the chain saw in his hand. He had not switched on the power. He waited for a moment and stretched himself to be closer to the top of the trailer, straining to discern the sound he thought he had heard. There was no doubt about it, there was someone in the trailer.

'Chief,' shouted the fireman with the saw, 'there are people in there.'

'Ask them if they are all right', Johnson shouted back.

'Hello in there', the fireman enquired.

'Yes! yes!' Shamon Kazi's weak voice responded.

'Is anyone hurt in there?'

'Yes, my wife. She cannot move', replied Kazi. 'You see the branch in the window, she is fixed with that and she cannot move.'

'Okay, Pop, you hold on there, we'll get you out, no problem', the fireman reassured Kazi.

When the information about the trapped woman was related to Johnson, he thought it through for a while and knew that if the trailer shifted when the branch was cut it could easily crush the woman to death. He decided the cables he had strung up would do the job provided there were no more mud slides. They had to take a chance and hope for the best.

'Cut the branch,' said Johnson decisively, 'but do it gently.'

The chain saw roared into action when the fireman pulled the cord. Pieces of bark began to fly through the air, followed shortly by wood and sawdust when steel met wood. Simon Carter held his son close to him and braced himself for the unexpected. The steel invaded the wood, severing the lifeline to which the life of Shamon Kazi and his wife had dangled through the night.

'Timber!!' shouted the fireman, when he saw the branch was almost free from the fallen tree. In an instant, there was a snap. The branch separated from the oak tree the trailer sagged and fell into the bosom of the straining cables attached to the two powerful red rigs. A roar of approval went up from the onlookers, showing their relief. For Chief Johnson, the job was only partially done. He now had to get the trailer away from the trench and attend to the people inside.

'Sam, Pappy, remember,' shouted Johnson to his two trusted men, 'when we start this final stage, you two must really work together.' Johnson rubbed his hands together to dispel his nervousness.

'Sam, you reel in at the exact same time that Pappy releases. Okay?'

The two men showed acknowledgement and positioned themselves on their respective rigs ready to rescue the trailer and its occupants.

'All right boys, let's do it', shouted Johnson.

Sam began to rewind the paid-out cable at the same time that Pappy released more cable from his spool. The two firemen worked like clockwork, operating at exactly the same pace, and watched the trailer slowly moving towards Sam's number one engine. Branches and twigs broke off from time to time when they brushed against the moving trailer. Occasionally, the trailer got caught on a stout branch that had to be cut to allow progress to be made. When the trailer was quite close to Sam's engine, Johnson made him drive the rig forward. Pappy kept pace by paying out more cable. Finally, Johnson instructed the two men to set the trailer down. The men gradually loosened the tension in the cables and slowly rested the trailer on the ground. Out of the window protruded the sawn-off branch from the oak tree, which was still tightly wedged in the trailer, announcing its own phallic connotation to the relieved onlookers.

Simon Carter turned towards Chief Fire Officer Johnson and shook hands with him. 'Congratulations Chief and well done', he said and quickly turned and headed for the trailer. There were people injured in there, so his work was just beginning.

The rain, which had been falling since early afternoon, had now stopped completely. There was a cool-refreshing breeze blowing when the firemen opened the door to the trailer. Simon Carter and the two ambulance men stepped in gingerly and were confronted by some unusual scenes.

There was a gaping hole in the roof of the trailer, as if a giant hand had punched the roof in from the outside, bits of metal and wood jaggedly hanging downwards. In the far corner of the trailer, behind what used to be a dining table, now shattered into bits, was a middle-aged woman of about forty. She was in a strange position, pinned back behind the shattered table, with the branch of the tree seemingly lying across her lap. She was extended against the wall, neither lying down nor sitting, but securely pinned back by the branch without any room to manoeuvre. On the floor all around her were pieces of broken glass, and various sizes of twigs, branches and green leaves. Part of the floor had buckled, having submitted to the forces that had been exerted on the trailer during the night. Beside the woman stood a slightly balding short man of about fifty-five. He stood absolutely still, his clothes dripping wet as if he had just emerged from a pool, with his left hand on the woman's shoulder. A door leading into another compartment of the trailer had come off its hinges and fallen against some object behind it. Everything was wet.

'Chief!' shouted Carter, who had realized that nothing could be done until the branch was removed.

Johnson was beside the doctor within seconds. They would have to saw off the branch in sections. 'Pappy, bring some rope and a saw', said Johnson.

The two ambulance attendants led the short man out of the trailer, followed by Simon Carter. As they exited, the firemen entered and went to work to free Shamon Kazi's wife. The ambulance sped towards St Agnes Hospital without its sirens but only the flashing blue lights. In the back were Juliana Kazi, now completely sedated, and, lying on a stretcher, Shamon Kazi, one of the ambulance attendants and Simon Carter.

Back at the farm, Chief Johnson held the hand of John Carter. He inspected the trailer and thought of Doctor Carter's last words to him when the ambulance pulled away.

'Chief, I entrust you with my boy, make sure you take good care of him.'

Turning to his son, Carter had added, 'I love you son.' He had then jumped in the back of the ambulance and slammed the door before it sped away. Johnson continued his inspection, reflecting on the doctor's expression of his love for his son.

* * *

Maureen Carter paced the floor of the living room. She had settled the gypsy boy in one of the guest rooms where he slept comfortably with the aid of the small white tablet that Maureen had given him. Katherine Carter had refused to go to bed, promising her mother that she would do so as soon as her father and her brother returned safely. She now slept peacefully on the couch, covered with a small yellow duvet. Maureen looked up at the old antique clock and for some reason looked at her own wristwatch, as if she doubted the antique clock's pronouncement of time. Both clock and watch agreed that it was three forty-four in the morning. They had been gone a long time, she thought, hoping for the best but preparing herself for the worst. She paced into the kitchen and poured herself half a cup of hot black coffee. She brought the coffee back into the living room and sat in the rocking chair next to her sleeping daughter. Maureen gathered her nightgown around her and gave the belt a tug. She sipped the strong, hot coffee and watched her sleeping daughter. She thought of her husband's unusual behaviour earlier at the dinner table and decided to backtrack.

Maureen went into tape-recorder mode and played back the day's activities. *Who is Jack Dawson? The call that had come in the afternoon said something about urgent. The call couldn't have had anything to do with Simon's work because he could have been reached at the hospital. She knew of Dr Dawson, the gynaecologist, but his first name was Henry. Could Jack Dawson be a relation? He would have said so. Why was Simon so agitated during the evening? He seemed fidgety, totally out of character. The second telephone call during supper. Yes, it was the same voice. Why did Simon look so frightened? They had never had secrets from each other and although he preferred to answer some telephone calls in his private study, last night's call did not seem to fall into that category. What could it be that's got Simon so shaken?*

The tape recorder in Maureen's head was still playing when Simon Carter walked into the living room with his son. Maureen Carter almost jumped out of the rocking chair. She hugged her son, and then, adding a spice of 'womanly emotion', hugged her husband and kissed him affectionately.

'Tell me there are no fatalities,' she said to her husband, with her arms still around his neck. 'None', replied Simon Carter.

'The boy's mother?'

'She is at St Agnes, nothing serious, a few lacerations and a fractured sternum.' He continued, 'I feared the worst but it worked out okay.'

'Thank God', said Maureen, finally releasing her husband. 'I'll run you both a bath', she said and disappeared.

Simon Carter looked at his son and put out his hand. 'Shake, Partner', he said. The boy shook his father's hand firmly and looking straight at him said, 'I am very proud of you, dad.' As an afterthought he added, 'And Chief Johnson too.'

'Yes, he was very good, wasn't he?'

26

'Were you frightened at any time tonight?' asked the boy.

'Most of the time', replied the doctor.

'So was I', concurred the boy.

'Let's wash off this grime', said the doctor. They walked out of the living room together and headed for their respective bathrooms.

* * *

The Hood Acre was officially classified as a night club but in reality it was a twenty-four-hour establishment. Food was available at all times during the day or night and, although alcohol was only supposed to be served between the hours of eleven in the morning and four the next morning, no one seemed to pay any attention to the other seven hours.

Rosalynn Brando had planned to leave at around two this morning, hoping that Mickey Steiner would see her home safely. It was now three fifteen and she was enjoying herself too much to care. The four of them, Steiner, Rosalynn, Stumpy and Jacqueline, had moved from the Blue Room to The Fantasia, one floor above. The famous Fantasia was the one dance hall in the city that, like a magnet, attracted the rich and famous - politicians, businessmen, doctors and dentists, judges and high-powered lawyers, stockbrokers, bankers and financiers. Mixing on a regular basis with these rich and powerful were the gangsters and hoodlums and their women associates. The Fantasia had character. It had been designed for effect. It seemed to take everybody in and blended them all into one happy bunch regardless of the degree of wealth, power, creed, colour or sex. It was Jack Maldini's answer to the great and the good of society who had looked down on him because of his criminal past.

Stumpy Lazarus grabbed the hand of the blonde and practically dragged her from the table to the dance floor. He had never been a good dancer, but when he was in the mood he'd try anything and tonight he felt like dancing. Stumpy held onto the blonde girl and shuffled his feet clumsily. It was obvious Jacqueline was feeling awkward and uncomfortable about the way in which Stumpy was pushing and pulling her on the dance floor. She made several attempts to slow Stumpy down and to refine his dancing routine but to no avail as Stumpy, in an exhilarated mood, fumbled around the dance floor.

Mickey Steiner was intrigued by the lyrics of the music to which the dancers on the floor were merrily twirling and concentrated on the words. He took Rosalynn Brando's hands into his and gently stroked the back of her hands.

'Listen', he said.

Rosalynn listened, not fully catching the meaning of Steiner's intentions.

'It makes sense, doesn't it?' asked Steiner.

'What does?' asked Rosalynn.

'The song. The words. Listen.'

Rosalynn tuned in to the words.

Everybody wants to go to heaven but nobody wants to die - crooned the vocalist, the bass guitarist backing him up with some wonderful strings.

'Oh!' exclaimed Rosalynn, after she had taken in the full meaning of the lyrics.

'I see what you mean.'

'Why is that?' asked Steiner. 'I mean, why is it that everybody wants to go to heaven but nobody wants to die?'

Rosalynn Brando thought about Steiner's question for a long time - indeed why? The only answer she could honestly come up with was the answer that she eventually blurted out loud. 'It must be the uncertainty of the transition or passage that frightens people, not the dying.'

Steiner thought about the answer and nodded his head in agreement. 'Shall we go?' he asked.

'Yes', she replied simply. Rosalynn Brando was chaperoned out of the Fantasia by Mickey Steiner while Stumpy Lazarus continued to twirl the blonde clumsily around the dance floor.

CHAPTER THREE

The cool, early morning breeze, freshened by the overnight rain, blew refreshingly through the kitchen. Maureen Carter sat across the table from her husband and watched the lace curtain in the window fluttering to the dictates of the breeze. She held her coffee mug in both hands with her elbows on the kitchen table. She could feel the 'peace' that had settled over the house after the chaos of the night. The two children and the gypsy boy were now all fast asleep. She sipped coffee from her mug and looked questioningly but lovingly at Simon Carter. The question was written all over her face - she didn't have to say a word.

'I think it's time for me to explain', said Simon Carter simply.

'I just want to be of some help if you are in difficulty. I'd like to share the burden', replied Maureen Carter, her eyes moistened by the tears which she was unwilling to shed.

Simon Carter started slowly.

'It all began three months ago when Ben Swinton came to dinner. You will recall we had a wonderful time, but after he had left you said you'd detected signs of nervousness and worry in his behaviour. Well, he had a private chat with me that night. He was desperate and needed our help.' Carter sighed and drank from his coffee cup. Maureen sat quietly opposite her husband, arms folded across her chest and intent on hearing every word. She asked no questions; neither did she make any comments.

Simon continued. 'Ben's problems began with the incident at the hospital. You know the details so I will not bore you with that; except to say that "Obstetrics" are investigating the matter and it doesn't look good for him. It is possible he may be struck off.'

'But everybody knows the baby's death was an accident', said Maureen. 'An accidental umbilical strangulation.'

'Well, they believe Ben could have prevented the baby's death if he had been completely sober. There was excess alcohol in his blood as the tests showed', Simon countered. 'The fact is, all this had affected Ben so badly that he became reckless.'

'Oh!' interjected Maureen.

'That evening after dinner, Ben confided in me that he had become desperate after the initial hospital investigation had raised the question of excess blood alcohol. He had contemplated suicide at first, but had thought better of it and had decided to go out and drink instead.' Carter paused, picked up the coffee cup, changed his mind about drinking it and placed the cup back on the coaster.

'He had spent days drinking and gambling', he continued. 'Surprisingly, he had won a lot of money initially and got carried away by events.'

'How much is a lot of money?' asked Maureen.

'Two hundred and thirteen thousand dollars.'

'Wheew!' blew Maureen.

'Anyway, 'Simon continued, 'several days later he had lost all his winnings and was in debt by eighty thousand dollars. He had managed to pay thirteen thousand dollars to his gambling creditors and needed a further sixty-seven thousand. There had been threats, threats he believed to be serious involving his life.'

'My God, how frightening', said Maureen.

'Well,' continued Simon, 'he needed me, he needed us. He wanted me to stand as a guarantor for the $67,000 while he arranged to obtain the money from the trust fund his father had set up for him.' Simon placed his hands together and leaned forward prayerfully.

'I should have discussed this with you prior to signing the documents but I didn't want to worry you, I am sorry.'

Doctor Carter looked into his wife's eyes and discovered what he had always known - complete love and understanding.

'So, where are we now?' asked Maureen.

'The thirty-day deadline ran out on Wednesday night. Strange people came to see me at the hospital on Thursday morning. And you know about the telephone calls of course.'

'So where is Ben?' Maureen enquired.

'That's the surprise, I don't know', replied Simon Carter. 'I have tried on several occasions to telephone him; so far I've not been able to contact him. I am worried for him, not because of the money but because of the thought of suicide.'

Maureen Carter was a practical woman. She had been brought up to use her mind. When she was a child, she often played games of

30

'Solution' with her father. These were games she had enjoyed.

Colonel Parkinson, Maureen's father was an army engineer. The colonel had travelled the world solving engineering problems for the army. Because of his long absences from home, he had treasured every moment with his daughter and he had introduced the games of 'Solution' that he knew his daughter enjoyed, to allow them the opportunity to share each other while at the same time putting their minds to active use. Maureen could remember the bridges the colonel had built over ravines in south-east Asia; the rivers that were to be crossed by tanks and heavy artillery in the dead of night; how to find sustenance in unfamiliar territory, where good food and poisonous food were available side by side.

Maureen looked at Simon and smiled. The game of 'Solution' that she had enjoyed with her father was now going to be put to use to assist her husband, except this was no game.

* * *

Ben Swinton was not sure whether he was dreaming. The knock on the door sounded faint and far away. He opened his eyes and lay still, feeling every sharp needle that was pushed into his brain and other parts of his body. His eyes burned red and hurt as if they were boiling on hot coals. The knock in his head suddenly found its rhythm with the actual knocking on the door. He realized he was wide awake. The knock came again, now louder than before. He decided to answer the door and stumbled in the darkened room, tripped over a table and went sprawling head first against the door. When his head collided with the door, the little gremlins seemed to intensify the drumming in his head that had now become routine over the past few days. He struggled to his feet, using the walls for supports and finally yanked the door open.

The young man at the door looked familiar. Ben Swinton rubbed his eyes and tried to focus more fully, trying to remember where he had met the stranger. He leaned against the frame of the open doorway to support himself and filled his lungs with the fresh early morning air. The moist air tasted sweet and fresh.

'Yes!' said Swinton, staring at the stranger.

'I've been worried about you sir,' said the young man softly 'and

31

wondered if you needed anything before I go off duty.'

Memories of his conversation with the desk clerk came flooding back to Swinton. They had spoken for the first time on the night that he had checked into the motel. He could recall his request at the time not to be disturbed and remembered the young man's gratitude when he had tipped him. The man had seemed pleasant and helpful and had shown concern about Swinton's health, considering his drunken state.

'What day is it?' asked Swinton, running his hand through his matted hair.

'It's Friday morning, sir.' The young man looked at his watch and added, 'Five fifteen. I normally leave at six. It seems no one has seen you since you arrived last Tuesday night and I wondered if you were all right.'

'Thank you. I am fine,' Swinton replied.

'Can I get you anything before I go off duty?' said the young man, quickly surveying the dishevelled room. He could see the empty whiskey bottles littering the floor. Next to the pillow, the half empty bottle seemed to announce loudly the activity that had gone on in the room over the past couple of days and nights.

'I could get you some coffee,' the young man said kindly, 'and arrange breakfast before I leave.'

'Coffee would be nice.'

'I'll be right back', announced the young man as he turned away from the door and walked towards the main entrance of the small motel.

Ben Swinton watched him disappear into the building and shut the door. He fumbled along the wall for the light switch and illuminated the room with a flick. He sat on the dishevelled bed, both elbows on his thighs and head in hands. The gremlins were still there, pounding loudly in his head. He had to talk to somebody, he thought. He had sacrificed too much to throw it all away like this. There had to be a better way.

The coffee tasted strong and hot. Swinton always drank coffee black and appreciated the aroma wafting from the cup in his hand. He sat on the bed and watched the young man moving silently across the room. It suddenly occurred to Swinton that the man was making an attempt to tidy the room.

'What is your name?' asked Swinton.

The question froze the young man in his tracks. In his hands, he held the pair of shoes and the soiled shirts he had gathered from various corners of the room.

'Tom', the man replied. He piled the dirty clothes neatly at the foot of the bed and arranged the shoes on the shoe rack.

'I am sure your duties in this motel do not include cleaning rooms,' said Swinton, watching the young man, 'so why?'

The young man deliberately ignored Swinton's last question but instead elaborated on his answer to the first question.

'Actually, my full name is Thomas Bakersfield. Some people call me Thomas but I prefer Tom.' He emptied the ashtray and began to collect the empty whiskey bottles scattered over the floor of the room.

'And, no! My duties do not include cleaning rooms, Doctor Swinton.'

Swinton sipped the coffee more urgently and seemed to be enjoying it. The headaches he had suffered for the past few days seemed to have eased and the coffee certainly wasn't doing him any harm. He cradled the cup in both hands and sipped.

'You are forgetting something', said Swinton. 'My question was, why?'

Tom Bakersfield had somehow transformed the state of the small motel room to something more respectable. He pulled a chair and sat down.

'I have worked here for almost three years,' he started slowly, 'and I've seen and studied people as they come and go at all hours of the day and night.' Leaning forward, he continued. 'I could tell as soon as I saw you on Tuesday night that you were in some sort of trouble. Please forgive me if I am intruding but I think you may want to talk to somebody,' he drew in a sharp breath, 'and it might as well be me', he concluded, refilling Swinton's now empty cup.

It was as if the young man could read his thoughts. Swinton sipped the hot coffee and looked at the stranger. He desperately needed to resolve the problems that had been eating at him. It might not be a bad idea to open up to this young man. He looked at Bakersfield over the cup, sipped the coffee and made his decision to tell him as much as he could, but first he had some questions of his own.

'How old are you, Tom?' asked Swinton.

'Twenty-six.'

'And you've been working here for three years, so what did you do before that?'

'Joined the Marines after high school, served two years in south-east

Asia. When I returned home there were some difficult times until I met Marie.' Bakersfield paused. 'She is my fiancée, due to be married next June. She is the best thing that ever happened to me. You see, after Nam, I felt so confused I even considered ending it all.'

'You mean suicide?' asked Swinton.

'Yes, suicide.' Bakersfield showed embarrassment.

'Is that the reason for your concern?' asked Ben.

'I suppose it has something to do with it,' Bakersfield replied honestly. 'You see, when you've been through it, you can sometimes read the signs.'

'Was Vietnam that bad?'

'Let's just say that after my tour of duty, I didn't think life was worth living, until I was rescued by Marie.'

'I take it you are now off duty. Shouldn't you be going home to Marie?'

'Indeed, I was off duty at six,' Bakersfild smiled, 'and since then, time has been all mine.'

Swinton looked at the young man and decided it was worth sharing some of his problems with such a man.

'Up until about four months ago, I was a very happy doctor, an obstetrician.' Ben paused, clasped and unclasped his hands nervously, 'Until a baby died on my watch.' He picked up the coffee cup and drank; an attempt to settle his voice which was beginning to shake. 'It should have been a normal, straightforward delivery and it seemed so until the complications began. I did everything humanly possible to save the baby and the mother. Unfortunately, I only managed fifty per cent of the task, because the mother survived but the baby died.' Ben was crying.

'It's all right, Doctor Swinton.' That was all Bakersfield could manage to say as he watched the doctor.

'It was a little girl, a beautiful, little, dead girl', Ben sobbed.

Bakersfield produced a box of tissues and passed it to Ben Swinton who pulled two sheets and dabbed his eyes.

'Life can be so fragile', said Ben, blowing his nose and trying to compose himself.

'So what happened?' enquired Bakersfield.

'Negligence, incompetence, unfit for duty,' said Ben, 'you know the words.'

'But it was an accident!' Bakersfield sympathized.

Chapter Three

'No!' Ben said sharply. 'Not if blood tests reveal alcohol in your blood.'

'Are you saying you were drunk?' asked Bakersfield.

'No, I am saying there was a trace of alcohol in my blood, as shown by the tests.'

'Be honest with yourself,' said Bakersfield frankly, 'was the baby's death your fault?'

Ben Swinton glared at Tom Bakersfield for a long time.

'No!' he replied emphatically.

'That's good enough for me', said Bakersfield. He could feel the doctor's honesty and added, 'Why then are you torturing yourself? I have gone through what you are going through and I think I speak from experience. I felt the same sort of guilt when I first killed a man in Vietnam.'

Ben Swinton looked up at the young man. The man's eyes looked directly at him but somehow Swinton sensed he was no longer in the room with him.

'What happened?' Swinton asked, showing curiosity and interest.

'We had taken two Vietcong prisoners near Quang Tri after a fierce fire fight. We had sustained heavy casualties and everybody was jumpy. One of the prisoners shoved a sharpened bamboo stake into the kidney of our radio officer and escaped. It took the better part of an hour before I caught up with him.' Bakersfield was smiling. A strange, unreal kind of smile tinged with sadness. 'The Vietnamese was hiding in thick undergrowth. I wouldn't have seen him had he not coughed. Actually, I seemed to sense it rather than hear it. When I turned and levelled my M16 carbine, he slowly stood up and raised his hands. He was still holding the bamboo stake, covered with the radio officer's blood.'

Bakersfield laughed hideously, then added, 'I shot him, twice, close up.' He wiped his face with both hands. 'After that I turned and walked back to my unit.'

'What did they say to you when you rejoined them', asked Ben.

'No one asked,' Tom Bakersfield said simply.

'And you never told them?'

'No.'

'But that is cold-blooded murder!' Swinton shouted.

'That's what I told myself at first and for a long time after that.'

'What do you tell yourself now?' asked Swinton.

'It was war', replied Bakersfield. 'By the way, the radio officer died', he added.

'I think I understand, although I find it difficult,' Swinton said.

'I've never discussed what I told you with anyone, not even Marie.' Tom Bakersfield stretched himself and placed both hands behind his head. 'All right, so the baby died and they say you are guilty. Is that the reason for these bottles?' Bakersfield nodded in the direction of the empty whiskey bottles he had piled neatly in the corner of the room.

'That's not all'. replied Swinton 'I have been irresponsible. I got myself in trouble and let down a good friend.'

'Now, that doesn't sound good.'

Swinton then proceeded to narrate the full story to Tom Bakersfield. He told him about the gambling debt, his plans to use some of his trust fund to settle the debt and about the medical investigation that could lead to his possibly being struck off.

Tom Bakersfield listened patiently to everything that Ben Swinton told him. He stood up and smiled, 'I'll be right back with some breakfast. Tidy yourself up, and Doc, please don't drink any more, I think you've had enough to last you a year.' He walked out of the room and shut the door.

* * *

Shamon Kazi sat next to his wife's bed in the hospital and watched the nurse preparing her injection. He hadn't slept much, but he felt good within himself and in the knowledge that his boy was safe in Simon Carter's house and that his wife was now comfortable and in good hands. His spirits were high as he looked through the large hospital windows and saw the sun easily breaking through the sparse clouds that, after the deluge, had shed their defences and offered no resistance. He soaked in the rays of brilliant sunshine and with a smile on his face thought of his five horses in the field. It suddenly occurred to him that he had not had time to attend to them the day before, since the rain began.

Kazi got up from his chair and approached the nurse. He noticed his wife was still asleep, so he whispered his message into the nurse's ear, thanked her profusely and jauntily walked out of the hospital with one thing in mind. He was going to attend to his horses. Shamon Kazi stood in front of the large hospital and appreciated the rows of ambulances that were neatly parked in readiness for any medical eventuality. He looked almost funny in the borrowed, slightly oversized clothes that had been lent to him by the hospital and realized all of a sudden that he had no means of getting back to the farm. Undaunted, he started walking without considering the long journey ahead of him. He knew the way and guessed it would take him several hours of walking, although he had no idea of the number of miles involved, which as the crow flies would be about fifteen miles.

* * *

The shrill alarm clock on the bedside table jolted Jack Dawson back to life at exactly seven o'clock. He sat up immediately and let the alarm ring for a few more seconds before silencing it. He rubbed his eyes, stretched and rolled out of the bed. In the kitchen, he turned on the radio and switched on the kettle. The flat was small but unlike his office it was immaculately decorated, clean and tidy. Jack Dawson had never married, preferring the loose and convenient arrangement he had with the one woman he had been seeing for the past twelve years. On this Friday morning, he was happy to be alone. He parted the curtains in the living room and opened the windows to let in the fresh morning breeze that accompanied the warmth of the sun.

The pleasant voice of the female radio announcer commented on the soft music which was just tailing off and prepared her listeners for the next sequence of tracks which would follow after the seven thirty news interlude. Dawson increased the volume slightly, poured himself a glass of orange juice and with coffee and juice in hand settled down on the sofa and picked up the red folder.

The meeting was at ten o'clock this morning. He had already prepared his notes and knew all the figures, but he went through the file page by page to refresh his memory. He had used the same folder for several years, inserting and deleting the plastic sleeves that contained the sheets of paper as old accounts closed and new ones began. Each page showed a small passport size photograph, in color, at the top right-hand corner, the name of the 'client', as Dawson preferred to call them, followed by two addresses in most cases, although only one address in others, and a series of dates and figures. The figures were entered neatly in two columns. Under the column headed credits, the entries were in black ink and under the debits column, red. After skimming through all the pages - sixteen in all - he turned back to the beginning and read the summary sheet.

The soft, pleasant voice of the radio girl was back. Dawson listened, as the next song was given the necessary accolade. *'I promise you, you will enjoy this new song which has been scaling the charts over the past three days'*, she intoned, *'and think about the lyrics as you enjoy this beautiful song.'* She concluded the introduction by inviting listeners to call in with their views and rattled off two telephone numbers, toll free, of course. The song began quietly, with an instrumental opening and slowly built up in volume as the lyrics joined in,

'We are in a beautiful world and life is good to us. We have all the pleasures and a small price to pay. No matter how long we live, in the end we must move on. Is this all there is, or is there a heaven? Everybody wants to go to heaven, but nobody wants to die. . .'

Jack Dawson tapped his feet to the music and agreed with the radio girl that this song was indeed very good. He waited for the song to finish completely before he turned his attention back to the red folder. Dawson flicked through a few pages and examined the details on the sixth sheet. He rubbed his unshaven chin, peered at the picture on the page - a gray-haired, elderly, respectable looking gentleman of about sixty-five - and read the details:

Judge James C Colman
25 Appleton Mansions
Corsegrove Heights
Corsegrove 64007

The Federal Courts
The Federal Buildings
Room 36A

Date	Credit	Debit
03/16	$13,375	-
03/23	$10,000	-
04/12	-	$6,750
04/28	$9,220	-

Jack Dawson flicked through several more pages and stopped at the fourteenth page. On the page were two different pictures, one of Ben Swinton, below which was listed his home address and St Agnes

Hospital, followed by a series of dates and figures. The final figure in the debits column showed $67,000 and against that 04/12. The second picture was that of Simon Carter, followed by home and work addresses and the word *'Guarantor'*, written in capitals. He looked at the picture of Simon Carter for a long time and muttered, 'poor bastard'. Jack Dawson closed the red folder, finished his coffee and headed for the shower.

CHAPTER FOUR

Maureen Carter had not had much sleep when the soft alarm bells woke her at six thirty. She quickly got out of bed and reset the alarm to seven thirty for her husband. Her first thoughts were of the gypsy boy in the guest room. She quietly opened the door to the guest room, anticipating the boy to be still fast asleep, only to find the room empty. She entered the room, and was surprised by how little evidence there was of the boy's presence from the night before. The bed had been made, the pyjamas that had been borrowed from her son were neatly folded at the foot of the bed, and every item in the room was in its place. The only sign of the boy's occupancy of the room were the still damp, well-worn trainers which were against the wall. Maureen began to comb the house, from the children's rooms to the other guest rooms, upstairs and downstairs, but there was no sign of the boy. She decided she would have to wake her husband and drew back the curtains. In the middle of the spacious back yard, among the flowers and garden ornaments, sat the gypsy boy.

Kazeem Kazi sat in the middle of the garden, cross-legged and bare-footed, his left arm loosely beside him and the splintered right arm across his lap. He sat absolutely still with his back to the house as Maureen watched him. After several minutes, the boy lifted his head and looked up to the sky, then down again. He repeated this sequence for about five minutes, all the time watched by Maureen. Finally, he stood up slowly, and in the same place where he had been sitting, he did three full turns and jumped. Maureen quickly moved behind the gathered curtain as the boy turned and started to walk towards the house. She pretended she had not seen the boy's activities in the garden and showed surprise when the boy walked into the house.

'Oh! There you are young man, how are we this morning?'

'Fine Ma'am'. replied the boy 'I was just praying and it's okay that you watched.'

Maureen Carter felt slightly ashamed for trying to hide when the boy had turned, and, looking fondly at him, said, 'Thank you Kazeem.'

By the time the rest of the Carter family gathered around the breakfast table, Maureen had changed Kazeem's head bandages and re-splintered the broken right arm. He had completed his ablutions and was dressed in a pair of blue jeans, sneakers and a light green shirt - all borrowed from John Carter's wardrobe. He looked quite handsome.

'You'll be coming with me young man', said Simon Carter. He sipped his grapefruit juice. 'We'll take a proper look at the head and organize a cast for your arm.'

'Thank you sir', said Kazeem. 'John's mum told me about my mother and everything.' He may have been young and quite simple but the boy's eyes said it all. He was grateful and didn't bother to hide it.

Simon Carter reversed the car in the driveway and, with Kazeem next to him, waved goodbye to his family and began the journey to the hospital. He was thinking of the Kazi family and their present predicament. The trailer in which they lived had virtually been destroyed. He would have to have a word with the boy's father sometime this evening to see what could be done to help. As always, his mind was separating later activities into slots.

At the hospital, Simon Carter parked the car in his designated parking bay and entered the building by the side entrance. Over the door, the sign read *Hospital Personnel Only*. He entered the elevator, while holding the gypsy boy's hand, and said good morning to the two staff nurses. In the elevator, one of the two nurses pressed the button for the second floor and asked Simon Carter for the floor of his choice. He was thinking about the two visitors from the day before and the unfinished conversation with Jack Dawson and did not hear the nurse's question. The nurse repeated herself, looking rather strangely at Doctor Carter.

'Oh! sorry,' he came awake, 'four please', he said. The nurse pressed four and all four occupants stood in silence until the sound of the bell signified their arrival on the second floor. Carter wished the two girls a good day as they departed the elevator and the door closed. He folded his arms and observed the gypsy boy as they went up.

'I think it would be nice to see your mother first, don't you?' Carter asked the boy just as the elevator bell rang again to signify their arrival on the fourth floor. Kazeem Kazi's face lit up.

'Okay, come on then', said Carter striding into the ward, closely followed by the gypsy boy.

* * *

Rosalynn Brando parted the curtains and ushered in the sunshine. She stood fixed at the window and marvelled at the wonders of nature; the contrast between yesterday's very wet conditions and today's brilliant sunshine. She found herself reflecting on the question that Mickey Steiner had asked her and wondered if there was life beyond this. She turned her head when the strong arms of Mickey Steiner enveloped her and smiled at him.

'I hope I didn't wake you?' said Rosalynn, turning to face him.

'You should have'. replied Steiner. 'Don't you think it's selfish of you to keep a beautiful day like this all to yourself?' He kissed her, lifted her gently off the floor and wheeled round.

Rosalynn giggled, 'I feel as wonderful as I did when I was a child', she said.

'That's good', Steiner said with a broad smile.

'Let me make you breakfast.' Rosalynn tweaked his nose. 'I've wanted to cook for you since I first met you and this is a glorious day to do it', she said and waltzed into the kitchen.

Mickey Steiner settled himself on the comfortable sofa in the living room and picked up the glossy magazine on the table in front of him. He flicked carelessly through the pages and replaced it on the table. The picture on the cover suddenly caught his eye. He leaned forward, looked at the picture closely and picked up the magazine again. *Fashion Gazette*, he read the cover title, stared at the picture and began reading more closely. *Rosalynn Brando's designs stun the nation, page sixteen.* He turned the pages. Under the heading, *Brando captures the hearts of America's women, by Maureen Crompton*, the article covered Rosalynn's designs in detail, making comparisons with some of the most famous designers in the country, and finished with a brief on the designer, finally concluding, '*it is believed Charles Brando was utterly devastated by their divorce and is said to be seeking a second chance.*' Steiner replaced the magazine on the table and walked into the kitchen.

They chose to eat at the small kitchen table instead of the dining room.

'Maureen Crompton seems to think very highly of you', offered Steiner as he enjoyed the simple but tasty breakfast of waffles, eggs and bacon.

Chapter Four

'Who?' enquired Rosalynn.

'I just read an article in the *Fashion Gazette*.'

'Oh, that,' she said humbly.

'She said Charles was utterly devastated by the divorce and wants you back.' Steiner looked into her eyes. She looked so natural, so feminine, so good.

'She seems to know a lot', Rosalynn said, smiling.

'Well, do you want him back?' pressed Steiner.

'No', she replied simply.

'Thank you for a wonderful night and a wonderful breakfast.' He tore a sheet from the pad on the sideboard and wrote down a telephone number. 'Please call me, anytime.' He kissed her and walked out of the kitchen.

Rosalynn Brando had no doubt that she had fallen in love again. She started singing as she cleared the breakfast table.

* * *

Jack Dawson arrived at the Hood Acre at exactly nine fifty-five. He entered the building through the little known private entrance secreted near the delivery gates. The meeting was scheduled for ten o'clock in one of the Red Rooms on the third floor. He skipped quickly up the spiral staircase and acknowledged the security officer's greeting with a nod. Dawson stopped at the door, placed his briefcase on the floor and arranged his tie. He took in a deep breath and entered the room.

The center of the room was occupied by the highly polished, round mahogany table surrounded by six comfortable chairs. Along the walls, the paintings were originals of the works of emerging but not well-known artists of the time. The low ceiling and the arrangement of soft lights cut into the panels of the wall created an intimate feeling, making the room seem smaller than it really was. On the floor was a deep plush red carpet.

Only three of the six chairs were occupied. On the table, in front of each one of the seated occupants, was a red folder, identical to the folder Jack Dawson carried in his briefcase.

'Good morning Jack,' the man in the middle greeted Dawson, 'right on time as always.' He motioned Dawson to sit down.

'Thank you Mr Maldini', said Dawson, settling himself in the middle of the three empty chairs, directly opposite Jack Maldini. He opened the briefcase and produced the red folder, placing it on the table in front of him.

'Shall we begin?' asked Maldini, looking around the table, first to Sam Templeton on his right, then to Jake Watson on his left. The two men nodded.

'Let's begin with the judge', instructed Maldini.

Jack Dawson opened the red folder and flicked through the pages. When he reached the sixth page, he flattened out the sheet with his palms, looked up at the three men and told them where they would find the judge. He waited for the three men to find the judge in their respective folders and began to brief them.

'He's up twenty-five thousand.' Dawson looked down on the page. 'Twenty-five thousand eight hundred and forty-five to be exact.'

'What happened on the twelfth of April?' asked Templeton.

'He was very drunk that night and made some very stupid bets. We tried to cover him but it would have been too obvious, so we let him play his hand. In the end he took the hit and finished up losing almost seven grand.'

'That's fine,' said Maldini, 'just keep him happy and make sure he keeps winning. We have him covered for a hundred grand.' He pulled a white handkerchief from inside his coat pocket and blew his nose loudly.

'Yes sir, Mr Maldini', Dawson said enthusiastically.

'What about the doctor?' asked Maldini.

Dawson flicked through the pages and announced confidently, 'page fourteen'.

The others around the table turned pages until eventually everyone was looking down in their red folders on Ben Swinton and Simon Carter.

'Have we got the sixty-seven grand?' asked Maldini.

'That was due yesterday', Dawson croaked. 'I sent the boys down to see him at the hospital yesterday morning,' he looked at the three men around the table, 'but he doesn't seem to have it yet.'

The silence in the room was deafening. Sam Templeton reached for a cigar and clipped the end. Dawson rushed out of his chair and scrambled around the table to light it, his hands shaking. He lit the cigar for Templeton and returned to his chair, all the time watching the three men.

'But he doesn't seem to have it yet.' Maldini repeated Dawson's last words as he turned to Jake Watson and then to Sam Templeton. The three men began to laugh, the laughter causing Sam Templeton to choke on the smoke of his huge cigar. Suddenly the room was silent again.

'Did we pay you your wages last month?' Maldini asked Dawson.

'Yes sir, Mr Maldini', replied Dawson.

'Now imagine me saying to you, Jack, we can't pay you your wages because we don't seem to have it yet.' The laughter around the table began again before Maldini finished his sentence.

'Jack', Maldini was serious all of a sudden. 'There can be many reasons why a person can't pay a debt', he stared at Dawson, 'but if you ever tell us that the client can't pay because,' he quoted Dawson 'he doesn't seem to have it yet', then we'll have to consider finding a better person to do your job.'

The three men glared at Dawson as he squirmed uncomfortably in his chair.

'Okay,' said Maldini, 'who are we after?' He looked down on the page in front of him and continued, 'I take it the guarantor is our man', he concluded.

The meeting proceeded with a full briefing by Jack Dawson on all of the clients in the folders. The final figure was tabulated and agreed upon; a final credit balance of $472,339 to be collected. Seven new clients were added to Jack Dawson's list when the meeting was drawn to its conclusion by Jack Maldini.

When Jack Dawson opened the door to leave the room, Jack Maldini called him back.

'About this doctor,' he said, pointing to Simon Carter's picture, 'don't do anything until we tell you.' He then handed him the brown envelope, patted him on the back and sent him out of the room.

When Dawson was gone, the three men reviewed the morning's meeting and came to the conclusion that everything was going well. They touched on the subject of the two doctors and decided they might be of more use to them in the future. They would wait and decide at their next meeting what should be done. Jack Maldini pressed the secret button under the table and ordered the customary drinks which signified the end of the monthly meetings. Outside the Hood Acre, Jack Dawson sat in the car with the brown envelope in his hand. He tore the envelope open and started counting the money - $40,000 - all in thousand-dollar bills. Dawson was sweating but he knew he and his boys had earned it. He switched on the ignition and drove out of the car park.

* * *

Shamon Kazi walked like a man possessed. Besides his family and his horses, walking was the one pleasure he always enjoyed. And on this glorious morning, he seemed to glide along effortlessly, his short legs whittling away the miles, with a song in his heart and his horses in his mind. He knew each one of the animals well and had always treated them like his children. Kazi felt a twinge of guilt for not having thought of their safety during the night. How had they managed to survive the awful conditions of the night before? The chestnut would guide them to safety, he thought. She was a three-year-old, but she had the protective instincts of a female animal. Kazi had often watched the beautiful filly at play with the others and felt confident that her intelligence would help her to guide the small herd to a place of safety.

Having grown up with horses in his native Hungary, Shamon Kazi's knowledge of horses was second to none. His father had taught him, even when he was a child, how to heal an injured horse, how to communicate with them and how to ride them. He had won gymkhana competitions since the age of fourteen and seemed to have an unusual rapport with horses. His instincts, knowledge and experience all told him that the chestnut filly was something special. She would be a fitting gift for a king or queen.

Kazi began talking to his animals as he walked, the conversation more cerebral than verbal. He focused on each animal; praising, cajoling, sympathizing where necessary and loving. Before long he had gone through his personal communication and cerebral bonding with three of the five horses.

'Aaaah! Talisman!' the words were uttered out loud, involuntarily. His bonding was beginning with horse number four. Talisman, the black gelding. A powerful horse with a beautiful, shiny jet black coat, now three years old. Shamon Kazi was not walking any more, he was floating home to his farm, a smile on his face and the morning sun on his back.

The wall of water hit him full in the face and drenched Kazi from head to toe, as the black Chevrolet swished through the puddle and continued on its way speedily towards the heart of the city. Jack Dawson looked in the rear view mirror and bellowed with laughter. He gazed at the drenched man's futile attempts to shake the water from his clothes. Shamon Kazi stood by the roadside and stared at the vehicle until it turned to a speck in the distance, his thoughts rudely interrupted by the driver's foolish action. Now, where was he, he thought as he removed the wet shirt and discarded it. Kazi felt no anger. He reorganized his thoughts, resumed his private conversation with his beloved Talisman and turned to walk towards the farm, shirtless.

Shamon Kazi was within sight of the farm when the discarded shirt probed his thoughts. The wet shirt he had left by the roadside did not belong to him. It had been loaned to him by the kind people at the hospital. He would have to retrieve it, two-and-a-half miles down the road. Kazi turned around and retraced his steps. He had finished his conversation with all the horses and was now concentrating on his wife and son. The boy had done well. He would have to find out from him how he had managed to help his mother, and also how he had got away from the trailer. Kazi's thoughts suddenly shifted from his own family to the doctor's family. He had never met the parents of the two children who often stopped at the farm to enjoy the horses, until the father helped Kazi's family in the middle of the night. The young girl was so friendly and so polite. Kazi could see the girl in his mind's eye. She had fallen in love with the chestnut filly and desperately wanted the horse for her birthday. *Birthday!* Shamon Kazi suddenly became aware of the fact that tomorrow was Saturday, the day of the young lady's birthday. What had he thought before? That the filly would be a fitting gift for a king or queen? This special chestnut filly could only belong to one special person, the little girl, whose father had saved his wife and helped his son in the middle of the night.

Shamon Kazi had arrived. He had no idea how he had covered the two-and-a-half miles in such a short time, but there, at the roadside lay the wet shirt just as he had left it. Kazi bent over, picked up the shirt and wrung it out. He draped the now damp shirt over his left shoulder and began to sing one of the famous gypsy songs that only he seemed to know. He sang loudly as he floated on air, back to his farm.

* * *

Jack Dawson slowed the car and merged with the city center traffic. He had forgotten all about the insignificant tramp he had soaked so timely out on the country road. His mind was now on today's calculations of commissions for his two muscle men. He had to have a word with Steiner. It was Mickey Steiner's idea to take it easy on the doctor and allow him a few more days. Dawson sat in the early afternoon traffic and visualized Jack Maldini's face as he echoed his words *but he doesn't seem to have it yet.* That Maldini is a dangerous man, thought Dawson as he inched the car forwards along with the afternoon traffic. Dawson made a mental note to be sure never to cross Maldini. The man could be kind and even friendly but he had an underlying dark streak. Many stories had been told about how Maldini had ended up in prison, how he had managed almost to run the prison, along with the prison governor with whom Maldini is said to have shared dinner once a month while a prisoner.

The long, loud blast of the horn from the car behind catapulted Dawson from the prison governor's dinner table back to the mayhem of the afternoon city center traffic. He caught sight of the burly, bearded driver of the car behind, and gunned the motor to catch up with the vehicles ahead. He swung left on Charcoal Street, avoiding the city center, and entered Carvel Avenue from Pebble Street. He eased the Chevrolet behind the gray Buick and knew that the two boys were upstairs in the office. He picked up the brown envelope Maldini had given him earlier in the morning from the seat next to him and stepped out of the Chevrolet.

Stumpy Lazarus had just finished a detailed account of his exploits the night before and was pressing Mickey Steiner to tell him all about his night with Rosalynn Brando.

'Stumpy,' said Steiner, while he examined the day's mail, 'a gentleman never discusses his private moments with a lady.'

'Jacqueline is not a lady', Stumpy said and laughed.

'Well,' Steiner looked up from his mail, 'maybe if you acted like a gentleman and gave her a chance, she might just surprise you.

48

Chapter Four

Besides, I thought she was a nice girl.' He returned his attention to the mail and started writing the date on the top left-hand corner of each of the envelopes.

Stumpy Lazarus was nursing a headache from his evening's drinking and the lack of sleep and did not appreciate Steiner's comments. He was about to light the short fuse of the temper that he was famous for, when Jack Dawson opened the door and waved the brown envelope at the two men in the office.

Dawson removed his jacket as soon as he entered the office and asked Stumpy to pour him a cup of coffee. He placed his briefcase next to his desk, put the brown envelope on the desk and pulled out a small black diary from the top drawer. He sat down behind the desk and produced a large A4 pad and began writing. Mickey Steiner watched Dawson busily checking and cross-checking figures from the black diary and making short notes on the pad. Dawson acknowledged the cup of coffee Stumpy Lazarus set in front of him with a nod and continued his frenzied tabulation. Finally, he picked up the brown envelope and tore it open. Two tightly bound bundles of notes fell on the table in front of Dawson. He picked up one of the bundles and, holding it in his left hand, flicked the bills between his right thumb and forefinger.

'Boys,' said Dawson happily as he tore off the paper band holding the bills together, 'you have earned this.' He counted ten one-thousand-dollar bills and handed them to Mickey Steiner and passed the other ten thousand to Stumpy Lazarus.

He picked up the second bundle, placed it back in the brown envelope and shoved it into his briefcase.

'About the doctor,' he said, 'we are going to give him some time.'

Jack Dawson had changed his mind about being angry with Mickey Steiner and took credit for the generosity he was showing towards the doctor. He briefed the other two men about their assignments for the following week, supplying them with new names and addresses from the red folder. When the briefing was completed, Dawson pulled out a bottle of whiskey from the bottom drawer of his desk and asked Stumpy to fetch the glasses. It was Friday and the sun was shining after yesterday's heavy rains. They could all have a couple of drinks and call it a day.

CHAPTER FIVE

Maureen Carter was grateful for the week's vacation she had taken because of her daughter's impending birthday. She was not due back at the hospital until Monday and had managed to confirm all invitations for the surprise birthday party she had meticulously planned for her daughter with the help of her son. Her only regret was that she had not had the time to discuss the horse her daughter wanted with her husband because of the previous night's chaotic activities. She made a mental note of what she could do later in the evening when Simon returned, and began tidying the house.

It took Maureen Carter a little over an hour to complete her morning's domestic chores, finishing with the kitchen. She washed her hands and dried them, poured herself a fresh cup of coffee and sat at the kitchen table with the pad and pencil. She was alone in the large house, having sent the children off to school and Simon to the hospital. The pencil began to glide across the paper, transcribing her thoughts. Maureen had been thinking about the details of her conversation with her husband during the early hours of the morning, while cleaning the house, and was now ready to begin her game of 'Solution'.

The game was wonderful in its simplicity. It went as follows: First: think of the problem and decide whether it really is a problem worth solving. Select *yes* or *no*. Second: if *no*, discard the problem and consider it solved. If *yes*, assign a numerical designation to the problem, ranging from *one* to *five*; A designation of *one*, representing problems of the lowest priority and *five*, representing problems of greater magnitude, demanding greater thought and planning. Third: determine whether the problem can be solved alone or whether it requires assistance from others. Select *yes* or *no*. Fourth: if *yes*, assign the letter (A) if three or less, or (B) if four or more. Fifth: assess the degree of confidentiality, where the problem involves others and assign a roman numeral, (i) for low or moderate level of confidentiality or (ii) for high level of confidentiality.

Maureen could almost feel her father's presence in the kitchen as she began to categorize the problem confronting her husband and, in essence, the well-being of her whole family. On the pad in front of her, her little jigsaw puzzle revealed:

1.Yes 2.(5) 3.Yes 4.(A) 5.(ii).

Her father's famous words rang in her mind, '*Maureen, my darling, the brain in your head is a wonderful thing. If you harness it, there is no problem you can't solve.*' She could remember the hugs that usually followed the words and smiled. Maureen sat at the table and began to concentrate. The process of selecting and deselecting began almost immediately. She tapped the table with her fingers and bit the end of the pencil occasionally as names flashed through her head. Some were pondered upon for long periods and then rejected while others came and went in a flash. She got up from the table and paced the kitchen floor, pencil in mouth. The name came up again and again, meeting every criterion that Maureen threw at it. The only question left to answer: was she in the country and able to help?

Maureen Carter reached for her handbag and took out her personal diary. The degree of confidentiality was (ii), and she knew she could trust her. She flicked through the diary and stopped at S. She ran her finger down the list of names and found her.

She was listed in the diary as Jennifer Broxburn Singleton. Broxy, as Maureen had always called her friend, was the ideal person to be contacted for the plan that Maureen had in mind. She reached for the telephone next to the refrigerator and dialled the number in the diary, long distance. Maureen Carter seemed anxious. She listened to the ringing tone and began counting after the third ring, four, five, six; she was about to replace the receiver when she heard the click of the answering machine.

'Jennifer and Robert are not in right now, but please leave a message and a number and one of us will return your call as soon as possible, chow', followed by a long tone.

'Broxy,' Maureen began, 'this is Maureen Carter.' She paused. 'I must speak to you honey.' She thought of something to say and decided simply to leave a number, starting with her area code, followed by her seven-digit number. She then added, 'Love you lots', and hung up the phone. Maureen returned to her pad on the kitchen table and made a tick, signifying the completion of the first assignment. Assignment number two would be to find Ben Swinton.

* * *

Ben Swinton had enjoyed the substantial breakfast that Tom Bakersfield had produced. Having showered and shaved, he was now dressed in a navy blue suit, light blue shirt, offset by a red silk tie with dark blue dots. He walked out of room 202, turned and inspected the room for the final time and shut the door behind him.

'Wow!' said the young, pretty receptionist. She was looking past the two new arrivals and stared unashamedly at the tall, handsome man walking towards the reception desk. The other two women who had arrived at the desk and just finished the process of checking in, turned their heads automatically, reacting to the receptionist's exclamation, and showed their embarrassment for having been so obvious. Ben Swinton knew immediately that he had attracted attention. When he arrived at the desk, the two young ladies parted the way for him to have access to the receptionist. Swinton stepped forward to the desk, stood between the two women and placed his holdall on the floor.

'Doctor Ben Swinton, Room 202, checking out please', he said.

The receptionist nodded her head, still staring at Swinton, and began processing the doctor through the computer.

'Sir,' said the receptionist, looking at the doctor's details on the console in front of her, 'we expected you to be with us until Monday,' she said with some familiarity to impress the other two women. 'We don't normally make refunds, but I can make an exception in this case, considering that today is only Friday.'

The lady standing to Swinton's right, looked admiringly at the tall doctor, removed her glasses and self-consciously brushed her short, blonde hair with her right hand.

'A refund is not necessary, but thanks for the offer anyway'. Swinton then placed the key to room 202 on the desk and picked up the holdall. 'Thanks again', he said and turned to walk to his car. He was thinking of the seventy-mile drive south just as he reached the doors and decided it would be a good idea to telephone Simon Carter. Ben Swinton turned around. All three women at the desk were staring at him sheepishly. He walked back to the reception desk.

'Is there a phone I could use?' he asked the receptionist, searching his pockets for change.

'Oh, yes doctor', she replied, reaching behind the desk to produce a telephone. 'You may use our courtesy phone'. She placed the phone on the desk in front of Swinton.

'I am afraid it's long distance', said Swinton.

'That's not a problem, doctor', replied the receptionist with great emphasis on the final word. The blonde woman, glasses still in hand, was now positively swooning. The receptionist glared at her disdainfully.

Ben Swinton dialled Simon Carter's number and waited. Maureen Carter picked up the telephone on the first ring.

'Ben!' Maureen shouted with delight and relief. 'Where are you?'

'About seventy miles north of you,' Swinton replied, 'in a motel.'

'Are you all right?' asked Maureen. 'We've been worried about you.'

'Fine', Swinton said self-consciously, the three pairs of eyes boring into him.

'I should be with Simon and you within two hours,' he paused, 'if I haven't worn out my welcome.'

'Don't be silly Ben', replied Maureen. 'Simon is still at the hospital but he should be home just about the time you arrive. It'll be so good to see you.'

'See you soon, and Maureen, thanks.' He concluded the conversation and hung up the phone. Ben Swinton thanked the receptionist, smiled at all three women and headed for the door, feeling much better within himself. Just before he reached the door, he heard one of the ladies at the desk say, 'He'd be welcome in my world anytime.'

Ben Swinton drove away from the motel, thinking about Tom Bakersflied. He was grateful to the young man. He swung the car onto the Interstate highway and drove south.

* * *

Juliana Kazi had had a restful and comfortable day. The visit from the good doctor and her son had settled her mind and she had slept comfortably throughout the afternoon after they had left. The doctor had explained to Juliana the full extent of her injuries and reassured her that recovery would be speedy and complete. With regard to her son, he was a healthy young boy so the broken hand should heal well without complications. The head wound had been thankfully quite superficial as shown by the X-rays. The only uncertainty, as the doctor had explained, was the condition of the trailer and where the Kazi family would live after she was discharged from the hospital. In the meantime, the boy and his father were quite welcome to live with the doctor's family.

Simon Carter walked into the ward at six thirty in the evening, stethoscope draped around his neck and Kazeem Kazi by his side. Kazeem Kazi's right arm was in a cast, extending from just below the elbow to his hand, the cast wrapped around his hand in such a way that only the ends of his fingers and the thumb showed. Juliana Kazi smiled wholeheartedly at the two newcomers and tried with great effort to sit up in the bed. Carter motioned her to remain still, adjusted her pillow and informed her that his day was finished at the hospital and that he was going home with Kazeem, provided the boy and his mother had no objections. Having children of his own, he knew how important it was to allow mother and child to share a few private moments and excused himself with the plausible excuse of some last-minute hospital paperwork. He winked at Kazeem and left the two to themselves.

Kazeem Kazi proudly displayed his newly prepared cast to his mother and informed her of his bravery during the casting. He was pleased for the opportunity to stay with the doctor's family and especially happy to be with his friend John. Yes, he would behave himself, he assured his mother and no, he would not neglect his prayers. When they saw Doctor Carter approaching the bed, the boy gingerly hugged his mother and assured her that he would be coming to visit. Doctor Carter once again reassured Mrs Kazi of her son's total security, and with his arm around the boy's shoulder, said their goodbyes and walked out of the ward.

When Simon Carter started the car, his sole intention was to find Shamon Kazi and discuss his offer of a place for him and his boy for the time being, at least until Mrs Kazi was well enough to be released from the hospital. He chatted with the boy as they drove out of the city and headed towards the farm. Between the hospital and the farm, Carter built up a reasonably good profile of the gypsies. He discovered that the boy was not at school. The family had worked their way from the southern parts of the States, working on farms when possible or joining circus teams when Shamon Kazi could find work with the various touring circus teams that crisscrossed the United States. The boy talked proudly of his father's expertise with horses and described to Simon Carter how to tame wild horses. He tried to demonstrate to Carter the various techniques and sounds used to cajole an unwilling or a lazy horse to do the rider's bidding. The boy's facial expressions and the sounds he made caused Carter to laugh, and when the boy realized the doctor was happy, he shared the moment with him as they both giggled and laughed, like two happy children, in the privacy of Simon Carter's car as they drove to the farm.

Simon Carter could not believe his eyes when he arrived at the farm and switched off the ignition. He looked at the boy beside him as if for confirmation of his own sanity, and then at the display ahead. He could accept the broken, twisted trees, the shifted, uneven landscape and the muddy pot-marked surface that gave the appearance of being on the moon, but the rest of what he saw made him doubt his sanity.

In the middle of the farm, with the backdrop of a beautiful sunset, stood a man. Shamon Kazi, Carter surmised, surrounded by five beautiful horses, circling. He rubbed his eyes, looked at the boy totally at ease beside him and looked ahead again at the unbelievable spectacle. This is not a dream, he thought. He opened the door gently so as not to disturb his surroundings and stepped gingerly out of the car. He did not look at the boy but he could feel his presence as the two of them quietly moved forward and sat on the hood of the car to absorb the extraordinary scenes ahead of them.

It was unreal, surreal, a moment of incongruous mixture of reality and madness but somehow believable. The horses kept circling; as if orchestrated by some unseen conductor, first one way, then the other, walking, then trotting and then at a gallop, but in synchrony at all times.

Shamon Kazi suddenly raised his hands above his head and clapped. The chestnut filly broke rank, reared up and galloped away, followed by the gelding with the shiny black coat and the other horses in pursuit.

For some unknown reason, Simon Carter found himself clapping. He jumped off the hood of the car and walked towards the mysterious horse trainer. Shamon Kazi approached him, shirtless and smiling. The two men met in the middle of the field and shook hands. In an instant the boy had joined them. Shamon Kazi embraced his boy with pride as Simon Carter watched father and son with admiration. He could understand the emotion and the exchange of love between the two gypsies as his own thoughts drifted away from the field to his son. Shamon Kazi was about to invite the doctor into his home when it suddenly dawned on him that he had no home. He cast his eye over the mangled trailer and was about to issue his apologies to the doctor when Simon Carter interrupted him with a wave. Carter invited the horse expert to join him in the car. They sent the boy to gather in the horses, an excuse for privacy between the two men, and settled themselves down in the front seat of the automobile.

'Mr Kazi,' Simon Carter was unsure of how to begin, 'your wife sends you her best wishes and I am pleased to say she has had a comfortable day.' Shamon Kazi was completely relaxed. He sat next to the doctor, shirtless but without embarrassment, and exuded some strange sort of confidence that Carter could not quite fathom.

'Doctor,' Kazi began, 'I have lived an enjoyable, simple life. Today, again, it seems I have nothing in this life, but don't be fooled because I have everything that matters to me in life.' Simon Carter looked curiously at the gypsy as he listened. The gypsy meant every word.

'You know why I am so happy?' he asked Carter, not really expecting an answer. 'Because I have him', pointing to the boy frolicking happily amongst the horses, 'and my wife is alive, thanks to you and your wife and that good man. What's his name?' Kazi took in a deep breath and tried to remember.

'Fire Chief Johnson', Carter assisted him with the name.

'Good, good, man,' Kazi praised the Chief, 'I will find him and I will thank him for the life of my wife and me too.'

Carter was mesmerized by this incredible man. The man had practically lost everything. He had no home to go to, obviously no clothes to change into, probably no food and most likely no money. His wife was ill in hospital and his son had sustained injuries. Most people would have considered such a situation almost unbearable. Who was this man?

'Mr Kazi,' Carter had come here for a reason, 'I have sought permission from your wife for your son to live with my family while she is still in hospital,' adding diplomatically, 'but I think it's only proper that I ask you too.'

'Doctor,' Kazi looked straight into the doctor's eyes, 'do you know anybody on this earth who can say no to an offer like this?' he laughed,

'I can only say thank you for now, because, how you say it in America...?' Kazi racked his brain, 'I am at the rock bottom.' They could both see the funny side of this shared experience as both men roared with laughter.

'Will you be my guest?' Carter suddenly asked the gypsy horseman.

'I am already your guest', Kazi replied instantly. 'You have offered to look after my Kazeem,' adding, 'I will be with my horses, but I thank you.'

After several attempts, Carter struck a bargain with the gypsy to accept some blankets, a camping tent from his garage, some clothes and some food. Simon Carter drove away from the farm with the gypsy boy next to him. In his heart, he felt certain that he had made a very special friend.

CHAPTER SIX

Mickey Steiner was in a contemplative mood. He drove through the fashionable north side of the city and headed south towards the appropriately named Sheen River Crossing. The beautiful sunset, the river and the bridge merged to paint a picture of tranquillity. Steiner avoided the queues of traffic at the manned toll booths and threw in the change at the automatic receptacle. With the bridge behind him, the powerful V-8 engine of the Buick responded immediately when Mickey Steiner pressed the accelerator. The speedometer registered the engine's capability by rising steadily. At seventy-five miles per hour, Steiner pressed the cruise control button on the dashboard and settled back comfortably to enjoy the scenery. The powerful engine consumed each mile in less than a minute. He was familiar with the route and as always he had calculated the journey time and expected to cover the one hundred and eighty miles in less than three hours, from door to door. He had made hotel reservations the night before, expecting to spend the weekend away from home, after the conclusion of the initial business at hand.

The evening was pleasant and cool, twilight now passing as the sun moved west to embrace new longitudes and allowed darkness to blanket over Steiner's present location. He opened the window to the driver's side of the car, fiddled with the radio in the hope of finding some good jazz music for company and lit a cigar. The powerful engine hummed smoothly and willingly reached into its reserves when Steiner released the cruise control and pressed down on the accelerator once more. Eighty - eighty-five - ninety, the speedometer kept rising.

He decided to keep it there and reset the cruise control. He sped past the heavy trucks and slower cars on the highway, all heading south on this cool Friday evening.

Mickey Steiner arrived in the city by the lake at exactly eight forty five at night. He was familiar with his surroundings because this was his birthplace, the city in which he had spent his youth and had enjoyed many memorable experiences with his parents. He took the

Cosco River exit and headed south-east past the airport and found himself thinking of Rosalynn Brando, one hundred and eighty miles away to the north. Sometime in the future, it would be nice to bring Rosalynn to this city, but for the moment, he had a secret to keep. He manoeuvred his way through the city center and crossed the railroad tracks - the demarcation line between affluence and poverty - and entered the poor south side, where the city seemed to shed its fancy clothes and joined ranks with America's poor ghettos. Islands in the sea of affluence, crime ridden and torn - in a land where the dollar fuelled all.

Steiner drove on, his senses sharp and his body tense. He could feel the bulge in the shoulder holster and was reassured by the fact that out of the cold steel was the power to unleash hot lead to stop anyone who dared to challenge his presence on this 'island'. He thought of Stumpy Lazarus, took in the surroundings and understood why Stumpy seemed to view the world, and all within it, as enemies. '*When are you gonna learn that greed drives us all*', Stumpy had once said. The steamy, hostile atmosphere was as stifling as ever. His mind churned, trying to make sense of America's weaknesses, but at the same time he appreciated the fact that within this great country, opportunities abounded for all.

He slowed the vehicle and searched for the address, head turning left and then right until finally the number on the postbox announced itself - Thirty-three Maypole Street - Steiner deliberately drove past the house, circled the block and parked across the street. He waited in the car for several minutes and surveyed the neighbourhood. How many Americas were there, Steiner thought as he sat quietly in the car. Forget the global geographical separation of North and South America, he was thinking about America, the America - the USA. This was more like Nicaragua, the Favelas in Brazil, take your pick of any third world country. He felt slightly ashamed to be American, when he stepped out of the car and walked towards number thirty-three.

'Mrs Baxter,' Mickey Steiner addressed the gray-haired woman who opened the door, 'Mrs Jane Baxter?' He was asking, seeking confirmation.

'Yes', the woman replied, looking concerned and somewhat frightened.

'I am Steiner, Mickey Steiner, may I come in please?'

The gray-haired woman gasped, took a step backwards into the house, leaving the door wide open, and covered her mouth with her hands. Steiner watched her, still standing at the door.

'Come in! Come in!' said the woman, finding her voice.

Steiner stepped into the modest house and shut the door behind him.

'Sit, sit, please sit down, Mr Steiner', Mrs Baxter said excitedly as she dashed to turn off the portable black and white television. She moved across the room and peered her head around a door to look into another room and slowly shut the door. Turning away from the now closed door, she clasped her hands and pulled a rocking chair near to where Mickey Steiner was sitting and sat next to him.

'Mrs Baxter,' Mickey began, 'I've been meaning to come to see you for a very long time and I must say, I am pleased to be here.'

'This is a miracle, it sure is', replied the woman with a look of incredulity.

'How is Bruce?' asked Steiner.

'Fine, fine'; her words were long and drawn as if the answer she was giving was the opposite of the truth.

'Are you sure?' Steiner pressed.

'Well,' she sounded uncertain, 'things were never the same since the accident.' She paused. 'The doctors are helping and we keep praying, but things will never be the same, Mr Steiner.'

'Where is Bruce?' asked Steiner.

The woman pointed to the door that she had crossed the room to close, and added, 'He has been asleep for some time now, having had a somewhat difficult day.'

'Why didn't you let me know you were moving?' asked Steiner, pulling a long, bulging, brown envelope from the inside pocket of his coat. He passed the envelope to the woman.

'That contains every monthly sum I've been sending to you for the past ten months. They all came back marked, not at this address. I am sorry it took so long for me to get here, but it was difficult trying to trace you. There is twenty thousand in there.' He paused. 'I wish I could do more and in time I will.' He looked her straight in the eye and decided to get it off his chest.

'Mrs Baxter, after the car accident four years ago, my mother died instantly but my father was kept alive for eight days before he finally

Chapter Six

died. His final words to me were how sorry he felt for having been the cause of the accident. He believed he had seen a child in your car just before the collision and asked me to do what I could to find out what had happened to the child. He even made me promise.'

The woman sat quietly and rocked so gently in the rocker that the movement was almost unnoticeable. She was listening to Steiner's story with patience.

'Anyhow,' Steiner continued, 'after the funeral, I was able to find you easily, with the help of some friends. I discovered your husband had also died in the accident and found out about Bruce. Initially, it was difficult for me to be of help to you because I had difficulty with work,' Steiner rubbed his palms against each other, 'but all is fine now.'

'Mr Steiner, you are a good man and I've been dying to meet you. I am so glad that you are here today because I can tell you what's inside me.' She suddenly stood up, apologized for her manners and offered a cup of tea and cakes which Steiner gratefully accepted. Over the tea and cakes, their conversation continued.

'My son is crippled in there,' she motioned to the other room, 'and I know your father may have been the cause, but it was an accident, an accident pure and simple.' There was a certain finality about the way she said that. It was as if she had drawn a line under the matter and finished with it.

'Why did you move?' asked Steiner.

'Mr Steiner, I couldn't afford our previous home when Jack died', referring to her husband. 'Don't get me wrong, I appreciate all that you were doing, sending us money every month. I must let you know that you are the one who has kept my son in there alive, because without your help I couldn't have managed the medical bills.' She was looking at him, admiringly, gratefully.

'How old is Bruce now', Steiner wanted to know.

'Eleven, going on to twelve', Mrs Baxter replied, still looking at him.

'About this neighbourhood,' he wasn't sure how to phrase the question, 'well, do you feel safe?'

'We are living, Mr Steiner, but we are not living in America', she sighed. 'The shootings, stabbings and the drugs are all around us. There are times I dread going out, but it seems as if those horrible people out there have their own rules. They seem to have made a pact with Bruce and me because of his condition and they do leave us

61

alone. I must say there are times when some even help us.'

'Mrs Baxter,' Steiner was looking around the room and he could see the folded wheelchair against the wall, 'I get the impression that Bruce is totally dependent upon you and that the two of you live here alone, am I right?'

She nodded her head, 'We've been on our own for a few years now, although my sister-in-law visits when she can. She lives back east with her family and finds it difficult to come as often as she would want to.'

The envelope Steiner had given her was still lying on the table next to her and, realizing the value of the contents, she felt obliged to correct the statement she had just made.

'We are alone, as you say, Mr Steiner, but really we are not.' She was looking at the brown envelope. 'You have been with us for quite a few years now.' They talked late into the night, filling in the years that had gone by since the accident. She told him of her plans for her disabled son, the difficulties she faced, particularly with his education and her inability to have a social life of her own. As she informed him, she also showed interest in his own activities, his future plans, about his job up north, about his general happiness.

Mickey Steiner looked at his watch, realized it was almost midnight and apologized for having kept her awake. He stood up in preparation to make his exit, having first written down his full address and telephone number on the pad she produced, and asked if he could take a brief look at the sleeping boy.

'I'll try not to disturb him', said Steiner as he walked with the woman towards the closed door beyond which the boy was sleeping.

Mrs Baxter opened the door quietly and motioned Steiner to enter. At the base of the bed was a mechanical hoist, and at the far side of the bed a small computer on a table with connecting wires leading to the side of the bed, near the boy's pillow.

The room was tidy and unencumbered, obviously to allow for easy mobility. The small table on the right side of the bed was covered with several piles of comics. Steiner tiptoed forward and picked up several of the comics. He looked at the dark-haired boy sleeping peacefully and flicked through the comics. He turned to the woman, smiled and replaced the reading material back on the table and tiptoed out of the room. When the woman shut the door, Mickey Steiner smiled at her again and whispered, 'He seems to have chosen the best guardians.'

Mrs Baxter understood the comment even before Mickey Steiner rattled off the names,'Superman, Batman and Spiderman.'

'Please do keep in touch,' Steiner said to the woman as he stepped out of the house, 'and don't hesitate to call me if you need me.' He put out his hand to shake the woman's hand but found himself in a hug as Mrs Baxter stepped forward and embraced him, her arms around his neck, a kiss on his cheek and tears in her eyes.

Steiner walked briskly across the street, opened the door to the Buick and, with a final wave, drove away from the house with the woman in silhouette against the porch lamp. Within an hour of saying goodbye to Mrs Baxter, Mickey Steiner was asleep in a five-star hotel room in America, away from the 'island' ghetto.

* * *

Simon Carter drove home to a welcoming surprise. He recognized the black BMW and heaved a great sigh of relief in appreciation of the fact that his friend, Ben Swinton, was alive and well. He rushed into the house, closely tailed by Kazeem Kazi, to find Ben Swinton surrounded by his wife and the two children in the center of the living room. A sudden hush fell over the house as Ben Swinton turned to face the two newcomers. The two men just looked at each other, none daring to disturb the hush, with the other occupants of the room transfixed, seemingly waiting for their cue from either of the two men before injecting activity into the frozen atmosphere. Ben Swinton suddenly took two steps forward and embraced his friend as the others looked on.

'Don't you children have anything better to do?' Maureen Carter was taking control of her house. She was already in motion, taking the children in tow.

'Katherine, come and help me with supper, and John, go along with Kazeem and help him to settle in', said Maureen. 'And Simon, please fix Ben a drink, supper will be ready in an hour.' The living room emptied, with the exception of the two doctors who still stood in the middle of the room, speechless.

John Carter and his gypsy friend sat on the floor in John's room. He inspected the plaster cast on Kazeem's right hand and wanted to know the details of last night's events.

'That tree was huge Kaaz, awesome, tell me, what happened?'

Kazeem Kazi began to reflect on the events of the night before and began an incredible story, detailing his family's brush with death on a dark, rainy night. He had spent most of Thursday afternoon weaving carpets in the trailer with his parents. The incessant rain had prevented him from going outside with his father to work on the farm. Instead, they had kept Mrs Kazi company and helped her to weave the carpets which they sold to supplement their income. They had enjoyed the old man's stories about the old country where, in his younger days, Shamon Kazi's father had managed to bring several wandering gypsy clans together to form a large, stable community. They had earned their living in those days by gathering wild horses, training them and selling them to circuses which performed all over Europe. Shamon Kazi had been in the middle of these wonderful stories when the ground had begun to rumble and the trailer began to shake. Initially, they had thought it was an earthquake.

'What time was this?' asked John Carter, leaning forward with excitement.

'I don't know,' replied Kazeem, 'but it was already getting dark. My father went to try to find out what was going on but before he could open the door, the noise got louder and louder.'

'Weren't you scared?' asked John, his eyes almost popping out of his head.

'I saw the tree bending', continued the gypsy.

'You mean leaning,' corrected John, 'and then what?'

'Before I could warn my father, the big branch was coming through the window. It was like slow motion, but also very quick. It was coming straight through one of the windows and towards my mother and me.'

'Wow! This is scary. I don't know what I would have done, had it been me.'

In their excitement, the two boys had moved so close to each other their knees were almost touching.

'Crrrk!' Kazeem tried to imitate the sounds. 'The window broke when the tree hit it so I jumped and pushed my mother away from the middle of the room. She fell on the table and then rolled over against the wall. My head hit something, before one of the branches pushed me through the other door. I heard the lantern fall and smash and then it was dark everywhere.'

'How did you get away from there', John wanted to know.

'I don't know, I can't remember, I just kept running in the rain trying to find you to help us.'

'You are lucky you didn't fall in the hole you know, because nobody would have known, wow! scary', concluded John.

They could hear footsteps coming up the stairs and then a knock on the door. Katherine Carter was summoning her brother and his gypsy friend to come to supper.

* * *

Stumpy Lazarus picked up the telephone for the fourth time this Friday evening and once again dialled Mickey Steiner's number. He let the phone ring for a long time but like the previous attempts there was no answer. It was unusual for Mickey Steiner to disappear without telling his partner of his whereabouts and his absence on a Friday night, when the two men usually spent time in each other's company, made Mickey's absence even more bizarre. They had left the Carvel Avenue office at three in the afternoon, having enjoyed their celebration drinks with Dawson. Sure, they had not made any plans for the evening but there was nothing unusual about that. Under normal circumstances, there would be a message for Stumpy to meet his partner at one venue or another, or, failing that, Mickey's telephone would simply be off the hook, a method Mickey used whenever he felt the need to be alone. On this occasion, the telephone kept ringing but there was never any response. Something was definitely wrong. He had to do something, but what?

The taxi waited as Stumpy had instructed, the driver quite pleased with himself. He kept the engine running in front of Steiner's apartment block while Stumpy, dressed casually in tan slacks, maroon jacket and an open-necked white shirt talked to the building's security guard about Steiner's whereabouts. This was the third place the taxi had come to, having first tried the Hood Acre and then Simpsons, the popular cocktail bar which the two partners frequented on Fridays. Stumpy Lazarus was not having any success. All the security guard at Steiner's apartment could tell him was that he had seen Mr Steiner leave the building at about five thirty carrying a small holdall. Stumpy slumped back in the taxi and told the driver to take him back to his own apartment, the point at which he had first picked him up. Stumpy was determined to find his partner. He thought of contacting Rosalynn Brando but realized he had no idea where to reach her. It occurred to him that the only place he had ever seen Rosalynn was the Hood Acre. The taxi driver had already taken him there and he was sure that, had Rosalynn been in the Hood Acre, he would have seen her. The only place left to look was the Pepperdine. It was unlikely that Mickey Steiner would spend a Friday night alone at the Pepperdine, but Stumpy Lazarus remembered that almost three years ago when Steiner was feeling low, he had driven around the town for some considerable time and eventually ended up in the Pepperdine. It was the night that Mickey Steiner had met Stumpy Lazarus and probably saved his life.

As before, Stumpy Lazarus asked the taxi driver to wait for him when they arrived at his apartment. They had spent the last two hours combing the town for Steiner without success and the driver was beginning to show some concern about the meter reading which was by now registering the fare in triple figures. Stumpy Lazarus may not have been the brightest man around, but he had a keen sense of awareness, what might be called streetwise. He reached into his pocket and pulled out a small bundle of notes and peeled off two one-hundred-dollar bills. He passed the money to the driver and told him to keep the engine running.

Inside the apartment, Stumpy took off his jacket and strapped on his shoulder holster. He took out the gun, checked it and replaced it in the holster. The knife, which was a part of Stumpy's attire, was already secure in the sheath. He pulled on his coat and was about to walk out of the room when something prodded his mind. From underneath the kitchen sink, he reached for a small plastic bag and removed the Reid's 'my friend' knuckleduster .32. The weapon did not have a barrel because it fired directly from the revolver chambers. He preferred it as a back-up weapon since it was easy to conceal and could be used up close as a knuckleduster. He tucked the tiny weapon into his sock, turned off the lights and left the room. Stumpy climbed back into the cab, this time sitting next to the driver.

'The Pepperdine, on the east side', he told the driver.

'You mean the Pepperdine on Shackle Avenue?' asked the taxi driver, unable to conceal his anxiety.

Chapter Six

'That's the one', replied Stumpy, deliberately avoiding eye contact with the driver.

'Okay sir', said the driver, engaging first gear.

Stumpy could see the driver's hand shaking as he joined the Friday night traffic and turned left to head east. The evening was pleasant and there was the usual Friday night buzz about the town as people prepared to enjoy a weekend break from the hectic week of work.

The Pepperdine had a reputation. It was one of the famous old buildings in the city. Once a respectable hotel in the thirties and forties, it was subsequently converted to a popular nightclub in the late fifties and early sixties. In time, as more immigrants moved into the city and the relatively well-off residents of the inner city migrated out to the suburbs, the building was bought by a mysterious property developer and given a face lift to become the east side's most popular discotheque and bar. It now had a reputation for attracting lower grade criminal elements, ranging from drug dealers, pimps, ex-convicts, hard-core bikers and prostitutes. It was the police department's nightmare and, situated in the tough east side, was slowly becoming a no-go area for the ordinary, respectable citizens of the city. It was unlikely that Mickey Steiner would be in the Pepperdine. In fact, he had once confided in Stumpy Lazarus that his presence in the building on the first day of their meeting had been purely by chance, because he had lost his way in a town that was new to him at the time. Stumpy Lazarus knew that it was unlikely he would find his partner in the tough east side but for some inexplicable reason he had to satisfy his curiosity.

The taxi driver was now visibly nervous. The structural change was quite stark, as buildings which were well constructed and meticulously maintained in the past, now stood crumbling, bearing witness to poverty's contribution to dereliction. Once again America transformed itself, its fancy clothes as always, deposited at the demarcation line where the affluent forgot about the poor and the poor battled over scraps on the ghetto islands. Stumpy Lazarus did not seem overly concerned as the taxi and its two occupants were slowly sucked into the bowels of a mammoth ugly beast. This was a jungle, a jungle within which only the toughest could survive. On the dimly lit streets, shadows appeared and disappeared just as quickly, in pursuit of dreams that led into dead-end dark alleys, where drugs took young, virile lives and cruel sexual diseases claimed some. Those left standing eventually succumbed to worthless two-cent bullets which screamed out of equally worthless, untraceable guns.

'Nothing changes', said the driver, more to himself than to his passenger, when he saw the colourful neon lights displaying the Pepperdine in all its glory. Beneath the neon lights, the lines of hopefuls were patiently waiting for tickets to enter the building for their usual Friday night dose of loud music and all the extras that came with it. The driver pulled over to the curb, some distance away from the main entrance, and clicked the meter to the off position. Stumpy Lazarus did not bother to look at the displayed fare. He fished out the wad of notes and peeled off another hundred-dollar bill and passed it to the driver. Stumpy replaced the rest of the bundle of notes into his inside jacket pocket, pressed the jacket down with both hands and stepped out of the taxi. As soon as Stumpy stepped onto the side walk, the taxi driver wheeled the car into a tight U-turn and sped away in the direction from which he had come.

Stumpy Lazarus was in his domain. He took his time to light the cigar and cast his eyes over the Friday evening crowd. He turned in the opposite direction, away from the crowd, and walked around the building through the alleyway that separated the Pepperdine from the Shackle Avenue liquor store and rapped his knuckles twice on the side door, which he knew opened directly into the back of the main bar. He watched as the cover of the peephole was slid aside and seconds later heard the sound of the heavy bolts being pulled back to open the heavy iron door. Within minutes of Stumpy Lazarus stepping out of the taxi, he was in the main bar of the Pepperdine, shaking hands, slapping backs and sipping whiskey with people he had known almost all his life but had not seen for some time.

CHAPTER SEVEN

Jack Maldini's twenty-fifth wedding anniversary was expected to be a big affair. Vivian Maldini was going to see to that. She had prepared the very exclusive guest list personally and, with just a week to go, most of the RSVPs had been returned with grateful acceptance. Her task this Friday evening, was to meet the caterers, the marquee company representative responsible for the three massive tents which were to be erected in the garden of the ten-acre property, and finally to crosscheck her guest list against the number of invitations returned. She had been concerned about security, but that problem was now Joe Lazlo's responsibility.

Across the table from Vivian, in the ostentatiously decorated dining room of the Maldini mansion, sat her two best friends. Barbara Lazlo and Elizabeth Templeton did not hide their excitement about the forthcoming party and today, with final preparations almost complete, they were happily sifting through the pile of accepted invitations on the table and enjoying their glasses of sherry.

They heard the chimes of the door bell and the conversation between the maid and the person at the door. The marquee company representative was a tall, shifty, mustachioed, middle-aged man of about fifty. He stood just inside the door and waited for the maid to return after announcing him. He seemed surprised when he saw the maid and the three ladies approaching. Vivian greeted the man excitedly and led the way into the garden, past the swimming pool. With the marquee man's assistance, they selected the locations for the three tents and agreed that the work, which according to the expert would take approximately four hours, should be undertaken the following Thursday morning. The man produced a shiny tape-measuring device, took several measurements and recorded his figures in a small notebook. When all was finished, he accepted the bottle of champagne which Vivian Maldini insisted upon and with a final, brief inspection of the location, said goodbye to the ladies and left. Not long after the marquee man, the catering arrangements were similarly concluded satisfactorily. The three ladies once again returned to the dining table and the pile of invitations.

* * *

Rosalynn Brando, picked up the gold-fringed envelope and pulled out the impressive invitation card. The envelope had arrived on Monday afternoon, at which time she had read the invitation and casually discarded it on the side table in the living room. She was used to being invited by the so-called high society and wealthy women who often bored her with their naive and sometimes tasteless conversations about clothing. The majority of such invitations, which came regularly from all over the States, sought her presence only to enhance and inflate the egos of the hosts. She particularly disliked the political invitations, where her presence was guaranteed to increase the prospective candidate's female vote tally by up to three per cent. As far as invitations went, her preference was for selected charitable engagements concerning the welfare of children and the disabled.

She read the invitation card very slowly; gold lettering embossed on an expensive-looking white card:

Mr & Mrs Jack Maldini Request the Pleasure of Rosalynn Brando & Guest to Celebrate Their Twenty-Five Years of Happy Matrimony.

At the bottom left-hand corner of the card was the address and at the bottom right, the date and time. Dress was informal, RSVP.

Rosalynn held the card in her hand for a few moments and picked up the telephone. She would accept the invitation if Mickey Steiner would accompany her. She let the telephone ring five times and replaced the receiver. Rosalynn put the invitation card back in the envelope and placed it on the center table in the living room. She did not want to forget to respond to the invitation but she would do nothing about it until she had spoken to Mickey Steiner. She felt rested, having slept contentedly after Steiner had left her earlier during the day. This was a good time to catch up on the designs she needed to complete for her trip to the West Coast.

The evening was cool and Rosalynn felt good at home. She changed into a pair of comfortable jeans and slipped on a light blue sweater.

Barefooted, she crossed the room and selected the music: slow jazz. Happy with the music and with fond thoughts of Mickey Steiner, she settled down at her desk and began to work.

* * *

Outside the Pepperdine, the crowds had thinned, only the stragglers and die-hard hopefuls waited. The gates had long shut, the buzz that an hour and a half ago hung so heavy outside the gates had now literally been shifted onto the enormous dance floor and into the adjacent bars. The Friday night trading had begun in earnest. From behind the bars, alcohol bottles were emptied into glasses with fantastic speed and regularity; beer fountains flowed continuously into a conveyor belt of empty beer glasses, which, when full, were emptied equally as fast into welcoming throats and the empty glasses recycled through the trading chain once again. On the dance floor, a mass of gyrating bodies heaved and swayed with the tempo of the music as the DJs waved their musical magic wand over the crowd.

On the fringes, large amounts of dollar bills exchanged hands with drug dealers passing their illicit wares and happily pocketing the rewards. The Pepperdine was in motion.

Stumpy Lazarus had seen it all before. Whatever Stumpy's faults were, drug dealing and the use of drugs were not part of them. He harboured a special disdain for anyone connected in any way with drug activity and never hesitated to make his feelings known about such matters. Tonight, his primary concern was to find his partner. Since entering the building, he had spoken to just about everybody who might have had an idea of his partner's whereabouts and had resigned himself to the fact that Steiner did not want to be found. He sat at the bar alone and watched the busy bartenders filling their orders like chemists do with prescriptions.

Whenever he was alone in bars, restaurants and clubs, Stumpy's habit was either to sit with his back against a wall or face a mirror so as to see as much as possible behind him. Sitting as he was tonight facing the bar, he could see the two heavily bearded men in dark leather jackets approaching from behind, in the rectangular mirror behind the drinks dispenser in front of him. They were big, rough-looking men, not unlike Stumpy himself but much more sinister looking because of the heavy, dark beards and their dark clothing. At the bar, they stood one at either side of Stumpy, sandwiching him between them.

'Lazarus', said the one to his left.

Stumpy looked at him, sized him up with his eyes and ignored him.

'They say you are Lazarus, are you?' the man to his left pressed.

It would have been better to have left the Pepperdine when Stumpy had the inkling to do so. He did not know who the two men were and didn't really care because he did not like their looks. He assumed from experience that they were members of a bike club.

'What's the difference?' said Stumpy disagreeably, sipping from his whiskey glass.

'The Man says you're looking to buy some snow', said the biker to his right, who was weighted down by the heavy chain around his waist.

He knew what they meant. These men were trying to sell him cocaine. Stumpy's short fuse was about to be lit.

The music from the discotheque was now at a crescendo, making it difficult to communicate. Stumpy knew that once anything started, he would have to be quick or suffer the consequences. Flashes of a previous encounter which gave him the scar on his face shot through his brain. He wished he had left earlier.

'Tell the "Man", whoever he is, that I get my snow free in the winter,' said Stumpy, looking straight ahead but aware of the men's every little twitch in the mirror in front of him.

'What did he say?' asked the one on the left, leaning towards his friend on the other side, trying to shout above the music.

'He is a wise guy', the one on the right informed his mate, laughing loudly. 'He says he gets his snow in the winter for nothing, Joe.'

'Uh huh, I think we've got ourselves Mr Smarty Pants', said Joe, making room between himself and Stumpy by stepping back a pace.

The Pepperdine was about to live up to its reputation. Stumpy kept watch in the mirror and saw the tall black man in a long leather coat with a felt hat move away from his sitting position a few seats along the bar. Now that's a smart man he thought. The bartender closest to the three men looked up from the drink he was mixing. Having worked in the Pepperdine for a number of years, he could read all the signs that often spelt trouble. He placed the spirit bottle and the glass he was about to fill with the drink on the bar and ducked behind the bar as if reaching for something from the lower shelves and never reappeared.

The heavy chain smashed loudly and viciously on the bar, inches from Stumpy's left arm as Joe struck his first sudden blow. Stumpy Lazarus was off the stool and crashing into the second biker to his right just as the chain struck the polished wooden surface, his weight carrying both himself and the biker several feet away from the bar and onto the floor. Like a cat, Joe was already in mid-air after them. The chain whirled ferociously over his head in preparation for his second strike.

On the floor, Stumpy Lazarus was on his back on top of the second biker, his eyes wide open as the chain came down upon him. Seconds before the chain made contact with Stumpy's skull, he rolled left from on top of the biker on the floor and heard the painful animal-like scream of the fallen biker as the chain struck him across the chest and face. A thin fountain of blood shot up from the injured biker's face and arched in the air to form a pool on the floor.

A circle of spectators had formed around the three men. The biker on the floor reeled in agony, both hands on his face with blood now flowing freely between the webbing of his fingers. From the other side of the building, the music was now louder than ever, the majority of the people totally unaware of the vicious combat that was going on by the bar.

The heavy chain was whirling again over Joe's head with a frightening swishing sound. He stood in the middle of the circle of excited spectators preparing to do damage with the chain. Stumpy Lazarus eyed him intensely, his body tense and his mind trying to assess the direction of the anticipated blow. Joe moved forward slowly in a partially crouched position, chain whirling and totally focused on the man opposite him. Suddenly he lunged forward and swung the chain in an arc aiming for Stumpy's head. For a big man, Stumpy Lazarus was very quick. He ducked to his right as the chain swished over his head, the momentum of Joe's attack bringing him in close. Stumpy's left knee lifted as the biker came in close and felt the full weight of the knee in his belly. Joe groaned with the pain as he buckled to absorb the pain. Stumpy Lazarus hit him hard behind the head and sent the biker reeling, his chain rattling and gathering into a pile under his chin just as he fell.

The commotion was now attracting many more people, the circle of spectators growing quickly as onlookers jostled for more advantageous positions to view the combat between the two big men. Stumpy Lazarus did not rush after the biker when he fell. He took a few steps backwards, stepped over the first biker who was still lying on the floor, now in his own pool of blood, and prepared himself for the next attack which he was sure would come. He was not disappointed. Joe was up, wiping a trickle of blood from the corner of his mouth as a result of his fall over the chain which was now wound tightly around his hand. The bartender, who had disappeared behind the bar had now reappeared and stood behind the bar with his arms folded. This was nothing new, the Pepperdine was placing a few notches in its reputation.

The fighters circled cagily, each looking for a more advantageous position from which a telling blow could be delivered. Joe shook the chain loosely by his side and spoke for the first time since the fight began.

'You will die here tonight mister.' He inched forward, chain rattling.

'Welcome to hell', replied Stumpy, totally unafraid.

''Kill him, kill him', somebody shouted from the crowd, drawing approval and more sounds of 'yeah, yeah', from the onlookers.

All the time the music blared from the discotheque. Pinpricks of coloured lights reflected off the faces of the fighters and the spectators as strobe lights shot out their laser beams in conjunction with the loud music stoking up the atmosphere.

The fighters circled, Stumpy the more assured of the two. He hated drug dealers and he was going to make this man pay for trying to sell him the poison.

'Pick up your friend and leave,' Stumpy told Joe as they eyeballed each other, 'but before you go you will leave the snow you and your friend are carrying on the bar. Now what will it be?'

'Fuck you', shouted Joe as he swung the chain desperately.

Stumpy sidestepped and barely managed to avoid the chain which was aimed for his neck and punched the biker full in the face, causing his head to jolt backwards, his thick black hair flailing out like peacock feathers.

'That's just for starters son', said Stumpy as he took the bikers legs from underneath him with a vicious kick and sent him crashing against the bar with a powerful blow to the side of his skull.

'And that's for swearing, you bastard.'

Stumpy Lazarus moved quickly. He grabbed the biker's thick black hair just as he collided with the bar, grabbed the chain and wrapped it around the man's neck.

Joe was now pinned uncomfortably against the bar, his mouth wide open and gasping for air as the chain around his neck choked the breath out of him. Stumpy began to go through the man's pockets with his left hand, his right hand still holding firmly onto the chain around Joe's neck. Out of the biker's leather jacket came three small plastic bags of white powder, two more small bags containing red tablets and a switchblade engraved with the sign of a swooping eagle. He placed the items on the bar, placed his right foot in the small of the biker's back and shoved him forward, releasing his hold on the chain. Joe went crashing to the floor next to his injured friend, both hands around his neck in an attempt to free the chain for breath.

Stumpy was not finished. He reached down to the other biker, propped him up against the bar and searched his pockets, removing two bags of some white tablets and another switchblade engraved with a swastika. The contents of the two bikers' pockets were now displayed openly on the bar, with the two injured and humiliated men groaning and moaning with pain on the floor.

'Three whiskeys, doubles, without ice,' said Stumpy to the barman, 'and a large glass of water.'

The crowd that had witnessed the fight had now closed in around Stumpy and the two injured men on the floor, the attention of some of them focused enviously on the items on the bar. Translated into money, Stumpy knew that the contents of the small plastic bags on the bar would be worth several thousands of dollars. He also knew that those items put him in some danger because any one of the common drug dealers in the room would gladly kill to lay their hands on the drugs.

The barman lined the three double whiskeys side by side on the bar in front of Stumpy Lazarus and returned momentarily with a large glass of water which he placed next to the glasses of whiskey. Stumpy pulled some bills from his pocket and paid for the drinks. He picked up the bags of white powder, opened each one and emptied them on the floor. He then took the bags containing the tablets and threw them on the floor unopened. With his heel, he ground the tablets into the hard floor to the gasps of several of the onlookers. He then picked up the glass of water and slowly poured it over the powder and pills, stamping on the mixture with his shoes to make a total mess of the material on the floor. He knew he was making enemies but he didn't care.

'I figure this is a fair price for your snow and pills,' he said to the two men on the floor as he placed a glass of whiskey in front of each one, 'considering, as I told you before, that I get my snow free in the winter.'

Stumpy Lazarus picked up the third glass of whiskey, drank it in one quick movement and motioned the barman over. He leaned over the bar close to the barman and whispered something to him, at the same time slipping the one hundred dollar bill into the top pocket of the man's shirt. He worked his way slowly to the end of the bar and waited for the barman to bring the drink. By now Stumpy was standing at the entrance, against the small, folding door that opened behind the bar. He emptied the drink again with one quick motion, pushed the small door open and disappeared behind the bar and through to the back room.

The crowd which had gathered in front of the bar now erupted, as people began to describe to one another how they had viewed the fight and the subsequent events. No one seemed to notice the two injured men as the crowd began to disperse, their attention once again on the gyrating mass of humanity on the dance floor.

The barman picked up the two switchblades and tossed them in a bucket behind the bar. Some had won, some had lost, but the Pepperdine's reputation remained.

Stumpy Lazarus stepped out of the Pepperdine into the alleyway and looked at his watch. It was past four in the morning. He waited calmly for five minutes, watching for any unusual activity. Finally, he walked carefully out of the alley to the main street and looked for a taxi. The streets were much quieter now. He could see the two women engaged in conversation across the street from the nightclub and observed the tall black man with the felt hat smoking in the green Oldsmobile only yards away from them. Others on the street were walking away from the club, perhaps on their way home after a night's entertainment. He hoped a taxi would come along but he knew better. He watched as the two women climbed into the green Oldsmobile and lit a cigar.

The car moved slowly away from the curb on the wrong side of the street, crossed over to the right side and came to a halt directly in front of Stumpy Lazarus. In the driver's seat was the black man who had shifted position at the bar just before the fight began. Beside him was a young white woman with reddish hair, and in the back seat a pretty black girl. The rear window of the vehicle had been wound down. The black woman smiled at Stumpy and wondered if they could drop him off somewhere.

'No Ma'am, but thanks for the offer', replied Stumpy.

The muzzle of the pistol was pressed tightly behind Stumpy's right ear. He had not seen nor heard the man as he materialized from the shadows in the alleyway.

'Get in the car', he ordered, pressing the gun firmly against his head.

The black woman shifted along to the far side of the rear seat as Stumpy was pushed into the car, followed by the stocky, young white man with the gun. The driver accelerated quickly, while the black woman frisked Stumpy for weapons.

'He's packing a piece', said the woman, feeling Stumpy's gun in the shoulder holster.

'I'll take that', said the man with the gun, reaching inside Stumpy's jacket. He removed the weapon and tossed it to the redhead in the front seat.

'What do you want with me?' asked Stumpy, folding his arms across his chest in an attempt to conceal the knife inside the sleeve of his coat.

'Cover him up', said the driver to the black woman sitting in the back seat, ignoring Stumpy's question.

The girl placed a brown hood over Stumpy's head, pulling gently on the draw strings to make a loose fit around his neck.

Stumpy Lazarus knew the city well and tried to follow the route of the vehicle in his mind. He eventually gave up the exercise because of the many twists and turns, an attempt by the driver to protect his final destination. They drove through the east side of the city for almost half an hour before the Oldsmobile finally pulled up. Stumpy felt himself being pushed down a flight of stairs. Basement hideout, he thought. He could hear several locks being turned before he was shoved into a room, the door slamming behind him and once again the turning of locks. Total silence, they were gone. He removed the hood from over his head; the silence was now complemented by total darkness. Stumpy Lazarus knew he was in trouble. He sat on the cold, hard floor, his back against the wall, and pulled up his knees under his chin. They had taken his gun but he had the knife and the Reid's 'my friend' knuckleduster .32. He patted his trouser leg and felt the tiny weapon tucked into his sock. He was grateful that the gun did not fall out during the fight. Reassured, he settled back and closed his eyes; within minutes Stumpy was asleep. He had not had much sleep since Thursday night.

CHAPTER EIGHT

The Saturday morning sunshine broke through the early morning clouds with impunity and splashed its warm rays over Katherine Carter's bedroom, the room glowing with the paint of gold. Katherine lay awake in the bed, enjoying the tickling, teasing rays, and felt good to be alive. This was her special day, her sixteenth birthday. She had no idea what the day held for her but she felt sure that something special would happen. Her mother and father had never let her down. As far back as she could remember, her birthdays and those of her brother had always been special. What she hoped for was the horse that she had fallen in love with, but with the strange events of the past few days she believed time had not allowed her parents the opportunity to buy the filly.

Katherine resigned herself to enjoy the day however it turned out and jumped out of bed. She knelt down beside the bed as she always did in the morning and said her prayers. Today's prayer was for a special thanks and lasted slightly longer than the usual prayer sessions. She was reluctant to disturb the quiet of the house and stayed in her room, standing in front of her window to embrace the brilliant sunshine and the warmth it showered upon her.

Maureen Carter had been up much earlier this morning and had organized her troops for action. Her small army consisted of General 'doctor' Carter, Captain 'little' John Carter, Major Kazeem 'the gypsy boy' Kazi and Commander in Chief Maureen 'nurse' Carter. The troops had been up long before six, blowing balloons, hanging decorations, painting signs of birthday wishes and generally organizing the house and the garden for the afternoon surprise party. They were now ready for the guest of honor.

Maureen led the way up the stairs, closely followed by her troops. Katherine Carter was still standing in front of the window, enjoying the sun, and did not hear the door open. The Commander organized her troops quietly, sneakily, into the room and gently shut the door. Maureen faced the sneaky troops, put her left forefinger to her lip and raising her right hand began to beat time: one, two, three.

The room erupted to a discord of '*Happy Birthday to You...*'

Katherine Carter whirled around with great surprise and began to laugh at the motley collection of pyjama garbed troops. She waited for them to finish the brief song, rushed towards the group and found herself encircled with love.

The Commander led the way from the bedroom, down the stairs and into the kitchen, where the breakfast table had already been set.

'I can guess what's for breakfast,' said Katherine as she took her seat next to her father, 'pancakes, my favorite.'

The Commander was busy again, shifting plates of pancakes, eggs, sausages, syrup, juices and tea. All of a sudden, in the middle of the happy breakfast scenes, Kazeem Kazi looked at Katherine Carter and said to her, 'You will live long Katherine, Happy Birthday.'

Simon Carter looked at his wife, smiled and shrugged his shoulders.

* * *

Mickey Steiner stood at the desk of the five-star hotel and prepared to check out. He had slept very well, which in Steiner's case was very unusual. He felt good for having had the opportunity to talk with Mrs Baxter. He liked the lady and felt sure that he would be seeing her more often in the future. Now that he had her new address, there should be no difficulty assisting her with the monthly sums that he took pleasure in sending. He wondered what Rosalynn Brando would be doing on this beautiful Saturday morning and decided he would contact her when he returned. He thanked the polite hotel receptionist and left to collect his car.

The beginning of the journey north was uneventful and very quiet. It suddenly occurred to him that this was early Saturday morning. If the highways were going to be busy, it would not be until much later in the morning after most travellers had had their Saturday morning lie in. The ubiquitous trucks were there as always and one by one he passed them, hugging the middle lane of the freeway, the speedometer reading ninety. He liked driving long distances because such long journeys allowed him the opportunity to think things through and organize his mind. He wondered what Stumpy Lazarus had done on Friday evening, knowing that Stumpy would have definitely tried to contact him to spend part of the evening in each other's company.

He moved from the middle lane to the far left lane to overtake the slow camper that seemed to be struggling with the slight gradient and returned to the middle lane after passing the camper. There was something unusual about the vehicle, so Mickey kept his eye in his rear view mirror. He reduced his speed to allow the vehicle to catch up. The sun's reflection made it difficult to see clearly but Mickey thought he could see sparks from beneath the camper. He kept his speed down and watched, his eyes glued to the rear view mirror. He was right. It happened instantaneously. What he had seen were flames licking the underside of the camper and occasionally throwing out sparks as the vehicle moved along. The occupants seemed unaware of the danger. He knew he had to do something and was preparing to flag the camper down when all of a sudden flames shot up all around the vehicle, fanned by the winds on the freeway. He could see the driver trying to slow the vehicle enough to pull over and observed the sudden rush of activity as truck drivers tried to manoeuvre heavy rigs in order to stop and offer assistance.

Mickey pulled to a stop a couple of hundred yards ahead of where the camper had come to a stop and watched as truck drivers rushed forward with fire extinguishers to try to put out the flames. The occupants of the camper had managed to scramble free. The battle was now on to save their vehicle and their belongings. He felt helpless as he watched the frantic scenes, but with the full knowledge that without a fire extinguisher in his car there was very little he could do. It was better to remain a distant spectator than to become a hindrance to those most able to help. He observed the truck drivers' futile attempts to save the camper, watched as the occupants of the camper were shepherded into trucks and eventually got in the car and drove north. He felt sorry for the people involved in such a freak accident on a beautiful Saturday morning and hoped that they were comprehensively covered by their insurance company.

The Sheen River seemed to welcome Mickey Steiner back home as he joined the queue of vehicles crossing the bridge. He looked at his watch. It was exactly eleven forty-five and he was feeling marvellous. The plan was to go home, relax for an hour or so, telephone Stumpy Lazarus and arrange to share a few drinks somewhere. He would wait until Sunday before contacting Rosalynn Brando.

* * *

Stumpy Lazarus opened his eyes in the dark room when he heard the key turning in the lock. He had been asleep for a while and did not feel as tired as he had been just before he was manhandled and thrown into this dungeon. He remained seated on the floor and waited for the door to open. Bright sunshine burst violently into the previously dark room, forcing Stumpy to shut his eyes. He covered his face with his hands and slowly opened his eyes, letting the light in by peeping through the spaces between his fingers. In a few moments, his eyes had adjusted to the light. He removed his hands from his face and looked at the two men standing in the doorway, both holding small calibre guns.

'Hello Lazarus', said the tall black man with the felt hat.

Stumpy looked at him, not saying a word.

'You put on quite a show last night,' the man continued, 'but you see, theatre costs money and you owe me, big time.' He laughed, showing two gold front teeth.

'Yeah! Big time', echoed the stocky white man next to him.

'I figure three sachets of snow,' the black man paused, calculating, 'two bags of whites and two bags of reds, oooohh,' he paused, 'all come to fifteen Gs, and that's generous, because retail street, you are talking twenty Gs easy.'

'Naahh Smokey, more than that', the white man chipped in.

'Now, how are we going to deal with that?' asked Smokey.

There was no point arguing with these two, thought Stumpy, knowing he was at a disadvantage. He decided not to say anything and sat passively against the wall.

'You must be hungry and I don't like a man to make decisions on an empty stomach so we'll have the girls bring you some food.' The black man was serious all of a sudden, angry. 'When you have eaten, you will then tell me how I get my money, fair?' He answered his own question, 'Fair'. He took a step back to allow his partner to shut the door and lock it. Darkness descended upon Stumpy once more as he listened to their fading footsteps.

* * *

Chapter Eight

The comfortable Ocean Pacific VIP lounge at the newly constructed airport was buzzing with activity. The airline's strategy of setting new landmarks was well under way on this beautiful Saturday afternoon. The invited guests, who comprised the mayor, members of the press and television and various dignitaries, were anticipating the arrival of the airline's special transatlantic flight from Zurich.

Sam Dixon stood proudly in the middle of the lounge and chatted with Robert Singleton while waiting for the opportunity to make his speech.

'Ladies and gentlemen,' the brief announcement came from the public address system, 'Ocean Pacific's director of operations will now brief you.'

The din in the lounge slowly melted away, the silence eventually punctured by Dixon's footsteps as he climbed onto the small, raised platform to begin his address.

'Ladies and gentlemen, honored guests, this is a proud moment in Ocean Pacific's short history', he began. 'The significance of flight OP 313 from Zurich,' he paused and looked at his watch, 'which will land here in exactly fifteen minutes, will bear testimony to Ocean Pacific's determination to break new ground in aviation.' He looked around the lounge at the flashing lights and heard the clicks of camera shutters. 'I am proud today, in my capacity as the director of operations for this great airline, to announce the first ever all female crew to fly a transatlantic passenger service.' He waited for the applause to die down.

'By an all female crew, I mean all female - from captain and copilot, through engineering, communications, all the way to cabin crew', he said proudly. 'As you all know,' his eyes searched the lounge, 'behind every successful man there is a woman, but today I can safely say that behind this successful woman there is a man.' He pointed to Robert Singleton in the crowd and continued, 'The record breaking captain of flight OP 313 is none other than the brave, intelligent and beautiful wife of Mr Robert Singleton, better known to most of us in the company as "Broxy." Ladies and gentlemen, Jennifer 'Broxy' Singleton will bring in Ocean Pacific's first all-female crewed transatlantic passenger flight,' he looked at his watch again, 'in ten minutes.'

Captain Jennifer 'Broxy' Singleton landed flight OP 313 on schedule at exactly 1500 hours. She was aware of the importance the airline attached to this particular flight and, although she did not wish to shirk her public relations duties, her desire was to go through the formalities and celebrations as smoothly as possible and spend the rest of the day with her husband in the peace and quiet of their newly acquired home in the suburbs. After what seemed like an endless period of photographs and interviews with the international and city's press corps and television, finally, duty done, Captain Singleton sat next to her husband in the station wagon and relaxed.

'What a hectic day', she said, kicking off her shoes.

'You realize you've made it into the history books don't you?'

'I'll trade a long, hot bath and a quiet dinner with you for that, although I must admit that I feel quite proud about what the girls and I have achieved today', Broxy replied. She adjusted the seat into a comfortable position and fell asleep immediately.

Jennifer Singleton slept through the thirty-five-minute journey from the airport and awakened when the station wagon pulled up in the driveway of her home. She slipped on her shoes, patted her husband gently on the head and walked into the house. She had been away in Europe for the past five days preparing for the record breaking flight. Now, at home, physically tired and emotionally drained, she flopped into the large sofa and let out a great sigh of relief. She threw her head back and began to unwind, ignoring the beeps of the telephone answering machine informing her of the recorded messages. She watched her husband carry in the luggage, disappear out of sight and reappear later to press the button on the answering machine. They sat side by side on the sofa and listened to the messages.

The first message was from Broxy's mother welcoming her home from her long trip and an invitation to dinner at her convenience, followed by the deep tones of Ocean Pacific's chairman, the legendary Roy Masterson, congratulating her for what he was sure would by now be a job superbly done. The next two messages were from Robert Singleton's law firm concerning ongoing criminal law cases.

'Broxy, this is Maureen Carter', came the fourth message. Jennifer sat up in the sofa. She had not heard from her closest friend since their happy meeting at Jennifer's wedding six months ago and eagerly awaited the rest of the message. 'I must speak to you honey', came the rest of the message, along with a telephone number, followed by 'love you lots'. The message had been recorded on Friday afternoon at two thirty-seven; it was now seven fifteen on Saturday evening. They listened to the final two messages which followed, one from Cooper's, the clothing company, informing Broxy about the coat she had ordered two weeks ago, and the final message from the gardener wondering when they wanted him to start the landscape work they had discussed. He was ready to start the work at any time.

'Maureen's message sounds urgent', said Robert Singleton. 'She is probably wondering why neither of us has returned the call.

'I'd better do that right now', said Broxy, reaching for the telephone.

* * *

Katherine Carter's sixteenth birthday party started at two thirty. Cars had been coming and going all afternoon and the spacious back yard was now full of youthful exuberance as fourteen-to-seventeen-year-olds giggled, laughed, danced and generally did what they did best, which was to have fun.

Inside the house, Maureen Carter was playing host to some of the parents who had accepted the invitation to stay for the party. Despite the size of the house, space was at a premium this afternoon, an indication of Katherine's popularity with her peer group as well as their parents.

Maureen Carter had planned the party in such a way as to allow the children their freedom to enjoy themselves. She, of course, had complete trust in them and, to avoid interference from the adults, she had surreptitiously nominated five of the seventeen-year-old girls and three of the seventeen-year-old boys as her special marshals in charge. The parents who chose to stay were segregated from the young ones and entertained inside the house. The marshals, along with Katherine's brother John, had organized the selection of music, the seating arrangements and the choice of whom they felt would be the best and most popular disc jockey. Kazeem Kazi had been put in charge of gathering all of Katherine's presents and placing them in her room. The afternoon was going splendidly and it was obvious everyone was enjoying themselves. Maureen Carter's only regret was her inability to acquire the very special present that her daughter wanted.

Simon Carter, Ben Swinton and others were engrossed in conversation with the chief executive of Nylander Electronics in the living room. William Nylander had been away in Saudi Arabia for the past year working on an important electronic guidance systems project. He had come home on short notice to consult the State Department on some delicate matters and was due to return to Jeddah via Washington in two days' time. When he had dropped his sixteen-year-old daughter Jill off at the party this afternoon, he couldn't resist the invitation from Maureen Carter to stay and spend some time with them. Nylander enchanted the small gathering around him with stories of the Arabic world. He told them of Bedouin sword dancers, of how the Bedouins spun yarn from wool from their camels, sheep and goats and derived the patterns and designs of the weavings from the desert environment.

'I have great difficulty imagining any greenery and wildlife in that region of the world', said Barbara Supple, whose daughter had been nominated as one of the marshals for the party.

'Mrs Supple,' Nylander turned to her, 'did you know that each autumn large flocks of greater flamingos arrive in the Gulf from southern Russia and northern Iran?'

'But the place is so dry and hot', challenged Barbara Supple.

'It is a fact that the character and traditions of Kuwait, for example, have been shaped by the sea.' Nylander picked up his glass and drank. 'I'd bet you thought you wouldn't find a fish in sight.' Everybody laughed.

'I have heard of desert camping and how exciting it can be', Ben Swinton said. 'Have you had the opportunity to try it?'

'Not so far,' Nylander replied, 'but it's something I've been meaning to do. You see, times have changed for the Saudis, Kuwaitis and generally the whole area of the Arabian Peninsula. It is the desire to return to their roots that forces the Bedouin to camp in the desert. By so doing, they remember the simpler days, when their forefathers lived in a land of uninterrupted horizons and the hardships of physical labor and inherent dangers of life which shaped their personalities.' The small gathering was now totally engrossed in Nylander's romantic description of open spaces, cool evenings, limitless horizons, no boundaries and fresh open air.

The calm, pleasant interior of the Carter living room received the sounds of the door bell and spread it monotonously across the room. The crowd around Nylander that had now absorbed other smaller groups of conversationalists seemed to be awakened from a dream, a dream of limitless space. Maureen Carter excused herself and moved to the door. She opened the door to an experience she would never forget.

In the front garden of the house, tethered to the birch tree, was a most magnificent horse. At the door, the short man wore a dark suit that Maureen recognized immediately as one of those she had included in her package to Mr Kazi, from her husband's wardrobe. Because of the man's short stature, he had made an attempt at some alteration to the suit and, as Maureen could guess, he had done a fair job at it. The man took off his hat and bowed.

'Mrs Doctor Carter,' said the man, 'my name is Shamon,' he paused, 'Shamon Kazi.'

'I know, I know, Mr Kazi', she was almost screaming and jumping up and down, like a little girl. They spilled out of the house like bees escaping from a bonfire, Simon Carter leading the way. The Arabian Peninsula was now truly thousands of miles away from here and from their minds as well. They had gathered on the front lawn, Shamon Kazi standing beside Doctor Carter, with all of the guests who had been in the house, in a semi-circle behind them and admiring this most beautiful specimen of a horse.

Shamon Kazi stood next to Carter with his hat in his hand. He cleared his throat and began to speak. He had not planned on a speech today. All he wanted to do was to bring the horse to the young girl who Kazi was absolutely sure would love the horse as much as he did.

'Doctor Carter, Mrs Doctor Carter, good people', he began. Shamon Kazi did not know it but he was giving his first official speech ever.

'I come here today because I must.' He paused, pulled a red hand-kerchief from his trouser pocket and wiped his mouth. No one moved or even twitched. They stood as one, eyes focused on this humble man and on the horse behind him and waited to hear what he had to say.

'Thursday night, the good doctor he saved my life and the life of my wife. No doubt in my mind at all, I know.' His voice croaked, tears slowly welling in his eyes.

'My wife, she is getting better and I am happy about it, so today, I come here to say a special thank you to the good doctor and his wife for also looking after my Kazeem.' He turned and walked over to the horse and led the animal forward.

'Doctor Carter, this special filly is for my little girl, your daughter. Happy Birthday', he said, presenting Carter with the horse.

John Carter came out of his room with the small present he had hidden for his sister and heard the clapping. He was sure it was coming from the front side of the house. There was no one in the living room so he followed the sounds until he stood in front of the large window and immediately recognized the horse. It was as if he had been shot out of a cannon. Within seconds he was beside his sister in the back yard. It was indescribable. Katherine Carter certainly couldn't run that fast and stay on her feet at the same time. The rest of the children just had no idea what was going on. It might have had something to do with instinct and survival because when the children saw Katherine Carter move the way she did, they must have thought run or die. It was like a herd of buffalo as they streamed out of the house and spilled onto the lawn.

Katherine Carter found herself in suspended animation. Moments ago, she had unofficially broken the world sprint record for fifty meters but now, face to face with the filly that she had dreamt about for the past few weeks, she couldn't seem to move her legs. She stood next to her father and looked at the horse. It was as if she was in a trance. Eventually, her energy and breath restored, she wrapped her arms around the horse's neck and whispered over and over again, 'Shamka, Shamka my love, Shamka.' She was crying. Tears of joy streamed down her face unashamedly. Maureen Carter found herself crying happily and joined the crowd which had now spontaneously started singing - *'Happy birthday to you.'*

Simon Carter led the way back into the house, his arms around the shoulder of his newly found friend. He took time to introduce Shamon Kazi to all the guests and produced a bottle of champagne to celebrate his daughter's special day. In the back yard the children were once again in celebration mood, the music a little louder than before.

Maureen Carter answered the phone in the kitchen and recognized Broxy's familiar voice instantly.

Chapter Eight

'What in the world is going on there', Broxy asked, listening to the loud music filtering down the telephone line.

'It's Katherine's birthday party', Maureen answered excitedly.

'Oh, sweetheart, you'll have to forgive me, I had forgotten', said Broxy with some regret, 'I'll make it up to Katy as soon as I can, and wish her happy birthday from both Robert and I.'

They agreed to speak again on Sunday, Maureen promising to call before hanging up the phone.

* * *

Stumpy Lazarus stood up and moved away from the wall in the dark room when he heard the women's voices outside. They were coming down the stairs, probably with the food that had been promised by Smokey earlier. He waited, arms folded, and closed his eyes when the door opened, flooding the small room with bright sunshine.

'You've got to eat sometime, big boy.'

Stumpy opened his eyes slowly, allowing them to adjust to the light. In front of him approximately four paces away, stood the pretty black woman who had placed the hood over his head in the car. Directly behind her stood the red-head-woman holding a small calibre weapon which Stumpy recognized as a Remington Elliot .22. An unusual weapon he thought, because the Elliot .22 had a ring that served as the trigger, with a curved trigger stop behind it. Unlike most modern day weapons, this particular make was a five-shot pistol. He made a mental note of that and turned his attention to the woman holding the tray of food.

'You will enjoy this,' said the woman, 'but I am afraid you'll have to eat your meal sitting on the floor since there are no tables.'

She set the tray on the floor, just inside the doorway, and stepped back.

'Bon appetite', said the redhead, waving the gun in the direction of the tray of food on the floor.

'Smokey will see you in an hour,' the black woman chipped in, 'so take your time and enjoy your food.' She flashed the attractive smile again, reminding Stumpy of how they had surprised him earlier in the morning. 'You'll find a smallflash light on the tray', she said, stepped back and slammed the door. Once again, darkness descended upon

89

Stumpy Lazarus. He moved forward slowly, shuffling his feet in order not to tread on the tray of food, and bent over when his foot made contact with the edge of the tray. Stumpy fumbled in the darkness for the flashlight, switched it on, removed the white cloth covering the tray and examined the contents of the plates.

Stumpy Lazarus was surprised. He had expected... well... what had he expected? Although he was hungry, he had decided prior to examining the contents of the tray that he would not touch any food they presented. He wondered if this was some kind of joke. Underneath the carefully folded napkin was a small slip of paper. Stumpy picked it up. He tried to read what he thought was the menu, found the exercise almost impossible and finally gave up, frustrated. He wished he had not wasted the educational opportunities that had come his way as a child and decided he would take Steiner's advice and attend adult educational lessons. For the moment, he would enjoy the roast chicken with orange, golden roast potatoes, peas and carrots and the large slice of pumpkin pie. He sat on the floor with his back against the wall, placed the tray on his lap and adjusted the flashlight in such a way that the light shone directly onto the tray. The food presentation had impressed him but the taste and smell were even better. Stumpy consumed everything on the plates. They meant it when they said 'bon appetite', he thought.

He was asleep when they came for him, the stocky white man leading the way, followed closely by the redhead and a mean, looking white man wearing a pair of sunglasses and black leather jacket. Stumpy sized him up, guessing his age to be about twenty-seven or twenty-eight.

'Okay, show time', the stocky man announced. 'Come on now tough guy, Smokey wants to see you.'

They took him up the concrete steps, past a collection of white plastic drums and through a small gate which opened into a sizeable warehouse. He was beginning to get an idea of the location. If he was correct, this warehouse should be situated in the old industrial part of the city, deep in the poorest part of the east side, generally referred to as the 'Rail Yard'. Nothing much happened here, except the few scrap metal companies which used the open spaces to store broken down vehicles, salvaging metal and rubber for recycling. The rail tracks should be nearby if he was correct, thought Stumpy. He guessed his position, which placed him almost five miles south-east of the Pepperdine.

They entered the small office at the back of the warehouse where Stumpy came face to face with Smokey once again.

'Hello Lazarus', Smokey looked up from behind the desk. 'I hope you found the food to your liking', he said, flashing his toothy gold smile.

'Yeah,' said Stumpy, 'I enjoyed the food, excellent and he meant it.

'Well now,' Smokey leaned back in his chair, still smiling, and folded his arms across his chest, 'I think we should talk money then.'

Stumpy could feel himself getting angry; the short fuse was being readied. He had to be careful though. Behind him, the two men who frogmarched him into the office had spaced themselves to either side of where he was standing. The redhead was the only one in the room with any kind of a weapon, the Elliot .22. She had positioned herself just to the right of Smokey, the pistol in her hand but not exactly pointing at Stumpy. He wondered where the door to the right of the girl opened to and hoped that he was right in his guesswork about their location. By the way, where was the black girl? Stumpy eyed Smokey angrily.

'I'd offer you a chair, but as you can see, we don't hang around here much', said Smokey. 'However, you may sit if you wish.'

To everyone's surprise, Stumpy immediately sat on the floor, drew his legs in close and braced himself with his arms, palms facing down on the floor to either side of his body.

'You were talking money', said Stumpy.

'Right, fifteen Gs to be exact,' replied Smokey, 'and believe me, you are going to see a lot of that little room until the money is in my hands, fair?' Stumpy knew Smokey would answer his own question and mimed the word as Smokey said it.

The long, loud whistle came first, followed immediately by two short blasts and then the slow clatter of wheels on tracks. He was right, he knew exactly where he was. Stumpy smiled at the black man in front of him, keeping his eye on the redhead.

'You couldn't spare a glass of water, could you?' he directed the question to the girl, 'Sister'.

The girl ignored Stumpy and turned her attention to Smokey, who was still flashing gold.

'Yeah, why not, Lucy get the man a glass of water', said Smokey. 'Might as well cool him down before he tells us how we get our money.'

Lucy turned towards the door beside her, and at the same time Stumpy's right hand left the floor, reached into his right sock and palmed the Reid's 'my friend' knuckleduster .32. He fired a single shot into the wooden floorboards and addressed Lucy.

'The next shot is for you, if you don't drop that Elliot.' He had moved closer to Smokey's desk and had all four of them in his sight. The girl was starting to turn.

Stumpy fired his second shot through the door, next to Lucy. He deliberately aimed the shot farther to the left of the girl, knowing that the knuckleduster lacked accuracy because of the lack of barrel.

He heard the gun drop and watched the girl's ashen face as she turned to face him.

'Now kick it over sister.' Be looked at the girl's terrified face and added, 'Lucy'.

Stumpy now had control. He was sure that there were other weapons in the room, so he made the three men gather in the center of the room, their backs against one another and facing in three different directions. He picked up the Elliot .22 from the floor and placed the knuckleduster in his left coat pocket. He was not worried about the girl, knowing that it was unlikely for her to have been carrying a second weapon. Besides, she was too terrified to do anything stupid. Stumpy checked the weapon to make sure it was loaded.

'Come on now gentlemen, don't make me ask you, show me the steel,' he said, 'one at a time, starting with gold teeth.'

Within minutes, he had disarmed all three men and, as he had correctly guessed, all three were carrying guns. He had no plans to stay in the warehouse any longer than was necessary but, in his world, certain rituals had to be followed for one to stay alive and on top of the pile. He expected the pretty black girl could return at any moment and who knows how many others could be coming. The three men and the girl were now all sitting back to back in the middle of the small office.

'Weren't we talking money?' said Stumpy to Smokey, who was by now so angry he was quivering. It was obvious the other two men were in shock and were just beginning to recover from the speed and surprise with which Stumpy had acted.

Stumpy motioned Smokey away from the small gathering and met him near the desk. He made him place both hands behind his back and instructed Smokey to draw his hands up as far as they could go. When Stumpy was satisfied, he placed the .22 into the man's armpit and pressed it tightly against the soft flesh, then started to speak to him very softly. He was almost whispering into Smokey's ear.

'How much do I owe you?' asked Stumpy, pushing the gun deeper into the flesh.

'Nothing', came the reply.

'How long have you been dealing drugs in this city?'

'Not long.'

'Shit man, I want to know, how long?'

'Two years,' Stumpy pressed the gun deeper, 'and a bit', groaned Smokey.

'Where are you from? And your answer better be the truth.'

'Chicago', replied Smokey. 'South side', he added.

'Okay Smokey, you son of a bitch,' whispered Stumpy, 'you've now tangled with Stumpy Lazarus and are about to get off light.' He paused. 'You know why?' The man shook his head, showing great discomfort from the pressure being exerted on the gun in his armpit.

'The food you served me this afternoon is what's saved your life. I don't care if you stay in this city or not, but I'll tell you this, if I find you dealing drugs here you and I will clash again and I can tell you, you may not live to tell others. This is my town.' He whipped the Elliot from under the man's armpit with such force that Smokey yelped like a dog and collapsed on the floor. He was walking away from Smokey when the door opened and the pretty black girl walked into the small office. For some inexplicable reason, Stumpy liked her.

CHAPTER NINE

Mickey Steiner stepped out of the shower, towelling his hair vigorously, when the telephone rang. He was happy to be home after the long drive. It would be Stumpy, he thought as he picked up the phone.

'Good evening stranger', the lovely voice of Rosalynn Brando came soothingly from the receiver. 'I tried to reach you last night.'

'Oh', replied Mickey, still rubbing the towel over the wet hair.

'I'd like to discuss something with you. Any possibility of sharing a drink tonight?'

'I'd like that', said Steiner happily, checking the time on the video recorder display. 'Be with you in an hour.'

'See you at eight', Rosalynn said and hung up.

He did not realize he had slept for over four hours. He plugged in the telephone answering machine and started to whistle quietly. The evening was cool and pleasant. Steiner dressed casually and quickly, prepared his laundry for the routine Monday collection and picked up the telephone to call Stumpy Lazarus.

There was no reply from the number so he decided he would telephone his partner later in the evening from Rosalynn's. He stopped to have a brief chat with the security guard at the desk and learned that Stumpy Lazarus had been looking for him the night before. Steiner stepped out of the building at seven thirty to begin the thirty-minute drive to Rosalynn's. It would be good to see her again.

He was surprised at how much he had missed her when he had been away and thought of telling her that when he saw her.

Rosalynn Brando opened the door and welcomed Mickey Steiner with a smile.

'I've missed you', said Steiner, kissing her softly.

'And I've missed you', she said, closing the door behind them.

Steiner strolled into the immaculate house, plopped himself on the couch and picked up the white envelope on the center table.

'That's what I wanted to talk to you about.' Rosalynn pointed to the envelope in his hand and sat next to him.

Chapter Nine

Steiner handed the envelope to her and watched her opening it. She pulled out the invitation card and handed it to him.

'I'd like to go but not without you', she said, and waited for him to finish reading the invitation.

'Do you know who Maldini is?' asked Steiner, placing the card on the center table. She nestled close to him, nodding her head.

'One of the richest men in this city,' she replied, 'the owner of the Hood Acre, the Pepperdine on the east side, KTMZ Radio and God knows what else.'

'You've done your homework', said Steiner, placing his right arm around her shoulder and drawing her close to him.

'Well, you've read the invitation, are we going?' She turned her head to look at him, her face close to his.

'If you want to,' he said, 'but I need to tell you a little more about Jack Maldini and about myself before you decide.'

'Before you do that, tell me, have you had dinner?' she inquired.

'No.' He kissed her. 'Have you?' he asked.

'I was hoping you'd say no because I'd like to take you to a special place. The food is out of this world and I am hungry. This will be my treat, I insist', she said.

'You're the boss.'

Rosalynn untangled herself from his grasp and reached for the phone. She made the reservation for two, nine fifteen and hung up the phone.

'I hope you like Italian', she said.

She returned to him, and stretched herself on the couch, with her head on his chest.

'Now, what about Maldini?'

Steiner looked into her eyes. 'How much time do we have?' he asked, smiling.

'Well, dinner is at nine fifteen.' She looked at her watch. 'It's now ten past eight. It'll take us approximately twenty-five minutes to get to the Romantica', she said winking at him. 'That's where we are eating,' she added, 'so you've got roughly forty minutes to tell me all about Mr Maldini and yourself and anything else you might have in mind.' She giggled and pinched him.

'Did you know that Maldini served five years in prison for murder?' Steiner rubbed his hand gently on her shoulder.

'Yes,' she replied, 'he is supposed to have shot his business partner when he caught him in bed with his previous wife. That's almost twenty-eight years ago, so?'

'So, it's how he did it that shows you something about the man.'

'How did he do it?' Rosalynn was curious.

'When Maldini found them, so the story goes, he undressed all the way down to his underwear, just as his partner was, and sat in a chair next to the bed. He then asked his wife to make a choice, him or the partner.'

'Okay.' Rosalynn did not seem to see anything unusual about that.

'Now this is the interesting bit', Steiner continued. 'Maldini produced a pistol from his collection of antique guns, a Colt Classic Peacemaker .45, placed a single cartridge in the chamber of the weapon, spun the chamber and asked his wife to take alternate shots at his partner and himself until the gun went off. You might say a game of Russian roulette with a twist.'

'Who was to be first?' asked Rosalynn.

'You guessed it, Maldini of course.'

'Apparently, the game went on for quite some time, Maldini threatening to kill his wife with the spare loaded pistol in his hand every time she tried to stop the game.'

'Are you saying that it was Maldini's former wife who shot the business partner?'

'Yeah, but it was Maldini who forced her to do it.'

'It could have been him who was killed', said Rosalynn.

'He took a chance and won.'

'Did all of this come out in the trial?' Rosalynn wanted to know.

'No, because Maldini lied in court and claimed that he had committed the murder. He was sentenced to nine years. His lawyers fought on the grounds of crime of passion. Anyhow, he spent five years in prison, but all the while managed to keep his business interests going.'

'What happened to his wife,' she corrected herself, 'I mean his former wife?'

'She moved to Europe, I believe somewhere in France, remarried and died mysteriously two years after Maldini went to prison.

'And about you, what do I need to know?'

Steiner released her from his grasp and stood up. He wanted to tell her all about himself but felt a slight discomfort now that he had the opportunity to do so.

'Do you have any idea what I do, I mean my work?'

She looked quizzically at him and shook her head.

'Should I be concerned about that?'

I think it's important that you know', he said, pacing away from her. She was staring at him, taking in his tall frame. There was no question in her mind that she loved this man and decided there and then that regardless of what was coming, it would not change her feelings for this quiet, handsome man.

Mickey Steiner had turned and was facing her again.

'I am a bounty hunter', he said.

Her eyes opened wide. 'You mean you kill people?' she asked.

Steiner laughed. 'Good heavens no', he told her, still laughing.

'Well, what does a bounty hunter do?' she asked, feeling more at ease.

He returned to the couch, sat next to her and began to give her details about how Jack Dawson, Stumpy Lazarus and the business in general operated.

'The truth is, we are all indirectly employed by Jack Maldini, although Stumpy doesn't know that.' He looked into her eyes. She was still there, calm, attentive and beautiful.

'As far as Stumpy is concerned, he works for Jack Dawson.'

'Are you disturbed by what you do?' she asked calmly.

'Sometimes,' he replied, 'depending on the individuals involved.'

'Then you must pick and choose your own assignments, that is, if it is possible to do so.' She held his head in her hand and kissed him passionately. 'It'll free your conscience', she concluded.

'You mean you don't mind what I do?' He looked at her, feeling much more at ease.

'No, I don't.' She was being truthful.

Mickey Steiner looked at her for a very long time. 'You know I am in love with you, don't you?'

Rosalynn's heart skipped a beat. 'I am glad, because I've been in love with you since I first laid eyes on you.' She was crying softly.

Steiner held her very tight and kissed her again. 'Come on,' he was pulling her to her feet, 'the Romantica awaits. It's your treat, remember.'

They walked out of the house, hand in hand, and drove away in silence.

* * *

Katherine Carter had had a wonderful day. She had hoped for a special birthday and had harboured no doubts about how special it might be, but her sixteenth birthday had surpassed her wildest dreams. Katherine hugged her best friend at the door and finally said goodnight. The children had all left, having enjoyed one of the best days in their lives. She walked into the living room, straight into the hands of Simon Carter.

'Thank you daddy,' she said, 'thank you so much.'

'I am happy for you darling.' Simon Carter looked at his daughter admiringly. 'But I am not the one you should be saying thank you to.' He pointed to Shamon Kazi. 'That's the man who made your day.'

Katherine rushed to Kazi, held the gypsy's hands in hers and made him a promise.

'Mr Kazi', she said.

'No, little one, Shamon', he replied, his hands still in hers.

'I promise to look after Shamka better than anybody else in the world. Oh, she is so beautiful, thank you, thank you.'

Maureen Carter's thoughts had returned to Thursday night. She was thinking about the conversation at the dinner table when her daughter had mentioned the name Shamka for the very first time. Maureen looked around the room at the few familiar faces now left and decided to ask her daughter the question that had been in her mind since that Thursday night.

'Sit down next to Mr Kazi darling', she said to her daughter.

Katherine took her seat next to the gypsy, still holding the man's hand.

Simon Carter turned to Ben Swinton, then to Nylander, whose daughter had already sought a lift home with friends, and finally to Shamon Kazi and winked at his wife.

'Gentlemen,' he said, 'I have a feeling my wife is going to surprise us all. I can see the look in her eye and experience tells me an important question cometh.'

Maureen picked up the champagne glass, found a small fork from the hors d'oeuvre tray and knocked the fork gently against the glass.

'Lady,' she bowed to her daughter, 'and gentlemen, I have a most important question to ask.' She looked at Katherine, smiling. 'We would all like to know how this lovely sixteen-year-old lady came to name this gorgeous horse.'

Heads started to nod all around the room. They were in fact all curious. Why such a strange name?

Katherine walked confidently into the center of the small gathering, looked at her mother accusingly and began to explain her special name for her special horse.

The name had come from her visits to the farm with her brother. She had, on so many occasions, listened to Mrs Kazi calling out to Shamon Kazi who seemed to be always with his horses. Shamon Kazi's refusal to respond to his wife's calls seemed to frustrate Mrs Kazi, who naturally kept repeating herself so frequently that in the end, what Katherine was hearing sounded like Shamka. On that rainy Thursday night at the dinner table, while they were discussing the possible purchase of the horse for her birthday, her experiences at the farm had naturally come to the forefront of her mind and she had chosen the name spontaneously. Shamon Kazi roared with laughter. He slapped his thighs exuberantly and, looking around the small gathering, nodded his approval.

'When my wife calls me,' Kazi said laughingly, 'I will always run to her.'

Ben Swinton leaned over to Nylander and whispered, 'How appropriate that this magnificent animal should be named, accidentally or deliberately, after this man who has cared for her so lovingly.'

Nylander leaned towards Swinton and whispered. 'That horse is a thoroughbred.'

'What's a thoroughbred?' Swinton enquired.

Nylander looked at him, bemused; and rubbed his chin, trying to find the words to explain. To him, it was obvious; all the signs were there to see.

'Well,' Nylander tried to explain, 'thoroughbreds come in all shapes and sizes. The best specimens will have excellent conformation, characterized by a refined, intelligent head, an elegant neck, well-sloped shoulders, a short, strong body with great depth through the girth giving plenty of "heart room", strong, muscular quarters with well-set tail, well-let-down hocks and clean, hard legs with a minimum of eight inches of bone below the knee.'

'Jesus!' exclaimed Swinton. 'How the hell can you tell all that just by looking at a horse?'

'Trust me,' said Nylander convincingly, 'I know.'

Swinton was unsure. Nylander seemed to know a lot about horses but Swinton felt he was none the wiser about thoroughbreds.

'Now,' said Swinton, 'can you tell me in plain English what a thoroughbred is?'

Nylander laughed.

'Okay,' he tried again, 'technically speaking, a thoroughbred is a horse whose parents are both entered in the General Stud Book in Britain or in the equivalent official thoroughbred stud books in other countries and who thereby qualifies for registration in the same stud book.' He lifted his glass when Maureen Carter did her rounds, filling his glass with champagne.

'Are you saying that the parents of this horse are entered in the General Stud Book?' asked Swinton.

'I doubt it very much, but they should be', replied Nylander. 'Nevertheless, I am sure the horse qualifies for thoroughbred status.' He leaned back in the comfortable chair and sipped the champagne, his thoughts far away across the oceans in the Arabian Peninsula. In a few days he would be back in Saudi Arabia, busy with guidance electronic systems and doing business with temperamental Arabs who could make phenomenal business decisions worth millions of dollars in split seconds over cups of sweet coffee. He thought about his good friend Sheikh Al Makhtoum Walhadi and smiled to himself, wondering what the Sheikh would make of this wonderful horse.

* * *

Rosalynn Brando settled herself comfortably in the plush leather seat and waited for Mickey Steiner to return. The Romantica was certainly the right choice for this evening's dinner. A truly romantic setting, decorated to titillate the heart strings of even the most unromantic soul. She stared at the single red rose in the long-stemmed flower vase, her mind floating peacefully in the peaks and troughs of the almost imperceptible background music which seemed to carry her gently on a journey of incredible tranquillity.

'Miss Brando.' The woman's sharp voice punctured the soft soap bubble within which Rosalynn had been floating so serenely, bringing her back into her seat with a jolt. Rosalynn lifted her head, her eyes locking with those of the intruder.

'Yes', she acknowledged and took in the expensively dressed middle-aged woman.

'Please excuse me for interrupting your thoughts. I really wish now that I hadn't come to you at this moment because I can see you were in some sort of a special place. I am deeply sorry.'

'It's quite all right', said Rosalynn smiling. 'Please sit down. I must be honest and tell you though that you have me at a disadvantage.'

The lady perched herself on the edge of the chair as if to signal her intentions not to stay for long.

'I am Vivian Maldini', she introduced herself, offering her hand to be shaken.

Rosalynn simply nodded her head and shook the woman's hand. She could see immediately that this woman was wealthy. It was unfortunate, however, that her wealth did not seem to accord her the taste and class that wealth alone could never buy. Underneath the excesses, there was a naturally beautiful woman who in Rosalynn's view did not need to complicate such natural beauty with any unnecessary encumbrance.

'Jack and I so very much wish for you to join us to celebrate our anniversary.'

'Thank you Mrs Maldini.' Rosalynn looked directly at her. 'I have every intention of doing just that.'

'Oh, I am so glad', said Vivian Maldini. 'We shall look forward to seeing you.'

She stood up and with a beaming smile scuttled away to her table.

Rosalynn Brando watched her go. What a pity, she thought. The woman seemed nice, she had most of what money could buy, but somehow she projected sadness.

'That could be none other than Maldini's wife.' Mickey Steiner was taking his seat next to Rosalynn.

'I guess we are definitely going to the party,' replied Rosalynn, 'and I can also tell that you weren't able to contact Stumpy. You are worried about him, aren't you?'

'I know I shouldn't be.' Steiner could see the waiter approaching with their starter. 'But for some strange reason, I feel a little uneasy', he concluded.

'Sweetheart,' Rosalynn felt comfortable using the word, 'Stumpy is fine, I know it.' She was smiling, the genuine, wonderful smile that comes from deep within the soul. Mickey Steiner was getting used to appreciating this beautiful woman's warmth. He immersed himself in the romantic atmosphere and began to share a most memorable meal with this most special woman.

When they left the Romantica, Rosalynn Brando was in good spirits. She felt slightly light-headed from the wine which had accompanied the superb meal and wished the enchanting evening to be prolonged.

'Cedar Heights', she said, feeling the effects of the bright moonlight which illuminated the car park.

'A wonderful idea', Steiner replied, knowing exactly what she meant. It was the highest point of the city from where the city presented a magnificent view, especially on a beautiful night. They drove in silence, Rosalynn's head resting gently on Steiner's shoulder, while the moon worked its magic on the two occupants in the Buick.

* * *

Saturday nights were always special in the Hood Acre. Tonight, however, the masses of human flesh filled every available space, forcing the management to adhere to the city's fire regulations by shutting the doors at exactly eleven thirty.

On the ground floor, the blackjack and roulette tables were doing a roaring trade and providing the excitement that the players and fortune hunters had come for. Couples and small groups of people who chose to enjoy a more sanguine evening, filled the four coloured rooms on the second floor and enjoyed the multitude selection of drinks which the management ensured were always available to its clientele. In the Fantasia, the city's elite could be seen, some with wives but most in the company of beautiful women who availed themselves to wealthy men in return for the most precious of commodities - the almighty dollar. The real action, though, was in the Red Rooms, where everything that happened concerned money. Money that was never physically seen, felt or touched but was emptied from one bank account or another and poured into other bank accounts dotted across the country and all over the world with the simple stroke of a pen.

The Red Rooms were all fully occupied tonight. In one of them, the specially organized poker game that had been meticulously arranged by Jack Maldini personally, was about to get under way.

Around the large mahogany table, all six chairs were occupied. On such special days, which occurred twice a year in the Hood Acre, Jack Maldini ensured his presence, and tonight he stood proud and eager to declare the game open officially. He held his prepared speech in his hand and waited for his guests to make themselves comfortable. The six beautiful waitresses, one to every guest in one of the six chairs, were upgraded to hostess status in the Red Rooms and were never referred to as waitresses. Maldini waited patiently for the girls to serve drinks, light cigarettes and fat cigars and finally withdraw to their stations, from where, in the course of the night, they would appear from time to time to respond to the gambling guests' every whim.

Jack Maldini cleared his throat softly and began the introductions. The room reeked with obscene affluence.

They had come from far and wide. Men who prided themselves in their ability to play the game of poker but more importantly thrived on the adrenaline rush they experienced in pitting their skills against those they perceived to be their equals.

The introductions began with the Argentinean beef magnate, Senior Pedro Munzon, a short, balding, bespectacled, tough-looking man in his fifties. He bowed his head in acknowledgement, 'Seniores,' he said loudly and sat back in his chair.

Next came Walter O'Reilly, a well-respected New York banker. Rumour had it that O'Reilly's parents had arrived penniless in the States from Ireland at the turn of the century and had managed to amass a small fortune by advising wealthy horse owners on how to breed quality horses for the racing industry. Walter was the third of five children, all of whom were educated at excellent American universities. In banking circles, he was revered as one of the nation's brainiest.

Simon Chen sat next to O'Reilly and bowed his head at the mention of his name. A small, wiry man, the Hong Kong property developer was believed to be a compulsive gambler who spent a great deal of his time travelling the world. He was a familiar face in Las Vegas and

Atlantic City, where he was said to have won six million dollars over a period of five days. His excitement at the prospect of the anticipated game tonight showed in his face as he looked at his adversaries around the table.

Jack Maldini looked at the next name on his sheet of paper. He hoped he would pronounce the name correctly the first time and prepared for the ordeal by sipping from the glass of water in front of him.

'Gentlemen,' he said, 'I have great pleasure in introducing to you tonight, Mister Andre Papadropolous.' Maldini seemed pleased with himself for getting the name right the first time. 'This is Andre's first visit to this wonderful country of ours,' he said, 'and I am sure it will not be the last.' He walked over to the Greek shipping magnate and patted him gently on the shoulder. 'Welcome to the Hood Acre, Andre, we are honoured to have you with us tonight.'

'God damn, Maldini,' shouted Stan Anderson, 'are we ever going to get a chance to play a game tonight?' The oil man was getting impatient.

'Hold your horses Stan.' Maldini looked at the Texan, smiling.

The Hood Acre was practically Stan 'Butch' Anderson's second home. Well, more or less. The Texan thrived on gambling. Besides oil, which he referred to as the 'blood of the earth', there was nothing he loved better than pitting his wits against other rich people who loved to gamble as much as he did. Butch viewed everybody who had made money outside oil as 'useless, no good bums', except, maybe, cattle men and those who worked in oil-related industries. He had no respect for politicians either, although he donated thousands of dollars to the Republican Party, simply to help ensure that Democrats were kept away from power, be it congressional, the White House or gubernatorial. He stretched himself, puffed on his cigar and waved Maldini to carry on.

'They say that "diamonds are a girl's best friend",' continued Maldini, inviting applause from the six girls in the room, 'but I can tell you this, diamonds are certainly our next guest's best friend.' He was referring to Jan Van Derpool, the Dutch diamond dealer. The good-looking, blonde man raised his hand to acknowledge the introduction.

'Shieeet,' Butch said loudly, 'diamonds my eye.'

Maldini ignored him and quickly began to read through the agreed rules for the night's game.

The game was to be Five Card Draw Poker. Minimum stake was set at a thousand dollars, with no maximum limit, although no player would be allowed to exceed the agreed million-dollar kitty per person. House rules would apply and at the conclusion of the game the overall winner would pay the normal five per cent commission to the Hood Acre. The total stake money of six million dollars had already been transferred into a secured account under Maldini's control and could only be released by Maldini producing an authority note bearing the signature of all six players and countersigned by Maldini and the manager of the nominated bank.

'Good luck gentlemen', said Maldini as the lights in the room were dimmed and the game lamps were switched on to illuminate the area of play. A sudden hush descended upon the Red Room as the first cards were dealt.

* * *

Stumpy Lazarus had never kissed a black woman before. It was not something he thought about and, never having been attracted to any women other than women of his own race, he resisted the urge to do so this evening. He sat next to the pretty black woman who had driven him across town from deep within the east side and felt good to be in her company. She didn't talk much during the drive, limiting her conversation with Stumpy to asking for directions and giving one-syllable answers to his questions.

When the woman had walked into the small office in the large warehouse, her initial reaction had been to turn and run. Stumpy had fired the single shot right through the door, which seemed to convince her that the man with the scar on his face was intent on keeping her in the room. She had turned and walked straight to the group of three in the middle of the room, sat next to the redhead and started to cry. Stumpy had spent some time to stamp his authority on Smokey, who was still lying on the floor by the desk, and the others, to ensure that any ideas they might have had of seeking revenge at a later date were thoroughly diffused. Satisfied that he had accomplished what he had set out to do, he brazenly told Smokey and his small group of several places where they were most likely to find him if they wanted to try their luck at anytime. He then announced that he needed a lift home, though not going as far as to tell them that he could not drive. He knew he wanted the company of the black woman and picked her to drive.

The two of them sat side by side in the car in front of Stumpy's apartment, neither saying a word but Stumpy doing his utmost to suppress the seemingly uncontrollable and strange urge of wanting to kiss the pretty woman. In the end, he thanked her for having been kind enough to drive him home, apologized for having upset her by firing the single shot through the door and left two one hundred dollar bills on the dashboard to cover what Stumpy referred to as 'fuel expenses and your time'. He opened the glove compartment, searched for a piece of paper and found an old receipt. He handed the paper to the woman and told her to write down a number.

She sat motionless.

'Please', said Stumpy after the fourth attempt. 'It'll give me great pleasure to see you again.'

The woman searched through her small purse for a pen. She wrote down the telephone number that Stumpy repeated once more and placed the pen and paper back in her purse. Stumpy Lazarus stepped out of the car and closed the door gently.

'What's your name?' he asked.

She looked at him, started the car and engaged the gear.

'Jurelene Patterson', she said with that infectious smile and drove away.

Stumpy Lazarus was dreaming when the telephone rang. He was wide awake by the fourth ring and lifted the receiver. It was Mickey Steiner. The conversation was brief but pleasant, both men happy to have found each other again. Stumpy fell back on the pillow. He had been dreaming about Jurelene Patterson when the phone had interrupted him. He closed his eyes with the absolute certainty that he would fall asleep within minutes. The past couple of days had been rough and he needed the sleep. He hoped the door to the dream would open again to let him in.

CHAPTER TEN

Robert Singleton was enjoying the late Sunday morning breakfast with his wife in the quiet of their comfortable home. This was a rare experience for the Singletons, who were both busy with high-powered careers which often took them away from home and kept them apart for days on end. He looked into the cool cerulean eyes of the airline captain and felt proud to be married to this dynamic woman. In contrast to the day before, Jennifer Singleton looked rested, fresh and vivacious. Their conversation centered around the logistics of the record breaking flight, and her fears of failure, which she believed would have been used by the most chauvinistic of men as a weapon against not just herself and the all woman crew, but against every aspiring woman on this earth. She was pleased with their achievement and seemed to be enjoying their success even more now that she had had time to reflect on their accomplishments.

'Can I tell you what I am most happy about this morning?' Broxy giggled, toast in one hand, a cup of tea in the other and both elbows, uncharacteristically, on the table.

Robert Singleton gazed at his excited wife who sat across the table from him and nodded his head in the affirmative.

'No schoolmaster or career adviser across this land will ever again dissuade any young girl who proclaims her aim to become an airline pilot, simply on the grounds that it is a man's domain.' She reflected on the statement she had just made and laughed loudly and happily. 'I can hear the girls' answer even now,' Broxy continued, '"But sir, Jennifer Singleton..."' She roared with laughter and spilled the tea all over the breakfast table, her joy shared by her husband.

After breakfast, they walked hand in hand into the back yard of the house to finalize the landscaping arrangements about which the gardener had telephoned. They agreed on what had to be done, Robert accepting the responsibility of informing the gardener to start immediately.

The ringing telephone summoned them back into the house. 'It's Maureen', Broxy whispered to her husband, covering the mouthpiece with her palm. She settled down for what he knew would be quite a lengthy conversation with her best friend; six months worth of information to be channelled both ways; digested, deciphered, analyzed, absorbed and enjoyed. Robert Singleton was happy for his wife. He walked over to her, took her left hand in his and gently kissed the back of her hand. Broxy waved at him and watched him disappear into his study to add the finishing touches to tomorrow's court cases.

Robert Singleton was completely engrossed in his work when Broxy opened the door to the study and walked in.

'Am I disturbing you?' she asked.

Robert looked up from the sheaf of papers on the desk, then at his watch.

'Of course not, darling,' he replied, 'come in, sit down.'

He had been working for almost two hours but it felt as if he had been at the desk for only a short time. He swivelled the chair around to face his wife who had taken the seat behind him. She was in a contemplative mood.

'Come on, share it'. He said kindly. 'What did Maureen say to turn you from the hot potato that you were earlier to a cold cucumber?'

'Apparently, Simon is in some kind of trouble', said Broxy, still reflecting.

'Well, don't hold back, trouble is my game', Robert said trying to cheer her up. 'I am a lawyer, remember?'

Indeed he was. Broxy perked up. It was as if she had been injected with a magic stimulant. In her head, the brain waves were crisscrossing and moving so fast she could almost feel the collisions. Why hadn't she thought of that? If Simon was in trouble, one of the best attorneys in the land was sitting right here in this house, right here in front of her, hallelujah!

'Come on.' Robert Singleton's 'lawyer's hat' was now firmly on his head. He had produced a pad from somewhere amongst the books and papers on the desk. In his right hand the ballpoint pen was primed, ready to attack the pad. 'Take it from the top', he said.

'I'll give it to you in brief, shall I?' said Broxy.

'Even better', replied Robert.

'Okay, here goes', Broxy started. 'First, Simon's friend gets into financial difficulty through gambling. The friend approaches Simon to act as a guarantor, just for a short while, thirty days to be exact. The thirty days expire, the friend has not come up with the money.' She paused to think. 'By the way, the amount involved is $67,000. Tough, rough people come out of the woodwork demanding their money from Simon. Obviously Simon is under pressure and naturally Maureen is quietly going bananas but doing her best to stay strong.' Broxy sighed and closed her eyes.

'Is that it?' asked Robert.

'That's it.' Her eyes were still closed, head back in the chair. She could hear the ballpoint pen attacking the pad.

'When did the thirty days expire?' asked Robert.

'Wednesday', she replied.

'Did she say anything else that you think might be important?'

'Well, she said she had thought of a plan and she wanted to see me as soon as possible.'

'Did she elaborate?'

'No.' Broxy shook her head.

'I am wondering about the legitimacy of the debt.' Robert was nibbling at the end of the ballpoint. 'What are you going to do?'

'I was thinking,' said Broxy, 'we haven't seen Maureen and Simon since the wedding.' Her eyes drifted to the framed wedding picture of the two of them cutting their wedding cake. 'It might be nice to use part of the two-week break I've got to visit. I could leave on Tuesday and you can join us on Friday.'

'Sounds fine.' Robert got up and placed the pen and pad on the desk. 'In the meantime I shall see what I can dig up to help.' She was out of the chair in an instant, captain's protocol firmly shelved elsewhere.

'Come with me Singleton', she teased, forefinger beckoning, and led the way to the bedroom.

* * *

They had all gone, and there was no evidence at all to show that they existed and that they had been here. The Carter household had opened its arms wide to friends; friends who had taken the trouble to bring some joy to a sixteen-year-old. Now, only the two were left. Simon Carter and Ben Swinton had just finished helping Maureen to clean the house; plates and glasses washed, carpets vacuumed, tables and chairs dusted and replaced and the kitchen spotless. Maureen had hugged them both and gone to bed, so finally, at two thirty on a Sunday morning, the two doctors sat across from each other in the quiet of the Carter living room, neither daring to talk of the trouble in which they had immersed themselves.

Ben Swinton spoke first. 'Simon,' he said, 'I wonder what I'd do if I were struck off.' There was no doubt about his anxiety. He had managed to share the joyous evening with the rest of the family and friends without showing a trace of the heavy load on his shoulders. All through the day he had been there to help, doing whatever Maureen asked of him without hesitation. Later in the evening, he had smiled quietly to himself and shrugged off the attentions of Mrs Supple, something that had not gone unnoticed by Maureen Carter. Instead, Swinton had concentrated on his conversation with Nylander whom he had found fascinating. He hoped someday it might be possible to camp in the desert like the Bedouins do. In the silence of this particular moment, he could not help but focus on his most pressing problems.

Simon Carter was sympathetic. He had no doubts that his friend would have done everything possible to save the baby. With regard to the alcohol in the blood, how much alcohol? Damn it! The man was an excellent obstetrician. If they insisted on striking him off, the hospital and the city would have lost a very good doctor indeed. 'We may have to seek legal advice on this', Simon found himself saying.

They looked at each other soberly, seemingly drawing strength and inspiration from one another.

'What happened when I was away?' asked Swinton.

'They came chasing me at the hospital for their money', Simon Carter passed the ashtray to Ben Swinton who had just lit a cigarette. 'That was Thursday morning. They were supposed to have come back on Friday morning but so far I've heard nothing from them.'

'I am so sorry to have involved you in this sordid affair'. said Ben, 'I've already arranged a meeting with my father's attorneys. I should be able to clear all this up by Monday evening.'

'I want you to promise me one thing.' Carter was looking directly into the eyes of his best friend. 'Regardless of what happens on Monday, the thought of suicide is definitely out of the question, promise me that, and I can assure you that Maureen and I will be by

110

you all the way through.'

It was as if Swinton had not heard Simon Carter's statements. He stared blankly ahead of him, the long ash on the cigarette between his fingers threatening to foul the recently vacuumed carpet.

'Ben!' shouted Carter. 'Did you hear a word of what I said?'

Swinton shook the ash into the ashtray and placed the half-smoked cigarette in the groove cut into the edge of the glass ashtray. He sat back in the chair smiling. Finally he spoke.

'I met a man', he said.

'What?' Simon Carter honestly believed his friend was losing his mind.

'Really I did.'

'And?' Carter waited.

'And, the thought of suicide is definitely out of the question', he quoted Simon.

Simon Carter believed him utterly. There was no doubt about the deep conviction with which the statement was made. Something must have happened. Carter wanted to know more but was somehow afraid to delve deeper into the mystery.

Ben Swinton volunteered the information. He told Carter about Bakersfield, about their conversation in the motel, the bottles of whiskey, the jungles of Vietnam, the radio officer and the Vietcong with the bamboo stake. He hoped someday it would be possible to introduce Simon Carter to the ex-marine who, somehow, in his own quiet way managed to drag him from the abyss.

They talked deep into the night, or was it morning, conversation changing all the time from one subject to another.

'Do you know what Nylander said to me?' Ben Swinton asked all of a sudden. 'The horse is a thoroughbred', he added.

'What's a thoroughbred?' Simon Carter thought he had a rough idea but was unsure.

'I was hoping you wouldn't ask that,' Swinton laughed, 'because the answer is too long and too complicated to say it in English.' He stood up, stretched and shook Carter's hand. 'Goodnight pal', he said and walked off towards the guest room.

* * *

Jack Maldini sat in the cashier's office in the Hood Acre. Across the table from him were Joe Lazlo and Jake Watson. The three men watched the cashier, pencil behind the ear, his cap perched on his head and busily stacking the bundles of notes in neat rows on the long table in front of him. The Hood Acre had 'minted' as much money as could be legally 'minted' by any legitimate business. He reminded Maldini of the telegraph operators in the old days. The men who contributed to building America by ensuring that communication lines stayed open, men who went about their business with dedication and were relied upon by newspapermen to get their stories through. No one seemed to notice men such as these. It occurred to Maldini that he did not know the man's name. He was sure that neither Joe Lazlo nor Jake Watson would know the name of the busy cashier and decided to put his assumption to the test. Maldini leaned over towards his two business associates.

'Tell me Joe,' he said to Lazlo, at the same time drawing in Jake Watson by looking at him, 'what's his name?' pointing to the busy man still counting and stacking up the bundles of bills.

Maldini was right, neither man knew the name of the cashier. He felt ashamed.

Jack Dawson was right. Jack Maldini had many sides. He may have had a dark streak but he was also unpredictable.

'Young man', Maldini called the cashier over. 'Who am I?' he asked.

'Mr Maldini of course', the cashier replied.

'And these two men?' He was referring to Lazlo and Watson.

'Mr Lazlo', the man bowed his head gently towards Joe Lazlo, 'and Mr Watson.'

'Have you been with us long?' asked Maldini.

'Five years last May', the cashier replied.

'Thank you.' Maldini felt embarrassed.

His mind went back to the old days. It was always this way. The world was full of people who got up every morning, sacrificed precious time, travelled back and forth to earn a living for their families, but men and women who generally remained anonymous. Maldini's eyes drifted to the long table now covered with the piles of bills.

'Do you two realize that it is people such as these,' he was once again referring to the cashier, 'who keep you and I rich and comfortable?

Chapter Ten

And we don't even know their names.' Jack Maldini was quite serious.
'From now on, I want this building closed to the public on the
twentieth of December every year. The only people who will have
access to the Hood Acre on that day will be the children of the
employees of this building, the Pepperdine, the radio station and the
cannery. The twentieth of December party will be our thanks to our
employees and every child will receive a present.' He looked at the
other two. 'We should have done this a long time ago.' Maldini got up
ready to leave the room. He walked over to the cashier who had just
finished bagging all the money and was making his last entries into the
ledger.

'What's your name?' asked Maldini.

'Frank Dimble.'

Maldini shook the man's hand and walked out of the office. He was
going to pay his last visit to the Red Room. His watch read five fifteen.

* * *

The security man opened the door to the Red Room for Jack
Maldini to enter. The room seemed no different from when he had
left it hours ago after his brief speech and introductions, except that
smoke now hung heavy above the occupants who seemed totally
unaware of his presence. He accepted the glass of brandy from the
pretty hostess and melted into the background. Maldini felt like a fly
on the wall. He looked at each of the players. They had been playing
for over five hours and yet none of them looked tired. He could not
tell from their demeanour who was winning or losing. No one spoke.
Maldini watched as Walter O'Reilly raised his glass to be filled almost
instantaneously by the leggy, blonde hostess who glided in from
amongst the shadows and just as quickly faded away into the shadows.
The dealer sat at the table with them, poised to deliver a card to
whoever had the right to demand one.

Jack Maldini was thinking how unreal the whole scene looked. Six
wealthy men, from different corners of the world, assembled in this
relatively tiny room, sitting for hours and hours doing nothing constructive but willing to lose millions without a care in the world. He
was looking at Simon Chen. The property developer from Hong
Kong sat passively between the New York banker, Walter O'Reilly, who

113

seemed bored, and the shipping magnate. Maldini smiled to himself, thrilled at his success in the pronunciation of the long unpronounce-able Papadropolous. Everybody from Greece must be something 'Opolous' or other, he thought. 'Right fellas,' the sound reverberated through the room. It was the Texan, Stan Anderson, 'I'll match the one hundred and fifty and raise it by another two hundred.' The oil man scribbled the bet on a piece of paper and passed it to the table controller, then looked confidently around the table, coughed loudly and picked up the glass filled with gin and tonic.

It was then that Maldini became aware of the fact that no one had spoken in the room for the whole time that he had been in there. There was movement at times, mostly from the girls who went about their duties in silence and the subtle movement by one player or another to peek at a card in front of him, but no one spoke. The con-troller had finished reading the figures that the oil man had passed to him and confirmed the bet thus, 'Gentlemen, the one hundred and fifty thousand has been matched by Mr Stan Anderson. I confirm that Mr Anderson has also now raised the stake by a further two hundred thousand.' The controller then opened a small, brown, leather wallet and placed Anderson's slip inside.

Jack Maldini watched as Jan Van Derpool signalled the light-skinned black girl to refill his glass. Of those six men around the table, five would finish this game having lost a million each. The dealers, the controllers and the girls, all of whom were replaced at two-hourly intervals, would have earned substantial amounts of money that would be paid as bonuses on top of their salaries. He, Maldini, was guaranteed his five per cent, which in this case was $300,000 regard-less of who won or lost. He looked at the pretty hostess next to him, smiled and thought of his wife. The anniversary party was on Saturday. He quietly walked out of the Red Room.

* * *

The honorable Justice James C Colman was in his sixty-fifth year of his life. Although quite distinguished looking he was prone to excess weight that caused his stomach to strain against the expensive striped shirts he was fond of wearing. In court, however, the excess fat was thankfully concealed when the judge was robed. The judge was a very

114

unhappy man this early Sunday morning. He paced the spacious balcony of his expansive home that nestled in the secluded Corsegrove Heights area at the base of the Corsegrove Mountains.

He had enjoyed his poker session last night and had been fortunate enough to have won thirteen thousand, a tidy sum which he believed now boosted his credit substantially. His anger, however, was caused by the rumour that had been circulating in some of the Red Rooms, in one of which he was busily teaching those upstarts a thing or two about the intricacies of the poker game. He would have to check with that nincompoop Maldini. If the rumour was true, that fool, that criminal, would have some explaining to do. Judge Colman smiled at the thought. He had often imagined Maldini in chains, standing in front of the bench in his courtroom ready for sentencing.

Jack Maldini had just gone to bed when the telephone rang. He reached over his wife to pick up the receiver. It was Judge James C Colman.

'Maldini!' shouted the Judge, 'What's this I hear about an important big game in one of the Red Rooms last night?' He paused. 'Are you implying that I am not important enough?'

'Judge,' Maldini tried to explain, 'your honour, it was a million dollar stake table, I didn't think you would want to involve yourself in a game like that.'

'A million dollars eh?' The judge's voice seemed to weaken considerably. 'Anyhow, you know my credit is good', he said and hung up the phone.

Colman entered the bedroom where his wife was still fast asleep. He loosened the belt and removed his morning gown, immediately releasing the wobbly stomach that seemed to want to burst through the pyjama top. 'What kind of a man plays poker for a million dollars?' he asked aloud, sliding gently into bed in order not to wake his wife.

Jack Maldini had replaced the receiver. He was now lying on his back, staring at the ceiling of his bedroom. The special poker sessions were getting better and better, he thought. He lay there, listening to Vivian Maldini's steady breathing and visualized all the four Red Rooms full of oil men, diamond dealers, bankers and maybe even kings and queens, all of them playing for million dollar stakes. Why not, he thought and began to drift into sleep, this is America, anything is possible.

Jack Maldini was fast asleep when Vivian Maldini woke up at nine o'clock. She removed her bible and rosary from underneath her pillow and quietly began to recite her prayers. She would attend the eleven thirty Mass alone.

* * *

Shamon Kazi stood in the middle of the field and watched the horses quietly grazing. He had had a most wonderful night with the doctor, his family and friends. For the first time he had tasted champagne. Kazi could not understand why so much fuss was made over this drink which to him tasted like dry wine which had been kept beyond its sell-by date. Oh, he had enjoyed the drink, but he simply couldn't understand the fuss.

He watched the chestnut filly. What had the little princess called her? Kazi tried to remember. *Shamka*. Kazi started to walk towards the horse. For some strange, inexplicable reason he had never bothered to name this particular horse although all the others had names. Besides the chestnut, his favorite was the black gelding, Talisman. Yes, Talisman was a special horse too but why had he given him a name and not bothered to find an appropriate name for the chestnut. Shamon Kazi believed in the order of things in this world. He had learned that from his father, his ancestors. Nothing in this world happened without a reason. If the gods had wanted him to name the chestnut he certainly would have done so. In a way, the horse bore his name as explained by the little 'princess' last night.

He smiled at the thought of ignoring his wife's calls. It was not something he had noticed until the little girl explained how she had come to name the horse. Kazi kept walking towards the chestnut. He was calling her; calling her softly by her name. He could see the horse's ear prick up. This was the test? Would the chestnut pass the test?

Shamon Kazi stood directly in front of the chestnut and began to speak. Kazi was not communicating in English. He held the chestnut's head in his hands and chanted strange sounding words. In between the chants he would occasionally mention the horse's new name and rub the animal's neck vigorously. After the vigorous rubbing, the chanting began again and so it went. Slowly, the other four horses

116

began to gather around the chestnut and the mysterious horseman. A perfect circle had formed, in the center of which stood Shamon Kazi and Shamka. He continued to chant. The horses began to circle around Shamka and Kazi, the new name of the horse now mentioned more and more frequently. Something special was happening.

The chestnut began to back away from the horseman, slowly. The circle of horses maintained their form but the circle widened. Shamon Kazi made strange noises, now calling the name Shamka much more frequently. To the naked, untrained eye, it was like a dance: some sort of orchestrated ancient dance with mysterious undertones. Shamon Kazi was smiling. He was satisfied. The name had been accepted. He would now find out if the horse had everything he believed it had.

'Shaaamka!' shouted Kazi all of a sudden. The filly cantered towards him, closely followed by Talisman and the other three. Shamon Kazi grabbed the horse's mane as she cantered by and swung himself acrobatically onto the horse's back. He rubbed the horse's neck gently, placed his head very close to Shamka's pricked ears and whispered the horse's name. Not a single soul saw what happened next, and had they seen it they would not have believed their eyes.

* * *

Maureen Carter sang while she prepared Sunday lunch for her family. Katherine Carter had set two extra plates at the lunch table for Kazeem Kazi and Ben Swinton. Maureen Carter sang because she was happy. Her daughter's sixteenth birthday had gone perfectly, capped by the wonderful surprise from the gypsy. Earlier today she had attended church with her family to say thanks to God for the wonderful life they enjoyed. She had kept her word and telephoned Broxy immediately after church. The conversation had lasted a long time and it had been good to share her innermost thoughts - joys as well as worries - with her very special friend. Broxy would be coming in two days' time and Maureen looked forward to that. All she had to do now was to feed her family and friends, take it easy for the rest of the afternoon and sleep well tonight to be ready for her hospital duties on Monday morning.

The lively conversation at the table was all about yesterday's events. Katherine Carter glowed with joy. Her father had arranged with the gypsy horseman to look after the horse for his daughter in the meantime. Shamon Kazi had gladly accepted the task but had made it absolutely clear that the chestnut filly was now owned completely by Katherine. He, Shamon Kazi, would only be the temporary keeper until such time that the young lady wanted to take full possession of the special horse, and, in addition, she would have access to her horse at any time, night or day.

Ben Swinton's thoughts were once again revolving around last night's conversations with William Nylander. He could not forget how convincing the man had sounded. For an electronics expert, he seemed to know so much about horses. His statement about the horse being a thoroughbred was conclusive; no ifs, buts or maybes, just pure certainty of fact. Swinton raised his plate to receive the slice of apple pie that Maureen was ready to place on the plate and almost dropped the plate when he heard the words again, this time from Katherine Carter's lips.

'Uncle Nylander said Shamka is a thoroughbred', she said excitedly. 'What's a thoroughbred?'

They were looking at one another around the table. Simon Carter smiled at Ben Swinton, remembering that he had posed the exact same question last night or rather earlier on Sunday morning and had received a 'goodnight' in response.

Somebody had to reply to Katherine, but nobody was sure, so Maureen Carter tried.

'Honey,' she began tentatively, 'a thoroughbred is a very special horse. A horse with good parents and very fine qualities.' She looked around the table for support but only managed to receive a wink from her husband. Ben Swinton was impressed. That's it, he thought. That's basically what Nylander was trying to tell him. Swinton was about to expand on Maureen's explanation, drawing on the information Nylander had given him, when he heard the gypsy boy.

'A thoroughbred,' said Kazeem Kazi somewhat apprehensively, 'is a horse that is good-looking and alert. It moves with great freedom and covers the ground easily with its stride when it gallops. They have great courage and much stamina which helps them to be good racehorses and show horses.'

Everybody around the table sat in shock and great surprise with the exception of John Carter who simply put his arm around his friend's shoulder.

'Way to go Kaaz', he said, as they all began to applaud. The boy had told them exactly the characteristics of a thoroughbred, simply, concisely and absolutely accurately without a lot of fluff. Shamka was exactly that.

Simon Carter sat with his mouth partially open. The boy was not in school and as far as Carter knew had never had any form of formal education. The eloquence with which the boy had just enlightened all around the table beggared belief.

Simon Carter could not resist the question. He coughed lightly before he began.

'Question, question,' said Simon, tapping his plate with his dessert spoon, 'Kazeem, your English is excellent,' they all knew the doctor was speaking the truth, 'where did you learn to speak such good English?'

The gypsy boy seemed embarrassed, unsure of what to say, his eyes punching holes through the tablecloth.

'Might as well tell them Kaaz', John Carter came to the aid of his young friend.

Maureen Carter was suspicious, a mother's instinctive suspicion which usually asks its own questions without words but screams loudly, *Okay, what have you been doing behind my back?*

The gypsy boy looked up from the table, looked to his friend who nodded quietly, and began to share a two-year hidden secret.

Kazeem Kazi had met John Carter just over two years ago, not long after the Kazis had settled on the farm. The gypsy could not ride a bicycle and took a fascination to John's ability to stay upright on the two wheels. They had shared their very first meeting sitting on the grass in the open spaces talking about bicycles and horses. It was then that they had made each other their secret promise. The deal was quite simple, John Carter was to teach Kazeem Kazi how to ride a bicycle in return for which Kazeem was to teach John how to ride a horse. The lessons had gone well, always in secret, the bicycle one week and horses the next.

The boys had progressed quickly, John soaking up all the information he could about horses and becoming very adept at riding while Kazeem felt happy in the knowledge that he had mastered the ability to do various tricks on two wheels. As a natural progression of their friendship, John Carter had begun to teach Kazeem Kazi how to read and write, how to work out mathematical sums and had given the gypsy an electronic calculator as a present. In return for the lessons, the gypsy had taught John Carter how to fish with the simplest of fishing tools.

The two boys had progressed to a point where they managed to spend every Wednesday afternoon, after John had finished school, in the city library where the librarian delighted herself by introducing the two boys to the most interesting books in her 'armoury'.

The Sunday afternoon 'bombshell' was unexpected. It had exploded loudly and accidentally over the kitchen table; a straight answer to a simple question, but an answer that carried a two-year secret of two young boys from totally different backgrounds sharing life in the most positive way possible.

Simon Carter wanted confirmation, not because of any doubts about the truth to the story he had just heard but rather to cement in his own mind the pride he felt. He and Maureen had brought up the children to respect the differences between the many peoples who inhabit this world. They had taught the children that from the humblest of people the most wonderful experiences could be gained provided one were open-minded. His son could ride a horse; his teacher, a gypsy. The gypsy could read and write; his teacher, John. He and Maureen had taught their children that variety was essential in life because it enriched the fabric of society and in essence humanity in general. Simon Carter looked at his son on this Sunday afternoon and felt as if he had climbed the highest mountain with his wife. The two looked at each other across the dining table, their spirits soaring high over the highest mountain. They had successfully planted their flag and it fluttered in the wind, shouting volumes for the world to see.

CHAPTER ELEVEN

Rosalynn Brando sealed the envelope and added it to the collection of post on the side table. Rosalynn and Mickey Steiner had accepted the invitation. They had had a wonderful Saturday evening together. Her spirits had soared to heights she never believed she could reach. She had floated on clouds when she had danced with Mickey at Cedar Heights to the soft music from the car radio. They had laughed and tickled each other like children. Saturday night had been a dream and reality all in one. But today was Sunday and her feet were firmly on the ground again.

She stretched herself on the couch and pressed the remote control. The television crackled once, twice, and splashed color all over the screen. She could not attune herself to the scenes at first but it soon became clear that something dreadful had happened. She sat up on the couch, reached for the remote control and increased the volume.

'We believe it was a small caliber weapon', the uniformed police officer was surrounded by a group of reporters, 'and no, we haven't found the gun. We'll issue a full report later this afternoon. This is tragic, really tragic', the police officer concluded and turned away from the reporters.

'And so once again, a drug-related murder in the Shackle Avenue area of this city, and now back to the studio', the reporter concluded.

In spite of the Sunday afternoon sunshine, the east side was in a gloomy mood.

Two youths had been found shot in the alleyway near the Shackle Avenue Community Center late Saturday night; both had been shot by a small caliber gun. In the pockets of one of the dead boys was a substantial amount of money and what was believed to be heroin. Word had travelled fast through the predominantly black population and the community was heavy hearted. The dead boys were fifteen and seventeen.

For several years, community leaders had been trying their utmost to remove the evil of drugs from the east side without much success. No sooner had they succeeded in the removal of one main dealer when another was easily installed by the faceless, ruthless men who

Shamka for the City

managed to control all drug activity in the ghetto. A significant event had occurred over the weekend, an event that had brought the issue of drugs and crime back to the forefront of the community's agenda.

The congregation spilled out of the east side Pentecostal Church, still incensed by the murder of the two boys, while those who earned their living in one way or another through the sale of drugs protested their innocence and blamed the community leaders for the lack of meaningful employment opportunities.

The tragic incident over the weekend was to shake the foundations of the east side to the core.

They gathered in the main hall of the Shackle Avenue Community Center, yards away from where the two boys had died violently on Saturday night. Most of the faces were black with a sprinkling of Latinos and whites who had also lived most of their lives in the city's east side. Their anger was undisguised, their fury only needing the right words to spark them into action. It came. Braxton Walker painted a picture with words.

Braxton Walker was a tough-minded, uncompromising, black man of twenty-eight. He had managed to escape the shackles of the east side with a full academic scholarship to a leading West Coast university and from there to a top medical school, from where he had emerged as a trauma surgeon. He knew upon graduation that he could have settled just about anywhere he wished in the United States but he had returned to the east side, which was the only home he knew and because it was the one place he felt he could make a difference.

Braxton Walker looked tired. He had been called to the hospital in the middle of the night when the casualties had been brought in. The fifteen-year-old boy was dead on arrival, so Braxton, two other surgeons and several nurses had toiled through the night in a desperate attempt to save the life of the older boy who had already lost a substantial amount of blood. Eventually, at four thirty Sunday morning, the seventeen-year-old boy had also died on the operating table.

Walker's emotions spilled from his brief speech like the blood of the two dead boys which had spilled through his fingers at the hospital the night before.

Mark Anthony of Julius Caesar fame would have been proud

122

because Braxton Walker managed to walk a tightrope, inciting the decent people of the community while at the same time making excuses for the drug pushers and the criminals by shifting the blame onto society's failure to notice their plight. The bottom line, though, was that two young men had died unnecessarily and, regardless of whatever excuses anyone might have had for being a part of life's detritus, it was still against the law of the land to trade in narcotics and to kill in cold blood; he then produced the list from his top pocket. He was going to name them.

'In this land of ours,' Walker shouted to the audience who had by now filled the hall and were spilling over into the corridors, 'every man is innocent until proven guilty by a court of law.' He waved the paper over his head. 'We are not here, therefore, to accuse the following people of murder, although murderers they may be.' He paused and looked all around the hall, his eyes red with tiredness and anger. 'We are simply telling them to take their poisonous drugs and their criminal activities somewhere else.' He wiped a tear from his eye. 'I came back home as a doctor to save lives, not to have the blood of our young ones drain through my fingers like it so frequently does.' Walker squeezed the small plastic container in his palm and watched the blood filter through his fingers and down his arm and, drop by drop, collect on the wooden floor. Some gasped, others shouted. They had gone mad, the crowd was absolutely incensed, screaming as one.

'Read the names, Doc, read the names!' they shouted.

Braxton Walker raised both hands over his head, his left hand still clutching the sheet of paper with the names, his right palm wet and crimson with blood.

'We all know who they are,' he shouted over the din in the hall, with their big, colourful coats, fancy cars and funny askew hats; can't read, can't write, but think they are the man.' The crowd yelled their approval with laughter and more shouts of 'read the names, now, now, read the names.'

Braxton Walker had whipped the crowd into a frenzy. It was now time to take on the drug dealers, head on. He slowly unfolded the single sheet of paper. The room had gone deathly silent. He began to read the list of eight, very slowly, one at a time:

Big Joe Kelly; Frank Biggles; Smokey 'White Shoes' Peters; Shoeshine Joe; Mo Franks; Sam 'Pretty Boy' Dingles; Joseph 'Tiny Bags' Moses & Paperbag

Jones.

The names did not surprise anyone in the hall; it was just confirmation of the facts as they were. Braxton Walker was not finished. He knew he was putting himself in danger by going public with the list of names, but he also knew that as one of the community's most respected citizens he would be protected by the people. He motioned to the young woman to come forward. She was the spokesperson for the east side Community Women's Association, a feisty, thirty-two-year-old, small woman named Christina Coomes. She hopped onto the small, raised stage and motioned for her two young sons to join her. The boys were eleven and eight:

'I'll be damned if I am going to sit quietly and let these drug pushers take the lives of my little boys', she screamed, at the same time pointing to her two sons.

'Enough is enough.' The crowd roared their agreement.

'Last night, two young lives were senselessly taken from us. Why?' She was really angry. 'So Smokey 'White Shoes' Peters and Sam 'Pretty Boy' Dingles and the rest of them, can ride in their fancy cars and wear their fine clothes.' She paused.

'We all know those dope dealers are not going to lie down and let us take away their fancy, comfortable lifestyle,' she was saying, her right hand balled and thumb pointing backward, 'so we have prepared ourselves.' She produced the thick folder, opened it and flicked through the sheets. 'These here are statements signed by many witnesses who will testify in court against those eight names the doctor just read out to you. All we are asking is for those men to leave our community before next Sunday morning or we'll damn well make sure that they are all sitting from the other side of the prison bars looking out.' The crowd showed its approval by clapping rapturously.

'Furthermore,' Christina showed determination, 'if those people have any ideas of threatening or harming the doctor or any members of this community because of the action we are taking, they'd better read their history books, because if one more decent person in this community dies in mysterious circumstances, we promise them a lynching in front of this very building,' she stabbed her finger vigorously at the floor, 'and that's a promise.'

The east side of the city had stood up at last. The silent majority had had enough and the gauntlet had been thrown down for the drug dealers to pick it up. No one knew exactly what would happen during the coming week but they all felt better when they streamed out of the community center and marched through the city streets; children in mothers' arms, toddlers on fathers' shoulders and young boys and girls who hoped for a chance just to live and grow every day without the fear that had become a part of their lives. They marched through the east side city streets in defiance and in the knowledge that they had the power to cleanse their community.

* * *

They cruised into the city from the south, all thirty of them riding three abreast, and crossed the Sheen River Bridge just before sunset. A moving mass of flesh, chrome, leather and hair; leaving in their wake, the acrid smell of smoke, the heavy smell of oil and the ear-shattering noise which lingered long after they had disappeared into the distance. The message had come through on Saturday morning. Joe Nickles and Pat Wenslow had been involved in a fight with some scar-faced dude in a place called the Pepperdine. Joe was not too bad but Pat Wenslow was in hospital with possible brain damage. The leader of the Eagles had summoned them so they rode.

They rode loudly through the southern suburbs of the city, screamed their way through the center of town and eventually crossed the railroad tracks to enter the belly of the mammoth beast, finally to be spat out on Shackle Avenue and into the Pepperdine.

The marchers had made their statement, issued their ultimatum, claimed a very small portion of their community back and had long since sought refuge in their modest homes. They had not anticipated a gang of motorcycle marauders to descend on their community on a Sunday evening, a day of mourning in the east side. The east side would have to sacrifice a little more blood if it was to heal itself; the leeches were out to demand it.

Like metal dragons, the menacing bikes stood guard outside the Pepperdine. Inside, Smokey Peters was in consultation with the heavily bearded leader of the pack. They had ridden one hundred and twenty miles to sort out the small matter of Pat Wenslow's health and to find out the person who was responsible for the damage. The rest of the pack were scattered around one of the bars in the

Pepperdine while others had disappeared into the pool rooms. Joe Nickles approached Smokey Peters and the bearded one, a broad grin on his face.

'Hello Braces.' He set the three bottles of beer on the table and put out his hand to be shaken by the bearded one. 'Thanks for coming, man, thanks.'

Braces was a big man, all twenty-one and a half stones of him minus the beard. He was feared and respected by members within the Eagles Organization but also feared by other gang members across the nation. His preference for the bright red braces he wore to hold up his trousers as opposed to belts eventually earned him the nickname by which he was now so well known in the bike set.

'You look worried.' Braces was eyeing Smokey Peters over the beer bottle from which he drank.

'It's this town,' said Smokey nervously, 'they are getting tough on us. Would you believe it, they've issued me an ultimatum to move within a week or else.'

Braces laughed, a deep, unpleasant laugh which seemed to come from somewhere deep within the mass of flesh, muscle and some fat. 'Or else what?' he enquired.

'Prison or lynching', replied Smokey.

'Yeah Brace,' Joe Nickles chipped in, 'they had themselves a speech and a march this afternoon, on account of two dead boys. Now they say they want a clean town; no drugs, no bother and maybe even no sex.' He found that funny and slapped his chest repeatedly and screamed with laughter.

'Was Pat Wenslow done here?' Braces changed the subject, wanting to know exactly where, in the Pepperdine, Wenslow had been injured.

'Yeah,' said Nickles, 'right by the bar.' He got up. 'I'll show you Brace.'

They all walked to the bar together, Braces carrying his unfinished bottle of beer. The bartender on the evening shift had just taken over and was wiping a few glasses in readiness for the evening trade when the three descended upon him.

'Three beers, on the house', said Braces to the barman, pulling a stool to sit between Smokey Peters and Joe Nickles.

'Three beers but on you', replied the young bartender. 'In the Pepperdine, on the house means on me and right now, I ain't got it.'

Smokey Peters opened his eyes wide in amazement; the young man was either too naive or too stupid. The only person he had ever heard talking to Braces in that tone of voice was a tough, no-nonsense Police Captain who, of course, had the full backing of the City's Police Force, the FBI, the National Guard and, if push came to shove, the whole US Army, Marines, Navy and the Air Force.

To Smokey's surprise, Braces simply produced a five dollar bill and placed it on the bar. He was looking around the place, and finally seeing his reflection in the mirror behind the bar, produced a small comb from his jacket pocket and started to comb his bushy dark hair and beard.

'Were you working late Friday night?' Braces asked the barman.

'Yeah, but not in here, I did the upstairs bar', replied the young man, placing the bottles of beer on the bar and returning the change to Braces.

'Who worked this bar?'

'Johnny, Johnny Ripples', replied the barman, showing irritation for the interrogation.

'Is Ripples working tonight?' Braces kept on with the questioning.

'Don't know, maybe, maybe not.' The barman moved away to rearrange the spirit bottles, hoping to put an end to the questions. Joe Nickles started to describe to Braces how Friday night's events had unfolded, twisting the ending to make it seem as if Stumpy Lazarus had smashed Pat Wenslow with the chain.

Smokey Peters felt uneasy, his sixth sense told him that something terrible would happen here this Sunday evening and frankly he would have preferred to have been somewhere else. The crazy, dark-jacketed, dark-bearded, long-haired, overgrown schoolboys could snap any moment. He wouldn't mind that, in fact he would like that, except that he didn't want to be around when all hell broke loose.

He had seen them in action before and, as much as he disliked their company, they were good to have around for protection in the seedy underworld drugdealing business. The people of the east side wanted him and the other boys out of town within a week, but if things got hot again and fear was put back in the hearts of the instigators of the afternoon's community hall meeting, he might, just might, be able to strut his stuff again and carry on with business as usual. He liked this city, particularly the east side, where, despite the pronouncements of

Lazarus, he was sure he had established himself and intended to stay.

Braces wanted answers and he was going to get them. He turned towards Smokey Peters, 'You were here, you saw the fight, what do you think?'

Smokey Peters was no fool; he had already lost about fifteen thousand dollars worth of merchandise because of the fight, money he hoped he would recoup in one way or another, but he was not about to tell the truth about Joe Nickles and add to his list of enemies.

'Yeah, I was,' Smokey replied calmly, 'but I had business uptown and had to leave early. From what I hear the troubles began not long after I'd left.' He looked at Joe Nickles, who returned the look with some semblance of appreciation.

In the two pool halls, the noise was getting louder and louder as the Eagles availed themselves of the selection of alcoholic beverages now copiously at their disposal.

The Sunday evening crowd was unusually thin, probably because of the city's somber mood and partially from the effects of the afternoon's community outpouring of grief and defiance. In addition to that, the menacing bikes which, like dragons, stood guard at the front of the Pepperdine seemed to underline the word 'trouble'.

* * *

Johnny Ripples had no idea what was in store for him when he walked into the Pepperdine with his girlfriend. This was Sunday, his official day off. The suggestion had come from Marsha Dixby, Johnny's longtime girlfriend, to share a few drinks at the Pepperdine before going to the movies, in her view a nice peaceful way to round off the weekend. In the car to the Pepperdine, they had discussed the unfortunate incidents that had taken place over the weekend. Johnny described Friday night's fight in detail to his girlfriend as they drove along, and showed his delight when narrating the manner in which Stumpy Lazarus had made waste of the illicit drugs. He was in two minds when they arrived at the club and saw the chromed dragons. Well, he thought, bikers often used the Pepperdine, maybe not in such large numbers but they came and went as they pleased and sometimes caused some trouble, so what?

Johnny Ripples shook hands with the young bartender. 'Hey Paul', he greeted Paul Stanton warmly, ordered drinks for Marsha and himself and began light conversation with his working colleague. Ripples deliberately avoided eye contact with the bearded giant who stared at him through the mirror. The man looked ominous, dressed all in black - and that included his shirt - heavy black beard, long black hair and a pair of very black dark glasses now on the bar in front of him. The only colour about the man was the two thin strips of red braces that peeped from beneath the open, black, heavy leather jacket.

Ripples felt uncomfortable. He picked up the drinks and turned to rejoin Marsha at the small corner table she had selected. From the pool rooms the sound of broken bottles could be heard in between the loud swear words that only the steeliest of reporters would have dared quote in any newspaper article. Once again the temperature in the Pepperdine was rising. Several things were happening at once, all under the gaze of the omniscient 'third eye'. The third eye was Jack Maldini's 'ace in the hole'.

Three years ago, on the advice of Maldini's chief security officer, the two clubs which, along with the radio station, and the tomato cannery operation constituted the Maldini empire, were fitted with the so-called 'third eye'. It was a complex network of strategically placed cameras, all connected to one nerve center where the activities of the people on the premises could be monitored at all times for, as Maldini put it, 'the purposes of protecting our clients'. In the Hood Acre, the nerve center of the 'third eye' was in a little-known room directly above the Fantasia. The 'third eye' in the Pepperdine had its nerve center in the basement, next to the wine cellars. From within this room, Rob Pascalis, the security officer on duty, watched the movements of the wild, drunken, leather jacketed bunch in every corner of the club. He had direct access to his boss, the chief of security, through the green phone, and a hot red line direct to Jack Maldini's home, office, mobile communications in the car and to his personal bleeper. Pascalis watched. He switched his gaze from one monitor to another and calmly smoked his cigarette. All his experience told him that this Sunday night was going to be one of the worst in the history of the Pepperdine, but at the same time he was unwilling to raise any false alarms. He sat and watched, smoking quietly and totally focused behind his 'third eye'.

* * *

Simon Carter was surrounded by three happy, excited children. The interior of the car was noisy and bubbling with the sort of excitement only children seem to possess. They were on their way from the hospital where John, Kazeem and Katherine had successfully lifted the spirits of Juliana Kazi. The good news was that she was responding to treatment very nicely and could be discharged within a week. The question, though, was where she would go after leaving the hospital, so Simon Carter was on his way to visit his gypsy friend to put forward certain proposals concerning accommodation for the gypsy family. Sunday lunch had been superb. Kazeem Kazi had dropped his bombshell about he and John Carter's two-year-old secret, Ben Swinton had long since returned to his flat to contemplate the problems that faced him on Monday morning, and Maureen Carter had finally retired with a book she wanted to finish before resuming work on Monday.

Shamon Kazi heard the engine of the car and emerged from his tent, a wide grin on his weathered face. He had finished his day's training of the horses and, having discovered what he had always known the special horse possessed, he was eager to pass the wonderful news to the doctor and his daughter. Kazi invited the doctor and the children into the tent.

Shamon Kazi never failed to amaze Simon Carter. Somehow, he had managed to turn the small camping tent into a reasonably comfortable home. From the destroyed trailer, he had salvaged usable items with which he had managed to transform the camping tent into a home. He offered one of the two chairs in the tent to Simon Carter and sat on the other empty chair. Kazeem Kazi had already taken his place on the floor next to the doctor, his legs crossed. John Carter and Katherine Carter followed his example and assumed the cross-legged position on the floor space between the doctor and the horse trainer.

'Katherine,' Shamon Kazi was looking at the girl, 'I am happy for you, very happy for you, because your lovely Shamka is a special one.' He clasped his hands, threw his head skyward and muttered some words which no one in the tent understood and proudly got up to offer his guests cups of tea.

'Shamon,' said Doctor Carter. He had long stopped calling the gypsy by his last name, 'please tell me,' Carter was choosing his words carefully, 'since yesterday, I have heard a lot about thoroughbreds, but I think you may be the man to tell me exactly what a thoroughbred is. So, what is a thoroughbred?'

Shamon Kazi's face was beaming. The doctor was asking him to talk about something he really knew about; horses, his life, his whole being, everything. He knew that he could not answer the question without rambling on. He knew just about everything there was to know about horses and he was not just thinking of thoroughbreds. He might as well have been asked to talk about the Arab or the Barb, or about the Quarter Horse, the Appaloosa or maybe even the horse and pony breeds of the Soviet Union. He was proudly passing tea to everybody, including his son, and still smiling.

'Doctor Carter,' the horse trainer was now ready to answer the question, 'a thoroughbred is the Sun, the Moon, the Earth and everything that is good,' the man was absolutely glowing, 'and I can tell you that Shamka is the best I have ever seen. She is a horse with heart,' he spread his arms apart, 'this big.'

'Could she win a race with other horses?' asked Katherine excitedly.

'Ho ho hooo.' Shamon Kazi's laughter seemed to answer Katherine's question, there was no need for words. He had seen horses as a child in Europe, he had ridden more than a hundred different horses and trained dozens of what he knew were excellent animals, but he knew that Shamka was a cut above any other horse he had ever known.

They had been with the horseman for more than two hours before Simon Carter realized how late it was. It had been the most absorbing two hours inside a tent with a man who seemed to live for horses. He had enlightened them all, entertained them with unbelievable stories of the old country and given them an insight into horses that none of them, except possibly the little gypsy boy, could have learned in a lifetime. Shamon Kazi had taken a special place in Doctor Carter's heart.

'Your wife should be out of hospital by next weekend Shamon. Have you thought of what happens after that?' asked Carter, when the two men shook hands by the car.

'Yes Doctor, tomorrow I will tell you my answer', the horseman said simply.

'Till tomorrow', said Carter.

Simon Carter drove away, wondering about life. How could a man with seemingly so little material wealth exude so much happiness and affect everyone in such a positive way. He concluded that life was much simpler than most people made it.

* * *

Rob Pascalis sat behind his 'third eye' and watched the two men closely. They staggered from the pool room, up the stairs and into the main bar. They shoved each other boisterously, shook the bottles of beer violently and sprayed the liquid in the air and on each other. Spontaneously, they interlocked their arms and began to dance in circles in the main bar. Other bikers began to gather around the two men, clapping and shouting loudly. '*Music, music*', they shouted.

'You heard the men,' Braces said to the barman, 'let's have music.'

The barman was now visibly worried. He could see that the big bearded man meant what he said and started to fiddle with the controls of the music system behind the bar.

'Turn it up', shouted Braces. The barman complied, filling the room with deafening sounds of, '*Don't step on my blue suede shoes*'. They were jumping, rocking, shouting, a dark mass of jacketed, bearded men, most of whom were already drunk and those not quite so guzzled beer at an alarming rate to reach the levels of those already inebriated.

Braces motioned to the barman. 'Give me the keys', he said, his eyes as cold as ice. The young man was unsure. 'Keys to what sir.' he enquired respectfully, fear oozing out of his face.

'To the premises', Braces said softly, leaning his massive frame forward over the bar.

'Security keeps those', the young man replied, wishing he were somewhere else.

Smokey Peters wanted out. He had made up his mind several moments ago when he read the fear in the barman's face, the kind of fear that naturally opens the adrenaline valves and screams for one to fight or flee. Smokey considered himself a tough, smart man and right now he pushed the tough part of his make-up deep in the recesses of his brain and shuffled the smart part to the forefront. The big man sitting next to him was an animal, an animal who had ridden over a hundred miles to deal with the people who had hurt Pat Wenslow and put him in hospital. He had come with his small army to settle a score and to wreak havoc on a community that had allowed it to happen to his brother, and now he was asking for the keys to the Pepperdine. It was time to go and Smokey knew that. He got up from the stool, draped his long coat over his left arm and offered his hand to Braces.

'Got to go brother,' he said to Braces, 'an engagement up town.'

Braces turned slowly to face the tall black man. 'Sit down', he said coldly.

'But Brace', said Smokey, 'duty calls', he appealed.

'Shut the fuck up and sit down,' Braces was looking ugly, 'and I ain't your brother.'

Smokey Peters withered back onto the stool, his coat sliding gently to the floor. He felt as if the gates of hell were opening and that soon he would be staring into the fire. Behind him, the band of marauders were not just stepping to the blue suede shoes, they were falling over them.

Rob Pascalis kept his eyes glued to the 'third eye' and picked up the green phone. He pressed the one button and waited. He could see the bright green light flashing and hoped it would be answered quickly.

'Maskins', the voice came over loud and clear when the green light stopped flashing. 'Jim, we've got problems', Pascalis told his boss.

'How big?'

'Very big', Pascalis informed him..

'Hit the Red,' Jim Maskins instructed Pascalis, I am on my way.'

Jim Maskins was Jack Maldini's right-hand man. As chief of security for the Maldini empire, the former Police Captain was respected and well liked. At the age of forty-eight, he stood six foot four, powerfully built and fearless. He did not appreciate the interruption this evening. The call he had received was going to take him away from his family on a Sunday evening, the one evening specially allocated to the family that he seldom saw during the week because of his hectic schedule. When the call had come, Maskins had been surrounded by his three boys in the living room of his suburban home, and in the process of losing the second of a competitive game of chess with his youngest son of sixteen. They were used to such interruptions, although hardly ever on a Sunday. Exactly fifteen minutes after the call had come, Jim Maskins had made his apologies to all three boys, kissed his wife and was speeding towards the Pepperdine in his red Volvo. He hated that part of town, but he had a job to do.

Six of the full complement of thirty security officers on the Maldini payroll were also bearing down on the Pepperdine from different parts of the city. They had all been easily reached by Maskins within minutes of the initial call from Pascalis. Jim Maskins drove, pleased with the systems he had put in place to handle emergencies of this kind. En route, Maskins made his final call to old colleagues in the police department. He did not believe the police would be needed just yet however. He was a cautious man and had taken the opportunity to alert them in preparedness for a possible call for assistance once he had personally assessed the situation.

Jack Maldini took the 'hot' call from Rob Pascalis in the Cadillac. He had rested well and enjoyed a fabulous meal with Vivian Maldini and the Lazlos around the pool until the telephone call came from the Hood Acre. The six million dollar card game in the Red Room was now at its most absorbing moment. The news was that all the six players had lasted well through the night, exchanging winnings and losses almost equally. The players had taken a break to rest and refresh themselves at seven in the morning and resumed again at nine. Since then, the knockout punch had been delivered to Simon Chen, Andre Papadropolous and 'Butch' Anderson. All three men had been dealt what they believed to be winning hands and they felt sure of the strengths of their respective positions, so they had battled against Senor Pedro Munzon. The Argentinean had taken them on, raising the stakes to the maximum limit and finally, with a stroke of genius, he had revealed a flush of spades to deliver his knockout punch to the Hong Kong property developer, the Greek shipping magnate and the pugnacious Texan. The game was now poised between O'Reilly, Munzon and Van Derpool, and Maldini was on his way to enjoy the finale when, all of a sudden, the red light started to flash on the communications unit in the Cadillac.

'Where is Maskins?' Maldini asked Pascalis.

'He is on his way sir', replied Pascalis. I found him at home.'

'Secure the chute and inform me as soon as Maskins arrives. Tell him I shall meet him in the bunker.' Maldini ended the conversation.

Joe Lazlo watched Maldini skilfully manoeuvring the Cadillac in a tight U-turn on the small country road, his thoughts graphically displayed on his chiselled face.

'What's up?' asked Lazlo, his right arm reaching for the seat belt in anticipation of the speed of the vehicle which he knew would follow.

'Bikers', said Maldini.

Joe Lazlo knew what that meant. There was no need to ask for an explanation or further elaboration. The word spoke for itself. Translated, it simply meant trouble.

He sat back in his seat and closed his eyes. He was thinking of past confrontations which had all been won and he knew this would be no different.

Inside the Pepperdine, the Eagle rockers had graduated from the blue suede shoes to music more to their taste and trade. Braces had somehow secured spare keys to the premises and the young barman had long been relieved of his duties on his orders; now replaced by two drunken members of the Eagles who taunted other members of the bike set to step forward and get drunk. The drinks were now truly 'on the house', as originally demanded by Braces.

Braces had given orders for all doors to be shut and locked, which they now were. He would not allow any of the few clienteles who had made the ill-fated judgement of enjoying their Sunday afternoon drink in the club to leave, so Johnny Ripples and Marsha Dixby stayed in their corner and watched the destruction of the interior of the club. In addition to Marsha Dixby, there were seven other women and twenty-two men in the Pepperdine, not counting Smokey Peters, Johnny Ripples, Paul Stanton and the Eagles. The plan was simple; the Eagles would stay and drink to their hearts' content, they would dance and please themselves in this sealed 'garrison' and finally rampage through the east side to show their dissatisfaction for allowing Pat Wenslow to be injured in their community. After that, they would find the hospital in which Wenslow was being treated and spend a moment or two with their friend and brother of the leader, before spreading themselves across the highway to ride south from where they had come.

One of the two drunken biker bartenders fiddled with the buttons on the music system behind the bar. When he found what he was looking for he turned the volume completely off and turned to face the surprised crowd on the other side of the bar. He spread his arms wide over his head, let out a howling scream and made his pronouncement with great satisfaction. 'Ladies and gentlemen, now dig some of this.' He turned round to fiddle with the controls, the volume almost at its absolute maximum. *'Baby you can ride my bike'* came the words, very, very loudly from the speakers, the sound hitting the occupants of the bar like blows. He had also opened a can of worms, figuratively speaking, because up until the time that he had made his brief pronouncement the marauders had not even noticed the seven women in the bar. The mention of 'ladies', followed by babes riding bikes, triggered the toughest of the Eagle bunch into action. All of a sudden they seemed to have discovered women on planet earth, seven of who were unfortunate enough to be in the Pepperdine with all doors shut and locked.

In the basement, next to the wine cellar, Rob Pascalis removed a shotgun from the rack behind him and checked the weapon. He hoped Johnny Ripples would not try to be chivalrous when the big brute with the heavy chain around his waist finally arrived at his destination, which happened to be the table at which Ripples and Marsha Dixby were sitting. Pascalis was wrong. Johnny Ripples was on his feet the moment the brute laid his hand on Marsha Dixby. For a moment all Pascalis could see on the monitor was the back of the dark-jacketed biker, the long hair and the massive upper torso. The man's frame had completely masked that of Ripples. The two seemed to engage in some sort of exchange. Pascalis watched his screen, the two men seemingly communicating, then like a rag doll he saw Johnny Ripples flying through the air only to crash against the nearest wall a few feet away from the table. Pascalis choked off the laughter which came out spontaneously. It was serious but also funny, his mind turning to the work of stuntmen he had seen in films. He watched the main screen. Johnny Ripples sat against the wall half bent with his chin on his chest and his left hand lying awkwardly across his lap. There was nothing the unconscious young man could do when the big, bearded biker walked away onto the dance floor with Marsha Dixby. The music was very loud, the vibrations felt by all in the bar except Ripples who seemed to have deserted his body for the moment.

Marsha Dixby was concerned about her boyfriend. She could see Ripples was not stirring and felt she needed to do something to protect him. She could see some of the other women trying to resist the attentions of the rough, unkempt bikers and watched their male partners sitting meekly in fear, having witnessed Ripples's solo flight through the air and the rough landing which seemed to have separated his soul from his body. She would use her head. There was no point offering resistance in such situations, it would be better to turn the tables. Marsha Dixby followed her instincts. She hoped it would work. Her woman's intuition told her that what she needed was time and so time was what she would buy. She looked into the face of the bearded brute, gathered her skirt with her left hand and swished it back and forth and began to dance seductively to the loud music. She had taken control, at least for the moment. She danced, moving very close to her bearded partner but always just managing to escape his claws when the drunken biker tried to grab her.

It had taken some time for Rob Pascalis to arrive at his decision. With the shotgun in his right hand, he was about to open the door and leave the secured nerve center when the girl's sudden change of mood drew him back into his seat. To his surprise, the music had suddenly been turned down to an acceptable level of volume and most of the Eagles were now seated, their attention focused on the pretty brunette who seemed to have mesmerized them. Marsha Dixby was giving them a show; she was dancing for her life and buying the precious time she so desperately needed. She moved skilfully around her clumsy partner, teasing, swaying, shuffling and laughing happily. From time to time she beckoned the other girls, who had by now escaped the attentions of their pursuers and were now in their seats, to join her. Pascalis watched the dancing girls in disbelief, now four, in control of the volatile situation, while the drunken bikers clapped and cheered them on. How much longer, thought Marsha. The locked doors of the Pepperdine at that time of the evening should be enough to raise the alarm. She would dance all night if she had to. She did not know it but she had a guardian angel; Rob Pascalis secretly willed her on, in the full knowledge that Maskins, Maldini and the others were on their way to her rescue. Against the wall, Johnny Ripples had not stirred.

CHAPTER TWELVE

The delivery boy was in a hurry. He pressed the button for the lift and waited; nothing happened. He tried again. Time was money so he pushed the door to the stairway and began the climb to the fifth floor. He took the stairs two at a time, holding his breath for long periods to shut out the smell of urine. On the third floor landing the two men who were preparing their fix for the evening, concentrated on the liquid they were heating in the spoon, and ignored him. He took in a large gulp of air and shut off his lungs again for the final climb to the fifth floor. The floor was in semi-darkness, the one operating bulb that was encased in a metal grille provided some illumination to make the numbers on the bleak doors barely visible. He ran along the corridor searching for the flat and rang the bell.

Jurelene Patterson and her flatmate had been cocooned in the flat the whole day. The redhead had suggested a home delivery meal for reasons of safety, so they had placed the order for their supper and waited patiently for the delivery boy who was now knocking loudly to attract their attention. The two women looked at each other apprehensively, the redhead rising to go to the door.

'Ask who it is before you open the door Lucy', Jurelene Patterson whispered to her friend who was now standing behind the door.

'Who is it?' asked Lucy Sharpe, eyes wide open and staring at her friend.

'Shakey's meal delivery for apartment five-one-six ma'am', replied the boy from the other side of the door. 'Get it while it's still hot.'

The two women nodded at each other uncertainly. Lucy carefully secured the security chain, slid the bolt back and opened the door just enough to peek at the boy. Satisfied, she opened the door and received the four small boxes of food, paid the boy with a twenty dollar bill and told him to keep the change. She slammed the door shut with her foot, passed the boxes to Jurelene and once again secured the bolt and chain on the door.

'I think we should get some help or get away', said Lucy, preparing to dish the food onto the two plates on the small center table.

'What about the police?' Jurelene suggested. 'It may be the best thing to do.'

'I don't think so.'

'Why not?' Jurelene challenged.

'Number one, it'll be our word against theirs. Remember we only heard things; we are not witnesses', Lucy argued. 'And two, how long do you think you and I will last after the court case, assuming it even gets to court?'

'But we heard them say they did it, Lucy.' Jurelene held the spoon full of rice near her mouth. 'We are talking murder here.' She shovelled the rice into her mouth and returned the spoon in search of meatballs on the plate.

'What about that guy, the one who gave us a hard time yesterday?' Lucy Sharpe tried to remember the name. 'That's it, Lazarus, the guy with the scar.'

'You are not serious', Jurelene replied. 'We hardly know the man. Besides, aren't you forgetting what happened yesterday?'

'The man has fallen for you, girl, you should have enough experience to know that.' Lucy studied her friend. 'He may be our only genuine chance, think about it.' They looked at each other and ate in silence, both thinking about the two unfortunate dead boys.

* * *

Stumpy Lazarus opened the two bottles of beer and passed one of the bottles to his partner. Stumpy was considering adult education classes. Something had happened to him yesterday and, out of the blue, he had asked Steiner about how he would go about registering for such classes. He had sat patiently, almost embarrassingly, and listened to Steiner's reasons for why he thought such classes would be good for him. In between the educational discussion, Stumpy had told Mickey Steiner about his search for his partner on Friday evening, the fight in the Pepperdine, the brush with Smokey and finally the strange feelings and the dream he had had about the pretty black woman. Unlike Stumpy, Mickey Steiner gave the briefest account of his weekend activities and simply told Stumpy how much he had enjoyed being in the company of Rosalynn Brando. The trip down south to Mrs Baxter's would remain his secret.

'I can now understand why you disappeared on Friday', said Stumpy, believing that Mickey Steiner had spent all of Friday and Saturday in Rosalynn Brando's company.

Steiner looked at his friend and knew that some sort of transformation was taking place. Something positive was happening. He did not know exactly why, but he was certain that the sudden change he was observing in his partner was not through fear or as a consequence of the fight, nor was it a result of his brief capture by Smokey. They watched the seven o'clock news together and were exchanging ideas about the most likely perpetrators of the previous night's murders across town when the telephone rang.

Stumpy Lazarus picked up the receiver and held it close to his ear without saying a word.

'Mr Lazarus.' Stumpy had not expected a call so soon from her.

'Yeah, this is Stump', he said, winking at Steiner.

'I was wondering,' Jurelene Patterson paused, 'I was wondering if we could meet tomorrow evening.'

Stumpy's heart began to beat faster than usual. This was not normal. No woman had ever dared to ask him for a meeting. When it came to his relationships with women, he told them, always.

'Sure, sure', he found himself saying, somewhat excitedly.

'I'll come to you if that's okay, about seven.'

'Seven is okay, you know the place, I'll look out for you.' He was smiling when he replaced the receiver.

This was a new experience for Mickey Steiner. He had never known his partner to be polite to any woman. His thoughts went back to how Stumpy Lazarus had introduced Jacqueline on Thursday night with a slap on the thigh in front of Rosalynn. In the office the next day Stumpy had made it clear that Jacqueline was not a lady. The man had never respected women, period. This new behaviour did not make sense to Steiner. The woman was black, according to Stumpy maybe even a prostitute. He hoped he would get a chance to meet her soon, possibly tomorrow.

* * *

Jim Maskins slowed the Volvo down on Shackle Avenue and dialled the three-digit number which patched him directly into the nerve center of the Pepperdine's third eye. He could see that the streets were almost deserted. Unusual, he thought, and checked the time on his watch, six fourteen. He informed Rob Pascalis of his arrival and took the messages that Maldini had left for him. The chrome dragons were now visible. Maskins deliberately drove past the motorcycles, counting as he went, thirty in all. He made a mental note. He drove to the end of the block, turned left on Pine, then left again on Spruce and entered the alleyway between the Pepperdine and the Shackle Avenue Liquor Store. Maldini had already given instructions for the chute to be secured, an instruction already complied with by Pascalis.

Maskins parked the car approximately fifty metres away from the Pepperdine and waited next to the so-called 'bunker'. He smiled to himself, a policeman's smile, and thought of how Maldini's experiences in prison had given his boss the idea for the construction of the chute and the bunker. He sat in the Volvo and thought of the story Maldini had told him about chutes and bunkers.

Jack Maldini had met an old-timer in prison, by the name of Old Man Slade. Slade was sixty-four at the time and seen by all the inmates as a father figure. He had taken a liking to Maldini in particular and had spent a great deal of time sharing the secrets of his criminal expertise with the then young Maldini. Slade's specialty was cracking the safes of prime banks, something he is said to have done successfully for over fifteen years before a jilted girlfriend assisted the police to trap him. According to Old Man Slade, the trick to the success of any operation was to ensure that there was always an escape route, no matter what sort of operation. The bunker was a secure place to hole up, if necessary, for days, and from there to gain access to the target, through the chute, and conversely to return safely after the job was done. Using this principle, Jack Maldini had constructed the Pepperdine chute and bunker under the guise of laying sewer lines. The only difference in this case was that the chute was to serve as an escape route in case of any future unforeseen difficulties in the Pepperdine. Tonight, it was to serve as a point of entry.

They were nine in all. Rob Pascalis looked at them as they popped out of the chute one after the other, Maskins first, followed by six of his colleagues all of whom he knew well, Mr Lazlo and finally Maldini. They crammed into the nerve center, Maskins and Maldini positioning themselves in front of the main monitor. They watched the bizarre activities in the main bar and quietly listened to Rob Pascalis. He briefed them fully.

There were a total of sixty-three people, all in the area of the main bar. Eight were women, the other fifty-five all men, no children. There were two employees down there, the on-duty barman and an off-duty bartender who was unconscious. The three dancing girls had been dancing for, Pascalis checked his watch, almost thirty five-minutes non-stop. Six of the bikers were too drunk to worry about, one lying in a pool of vomit near the unconscious man against the wall. The leader, it seemed to Pascalis, was the huge guy with the red braces.

'Who is the black man with the hat?' asked Maldini. 'Is he with them?'

'Not sure sir', replied Pascalis. 'He has been talking to the big guy with the braces for most of the time, but I can't say for sure if he is one of them or not.'

Pascalis then gave a brief account of the perceptible damage in the pool rooms and in the main bar. Quantities of alcohol had also been consumed.

Jack Maldini looked at Maskins, 'Well Jim, what do you think?'

Jim Maskins turned to face the others, Maldini at his shoulder. Maskins unhooked the small bunch of keys from his belt, crossed over to the far wall and opened the small wall cabinet. From the top shelf he removed the small bronze replica of the Pepperdine and handed it to Joe Lazlo who stood to his left. Lazlo placed the replica on the empty table beside him and watched with the others in silence as Maskins removed the two top shelves from within the cabinet. He pressed a small button and, with the others, watched the false wall slide slowly away to reveal the metal safe. Maskins began to turn the dial. They could hear the soft clicks, the sprockets falling into place one at a time. Within seconds the door to the safe was open and Maskins was reaching in for the laminated rolls of plans.

They all gathered around the table and watched Maskins unfurl the large plans, with the exception of Pascalis whose attention was still focused on the 'third eye'.

'Boss!' Pascalis shouted. The others turned their attention from the plans on to the large monitor and witnessed the changing scenes in the main bar. The brunette was still dancing, tired but dancing. At one of the tables, a short, pot-bellied biker with an American flag covering the back of his leather jacket had a man by the throat while a young woman, her blouse torn to reveal a lace-fringed, flesh-coloured bra, fought frantically with the biker in an attempt to assist her friend. The rest of the bikers were cheering. The woman sank her teeth into the biker's arm, bit leather to no effect and was shaken off by the pot-bellied biker who continued to choke the breath out of the man. The struggling woman tried again, this time on her knees. She sank her teeth into the biker's calf and bit, the resulting excruciating pain bringing a painful scream from the biker and causing him to release his hold around the man's neck. The drunken bunch screamed with laughter, taunted, whooped and encouraged 'Captain America', who having dropped his victim was now returning his attentions to the woman on the floor.

The sound of the breaking bottle punctured the music, diverting the attentions of the bikers from the pot-bellied biker and the girl on the floor to the huge man with the red braces. 'Leave her alone.' Braces was holding the top jagged half of the broken bottle, his face red with anger and authority. 'You,' he pointed to Paul Stanton, 'get some food, lots of it.' The young barman got up and walked past the brunette who had collapsed on the floor with fatigue and went in search of food. The ugly developments had been diffused for the moment but the atmosphere was full of tension. Jim Maskins had no doubt that it was only a matter of time before the next explosion. The men in the nerve center gathered around the table once again and quietly listened to Jim Maskins, pointer in hand, detailing his plan for the surprise which was to come.

* * *

This had been a momentous Sunday. For once, the people of this poor, forgotten community had spoken up. They had listened to the speeches with interest and showed belief that if they wished to change their community the power was theirs to do so. All they needed was encouragement. Braxton Walker sat in his tiny study, pleased with the day's accomplishments. He was sure that the coming week would prove to be a turning point in the long, sad and painful history of the east side community. Change was possible, but it would only begin if the community could rid itself of the poison of drugs. The long journey to recovery would have to start with the eradication of the parasites. He had named them in public and he was pleased about that. Braxton Walker had no way of knowing that while he plotted the eradication of the parasites, extraordinary events were unfolding in the Pepperdine Club just a mile away from the room in which he now sat. The leeches were attempting to demand their share of the community's blood. How much more blood would pass through his hands; only time would tell. He was concerned about Christina Coomes. The woman had grit. She had jumped on the stage and spoken her mind, expressing her concerns without fear. There was no doubt that the majority of the members of the east side community shared her views. If that was true, it meant they really had power, power that could transform their community, power that could drag the ghetto island into the mainstream of American society, tear down the invincible barrier that began at the railroad tracks and slay the mammoth beast. Walker picked up the telephone and dialled the number; he was thinking of a new strategy.

Christina Coomes answered the telephone, her attention still focused on the scenes being played out on the television screen.

'Hi Braxton,' she said excitedly, 'so you are watching it too.'

'Watching what?' asked Braxton Walker.

'Your Community, Channel Eight.' She could hardly contain herself.

Braxton Walker reached for the remote control, pointed it at the television and began to search through the channels. Within seconds he had brought the Pepperdine into his living room. He was looking at the masses who had gathered in front of the nightclub and at the shiny, chromed machines. The doors of the building seemed to be shut. On Shackle Avenue he could see that the police cars had blocked the avenue on either side of the massive building. The crowd was being held back from the building by uniformed officers.

'What's going on?' he asked the woman at the other end of the telephone line.

'Don't know exactly, Doc, but it seems a motorcycle gang is in town. They have taken over the Pepperdine, sort of like what happened years ago somewhere in California, you remember.' She paused to listen to the television announcer. 'There, can you hear that?' The announcer was giving viewers a chronological account of such incidents in the past, mostly in small towns in California and Oregon. Attempts were being made to find out why the bikers had selected the east side and particularly the Pepperdine.

'By the way Doc, well done this afternoon. It was a moving speech.'

'The credit belongs to you', said the doctor. 'Actually I called to discuss some fresh ideas. Could you set up a meeting with the community leaders for Wednesday evening at seven?'

'Okay,' replied Mrs. Coomes, 'at the community center, seven o'clock, Wednesday.'

'And Christina, keep that file in a safe place, you know, the file with the sworn affidavits, and take care of yourself. See you Wednesday.' Walker put the telephone down and returned his attention to the television screen. For the first time in months there were uniformed police on the east side streets; things were changing already.

* * *

Paul Stanton was rummaging through the kitchen for various food items, unsure of what to prepare to satisfy the demand that Braces had made. He was a bartender not a cook. He was thinking of sandwiches; tuna, ham, cheese and items of that nature. He turned, with the two loaves of bread in his hand, to face the tall security guard, the rifle in his right hand and his left forefinger to his lip.

'Sssshh.' The sound came quietly from the man, then the motion for Stanton to follow. Paul Stanton dropped the two loaves of bread on the wooden kitchen bench and followed the man without hesitation. They exited the kitchen through the swing doors, along the narrow corridors, down the narrow stairway and into the wine cellar. Rob Pascalis opened the hidden door to allow Stanton's escort to step inside the nerve center closely followed by the barman. Jim Maskins stepped forward to meet the barman.

'Are you all right?' Maskins asked the barman.

'I am fine sir,' Stanton replied, 'those are a bunch of animals down there.' He could see them on the monitor.

'What can you tell us?' asked Maskins.

'They rode in earlier this afternoon, started acting crazy and demanded the keys to the building.' Stanton was looking at the screen. 'The big guy with the braces is the leader.' He smiled, 'That's his name, Braces.'

Jack Maldini stepped forward, 'How did they get the keys?'

'Braces found them hanging on a peg behind the bar', replied Stanton.

'Why weren't the keys with Security?' Maldini wanted to know.

'We had just opened for business, sir.' Stanton looked concerned. 'I tried to find Rob but I didn't know where he was so I hung the keys behind the bar and waited for him to return.' The barman looked apologetically at Rob Pascalis.

'That's okay, son.' Maldini was satisfied. The fact that the barman did not know where the security man was indicated that he had no idea about the third eye, that was a good sign.

'Now listen son,' Maldini said to the young man, 'you are not to mention the existence of this room to anyone, ever.' He patted Stanton on the shoulder. 'And well done, you handled yourself well today', he concluded.

Jim Maskins hoped the plan would work. He had already briefed the police and expected them to have secured the perimeter of the building. If he could help it, he would keep the bikers in the building and ensure the safety of all innocent participants in this affair. His main aim was to get his hands on the man they called Braces, for once he had him, the rest of the bunch would be relatively easy to deal with. He had already dispatched two security officers with shotguns into the kitchen. They could be seen crouching in their positions on the right monitor. It was just a matter of time. If Stanton did not return with the food Braces had ordered, someone would have to come into the kitchen for it. He would give them some time but if things didn't go according to plan he would enter the bar with his men to subdue the gang.

They watched the main monitor, their attention on Braces who was removing a small gold case from his jacket pocket. Braces placed the case on the bar and took a handkerchief from his pocket. He wiped the top of the bar with the handkerchief, opened the small gold case and shook some of the white powder onto the bar. Ceremoniously, he returned the case into the jacket pocket and began to split the powder into thin strips, six in all. The two nominated biker bartenders looked at each other hopefully, one of them wiping his mouth with his hand in anticipation of the reward he hoped would come his way.

Maskins turned to Maldini, 'They are drinking and doing cocaine at the same time', he said. 'What a bunch of nutcases.'

Braces held a crisp dollar bill in his hand. He shifted his massive frame away from the bar and paced the floor. The music had stopped. All eyes in the bar were focused on him. He circulated through the bar, dollar bill in his left hand and the right thumb hooked into the thin red brace. He turned suddenly, pointed to the two bikers behind the bar and sent them off to the kitchen to speed up the preparation of the food. The two men scuttled off and disappeared through the small door behind the bar under the gaze of the small crowd in the nerve center. Maskins smiled and waited. In the main bar, Braces strolled regally amongst the frightened hostages. His biker comrades, heads raised reverently towards their leader, waited in the hope' of being chosen to receive the reward. It was not the white powder that mattered because most of the bikers carried their own stashes of cocaine and an assorted mixture of pills and marijuana. What was important was to be chosen by the leader and offered a 'hit' from his own special golden case. It was an honour, an affirmation of the leader's satisfaction with certain members of his entourage.

The two bikers entered the seemingly empty kitchen and looked at each other in bewilderment. On the wooden bench were the two loaves of bread along with several tins of canned beef, tuna and thick chunks of cheese. They moved towards the food and froze instantaneously when the muzzles of the shotguns made contact with each left ear.

'You can scream and meet your maker today or follow my instructions', said one of the two security officers. He was serious. 'It's Sunday, a good day to die', he added.

'Now move', the second security man whispered.

The two bikers were tied, gagged, blindfolded and dumped in the far recesses of the wine cellar.

Smokey Peters watched Braces making his nominations. He hoped he would not be chosen, for although he made his living selling drugs, he had first-hand experience of the damage drugs could do to the mind and body and preferred to pass it to others while he collected the financial rewards. Braces was standing next to 'Captain America', the biker with the large American flag on his back. He had rebuked the man for making advances at the woman with the torn blouse so this was a good time for appeasement. He tapped 'Captain America' on the shoulder and sent him off to await his return at the bar. Four other bikers were similarly chosen with a simple tap. The final choice would have to be special and carry the element of surprise. It was Braces's way of telling his 'subjects' that he was not an ordinary man. His ability to pull surprises made him unpredictable and, with that unpredictability, naturally came the uncertainty which was created in the minds of his followers, thus making him a leader to fear and respect.

Johnny Ripples was stirring. Braces watched him coming to life.

'Ha! The dead awake,' said Braces, 'just in time to watch the beautiful dancing maiden of a girlfriend get stoned. Welcome to the living', he said to Ripples and walked to the brunette who was still lying on the floor. He bent his massive frame over Marsha Dixby and tapped her on the shoulder in the same manner that he had chosen the five bikers. 'Now come with me my child.' Braces snatched her off the floor and carried her effortlessly towards the bar.

'If that man forces the young woman to take the drug, I swear I'll kill him where he stands', said Joe Lazlo calmly reaching for the .38. There was no doubt in the minds of those in the nerve center that Lazlo meant what he said. The man never talked much but he had a reputation for being very fair. With the exception of Jack Maldini, few people knew of Joe Lazlo's past.

Six years ago Joe Lazlo had lost his first wife to malaria on a trip to Mexico. Following his wife's death, Caroline Lazlo, his nineteen-year-old daughter had died from an LSD overdose seven months later. According to official reports, death by misadventure, although others believed her then boyfriend, a self-confessed playboy, was in some way connected with administering the drug at a party. The two incidents affected Joe Lazlo so badly he dropped out of circulation for a few years until Jack Maldini convinced him that life was for the living and that he had to try to become a part of the human race once more. He had remarried, taken an active interest in the Maldini empire and once again began to work hard, something which he found occupied his mind and lessened the grief he still felt. Because of his daughter's death through the use of drugs, Joe Lazlo had a powerful hatred for those who indulged in the use or the sale of drugs. He watched the screen. Braces's life was on a thread. The man could live or die depending on what he did to Marsha Dixby.

Jim Maskins dispatched his security officers - two to the kitchen, two

148

to the mezzanine, the final two to the pool room from where they would appear up the stairs which led directly into the main bar. All six men were armed, three with shotguns and the other three with rifles. They were to take their positions and wait for Maskins's signal. Jack Maldini and Joe Lazlo would be the bait, with Maskins coordinating the plan. Rob Pascalis would remain in the third eye and monitor the movement of the bikers with the assistance of Paul Stanton who had by now recovered from shock and was eager to play his part.

Braces was ready for the ceremony. He removed the tape from his jacket pocket and inserted it in the tape player behind the bar. On such ceremonial occasions every biker was required to remain on their feet, no matter how drunk or stoned they were. Braces waited and watched as the drunken bikers were picked up from the floor by their colleagues and propped up, most of them between two men, some with their arm around a slightly less drunk colleague. The bizarre scenes were watched by the hostages, half confused, somewhat intrigued and generally uncertain about what was to follow.

Braces pushed the button on the tape player and the music began:

We are the Eagles, we are the Eagles,
Fly free and easy, soar above the rest.
No law but our own, so we vote for no other,
But our leader, our only leader, who we choose.

Jack Maldini looked at Joe Lazlo and began to laugh. Paul Stanton wished he had a camera to record the extraordinary scenes being played out in the bar while Pascalis and Maskins just stared at the monitor. The bikers sang, in discord, loudly and proudly.

'Captain America' was first. He proudly received the tightly rolled, crisp dollar bill and bent over the bar. He lined it up with the first line of the six rows of white powder, the rolled bill close to his nose; he sniffed. In an instant the line of white powder had disappeared. He stood away from the bar, wiped his nose with his left hand and handed the rolled bill to Braces who took it with some aplomb and to rapturous applause and shouts of bravo from the rest of the dark, jacketed bunch. Line by line, the white powder vanished from the bar, the proud and grateful recipients taking their places in the crowd to accept the back slapping and congratulations of the rest of them.

Braces now stood face to face with Marsha Dixby. She showed no fear. She had already resolved in her mind that she would not be a part of this ceremony; they would have to force her. Braces handed her the rolled bill. Marsha Dixby stood firm, arms folded across her chest and shook her head. Braces pushed the rolled bill closer to her face, his own face showing some colour, the beginnings of anger but controlled. He knew that defiance from this woman, successful defiance that is, would open the floodgates for any of the Eagles to challenge his authority at any time. The woman would have to take the final line of white powder, preferably without force, but if necessary he would make her take the final line and all the powder in the gold case. Marsha Dixby stood there, dwarfed by the giant but unflinching.

Jim Maskins had seen enough. He picked up the microphone and checked the monitors. His men were all at their positions; it was time to meet the enemy so he counted down the seconds and watched Maldini and Lazlo exit the nerve center. Maskins could see the two making their way through the wine cellar, then through the kitchen. He waited for the two men to reach the door that led directly into the bar and spoke calmly but assuredly with the microphone close to his mouth.

'Philip Green, or should I call you Braces,' Maskins's voice boomed through the main bar, 'Mister Maldini, the owner of the Pepperdine has a proposition for you.' Maldini and Joe Lazlo appeared like ghosts from behind the bar, their hands in their pockets. Maskins continued, 'The gentleman in the dark suit is Mister Maldini and next to him Mister Lazlo. I'd be most surprised if you've never heard those names.' Some of the bikers charged forward having absorbed the initial surprise and now realizing that the two gentlemen were unarmed. Suddenly, like puppets on a string, the surging group froze in their tracks, the clicks of cocking guns bringing them back to their senses. Braces looked around him; two had appeared from the stairway leading from the pool rooms, the shotguns cocked and ready; two more had materialized in the mezzanine with rifles at the ready and two more armed men behind the bar alongside Maldini and Lazlo.

'Now, Mister Green, you will listen to Mister Maldini's proposal.' The matter of fact statement came from the Maskins microphone.

150

'What do you want?' asked Braces with an air of bravado.

Marsha Dixby saw her chance. She dashed away from the bar, making sure to avoid the large group in the center, and joined her boyfriend who was now fully conscious.

'First, my keys', said Maldini.

Braces produced the keys to the Pepperdine and threw them on the bar.

'Thank you', said Maldini, picking up the keys.

'Mister Green,' Jack Maldini deliberately refused to call the man Braces, 'it seems to me you are in charge of these gentlemen here.' Maldini waved his hand over the mob of angry bikers, those high on drugs still showing signs of wanting a fight but unsure of how to proceed because of the menacing weapons pointing at them. 'I heard your anthem and they sang clearly that they chose you, so here is my proposal.' Maldini sat on the stool directly opposite Braces, stretched his hand out to Joe Lazlo over the bar and took the Smith & Wesson Pocket .38. The single action revolver with a three and a quarter inch barrel was the perfect weapon for what Jack Maldini had in mind. He carefully removed all cartridges, spun the chamber and reloaded the weapon with a single cartridge and spun the chamber once again.

'A leader has to be brave,' Maldini said to Braces who was watching him carefully, unsure of the man's intentions, 'especially at times when regardless of the size of his army or the number of his followers he faces the challenge alone.' He smiled at Braces, 'You came to me, sir, so this is my proposal.' Maldini put the .38 to his own head and pulled the trigger. The hammer struck home on an empty chamber, followed by a loud click and a gasp from a woman somewhere at the back of the room who immediately fainted and crashed to the floor, scattering chairs as she fell. Maldini gave the chamber a whirl, turned the butt of the weapon away from himself and handed it to Braces.

'Your turn', Maldini told the giant.

'You are crazy!' The big man held the gun, his eyes bulging.

'Yes I am,' said Maldini, 'but not crazy enough to force defenseless young women to take drugs they choose not to take. Your turn.'

Rob Pascalis looked at Jim Maskins and back at Maldini whose face filled the monitor in front of him. He had heard rumors about Jack Maldini. In fact most people who worked for Maldini had heard rumors about how the man handled serious affairs. Today he was seeing it for himself. He could see that even the bikers were impressed. They were waiting for their illustrious leader to take his turn. He dared not let them down.

Jack Maldini removed his watch from his wrist and placed it on the bar.

'As a leader you must know that time matters,' Maldini told the biker, 'so we'll limit our thinking time to exactly one minute.' He turned to the armed security officers behind the bar. 'His time starts now. If he takes more than a minute, shoot him.'

Braces held the gun in his huge paw. He was unsure of what to do. He cast a quick glance around the bar and saw the disappointed faces. These were his men. He put the gun to his temple and pulled the trigger. Nothing happened. The hammer struck the empty chamber with a click. Braces had taken his turn with twenty seconds to spare. His entourage cheered their leader and watched Jack Maldini's next move, silence once again blanketing the area of the bar. Jack Maldini removed the single cartridge from the chamber of the .38 and gave it to Braces. 'A present for a brave man', he told the biker who took the bullet from Maldini with some disdain.

'I am going to crush you', said Braces.

'There'll be plenty of time for that,' replied Maldini as he reloaded the .38, this time with two cartridges. He spun the chamber, pointed to the watch on the bar to start his one-minute countdown, placed the gun to his head and pulled the trigger - *a loud click*. He spun the chamber again, handed the gun to Braces and pointed to the watch to begin the one-minute countdown. Beads of perspiration had formed on the giant biker's forehead. He held the gun nervously, trying to figure out a way to escape his predicament. He would have to pull the trigger because Maldini had already had his turn. Silence reigned, the tension unbearable for some and the men in the third eye glued to the monitor.

'I ain't playing your stupid game.' Braces was frightened. He held the gun, sweat pouring down his face which had now gone bright red.

'Twenty-five seconds', said Maldini, his eyes focused on the watch.

Braces fidgeted, looked across the bar to his men and then to the tall black man who was smiling broadly. Smokey Peters was watching the demise of the leather king. He could not believe that he was seeing fear in the man's face. Braces was the one who put fear into people who challenged his authority not the other way round.

'Ten seconds', Maldini's voice cut through the silence.

Braces started to cry. The seconds were ticking down. He panicked, levelled the gun at Maldini's heart and pulled the trigger.

Click. The hammer struck the empty chamber, followed almost immediately by the loud rifle report. The bullet caught Braces in the chest, spun him off the stool and dumped him on the floor next to Maldini's feet. He was still breathing, the trickle of blood drawing a jagged line from the corner of his mouth, over the thick, dark beard and onto the floor. The security officer did not shoot to kill. Braces would have to answer for his crimes.

'Stay where you are', the Maskins microphone came to life. 'You will be escorted out of the building.' They were subdued. The sight of their leader crying had taken the stuffing out of the tough bunch; most were angry because he had let them down, some were ripping the eagle insignias from their jackets.

On television, the Pepperdine incident had captured the audiences for Channel 8. All across the city, television screens burned bright with the news. Simon Carter and his family watched the dark-jacketed bikers being marched from the club and into the police vans. Stumpy Lazarus sipped beer in front of the television and allowed the cameraman to escort him through the familiar areas of the club. Judge James C Colman watched the scenes with his wife and knew the courts would be busy from tomorrow. At the far side of town Rosalynn Brando was prepared for bed but she felt obliged to watch the conclusion of this saga. Doctor Braxton Walker celebrated the fact that a potentially explosive incident had ended peacefully and Christina Coomes finally tucked her two sons into bed with hope in her heart. The police had actually come back to make arrests in the east side. She hoped they would come again for the infamous eight if they decided to stay in the community. She was about to turn off the television when she saw him. Smokey Peters filled the center of her television set. The man was strolling confidently out of the Pepperdine, hat as always askew and a cigarette in between his fingers. 'Swine', she said and switched off the set.

* * *

As a rule, there were never any card games in the Red Rooms in the

Hood Acre on Sundays. But this game had not started on a Sunday. They had been going at one another since Saturday night; three had been knocked out by Sunday afternoon and the three who were left were showing incredible skills in a game that had swung first in O'Reilly's favor, then Van Derpool's. Senor Munzon had lost almost all of the three million he had won from the three previous losers but he had slowly clawed his way back with some deft card playing, a mixture of bluff and quality hands, and he was now once again in the strongest position with almost four million at his disposal. The table controller consulted all three players. They could put the game on hold and resume on Monday evening, they could continue throughout the night until someone eventually won or they could take a break for two hours and return to play after they had refreshed themselves. They opted to place the game on hold and resume on Monday night, so at ten fifteen on Sunday night the table controller had called an end to play and secured the Red Room.

CHAPTER THIRTEEN

Monday morning broke bright and hot. The heavy rains of Thursday seemed to be the last for the end of winter. Spring was now ready to stake its claim. Doctor Ben Swinton woke up early, having had a long, refreshing sleep in anticipation of the difficult day ahead of him. He would meet with his father's attorneys at nine that morning, followed by a meeting with his bankers at eleven thirty, then on to the hospital for a brief meeting with the head of obstetrics at two thirty. Simon Carter had suggested lunch at the hospital canteen for one thirty, if time allowed, otherwise he would eat alone and telephone his friend later in the evening. Swinton checked the time, 6.58 according to the kitchen clock. He knew the seven o'clock news was imminent so he carried his coffee and the plate of toast into the living room and turned on the television.

The seven o'clock news began with vivid pictures of severe floods and mud slides in the Central American countries of Honduras and Nicaragua. Swinton watched the pictures and focused his attention on the pregnant woman who was trying to claw her way onto higher ground while dragging her toddler along at the same time. Not for the first time, he considered settling in some third world country where he could donate his medical services for the benefit of those who would appreciate it most. The newscaster was moving quickly through the chain of grim news. In Japan, somewhere called Kyushu, south of Osaka, an earthquake had registered 7.2 on the Richter scale. Damage, however, was slight. The President of the United States was preparing for yet another trip to the Middle East and finally, a motorcycle gang had taken over a nightclub in the city for several hours; the siege had finally ended late Sunday night without fatalities. The gang, approximately twenty-five to thirty in number were now in the county jail waiting to be arraigned in court. Swinton turned off the set and picked up the medical journal, wondering whether he would be able to practice his profession in some other country if he were struck off.

Ben Swinton entered one of the tallest buildings in the downtown area of the city just before nine. He wanted the sixteenth floor, the offices of Anderson and Tate, Attorneys at Law. The pretty young secretary was expecting him.

'Please make yourself comfortable Doctor Swinton. Mr Tate will be with you in a moment', she said and vanished from sight. Swinton looked around the office. There was nothing cheap about this place, he thought, and wondered how much the hour and a half or so of their time would cost him. Maybe he should have studied law. Well, they get debarred too, don't they? He was playing mind games when Patrick Tate walked in, his hand outstretched. Swinton had expected a much older man. Instead he shook hands with a thirty-two-year-old, well-tanned, fit-looking lawyer.

'Doctor Swinton,' the man announced, 'I am Patrick Tate, please come into my office.' He led the way into the plush office and offered the doctor a seat.

'Coffee?' asked Tate.

'Please, black', replied Swinton.

The secretary reappeared with an expensive silver tray and poured coffee for both men. She checked with Swinton to make sure that he was happy with the coffee and left the office, quietly shutting the door behind her.

'Doctor Swinton, your letter was very specific', Patrick Tate began, opening a thin blue file. 'You require sixty-seven thousand dollars from the trust account to which you are the sole beneficiary.' He looked at the doctor. 'You appreciate, of course, that we would require approval from the trustees.'

Swinton looked surprised. He had not anticipated that. The trust was his, so why would it be necessary to involve anyone else.

'I take it you don't quite understand', said Tate. 'Let me explain'. He sat back in the comfortable chair and took his time to give a broad introduction to the principles of trusts.

'A trust is a legally enforceable obligation placed by one person, in this case your father, who is the settlor, on another person or persons, who are referred to as the trustees. The trustees have an obligation to deal with the trust fund in certain specified ways for the benefit of the beneficiary, who in this case is you.' The lawyer looked at Swinton as if to ensure that the doctor understood what he was saying.

'The actions of the trustees are defined in the trust deed.' He pushed the paper towards the doctor.

'How many trustees?' asked Swinton.

'Three', replied Tate. 'The first trustee is your father, the second is your mother and the third, your father's brother, a professor David Swinton, now residing in Jacksonville, Florida.'

'Are you saying that all three will have to give their approval before the required funds are released?'

'I am afraid that is the case. I could have the papers drawn up and sent to them for their signatures, with your authority, of course.'

Ben Swinton was in a dilemma. The trust had been set up for him and the fund was his but he did not relish being in a position to explain to his parents and, as he had just discovered, to his uncle why he needed such a large amount. He handed the deed document back to the lawyer and rubbed his chin. He would have to think about it. He stood up, thanked the lawyer for his time and turned towards the door.

'Don't you want to know the fund value?' asked Tate.

Swinton turned to face the lawyer. 'Right', he said.

'Three million, two hundred and eighty-four thousand, four hundred and twenty seven dollars (US) and eighty-six cents.' The lawyer handed Swinton the piece of paper on which he had written the figure, shook hands with the doctor and said goodbye.

Ben Swinton exited the building. 'Three million blah, blah, blah', he said aloud and inserted the key in the ignition. He did not seem excited, nor concerned with the figure the lawyer had given him. All he needed at the moment was sixty-seven thousand to get those people off his back. He could call his father or better yet approach his mother first. Why did everything have to be so difficult? He was approaching the hospital when he remembered the eleven thirty bank appointment. It was now ten fifty. Why not, he thought and turned the car around. The bank might extend him the loan if he could put some sort of collateral against the loan. After all he owned his flat outright. He was not sure of the value but he believed the flat was worth somewhere in the region of ninety thousand. That's it, he would discuss the matter with the bank and keep his parents out of this. Ben Swinton parked the car and strode confidently into the building. He was going to keep his eleven thirty appointment with his bankers.

* * *

The hot early morning sun beat down on Shamon Kazi's bare back. He could feel the sweat trickle slowly down his neck and make its way down his back as if on a charted course, destined for a predetermined point somewhere on his lower body. He had spent some time searching for the oak tree under which he had buried the small metal box. The tree was no longer standing as a result of Thursday's heavy rains and winds but eventually he had found it lying on its side, apologetically it seemed, for having succumbed to the winds. Shamon Kazi had come to dig, his spade poised for the task at hand, but there was no need. Tangled in the mud-coated roots, he could see the small metal box, mud-coated but intact. Kazi reached into the mud, separated the roots, picked up the metal box, slowly brushed away the mud with his hands and carried the box into the tent. Inside the tent, he placed the metal box on the floor and slowly removed the key from his pocket. He had not laid eyes on the metal box or the contents for the past two years. Kazi was excited. He did not own much in this life and material things had never mattered to him, but today, he was excited and the excitement made him feel good. He inserted the key into the lock and turned it, took in a deep breath and lifted the lid. The small oilcloth was undisturbed. Kazi lifted it, folded it neatly and placed it on the floor near the box. He could now see the prayer cloth underneath which he knew the cross would be. There was no need to rush this affair, after all it had taken over two years to pull the metal box from its hiding place. Kazi placed his right hand over his heart, closed his eyes and began to pray the prayers of his ancestors, to ask for guidance and protection but most importantly for wisdom in decision making because soon he would have to dispose of his most prized possession besides his horses to safeguard his family. He had already seen the new trailer he wanted to buy to replace their old home and he wanted to make sure that the new trailer was in place, the old one removed and all necessary preparations made to welcome his wife back to the farm. Shamon Kazi knew that after praying whatever decision he took would be the right one.

Slowly, he lifted the prayer cloth to reveal the cross, a most magnificent silver cross encrusted with eight beautifully shaped diamonds, four down and four across. In the heart of the crosss sat a large ruby stone. Kazi gazed at the cross in silence, his mind in a daze, flooded with visions of his father's face and the words which had accompanied this wonderful gift.

The story had been told to Shamon Kazi simply, with pride but without fanfare. That was twenty-five years ago, just before his father had died. Ramnesh Kazi had summoned his only son to his bedside in the full knowledge that he would not last through the night. In true gypsy tradition, he had asked for the special moment with his son, alone, and he had shared the proudest moment in his lifetime with Shamon Kazi. The cross had been a present from the king of Prussia, in appreciation for devoted service in the care and transport of prized horses in the king's herd. Ramnesh Kazi had treasured the cross and on his deathbed had wanted to ensure that his most prized possession would fall safely in the hands of his only son. Ramnesh had wished his son well, embraced him with the little energy he had left and handed him the metal box containing the cross and the prayer cloth.

Shamon Kazi picked up the cross and examined it. Despite his prayers he was in a quandary. He was sure the cross was valuable enough to cover sufficiently the cost of the new trailer but deep in his heart he did not wish to part with it. He would have to seek advice from his friend, the doctor. It would be wise to do so. Kazi replaced the cross in the metal box, placed the prayer cloth over it and secured it in his satchel. It was time to see to his horses. He walked out of the tent and gathered the five horses around him. This was routine. He began to put the horses through their paces. For the first time in his life he did not seem to have the enthusiasm or the excitement that he felt naturally when he gathered his horses around him. It was as if the animals could sense Kazi's lack of enthusiasm. Shamka showed no interest in the horse trainer's instructions and reared up on several occasions. Talisman simply wandered off with the others and trotted aimlessly around the farm. Shamon Kazi knew there would be no communication with the horses today so he gave up and returned to the tent. He would rest and meet with the doctor in the evening to seek his advice. Shamon Kazi thought about his wife and his son and drifted into sleep with the vision of his father riding fast over the plains, coming towards him.

* * *

Mondays were always busy at the hospital and on this particular Monday, the day on which Maureen Carter was returning to work after her brief vacation, Simon and Maureen Carter had been up half an hour earlier than normal. Simon Carter had telephoned the head of his children's school on Sunday night with a special request. Would he allow John to attend his lessons with a friend, a friend who might soon be enrolling at the school? The request had been granted so on this Monday morning preparations were made to see the three children off to school before Maureen and Simon left for the hospital. The conversation in the car centered around Shamon Kazi and his family. Simon Carter wondered how he could be of assistance.

'We should have approached the department of social welfare', said Maureen. 'Actually it is not too late to do so. When I have some time today, I shall arrange for someone to go and interview Mrs Kazi. The hospital ought to be able to assist them.' Maureen had hit on something positive. That would be a good place to start because it was an emergency.

'I wonder if Shamon had any sort of cover on the trailer.' Simon looked at his wife. 'When I spoke to him yesterday, he seemed to know what he was doing and assured me he would let me know today.'

'If all fails, they can all live with us for as long as they wish', said Maureen. 'After all it's not as if we'd be cramped for space.'

Simon Carter looked at his wife lovingly. 'Didn't I tell you, you were beautiful?'

'At the moment I don't feel beautiful. By the way, Broxy arrives tomorrow evening', Maureen remembered. 'What about the people who came to see you at the hospital? Is there any chance they might come again, say today?'

'Ben is dealing with that today', replied Simon. 'It should be all over by this evening or tomorrow.' He sounded confident.

Simon Carter slid the car into the parking bay and entered the hospital, holding his wife's hand. They parted on the second floor and within minutes immersed themselves in the busy hospital atmosphere. Maureen Carter spent the morning coming up to speed with events that had taken place within the hospital during her week's absence. She was happy to learn that one of the two most critical patients she had been concerned about had made remarkable progress and was now off the critical list. The other patient was now stable but still on the critical list so she had checked in on the old man to ensure the necessary procedures were being followed and she had stayed with him to offer encouragement and the nurse's touch so vital in patient recovery. She had it in mind to find some time to spend with Mrs Kazi whom she had not met but had heard so much about since Thursday night.

Juliana Kazi woke up at three in the afternoon to find the woman sitting next to her bed. She could tell from the lady's uniform that she was one of the senior people in the hospital and wondered why she was sitting there, more like a visitor than someone at work. Maureen Carter smiled at Juliana Kazi, a familiar, warm smile, and offered her hand to the gypsy.

'Mrs Kazi,' Maureen shook her hand, 'I am Maureen Carter, one of your nurses.'

The gypsy woman nodded her head and stared at her. The name rang a bell in her head and brought a bright smile from Juliana Kazi.

'You are Doctor Carter's wife, the kind lady who has looked after my Kazeem.'

'He is a lovely boy, a lovely boy indeed, and we are happy to have him with us.'

'I hope he has not been much trouble for you.' Juliana raised her eyebrow, the sort of signal that mothers understood between one another. 'How can we thank you?' Her eyes were tearful but full of appreciation and admiration for the slim woman.

'You have already thanked us Mrs Kazi and frankly we are the ones who must thank you for sharing your son with us.' Maureen was being truthful. The two women talked and as time went on they seemed to feel closer and more comfortable with each other. Juliana Kazi gave Maureen an insight into the events of the frightful Thursday night, the fear she had felt and her resignation to the fact that her son might have to grow up without her. She told Maureen about how much she had enjoyed seeing Katherine at the farm from time to time and how she had wondered about the young lady's mother. Now she was happy, because fate had brought them face to face and as she had always believed, the mother of Katherine was as she had envisioned her in her mind's eye.

'When you are much better and stronger, you must come and visit,' said Maureen, standing up to return to her duties, 'and I will not take no for an answer.' Maureen laughed, gave the gypsy a gentle hug and walked away towards the far end of the ward.

Juliana Kazi watched her walking away, full of admiration and gratitude. She wished she could return the invitation someday, bake the woman some wonderful heavy dough bread, cook a very special goulash and make her welcome in her home. Her mind suddenly turned to her own present predicament. In a few day's time she would be leaving the hospital, for where? The trailer had been destroyed. As far as she knew Shamon was living in a tent loaned to him by the kind doctor and his wife; the boy was safe with them for the moment but in a few days the family would be together again, then what! Juliana Kazi was uncertain about her family's future. She placed her head on the pillow, closed her eyes and began to wonder how the future would turn out for them. Something seemed to stir in her all of a sudden; her eyes still closed she smiled hopefully, a calm feeling came over her and she knew that somehow Shamon Kazi would not let her down. He had never let her down and he would not let her down now. Quietly, she fell asleep.

* * *

Ben Swinton hummed to the music coming from the radio and manoeuvred through the afternoon traffic on his way to the hospital. He was feeling much better because his discussions at the bank had been very positive. The bank would be most willing to lend him the sixty-seven thousand dollars provided he could put up his flat as collateral. The bank had recently instituted a new lending scheme for doctors and dentists in the city, a new idea to attract many more qualified medical professionals into the city and, of course, to encourage such high earners to place their business with the bank. The loan would be granted at a low interest rate of 3.25% over ten years with the option to pay off the full loan amount without penalties at any time within the ten-year period. Once the deeds to the flat were examined and found to be in order and, if the value was, as the doctor believed, in the region of ninety thousand, the funds would be released into Swinton's account within a matter of days and that was that. Swinton felt good because there was no longer any need to involve his parents or anybody else in this arrangement. His next appointment was with the head of obstetrics but before that he hoped to share lunch with Simon Carter to inform him of the good news. He hoped Simon would be free to join him in the hospital canteen.

Simon Carter strolled into the canteen at twenty minutes to two and greeted his best friend with an apology for being ten minutes late.

'I would have been worried if I'd found you sitting here when I arrived,' said Swinton, 'simply because one would have got the impression that there is not much going on in this establishment,' he laughed. 'Lunch is on me, come on before I change my mind.' Ben Swinton led the way to the food counter. He was ebullient.

The two men ordered their meal, Swinton picking up the tab and finding a corner where they could talk more privately. Simon Carter listened patiently to Ben Swinton's account of his Monday morning activities and breathed a sigh of relief when Swinton told him of the positive response from the bank manager. Swinton hoped to have the whole thing cleared up by the coming Friday.

'And a lesson learned', Swinton concluded.

'Hallelujah!' Simon Carter was sharing his friend's joy.

They spent the rest of the lunch break discussing the two thirty meeting with obstetrics when, suddenly, at ten past two, Simon Carter was bleeped to attend to an emergency. He was on his feet in an instant. 'Good luck', he said to Swinton. 'Come home for supper at eight, much better food than this.' He pointed at his plate and rushed out of the canteen.

Ben Swinton finished his meal alone. In about ten minutes' time he would be sitting alone in a room with the head of obstetrics, once again going over the unpleasant affair. His future was in their hands. Why was he being put through this? His mind flashed back to his conversation in the motel room with Bakersfield. The man had believed him when he had told him in all honesty that the baby's death was not his fault, so why was it so difficult for those who mattered to believe him? He would tell them the truth again, once and for all, and if they chose to believe him, fine; if not, he would walk away from them and try to rebuild his future in the best way possible. That Bakersfield was one hell of a man, he thought, and walked confidently into the room to face his tormentors.

Ben Swinton sat across the table from them, his head clear and his heart pounding. He was ready for what was coming so he looked at the three men. He knew them all. They had chosen to hold the meeting in the Chief Administrator's Office. Swinton could see the framed pictures of eminent professors of obstetrics on the wall along with the pictures of great surgeons who had served in the hospital over the years. They were all great men, most of whom were dead but one or two still living but retired. He could feel the cold, hard eyes of those men along the wall boring into him. Not a word had been said but he could hear clearly in his mind the pronouncements which seemed to come from each one of the pictures along the wall - *guilty, struck off! guilty, struck off! Shame!*

'Doctor Swinton', the Chief Administrator's voice shook him back to life. Swinton sat bolt upright in his chair, his chest fully open and ready for the assault he expected to come at any moment. He had already heard it from those along the wall so all that remained was verbal confirmation from the other three in the chairs opposite him. The Chief Administrator was taking his time. He looked to his right and acknowledged the nod from the Chief of Obstetrics, Professor David Cudgeon, then to his left at the Chief of Surgery and Internal Medicine, Dr Ham Schluum who also nodded.

'Doctor Swinton,' the Chief Administrator was ready to lower the boom, thought Swinton, 'we owe you an apology.' What? Ben Swinton shook in his chair. 'We owe you a very great apology for having put you through this.' Swinton looked at the three eminent men. Were these men nuts? He had come here to defend himself so what were they talking about? He looked past the three men to those on the wall. He could swear those along the wall were smiling, their faces now serene and kind.

'Sir,' Swinton found the word from somewhere deep in his throat, 'I don't understand.'

The Chief Administrator was finding this difficult so Professor Cudgeon came to his aid. 'Doctor,' he said simply, 'there was a mix up in the blood samples. The sample we thought was yours belonged to a patient, a blunder, a great blunder indeed. You do, of course, have every right to lodge a formal complaint,' Cudgeon cleared his throat, 'and I can assure you personally that any complaint you lodge will be considered without bias. Please accept our apologies. We are naturally, considering some sort of compensation; in the meantime we would like you to return to your duties as of next Monday.' He lowered his glasses. 'We feel a week's holiday with full pay will give you some time to get over the shock.' Cudgeon then handed Swinton the envelope. 'This is a formal letter of apology from the hospital. We hope you will accept it.'

The three men got up, walked around the table and, one by one, they shook hands with Ben Swinton and left the room. He held the envelope in both hands, walked over to the wall and closely examined the pictures. Ben Swinton wondered what experiences they might have gone through during their long years of service to the medical profession. He walked over to the window and gazed out onto the hospital forecourt. Nothing had changed; he could see the nurses coming on duty while others were leaving, the ambulances stood in readiness and the odd doctor, stethoscope draped around the neck, walking briskly to one wing or another. His future had hung in the balance in this quiet room but he had survived the trauma. Tonight he would enjoy the supper that Simon Carter had promised and ensure that his blood had some alcohol in it.

'Thank you', he said quietly as he walked past the pictures on the wall and shut the door behind him.

* * *

The day had been busy, as Mondays usually were, and Simon Carter was feeling exhausted. He had already dropped Maureen Carter off at home and was continuing on to meet with the gypsy. The news wasn't too bad, according to Maureen. The Social Welfare Department had been contacted by the hospital after a lengthy interview with Juliana Kazi and someone from Social Welfare would be coming on Wednesday morning to assess Juliana Kazi's needs. It was unlikely that Juliana would be released from the hospital before Friday so the critical days would be Wednesday and Thursday. He and Maureen had already put their own contingency plans in place. If by Friday evening the accommodation arrangements were still uncertain, they would simply insist that the Kazis move in with them. They had taken into account the fact that by then Broxy and Robert would also be their guests. There was plenty of room for all.

Simon Carter tooted the horn once, twice and pulled up several metres away from the camping tent which was now Shamon Kazi's shelter. Carter stepped out of the car and watched Shamon Kazi walking towards him. Something was wrong this evening; the man did not seem himself. Unlike the Shamon that Carter had become used to, the man approaching seemed somber and downhearted. Simon Carter met the gypsy halfway and shook hands with the man.

'I get the feeling all is not well tonight', said Carter.

'Doctor Carter,' the gypsy looked at Simon, 'I have been waiting for you, I need your advice, please come in with me.' He led the way into the tent and offered the doctor one of the two chairs. Shamon Kazi then reached for the satchel and placed it next to him. They sat facing each other, neither of them saying a word. The shrill whistle from the boiling kettle cut through the silence like a knife. Shamon Kazi had anticipated the doctor's arrival and the kettle was reminding him of his position as the host. Kazi got up to silence the kettle. Methodically, he produced two cups of tea and handed one of the cups to Simon Carter. The doctor accepted the cup. He felt he had to say something.

'Kazeem went to school today with John', Simon Carter said cheerfully. 'I am sure he'll have a lot to tell us this evening, I look forward to that.'

'Doctor Carter, yesterday you asked if I had thought about where we will stay when Juliana comes back from hospital.' The gypsy held his tea in his left hand and rubbed his right hand gently over the satchel next to his chair. It was as if he had not heard Carter's statement about the gypsy boy's first day in a formal classroom.

'I have found a new home for my family.' He paused and looked sadly at the doctor. 'I think I can buy it, but I am very sad.' The man was not making any sense; Simon Carter was confused. The gypsy needed a new home; Carter was running the whole thing through his mind again; the man had found one that he thought he could buy. Under normal circumstances most people would be ecstatic but his friend was sad.

'Why?' Carter asked the gypsy.

'Because the price is too high', the gypsy replied.

Now this was getting really confusing. Hadn't the gypsy said he thought he could buy it? If the price were too high one would not consider buying it. This conversation was leading nowhere. Simon Carter decided to cut through the fog and bring the conversation down to straightforward logic, one question at a time, from A to B and

166

then to C and so on.

'Shamon,' Carter was going to try to be logical, 'you started by saying that you have found a home, is that correct?'

'Yes', the gypsy replied.

'And you did say that you think you can buy it?' Carter raised his eyebrow questioningly.

'Yes.'

'Now, this is where you lose me Shamon, because you want a new home, you have found a new home, you think you can buy it but you are sad.'

'Yes.'

As an undergraduate at university, Simon Carter had enjoyed Logic. Everything was so straightforward and clear. He wished he and Shamon were sitting in one of those lectures today because it would be most interesting to listen to the arguments.

'Can you tell me why you are so sad, my friend?' Carter had come to the end of the track. He was already exhausted from the busy day at the hospital. It was time for him to shut up and let the man explain himself or let the man quietly work through his sadness.

'I told you I needed your advice', Shamon Kazi was speaking again.

'Sure, just ask,' said Simon, 'and I hope I am worthy', he muttered under his breath.

The gypsy got up, walked to the far corner of the tent and returned with a medium-sized cardboard box. He placed the box between Simon Carter and himself. Slowly he reached into the satchel and brought out the small metal box and placed it on the cardboard box. He looked at Carter, who was by now perking up again with curiosity.

'Simon,' said the gypsy. It was the very first time Shamon Kazi had referred to the doctor by his first name and it sounded strange coming from him but Carter liked it.

'Yes Shamon', Carter answered to his name. He could sense something special was about to happen and he had moved forward on the seat and was now bent so far forward he seemed to hover over the cardboard box.

'I will show you something I have never shown anyone, not even Juliana.'

Hello! Simon Carter was now apprehensive, even a little afraid. He watched as Shamon Kazi opened the metal box and removed the oilcloth. Simon peered into the box. All he could see was the cloth with tiny inscriptions on it. Shamon Kazi slowly lifted the prayer cloth.

'Good God!' Simon Carter jumped off his seat, his eyes bulging. The silver cross gleamed in the light, diamonds shimmering and the large ruby in the heart, like a red eye, stared back at him. This was priceless, a museum piece, something that should not be touched by mere mortals. Simon Carter was breathing heavily. The gypsy picked up the cross, reached out to Simon Carter and gently placed the silver cross in his palm.

'My father gave me that,' said the gypsy sadly, 'and I am sad because I have to part with it to get my new home to shelter my family.'

'No you will not!' Simon Carter made it sound almost like an order. 'Do you have any idea of the value of this piece?' Carter was getting angry with his friend. Slowly he began to recover from the shock of seeing the exquisite cross, 'It is priceless.' Carter sat back down and calmly examined the heirloom. After some time, he gently returned the cross to Shamon Kazi who replaced it in the box and covered it with the prayer cloth and the oilcloth.

'You wanted my advice', Simon Carter reminded his friend about their conversation prior to the bolt of lightning striking a few moments ago.

'Yes Simon, I need the trailer but I also want to keep this,' he pointed to the metal box, 'because my father gave it to me.'

Simon Carter thought for a moment. He had succumbed to the fact that the logical approach to situations sometimes did not work so well when human emotion was introduced into the equation. He did not see why his gypsy friend could not have his trailer and keep his cross. The solution was simple. Simon took his time to explain the procedure they would have to follow.

'First we must have the cross appraised by an expert to have an idea of its true financial value.' Simon was speaking slowly. 'After that we must insure it for the financial value that we know the cross is worth, then we go to the bank and borrow the money for your trailer using the cross as collateral.' Carter was not sure if the gypsy could understand. 'How do you feel about that?' he asked his friend.

'You will guide me.' The gypsy had faith in his friend.

'How did you manage to keep this precious cross safe over the years?'

'Under trees', came the simple but true answer. Simon Carter could not help laughing. He could see Shamon Kazi returning to his old self again. The problem had been solved by the doctor, his friend, and all was well again. Tomorrow, he would enjoy training his horses once more.

CHAPTER FOURTEEN

The dark clouds were gathering and threatening rain by the time William Nylander stepped out of the shop on Lexington Avenue. He had arrived in Washington DC on Sunday night in preparation for the Monday morning meetings at the State Department and later in the afternoon at the Defense Department. Both meetings had gone well on Monday and Nylander was pleased for having accomplished all that he had come home to do on behalf of Nylander Electronics. His flight to Jeddah was scheduled for six o'clock eastern standard time from Kennedy Airport, so he had taken the shuttle from Washington and arrived in New York in time to collect the golf set he had chosen as a present for his friend Sheikh Al Makhtoum Walhadi.

William Nylander hailed the yellow cab and settled himself in the back for the journey from Central Manhattan to Kennedy Airport.

'Looks like rain', the taxi driver said inviting conversation.

'I hope it holds off until I am airborne', replied Nylander.

'Which airline, sir?' asked the driver.

'Saudi Air', said Nylander. 'Should be in Jeddah by tomorrow,' he hoped.

'Saudi Arabian Airlines, founded in 1945,' said the driver, scratching his head as if to extract the information he wanted manually and continued, 'first service, March 1947, I think the fourth, but I am not sure about that.' He turned to look at Nylander, 'It's a game I play with my kids, we know most of the airlines that come into Kennedy.'

They were crossing the Tri-borough Bridge when the dark clouds released their excess load of water. It came down all at once, a sudden heavy downpour that taxed the windshield wipers to the limit and very quickly slowed the traffic that began to bunch.

Nylander had been impressed by the driver's hobby and fished for more.

'What else can you tell me about Saudi Air?' he asked. 'Might as well know as much as possible about an airline if I've got to fly with them.' The inside of the windshield was beginning to steam up. The driver switched on the blower to dissipate the condensation. Again he

170

scratched his head. Nylander put that down to habit and waited for the man to come up with more information.

'They are based in King Abdul Aziz International Airport, Jeddah.' The man was right, that much Nylander knew.

'They have a fleet of about a hundred, a good mix too,' the driver continued, 'Airbuses, a wide Boeing range, one McDonnell Douglas DC-8F-54 and my favorite, the Gulfstream 11, 111 and IV.' The rain had almost stopped but was now spitting gently on the windscreen. They had left Manhattan behind them and were now into Queens.

'I don't think the rain will interrupt this evening's match.' The driver could see the sign showing the way to Shea Stadium. 'I love baseball and the Mets but I don't get enough time to go.' He was changing topics.

'So who's playing tonight?' asked Nylander.

'The Mets should beat the Braves.'

'Aren't the Braves from Atlanta?' Nylander was contributing his bit to the interesting man's efforts to make his journey a pleasant one.

'Yeah, the Atlanta Braves, if the rain holds out they should lose tonight', the driver said assuredly. 'What about you sir? I bet you miss the big games when you are over there in Saudi. No football, no baseball, no basketball, boy! Must be hard,' he concluded and pulled in front of the departure lounge. It was still drizzling when Nylander stepped out of the cab. He waited for the baggage handler to unload the luggage and the golf clubs from the trunk, thanked the driver for the pleasant journey and tipped him handsomely.

'You are right about one thing, I do miss the football season.'

The baggage handler led the way to the Saudi Air desk. Within minutes Nylander had been processed, his luggage checked in along with the golf clubs and handed his boarding pass. He had plenty of time before the flight was announced so he took the opportunity to make final contact with his wife and daughter. Mrs Nylander was grateful for the call. They hoped to see each other again in July when their daughter Jill was on holidays from school. Jill was not at home this afternoon but she could be reached at the Carter's, where she was revising for exams with her friend Katherine. Mrs Nylander provided the Carter's number which Nylander jotted down on the back of the ticket folder; they said their goodbyes, Mrs Nylander wishing him a safe flight. William Nylander dialled again, this time in search of his daughter.

'Hello Uncle Nylander', Katherine Carter said cheerfully into the phone.

'Katherine, hello!' Nylander was happy to be talking to the young girl. 'Mrs Nylander tells me Jill is with you. I am at Kennedy Airport, just about ready to leave for Saudi, just wanted to say goodbye to Jill.'

'She's right here, sir', said Katherine.

'Oh, by the way, before you go Katherine,' Nylander was talking quickly, 'thank you for a wonderful party last Saturday and take special care of Shamka, she is one of a kind,' Nylander concluded.

'Thank you Uncle Nylander, I will', said Katherine. 'Here is Jill.' Katherine handed the receiver to Jill Nylander.

'Hello Daddy.'

'Hi darling,' Nylander replied, 'I'll be boarding my flight in a few minutes and thought I'd say goodbye to my favorite daughter.'

'Oh Daddy,' Jill said sweetly, 'I love you too. Don't forget to send me a letter as soon as you arrive. I shall look forward to that, and daddy, have a safe flight.'

The announcement came loud and clear:

Will passengers for Saudi Air flight SV234 to Jeddah please proceed to gate thirty-eight. Last call, last call.

'That's my flight Jill, got to go. I promise I'll write within the first week.' He was about to put the phone down when he remembered something, 'And Jill, do take good care of your mother, bye.' Nylander hung up the phone and made his way quickly to gate thirty-eight.

William Nylader settled himself comfortably in the first-class seat. He planned to catch up on lost sleep during the long flight. He removed his wristwatch and began to alter the time from 5.55 eastern standard time to 1.55 sun time to accommodate for the eight hours that he would be losing. He was already making the mental transition from the United States to Saudi Arabia. The rest of the physical trans-formation was up to the pilots. Nylander picked up the flight pack and found himself thinking about the taxi driver. He was sitting in the first-class compartment of an Airbus A300-600. The Airbus operated a two-class configuration seating 258 passengers. Nylander knew the flight was full this evening. Therefore there were 257 passengers along with him, plus cabin crew, pilots and engineers. He looked around the compartment, a mixture of Arabs, Westerners and a small contingent of Japanese men who were talking excitedly amongst themselves. They were airborne at exactly 6.07, heading east.

* * *

Stumpy Lazarus wore a charcoal double-breasted suit, a button-down white shirt and a soft yellow silk tie. He had been looking forward to this meeting all day and waited on the balcony. Stumpy had said he would look out for her and from six fifty-five onwards he'd been doing just that, looking out. He had had an easy Monday with his partner. Steiner and Stumpy had left the city at five thirty in the morning and driven eighty miles to collect the thirty thousand that was due from the first client on the list that Jack Dawson had provided on Friday afternoon. The farmer and his wife had been at breakfast when the two men arrived. He was expecting them. The farmer's wife believed the two men were tractor salesmen who had come to discuss the new line of tractors and the various parts needed to keep their farm equipment in good running order. Steiner had taken the envelope the man handed to him, shaken hands amicably and both he and Stumpy had waved goodbye to the man and his wife.

'See you all again now', the farmer's wife had said and waved back. Stumpy and Steiner had worked their way back by stopping at an oil refinery approximately thirty miles outside the city. The manager of the refinery had seen them coming and, to save himself any embarrassment, he had picked up the envelope containing the fifteen thousand dollars he owed and had met the two men just outside the refinery gates. Again they had shaken hands amicably with the client and had driven away as smoothly as they had arrived. The two men had had lunch at Gringo's, a popular Mexican restaurant on the outskirts of the city at one thirty, made two more collections of twenty and thirteen thousand dollars and returned to the office on Carvel Avenue. The rest of the afternoon had been spent in the office with nothing much to do.

Stumpy Lazarus saw her drive up and watched as she parked the car. She stepped out of the car, looked up and saw him on the balcony and waved. Stumpy looked at the slim black woman, whistled softly to himself and beckoned for her to enter the building. They met at the elevator and entered the flat together, Stumpy stepping aside to usher

her into the flat. Jurelene Patterson looked stunning in the wine-collarless skirt suit with gold-effect buttons and jet pockets. She wore a comfortable pair of short-heeled shoes and carried a small, matching wine coloured handbag. The woman was just beautiful; her short black hair was combed neatly to one side and pinned just above the left ear with a tiny hair clip.

Jurelene Patterson stood in the middle of the living room and melted Stumpy Lazarus's hard heart with that disarming smile.

'Take a seat.' Stumpy felt like adding please but somehow he could not bring himself to say the word so he simply pointed to the sofa and sat down opposite the woman. They looked at each other, both unsure about how to start the communication. Mickey Steiner was right, his partner was going through a drastic transformation. Like a wild Bronco, Stumpy Lazarus was being broken by this slim, beautiful, black woman and yet she had not said a word.

'Can I get you a drink?' asked Stumpy, rising from his seat.

'Any soft drink,' said Jurelene, '7-up, orange, anything.'

Stumpy returned momentarily with a tall glass of 7-up containing ice and a glass of beer. He handed the woman the tall glass and sat down. He looked at her, sipped the beer and began to rub the scar on his cheek gently; Stumpy was nervous.

'Mr Lazarus,' Jurelene Patterson was getting ready to begin the conversation, 'I hope you don't mind my calling on you at such short notice.' She paused, sipped her drink somewhat nervously and continued. 'I am sorry for having contributed to your difficulties the other night.' She lifted her eyes, a whisper of a smile on the edge of her well-shaped lips.

'Forget it.' Stumpy was beginning to relax. The woman was not just beautiful, she was articulate and she sounded educated. When she had driven Stumpy from the east side to the flat the other night she had hardly spoken.

Tonight, Stumpy was going to find out a whole lot more about this woman that he had dreamt about.

'You know,' Stumpy was slowly gaining confidence, 'I am sure you came here for a reason. When you feel ready, you can tell me why, and by the way you can call me Stump.'

Jurelene Patterson was hesitant. This was only the second time she had met this man. Their first meeting had been orchestrated by

174

Smokey Peters, and now here she sat in the man's apartment completely of her own volition to try to seek his help for herself and her room-mate.

'You have heard what happened on Saturday night?' She paused and looked at him long and hard. 'I mean the murders on the east side.'

'Yeah, saw it on television.'

The door bell was ringing so Stumpy rose from his seat to answer it. It was Mickey Steiner and Stumpy let him in. He introduced Steiner to Jurelene Patterson, disappeared into the kitchen and reappeared again with a bottle of beer for his partner.

'About the murders on Saturday night', Stumpy was continuing from where they had left off. He suddenly realized the change in the black woman's demeanour. She was worried about the presence of Steiner. Within minutes Stumpy Lazarus had reassured her. She looked at the tall, handsome newcomer, liked what she saw and resumed their conversation about the murders of the two black boys on Saturday night.

'My room-mate and I know the person who killed the boys.' She clasped her arms about her as if she were cold all of a sudden. 'We are not sure but we think the killer knows we know.'

'As you say, you really can't be sure', said Steiner.

'Lucy and I were in the kitchen.' She looked from one to the other and felt the need to elaborate. 'Lucy is my room-mate, Lucy Sharpe. As I said we were in the kitchen when they came in the house. They had been drinking and didn't realize we were there so they started talking about what had happened and what they had done with the gun.'

'Who is "they"?' asked Stumpy.

She ignored the question. 'Lucy and I sneaked out of the kitchen and through the garage but there were two more coming into the house and they saw us.'

Mickey Steiner took the woman in tow. What she was saying was serious. If she truly knew the killer or killers of the two young boys then they were obliged to do something about it. Naturally, the woman was afraid for her safety and that of her room-mate so it was important to assure her of her well-being. She would have to have complete trust in them. After all, she'd come this far. If she couldn't trust them then she might as well put an end to the conversation right here and now and accept their word of promise that they would not mention what they had been told to anyone else. Mickey was looking directly at the woman. He could understand why Stumpy Lazarus felt the way he did. How could such a beautiful person - and he meant person, because the woman was physically beautiful but it seemed also that she was a good person but it seemed also that she was a good person. She deserved better, Steiner thought. Maybe she could still come out okay.

'Will you trust us?' Mickey Steiner had to know.

She nodded her head and flashed the most infectious smile, showing briefly a perfect set of very white teeth.

'Who did the killing?' asked Stumpy.

'Frank Biggles', she replied.

'Are you sure?' asked Steiner.

'When they came into the house,' she lifted her eyebrows, ' - you've got to remember they didn't know we were there and they were talking quite freely - Smokey Peters laughed and asked Biggles why he'd shot the boys.' She paused. 'Biggles replied, "because the two little fuckers thought they could cheat me and get away with it."'

'What about the gun, what did they do with it?' asked Steiner.

'It's under the floorboards in Biggles's bedroom, at least that's what he said.'

'And about the two men you think saw you coming out of the house, who were they?'

'Sam Dingles and Paperbag Jones', the woman chuckled. 'They call him Paperbag because he sells all his drugs in small paper bags instead of the small plastic bags that most of the others use.'

Mickey Steiner was curious. In a way so was Stumpy Lazarus but Stumpy left it for Mickey to make the enquiry because he was more articulate.

'Jurelene, how did you get involved with these people?' Steiner asked.

'It's a long story', she said and closed her eyes real tight. When she opened them they were full of tears. 'We just want out. Lucy and I need your help, please.' She started to cry. Mickey Steiner watched as Stumpy Lazarus cradled her in his powerful arms and consoled her. The man had fallen in love - a miracle. She had given them enough information to bring the boys' murderer to book. Mickey Steiner had no doubt that judgement day was coming, and soon.

* * *

When they had last gathered around the dinner table, which was only yesterday, Sunday, the gypsy boy had dropped the bombshell about he and John Carter's two-year secret. Supper would be ready in fifteen minutes in the Carter household and Maureen Carter was expecting Simon to return from visiting Shamon Kazi at the farm. Simon had invited Ben Swinton to join them for supper and the obstetrician was quietly reading in the living room. The two boys were excited because of the gypsy boy's experiences in a formal educational institution and the two could be heard reliving the day's experiences, sometimes too loudly, in John's bedroom. Katherine Carter had secreted herself somewhere in the house, probably reading the veterinary journals she seemed to be unable to do without. Any minute now Simon Carter should walk through the door and supper should begin. Maureen Carter was looking forward to supper.

Simon Carter entered the house at seven forty-five. By eight o'clock they had all gathered around the dining table and comments had started about the sweet aroma of roast chicken, corn on the cob, sweet potatoes and much more. The compliments would come later but for now Maureen Carter, apron on and looking motherly, was in charge of this evening's food distribution. Around the table once again was Ben Swinton who seemed happier and more talkative today than usual, all the Carters and Kazeem Kazi.

'So,' Simon Carter looked at Kazeem, 'when do I get to give you my autograph?' He was looking at the boy's right hand. The white cast was covered with signatures from the back of the hand to the elbow.

'At lunchtime they were queuing up, dad.' John Carter could hardly contain himself.

In just one day, Kazeem Kazi had won the hearts of the boys and girls at John and Katherine Carter's school. According to John Carter the pupils had queued up during their lunchtime to put their individual mark on Kazeem Kazi's healing right arm. Most of the children hoped he would become a registered pupil in the foreseeable future, a question which Simon Carter hoped to discuss with his gypsy friend and his wife later in the week when their accommodation worries had been successfully dealt with.

'I met your mother today', Maureen Carter informed Kazeem happily. 'Quite a woman too, I hope we can be friends, just like you two.' John Carter was nodding back agreeably at his mother, his mouth loaded with nutrition from the dinner table. It had been an eventful Monday for all of them, the children with their new friend at school, Maureen back to work after a week's break and the pleasure of meeting Juliana Kazi, Ben Swinton's vindication at the hospital and his positive news at the bank, both of which would be discussed in depth with Simon in private, and finally Simon's discovery of the cross at the farm about which he had said nothing to anybody.

'Broxy arrives tomorrow', Maureen reminded Simon Carter.

'Ah! And Uncle Nylander called today from New York', Katherine remembered. 'He was flying out to Saudi this evening, must be airborne by now.'

'I hope one day I'll get the opportunity to camp in the desert like the Bedouins do', Ben Swinton said remembering Nylander's stories of the Arabian Peninsula. He hoped to visit the Gulf States someday in the future.

They had enjoyed supper together, paid their compliments to the chef and scattered to various parts of the house to pursue individual goals. In the living room, Simon Carter watched the late evening news with Ben Swinton. They had missed the beginning of the story but it was obvious from the pictures of the bearded, dark-jacketed men, all handcuffed and paraded in front of the courthouse, that the law was now in charge of the events that took place in the east side club on Sunday evening. The next news item dealt with the police's attempts to catch the killer or killers of the two young boys. The police investigation centred around the weapon which had still not been found and an appeal to the public at large to come forward with anything at all that might assist in the capture of the killers.

Maureen Carter joined the two doctors in the living room. The news was finished and Ben Swinton had important news of his own so the television was switched off, cups of coffee circulated and all attention given to the obstetrician.

'It's all over', Swinton told them.

'What do you mean?' asked Maureen switching her gaze to her husband.

'I went in there this afternoon to defend myself. Instead they apologized to me, all three of them apologized to me.' Swinton began to laugh.

'Apologized?' Maureen could not believe her ears.

'Well, they had made a mistake. The blood sample which was supposed to have been mine turned out to be a blood sample from a patient.' Swinton was still laughing.

'What!' Simon was incredulous.

'Are you going to sue?' asked Maureen.

'I don't know, I don't think so', replied Ben. 'What I do need though is a drink, a very stiff drink.'

Simon Carter got up and walked to the drinks cabinet. He poured three brandies, handed one to Ben Swinton, another to Maureen Carter and raised his glass along with the other two. 'Thank God', he said and drank. They then talked about Swinton's visit to the bank and the likelihood of paying off his gambling creditors by the coming Friday.

'Don't you find it odd that since Thursday we haven't heard anything more from those people?' asked Simon. 'After Dawson's threats on the telephone, I expected them to have shown up on Friday or at the latest, today.'

'Maybe I'd better call them tomorrow', Ben Swinton suggested.

'It's me they are interested in', Simon grinned. 'I suppose I'd better call Dawson tomorrow morning but I must say I am surprised by his silence.'

Maureen Carter sat quietly and listened to the two men. She had made all her plans as far as the game of 'Solutions' was concerned. Broxy would be coming tomorrow, at which time she hoped to put her plan into action to save her husband and his friend. She would wait and play it by ear. The way things looked at the moment, it seemed as if there might not be any need for her to interfere in the matter, however. If it was necessary to involve herself and Broxy she was sure Broxy would not hesitate to help her. It really was now a matter of wait and see. It was getting late and she had to be at the hospital early in the morning so she put out both hands to her husband, pulled him up, bade goodnight to Ben Swinton and walked off with Simon Carter.

* * *

The table controller had prepared the Red Room under the watchful eye of the two security men. The six hostesses were at their stations and everything was set in readiness for the arrival of the card players who were sharing drinks with Jack Maldini and Joe Lazlo in the Green Room. Jack Maldini looked at his watch, 'Gentlemen,' he said, 'we begin at eight.' They had fifteen minutes to finish their drinks, compose themselves and begin again to pit their wits against one another for the six million dollar prize. It had been agreed that all six contestants would remain in the Red Room to see the game to its final conclusion but only the three surviving players would sit around the table of play. 'Butch' Anderson led the way out of the Green Room a few minutes before eight, a huge Texan hat in his hand. The security man opened the door and watched them entering the room one at a time - Maldini, the last to enter. Joe Lazlo had been left behind in the Green Room.

They settled themselves quickly. Around the table were Walter O'Reilly, to his left Senor Pedro Munzon and to the Argentinian's left, Van Derpool. Slightly further back from the table, three chairs had been arranged in a straight line for Simon Chen, Andre Papadropolous and Stan 'Butch' Anderson. The girls did their rounds quickly, ensuring that the three protagonists and the other three, now spectators, were all comfortable and served their chosen drinks. Jack Maldini once again melted into the shadows along with the hostesses and watched as the table controller took charge and began the game with the illumination of the play area.

Jack Maldini watched the three gamblers and wondered who would be the ultimate winner. Of the three players, Jan Van Derpool was the most difficult to assess. The Dutch diamond dealer sat calmly at the table, his face completely inscrutable. He picked up his cards, studied them briefly and placed them back on the table, face down. Walter O'Reilly looked at Senor Munzon with a wry smile on his face and waited for the Argentinean to study his cards.

'Your bet, Mr O'Reilly', the table controller announced.

Jack Maldini made his decision. He felt sure that Van Derpool would be the most likely player to walk away with the six million dollars.

'Have them call me when it gets really exciting', he said to the hostess next to him.

He opened the door quietly, acknowledged the security man's slight

180

bow of the head and walked away to join Joe Lazlo in the Green Room.

'What's going on in there?' asked Lazlo when Maldini sat next to him.

'It's begun,' said Maldini, 'and I have tipped the Dutch man to walk away with the pot.'

'How do you know?'

'Just a feeling,' replied Maldini, 'a real strong hunch.'

They could hear the soft music from the Fantasia and watched as couples left the Green Room to dance away the night in the room above.

'Jack,' Joe Lazlo turned to face his friend, 'I cringed every time you pulled the trigger last night,' he picked up the glass of martini, 'and wondered what I would say to Vivian if you blew your brains out.'

'It was a gamble Joe, a big gamble, but you see I have worked for everything I own and the way I figure it, if I can't put my life on the line for what I really believe in, then all this is worth nothing.' He waved his hand around the room. 'I'll tell you something else, if that bearded fool had had the guts to put the gun to his head and pull the trigger I might have given in to him because I would not have been able to try three bullets. It's all about bluff and self-belief you know, bluff and self-belief. That's why I believe Van Derpool will win the game in there."

'I have asked the police to confiscate the thirty bikes', said Lazlo. 'Those guys don't have any money so we can request the court to allow us to sell them to offset the cost of the damage they did and the drinks they consumed.'

'Fine.'

'I have also instructed accounting to make a payment of five thousand dollars each to all of the hostages along with a letter of apology for the inconvenience', added Lazlo.

'Make it ten thousand for the dancer and see if we can get her to come in for an interview. There must be somewhere in this organization we could use the services of a brave young woman like that, maybe the radio station or even here. Please see to that', Maldini concluded.

'Let's circulate', said Joe Lazlo. The two men got up and walked out of the Green Room. They were on their way to meet their customers, the people who brought in the money to make the Hood Acre the successful business that it was.

* * *

It was past midnight when Jurelene Patterson said goodnight to Stumpy Lazarus and Mickey Steiner. The two men walked her to the car, shook hands with her and once again assured her that they would be getting in touch with her and her room-mate within forty-eight hours. She was to do nothing but to wait patiently to hear from them. If for any reason she and her girlfriend felt threatened, they were to come to Stumpy's address where the doorman would be instructed to let them into Stumpy's flat even if he was not available. The two men stood on the side walk and watched her drive off. Jurelene Patterson stopped the car a few hundred metres from where the two men were standing. Her decision was on an impulse; she began to back up the car and finally stopped some distance away from them and jumped out of the car. She started to run towards the men. When she reached where they stood she suddenly threw her arms around Stumpy Lazarus and kissed him full on the lips. 'I'll call you', she said with that infectious smile and ran back to the car. Moments later the car had disappeared from sight.

Stumpy Lazarus stuffed both hands deep into his trouser pockets, licked his lips and calmly strolled back into the flat with Steiner close behind him.

'She kissed me', said Stumpy, his face bright with happiness.

'We'll stitch a plan together tomorrow, shouldn't be too difficult to retrieve the murder weapon from under Biggles's floorboards', said Steiner. It was late and they had more collections to make in the morning.

'She kissed me', Stumpy repeated.

Steiner ignored him, opened the door and stepped out of the flat. 'Goodnight.' He pulled the door shut, skipped down the stairs and left the building. He was thinking of Rosalynn Brando when he started the car. He would try and see her tomorrow.

* * *

The waitress came rushing to Maldini on the ground floor near the blackjack tables. She had no trouble locating him. She stood patiently beside Maldini and waited for him to finish his conversation with the suave gentleman and his lady companion and handed him the white envelope. Maldini tore the envelope open and read the two words: Six Red. He had requested that he should be informed when the game in the Red Room reached its critical stage; the code in his hand told him everything. The six million dollar game in the Red Room was at its most absorbing stage. He excused himself from his two guests, bounded up the spiral staircase, entered the Red Room and closed the door quietly behind him. His eyes quickly adjusted to the light and took in the heavy beads of perspiration on Walter O'Reilly's face; the banker's usual calm demeanour had deserted him, his face seemed redder than normal and he fidgeted with the pile of cards on the table in front of him. Maldini switched his attention to Senor Munzon. The man was like a block of ice, with the exception of the thin blue smoke that rose from the cigar in his mouth and danced lazily towards the ceiling. He showed no signs of life. He had both hands on the table on top of his cards. The gold watch on his left wrist peeped from underneath the cuffs of his shirt to remind all that there was plenty of wealth in beef. Maldini watched him and wondered what secrets Munzon held in the cards. Munzon was serious. He looked at the table controller, sat back in his chair and removed the cigar from his mouth. 'All in', he said and wrote the bet on a slip of paper and handed it to the table controller. Jack Maldini had arrived at a crucial time of the game. He knew what the Argentinean meant - he had just bet everything. If he won he could stay and battle on but if he lost he would have to leave the table. The table controller took the slip of paper from Munzon and confirmed the bet verbally and as always placed the slip in the small brown leather wallet. It was now the turn of the Dutchman. Maldini looked at him; Van Derpool kept his left hand on the cards and drummed the fingers of his right hand on the table; the diamond ring on his small finger sparkled as he drummed, shooting darts of light in different directions. Senor Munzon had shown gold; Van Derpool was now demonstrating the power of diamonds.

'Match it', said Van Derpool.

They were now back to O'Reilly who was sweating profusely. He unbuttoned the top button of his shirt, picked up the cards and looked, looked again and decided to try his luck. He wanted to see Munzon's cards and then Van Derpool'. For the privilege, he wrote his bet, also all in, on a slip of paper and handed it to the controller. It quickly disappeared into the brown wallet. It was time to show; Senor Munzon first, the cigar burning brightly and the blue smoke still rising. Munzon revealed his cards slowly - he was going to enjoy winning against some of the best card players he had ever encountered - first the ace of clubs, then the ace of diamonds. 'Butch' Anderson did not bother to summon the hostess to light his cigar; his face glowed yellow when he struck the match, causing the beef magnate to pause before revealing the third ace, a heart, followed by the king of spades and the king of diamonds.

'Three aces and two kings, full house for Senor Munzon', announced the table controller. The room buzzed with excitement as the occupants took the opportunity to shuffle themselves and prepare their minds for what was to come. Could the other two do better than a full house? The Argentinean beef magnate felt confident; all through the evening he had been successful whenever he had decided to challenge the others at critical moments. This was the one that mattered most. Could he knock out O'Reilly once and for all and weaken the diamond man enough for a final knockout punch and walk away with six million? Walter O'Reilly was smiling. He was looking at the Argentinean's cards; the beads of perspiration which had stood like huge pimples on his forehead had now dried up, an instant cure. The redness of his face had now toned down to a healthier pink, his eyes bright and eager. It was not his turn; they were waiting for the diamond dealer.

Jack Maldini folded his arms and watched Van Derpool. Earlier in the evening he had predicted that the Dutchman would be the most likely player to win the big prize. It was now time to find out. Jan Van Derpool's face was like a mask. He was still drumming his fingers on the table, his left hand on the cards in front of him. He seemed in no hurry. He had seen the Argentinean's cards; his thoughts were on O'Reilly, what was the banker holding? Maldini watched; the Dutchman revealed the first card, seven of clubs; not a sound as all eyes focused on the table. Second card, ten of clubs. The beef man puffed a cloud of smoke from his cigar, the cloud quickly consuming the thin blue line of smoke which was trailing towards the ceiling. So far so good, thought Munzon. He had not seen anything extraordinary, even his two kings were in control of affairs but there was a slight doubt in his mind. Could the diamond man be going for a flush, a flush of clubs? He watched the next card, eight of clubs. The room was like a cemetery, the occupants like ghosts who were afraid to make themselves known, silence their protector. Jack Maldini shifted his gaze from the three exposed cards in front of the Dutchman to the face of Walter O'Reilly. He could see the pimply beads of sweat slowly enlarging on the Irish American's face; the 'disease' which had been cured a few moments ago when Munzon revealed his cards was now coming back with a vengeance, accompanied by the telltale symptoms of redness of the face and twitchy hands.

Somebody called for a drink. The hostesses began to move again. The cemetery now had people, people who had come to bury the dead. Three had already died, their corpses stiff in the three chairs lined sombrely just a few paces away from the table of play. They were awaiting the burial ceremony, but they needed two more bodies; the sacrifice had to be made before all five losers could be mourned properly. The hostesses had retreated into the shadows, their duty done. Once again silence crept into the room, all eyes focused on Van Derpool. He flipped the card assuredly with his left hand; card number four, jack of clubs. A hostess giggled with excitement only to draw the cold stare of the table controller, a stare that seemed to shoot arrows into the darkened area along the wall from where the sound had come. Van Derpool took his time. He rearranged the exposed cards with his left hand - seven of clubs, eight of clubs, ten of clubs, jack of clubs. Tantalizingly, he left the slightest of gaps between the eight and the ten. Nine of any card would give the diamond man a 'straight', but if he had the *nine of clubs* O'Reilly would have to do something extraordinary to beat the running flush. Jack Maldini watched O'Reilly, the pimples of sweat now bursting on the banker's face to shed their load of liquid that now ran down the man's forehead and down his face. The Dutchman gently flicked the last card onto the other exposed cards. It landed squarely between the eight and ten - nine of clubs - a powerful running suit.

'Running flush for Mr Jan Van Derpool', the table controller said loudly and produced a small silver bell from the small box in which he had been placing the brown wallet containing confirmation of the bets. 'Gentlemen,' said the table controller, 'as per the custom of the Red Rooms in the Hood Acre, a running flush demands recognition.' He rang the small silver bell three times and returned it to the box. The six hostesses clapped.

'Cut the crap!' shouted 'Butch' Anderson. 'Let's finish the game, sign the paper and get the hell outa here.' The dead were beginning to stir; they were eager for burial.

The game was not finished. Walter O'Reilly had paid to see the other players' cards. Now that he had seen them it was up to him to better the other two players and collect the trophy of six million. O'Reilly shuffled his five cards, laid them down as one, face down and shook the hands of Van Derpool. 'Hopefully we shall meet again', he said.

'I declare Mr Jan Van Derpool the winner of this game. Gentlemen, thank you.' The table controller rubbed his hands together and held his palms outward, as if to say, this was your game, I had nothing to do with it.

Jack Maldini stepped out of the shadows and shook hands with each of the six players. There was one last formality. All six players had to sign the authority note which, along with Maldini's and the bank manager's signatures, would release the six million from the secured account into which it had been placed. They filed out of the Red Room at three o'clock in the morning on a Tuesday to return to their wealthy enclaves, enclaves they had carved for themselves in Texas, Buenos Aires, Amsterdam, Athens, Hong Kong and New York City.

Jack Maldini and the wealthy card players were gone. The security man at the door had now joined the table controller, the dealer and the six girls in the Red Room. They had all done their job well and some sort of congratulations was in order so the table controller asked them all to sit down around the table, the very same table around which the gamblers had gathered. He went around the table and poured each one of them a drink, finally pulling a chair to join them around the table. They all wanted to know, but no one said a word. The table controller moved Walter O'Reilly's discarded cards to the middle of the table, all five cards still face down. The six hostesses, each one of them beautiful, the security guard and the dealer all focused their attention on the five mystery cards in the center of the table and waited for the table controller to turn them over. He reached out suddenly, picked up the top card and slowly flipped it over; queen of hearts. They were eager to see the other cards so he deliberately kept them waiting. The table controller picked up his glass and drank, the others joining him as if compelled to carry on some sort of a bizarre ceremony. In time the controller revealed the second card now on top of the pile of four; queen of diamonds. They were all anxious so immediately he showed the third card, queen of spades, followed immediately by queen of clubs and the final card; the ace of spades.

'And to think I've seen people win thousands with three jacks, a three and a deuce', the table controller said sadly.

'Wouldn't you have called with a hand like that, four queens and an ace?' asked the tall, blonde hostess with the small tattoo of a sparrow on her shoulder.

'Sure would.' They spoke as one, finished their drinks and vacated the Red Room.

CHAPTER FIFTEEN

The Airbus A300-600 touched down at King Abdul Aziz International Airport in Jeddah at exactly five minutes past twelve - sun time. The flight had been long so William Nylander had used some of the time to complete a summary of his meetings at the State Department and the Defense Department necessary to brief the board of Nylander Electronics. He had wanted to watch one of the two movies on offer but instead decided to trade the movie for a well-deserved rest. Nylander woke up to find the Japanese group still in noisy and animated conversation. He wondered if the group had sustained their conversation all through the flight and prepared himself for the day ahead. He expected to be picked up from the airport, from where he would go directly to the office where he was expected.

Nylander was processed quickly through immigration, followed by routine customs checks, and whisked away by the company driver within thirty minutes of landing. The afternoon was hot but not unpleasant. He settled himself in the back of the company car and thought about his wife and daughter. Only hours separated them, yet they were thousands of miles apart. He preferred to think of the separation in terms of hours rather than distance because of the illusion of nearness that time seemed to create. He would telephone home in the evening to inform his wife of his safe arrival. His thoughts reverted to his conversation with Jill just before he was airborne and he smiled at the thought of having Jill and his wife in the Gulf during the summer holidays. There was no doubt in his mind that Jill would be prepared for the examinations she was studying for with her friend Katherine. The thought of Katherine Carter brought the horse to Nylander's mind. He opened his eyes and looked around at the passing scenery as the car sped towards his office. Several hours ago, he had been immersed in the western world - suits, skirts, yellow cabs, cramped spaces and skyscrapers - but now the scenery had changed to flowing white robes, traditional Arab wear, covered women and open spaces. He would have a chat with Sheikh Al Makhtoum Walhadi at the earliest convenience. He would tell him about Shamka. The Sheikh was a great lover of horses and a good rider. Nylander knew the Sheikh prided himself on owning some of the best Arab horses in the world and would appreciate good conversation about a horse Nylander believed to be a truly special specimen.

The driver pulled into the spacious courtyard of the electronics office complex and opened the door for Nylander. It was good to be back. He thanked the driver and entered the building.

'Good afternoon Monica.' Nylander greeted the head secretary of Nylander Electronics warmly.

'Good afternoon sir', Monica Pinkerton smiled at her boss. 'Welcome back, I hope you had a pleasant flight.' She was preparing the roasted green coffee with cardamom, boiled and strained with date palm. She handed Nylander the small cup filled with the coffee and watched as he drank. She was welcoming her boss in the traditional Saudi fashion, three cups of cardamom-infused coffee. Nylander drank all three cups and thanked his secretary.

'You have been converted', he said to the woman.

'When in Rome...', said Monica Pinkerton laughingly as she stepped out of the office with the coffee tray. 'Your afternoon schedule is on your desk', she added and shut the door behind her.

William Nylander sat behind his desk and began to read the schedule.

3.30 pm: Briefing - the Chief Engineer.

4.00 pm: Meeting with Abu Walid, Saudi defense

4.40 pm: Meeting with Max Boyles, Defense Attaché, American Embassy.

6.00pm: Return telephone call to Sheikh Al Makhtoum Walhadi at home.

Nylander smiled and looked at his watch, 3.03 pm. He reached into his briefcase and pulled out the file marked 'top secret' and began to read. He would busy himself until his first meeting.

* * *

Since the arrest of the Eagles on Sunday night, the east side seemed to retreat into its shell. The streets were much quieter than normal, and for the first time in months the odd police car could be seen on

Shackle Avenue. The Pepperdine was shut for repairs and would stay shut until Friday, according to the large posters pasted on the doors of the building. Commodity trading, as drug dealers liked to refer to their activities in the east side, had not stopped altogether but, with the naming of the main dealers on Sunday afternoon, trading was now being carried out with a certain amount of caution. The ordinary, decent citizens of the east side community had gone about their daily activities on Monday preoccupied with discussions about the murders of the boys, the meeting in the community hall and the descent of the Eagles into their community on Sunday night.

A microcosm of Monday in the community was now being played out in the Shackleton Barber Shop where arguments raged between clients, barber and client and barber to barber. The large wooden sign outside declared the barber shop as *Unisex, Multiracial and International Barbers*. However, the occupants were all male, black, and while usually several young men hung around the premises, today those in the shop were all adults. The proud owner of the barber shop used his clippers masterfully and talked.

'You know the police don't give a damn about this community, Joe.' The owner of the barber shop, John Dempsey, was making sure that one of his long-standing clients, Joe Logan, understood that. 'If them boys was white, cops would be crawling all over, trying to find the killers.'

'Tell the man, Johnny.' The shoeshine man waved his brush in agreement with John Dempsey.

'You are not telling me it was white folks killed them boys now', Joe Logan pointed out with his open-ended statement and looked to Dempsey for an answer.

'I ain't saying they pulled the trigger, but you know and I know that the little drug man down the street don't mean shit.' He took a towel and wiped his brow. 'The man in control of the drugs and the money don't live here, he lives across town. His children go to good schools, his wife ain't scared when she goes shopping and ain't nobody shooting at them.' He concluded his little speech with an air of satisfaction. Most of the men in the shop agreed with John Dempsey and showed it by nodding affirmatively or by the utterances of 'yeah, yeah'.

'So who are you going to blame, the man who lives across town or the fool who does the dirty work right here in the community for pin money?' Logan shot back.

They were all looking at him. The same people who had agreed with Dempsey were now nodding in favor of Logan's argument.

'The way I see it, Dr Walker was right.' Bob Taylor turned his head in the barber's chair to make his point. 'This community has to cleanse itself from within and to do that we have to start with the dealers. If we get rid of the drug dealers many good things will happen immediately.'

'Such as?' asked John Dempsey.

'Well, for starters, we'll remove such evil men away from our children. Secondly, by removing the drugs, our children will be more clear-headed. Clear-headed young people don't grow up robbing and killing,' said Taylor, 'at least generally speaking.'

'He's right Johnny', the shoeshine man shouted from his corner.

'And finally, clear-headed children can channel their energies into positive things.' Bob Taylor looked around the room. 'We, the adults, have a certain responsibility towards them and I say to you our responsibility starts with the removal of those animals from this community.'

'Bravo!' shouted Joe Logan.

'You know something,' John Dempsey was now in agreement with Taylor and Logan, 'our boys down from Edison High wanted to play a basketball match against the Roosevelt High boys across town, and you know something, them white boys didn't want to know because they didn't want to play the return match in this community.'

'Crime ain't got nothing to do with that.' The shoeshine man was getting excited. 'Them white boys is just scared of getting their asses kicked in a game of basketball with the best high school team in this city.' They all agreed with that, the historians amongst them quoting dates since God made the world, when Edison High did this and did that in basketball. They were all in agreement because they loved their community.

'I must say, though, that if my children lived across the tracks on the west side, I'd be worried for them to come on this side', said Logan.

They all agreed that they had blamed others for their problems for too long. It was time to look at the problems in the community and tackle those problems themselves.

'After all, charity begins at home', John Dempsey quoted the famous words.

* * *

Simon Carter had the Tuesday off because he was scheduled to be on call through the weekend. He had been able to sleep a little longer than usual and woke up at eight thirty to find the large house empty. The children had left for school and Maureen was already at the hospital. Simon entered the kitchen and found the note Maureen had left him on the kitchen table. He made himself a cup of tea, sliced a large grapefruit in half, sprinkled half a teaspoon of sugar on the fruit and picked up Maureen's note.

Good morning sleepy head, hope you slept well. Please pick up dry cleaning from Brambles, slips attached, and shop for the grocery items listed below. Remember to pick up Broxy from the airport at 4.30 pm. See you at 6 pm and have a good day, Love, Mo.

Carter knew the day would be busy. He intended to do all the things he had planned to do this Tuesday because once he got engrossed in the hospital during the rest of the week it would be impossible to do anything else for the next seven days. He arrived at the farm at exactly ten o'clock, as promised, and found Shamon Kazi dressed in a suit and waiting in front of the tent. Kazi carried a small satchel in his hand within which, Carter guessed, he had the small metal box containing the cross. First the appraisal of the cross, then to the bank, and from there to view the new caravan and arrange delivery, assuming the first meeting had confirmed his suspicions. He hoped he would finish all those activities before half past three by which time he expected to be heading towards the airport. Somewhere in between, he would try to collect the dry cleaning and do the shopping that Maureen had requested.

Simon Carter sat next to his gypsy friend and watched the jeweller. Simon had been assured that the man was the best in the city, a specialist gold and silver craftsman with connections to museums all over the United States and Europe.

'Doctor Carter, your telephone call sounded exciting, I have cancelled this morning's appointments just to see you so I hope I won't be disappointed.'

'I don't think so but you can tell us.' Carter turned to the gypsy,

'Shamon.'

Shamon Kazi reached into the satchel and produced the metal box; he removed the silver cross and hesitantly handed it over to the jeweller.

'Christ!' the jeweller exclaimed, holding the cross in his left hand and turning it under the light on his desk. He produced an eyepiece, held it to his eye and scrutinized the cross from every angle. Eventually, he pulled a soft white cloth from somewhere behind the desk and gently placed the silver cross on it. 'This is beautiful,' he said, 'glorious.'

'Well?' Simon Carter hoped for a positive answer.

'Doctor Carter, please allow me a moment to indulge myself', said the jeweller. 'Occasions like this come but once in a lifetime and I dare say that few men and women have set their eyes on this exquisite work of art.'

Carter looked at the jeweller, who seemed to have discovered new dimensions and was by now floating somewhere between the fourth and fifth. In his hand, a magnifying glass had replaced the eyepiece. He leant forward and invited the doctor and the gypsy to join him in the examination. He gently turned the cross over and began his explanation.

'Usually, pieces such as this will not carry any markings, but in this case it is quite easy to place the origins and also the period during which the cross was made.' He pulled a handkerchief and wiped his brow. 'The origin of this cross is English and I would say it was made somewhere in the late eighteenth century and early nineteenth century.' The lecture had begun. He was looking at the cross closely with the magnifying glass.

'See the leopard's head?' The jeweller tried to point it out to the other two. 'It was the first mark stamped in England.' He scratched his chin. 'That was in 1327, to prove that the silver was of sterling standard. You see, because pure silver is too soft to manipulate, copper, the only base metal that does not make it too brittle, is used to harden it. Initially, the sterling standard in England was 92.5 per cent pure silver but after 1837 the standard generally used was 90 per cent pure silver.' He was breathing heavily.

'Many markings came into being but the mark of the sovereign's head was added to the others in 1784. So, if the sovereign's head is shown and the leopard's head is crowned, then the piece was made between 1784 and 1821. Now you can see all that for yourselves. He handed the magnifying glass to the doctor and sat back contentedly.

'What about its value?' asked Carter.

'Priceless, I would have thought.' The jeweller was deep in thought. 'Frankly, this piece belongs in a museum, but if I were to place monetary value on it, I'd say in excess of a quarter of a million dollars.' He had it back in his hand, turning, twisting. 'Just look at that ruby, it gives you the shivers, doesn't it?'

'Would you be willing to give us your appraisal in writing, preferably on your headed paper?' Simon Carter enquired.

'Sure, sure', said the jeweller confidently. 'I could be more specific if you allowed me a couple of days, but I am happy to stand by my estimate. You are talking about a combination of pure silver, gold and a ruby setting all worked by quality craftsmanship; rare, very rare indeed.' He signed the paper and handed it to the doctor.

Simon Carter folded the paper and put it in his pocket while the gypsy secured the cross in the metal box and then in the satchel.

'Would you send me the bill for your services?' Carter said and extended his hand to the jeweller.

'Doctor, to have seen this cross today is pay enough, there'll be no charge for my services.' He shook the doctor's hand and then Shamon Kazi's and saw them to the door.

* * *

Somehow Simon Carter had managed to do almost all the tasks he had set himself on the Tuesday. After the appraisal, they had sat in the bank manager's office and watched as he gawped at the cross. He had pleaded with Carter and Shamon Kazi to allow his wife to see 'this amazing thing', and so they had waited for the bank manager's wife to arrive for her special viewing before locking the cross in a safe deposit box. Simon Carter had handed the key to the deposit box to Shamon Kazi and explained how he could gain access to the special cross, although, as collateral, it would have to remain in the custody of the bank until the secured loan was completely repaid with the added interest. The negotiations in the bank concluded, the two friends moved on to arrange for the delivery of the new trailer and for the removal of Kazi's old home from the farm. They collected the dry cleaning and finished Maureen Carter's shopping just before four and, with time pressing, Carter decided to drive to the airport with Shamon Kazi by his side.

Shamon Kazi stood alongside Doctor Carter in the arrival lounge. Broxy's flight had landed just before the two arrived at the airport so they waited patiently for her to appear.

'There, she is coming now', said the gypsy.

Simon Carter looked at Kazi suspiciously. Kazi was right and, although he had never met Broxy, he had pointed her out of the crowd of passengers who were entering the lounge.

'How did you know?' Carter was baffled.

'When I look at all the people,' Kazi explained, 'I see she is the best dressed lady and also the most beautiful, so I guess and I am right.' The man was back to his usual self.

Simon Carter stepped forward to embrace Broxy and then turned to introduce Shamon Kazi who bowed deeply, holding his hat in his hand. They proceeded to the baggage carousel to collect her luggage which Shamon Kazi insisted on carrying to the car.

'How naughty of me to forget Katy's birthday', said Broxy. 'From what I heard over the telephone last Saturday there must have been quite a party.'

'She has forgiven you but I regret to tell you that you missed a great party.' Simon Carter teased and joined the traffic leaving the airport for the freeway leading back to the city. 'Oh! And Broxy, congratulations, we read about the epic flight, we are very proud of you.'

They decided to drop Shamon Kazi off at the farm first. Broxy had found the gypsy charming and polite. Between the farm and the Carters', Simon managed to tell Broxy about the gypsies. She found the story about the horse particularly intriguing and hoped she would have a chance to see the special horse for herself.

'Saturday might be a good day to visit the farm and see this horse. Robert would love that.' Broxy folded her arms. 'That's if it'll be possible.'

I am sure something could be arranged with my gypsy buddy,' Simon Carter cast a quick glance at her, 'if the fee is right', he joked.

Jennifer 'Broxy' Singleton looked relaxed but she was thinking about her telephone conversation with Maureen. She, of course, did not know of the latest developments since that conversation on Sunday afternoon and wondered what Maureen had in mind. She had come prepared to assist her friend in any way possible. All she could do was wait until Maureen returned from the hospital. Jennifer Singleton walked into the house to be greeted by her two most favorite children.

* * *

Mickey Steiner and Stumpy Lazarus had promised Jurelene Patterson that they would do what they could to help find the killer or killers of the two boys. To have gone to the east side themselves, particularly after the incident in the Pepperdine on Saturday night, would not have been wise so they had resorted to the services of one of the extensive contacts they had cultivated in the east side community. They knew from information provided by Jurelene Patterson that Frank Biggles, Mo Franks and Big Joe Kelly usually travelled to a large mid-western city to account for the previous week's drug activities and returned with a fresh consignment of illicit wares. If the information was correct, Biggles's house should be empty this Tuesday afternoon.

The young black man posing as an electrical contractor parked the blue pick-up truck directly outside the house and strapped on his tool belt. He slung the two rolled electrical wires on his left shoulder and marched confidently to the door. He rang the bell and waited. No reply. He tried again, pressing on the bell hard and long. Silence. He walked around the house to the back and rapped loudly on the back door. The house was definitely empty. He walked around again to the front door and reached into his tool belt. Within seconds he was in the house with the door shut behind him. According to Steiner's information, the gun would be in the bedroom, somewhere under the floorboards. The electrician's instructions were simple. He was to verify that the weapon was where they had been told it was, to check the make and caliber if possible without touching it and to telephone his findings to Steiner later that evening. He paced the floor slowly, slipping on the thin rubber gloves and listening for hollow sounds and creaks. Nothing. He moved the heavy wooden bed, trying not to disturb much and rolled back the thin brown carpet. 'Bingo', he said quietly under his breath and removed the two loose wooden boards. He could see the rectangular plastic container. He knelt by the bed, next to the hole he had uncovered, opened the plastic container and stared at the multicoloured arrangement of pills, white powder in small plastic bags and bundles of dollar bills. On the floor, next to the plastic container was a Smith and Wesson pocket .22 revolver. He replaced the two wooden boards, rolled back the carpet and was about to move the bed into its original position when he heard the sound. A box of cartridges had fallen from somewhere underneath the bed. He slid under the bed on his back and ran his fingers along the small wooden railing which ran along the bottom edge of the bed. His hand made contact with another box of cartridges and then the shotgun. His instructions had been not to touch anything in the house but he could not leave the telltale traces of his presence so he replaced the boxes of cartridges and shifted the bed into its original position.

The telephone call came at five thirty in the evening. Mickey Steiner answered the call.

'Mr Steiner,' said the young black man, 'it's there, under the bed.'

'Thanks', Steiner replied and hung up the phone. He had no idea who he was talking to, because, as arranged with his contacts, he was to trust the information the caller would provide and use it as he wished.

Stumpy Lazarus looked at him anxiously.

'The gun is there all right', said Steiner.

This was turning out better than they had anticipated. They had no intentions of getting directly involved. All they had to do was to point the right people in the right direction and sit back and watch.

'Let's set it up.' Steiner picked up the telephone and handed it to Stumpy Lazarus.

He recited the number slowly and watched as Stumpy dialled.

Jurelene Patterson answered the telephone and listened to Stumpy's instructions. He reminded her of the fact that they were all uncertain about Frank Biggles's suspicions and the need, therefore, for herself and Lucy Sharpe to be particularly careful. If everything went according to plan, she and Lucy should be beyond suspicion and free to carry on with their lives by the morning. She could hear Steiner's voice wishing her luck just as Stumpy Lazarus hung up the phone.

They had one more important call to make. It was time for Steiner to inform his contact in the police department about the location of the gun, and most importantly the name of the suspected murderer. After that, they would wait.

* * *

William Nylander had skilfully woven his way through the afternoon meetings and had secured the necessary signatures the company needed to begin work on the two-year guidance missile systems project for the Saudi government. He had telephoned Sheikh Al Makhtoum Walhadi at six o'clock and to his surprise found himself invited to the Sheikh's home on the outskirts of Jeddah. The Sheikh had not set any specific time, realizing that Nylander had just arrived back in Saudi.

Nylander arrived at the villa at eight o'clock. He had known Al Walhadi for almost a year and, although the two men had met on several occasions at Nylander's home, this was the first time Nylander had visited the Sheikh.

The villa was designed in the form of a tent, six pointed spikes forming a complete circle and reaching skyward like fingers to Allah. He had seen this type of architecture before and tried to recall where he had first seen it. Nylander remembered it was in Kuwait, in the Dahiyat Abdullah Al Salem suburb. He admired the building, a beautiful white construction surrounded by lush gardens and tasteful fountains. He walked towards the main entrance, the heavy golf bag slung over his shoulder. He thought of Barbara Supple, something about the woman having great difficulty imagining any greenery and wildlife in this part of the world, and wished he could have brought that ignorant woman to see this wonderful building and its immaculate gardens.

'Welcome!' Sheikh Al Makhtoum Walhadi jumped down from the hammock, slipped on his slippers and met Nylander with a greeting in Arabic. 'How was your flight my friend?' he asked.

'Very smooth', replied Nylander. 'It's good to be back and I must say you are looking well.' Nylander placed the heavy golf bag on the floor.

'Yes, I feel well', said the Sheikh, eyeing the golf bag.

198

Chapter Fifteen

'This is for you', said Nylander, presenting the bag to the Sheikh. 'It might improve your game', he added, smiling.

'Only Allah could do that.' Al Walhadi accepted the gift with a smile. 'Come, my friend, I hope you are hungry.' He motioned Nylander into the interior of the villa and handed the golf clubs to the attendant who materialized from somewhere in the massive building.

After dinner their conversations continued. They had already discussed defense contracts, the global price of oil, American attitudes towards the Arabs and Islam and the role of education in the future of the Gulf States. Sheikh Al Walhadi enjoyed such meetings with Nylander because it reminded him of his student days in California; days which helped to shape his future and therefore his present enviable position as one of the most respected petroleum engineers in Saudi Arabia and, by inference, the world.

Something had caught Nylander's eye, so the Sheikh turned to join him in the examination of the framed picture on the wall.

'Falconry', said the Sheikh, walking over to the wall. He beckoned to Nylander and began to explain when and where the picture that showed the Sheikh in full traditional garb with a falcon on his arm was taken. They moved along the wall as Al Walhadi showed off his pictures of camel racing in the desert, pictures of horses and trophies that had been won by his horses all over the world.

It was Nylander's turn to impress. He told the Sheikh about the magnificent chestnut with the white face: a thoroughbred, the best looking horse he had ever seen and how confident he felt that over the distance of a mile or a mile and a quarter, the special horse would be the best in America and possibly the world.

'Impossible!' Sheikh Al Walhadi said emphatically. The Arab pride in horsemanship had been challenged. They had moved from the interior of the villa onto the cool, spacious verandah which skirted the villa and gave the building an air of openness. It was clear to Nylander that he had touched a nerve in the Arab and from now their conversation would be like jousting with each other.

'You say the horse is a thoroughbred?' The Sheikh looked at Nylander. 'You can show me the entries in the thoroughbred stud books?' It was meant as a challenge to Nylander.

'No', Nylander said without explanation.

'Then why are we talking about thoroughbreds?'

'Is registration the only proof of the quality of a horse?' Nylander probed.

'Of course not, but if we are talking about thoroughbreds, it would be a good starting point.' Al Walhadi's American education was showing through. The discussion was informal but in his mind it was a debate, a debate about what a thoroughbred is, and he was sure he would finish this debate as the victor.

'Have you ever looked at a horse or a falcon or a camel and thought to yourself, hhmmn, that's a special animal, or a special bird, without reading its history in some book or knowing its pedigree?' Nylander argued strongly.

'What you say is true,' the Sheikh was trying to find more ammunition for his argument, 'and one can certainly see an animal or a bird and think that it has special qualities, but to say that a horse is a thoroughbred and possibly the best in the world, without any sort of form or background information, is simply folly.'

'Sheikh, I am sure you have a phrase in Arabic for what we Americans call "gut feeling" and no doubt during your college days in the States and even now in business, you must have operated from time to time on gut instinct or a hunch.'

'Look Nylander,' the Arab was smiling, 'how many races has this thoroughbred of yours won?'

'None, as far as I know.'

'Fine.' Al Walhadi was ready to do a deal. 'When this horse of yours has won three races anywhere in the United States, come back and see me and we shall continue this discussion.' The debate was over, just like that, and Nylander knew it. After all, the Sheikh was quite correct, Shamka may have looked good to Nylander but that did not prove anything. They continued their evening's discussions, now focusing on geopolitics and the plight of third world countries.

William Nylander continued his conversation with Al Walhadi but his mind was no longer on the issues they discussed. If the Sheikh wanted proof, he would get proof. He was sure of the quality of the horse and, though untested, he felt convinced that the animal he had laid eyes on only a few days ago could turn out to be one of the most famous racehorses in the history of international horse racing. He could feel his pulse quicken as he thought about his first encounter with Shamka. They had all trooped out of the Carter front room to gather on the lawn. Even now he could see the gypsy, with the slightly oversized suit but dignified, standing there with that magnificent animal beside him. Nylander felt sure that the gypsy knew something the others on the lawn did not know. It was in his eyes, the way he communicated with the animal; effortlessly, naturally, as if they were of each other but yet each in its own space and time.

'You are not homesick already, are you?' asked Al Walhadi laughingly. 'I have been talking to myself for the past few minutes because you were far away in thought.'

'I was thinking about Jill', Nylander lied.

'She must be quite a lady now. I last saw her when she was twelve, how old is she now?'

'Sixteen.' Nylander replied, the smile on his face revealing his fondness for his daughter.

'Come.' Al Walhadi turned and made his way back into the confines of the villa. 'I will arrange a race for your horse', he said nonchalantly.

CHAPTER SIXTEEN

The evening was warm. The skies showed whispers of light that streaked through the heavens and exploded on puffy clouds to give the impression of a great work of art. In contrast, the east side wept with gloom as if an invincible shield had been erected to shut out the warmth of the sun.

Lucy Sharpe stood at the window and stared blankly into the gloomy street. Her mind, like the tight red skirt that wrapped her body, was wrapped around the plan that had been couched into her brain by Stumpy Lazarus and his partner.

The suddenness of the ringing bell startled her and made her jump. She turned from the window, hands on hips, to focus her attention on the thin, twisted black cord that led from the telephone to Jurelene Patterson's left ear. Lucy watched her room-mate, her head bobbing up and down like a cork on an angler's line as she took in the information filtering through the telephone line. She had an idea of what was being said but she waited, motionless, for the cork to bob for the last time and the receiver replaced, before she asked the inevitable question.

'Well?' Lucy asked.

'They are back', Jurelene Patterson replied. 'We are lucky, they want us to join them.'

Lucy breathed a sigh of relief. She moved forward and fell into the arms of her room-mate. Fear, like invincible electricity, flowed from one to the other and back again. They had been thinking about this evening, they had been briefed and they had rehearsed their roles in anticipation of what was to come. And, although they felt prepared and ready, the smell of fear, the thought of possible failure and the consequences that could result from such failure caused their embrace to tighten.

'I hope this works.' Jurelene Patterson untangled herself and wiped away the tears from her eyes.

'It'll work, it'll work if we stay calm and act natural', said Lucy with an air of some confidence. 'Remember we want our freedom and this is our chance.'

'Okay.' Jurelene had composed herself. 'Now, this is what they want us to do.' It took a few minutes for Jurelene Patterson to detail Frank Biggles's telephone instructions to her room-mate. According to Biggles, the journey to the big city had gone well. New instructions had been issued by those above him to try to expand the drug trade in the east side. Very 'important' people were coming down from the big city this evening and Biggles had instructed Jurelene to ensure that she arrived at the house at ten tonight with Lucy and two other girls whom he had named. The women would be expected to liven up the party and Biggles had made it clear that he did not want any foul-ups. This was business, pure and simple. Any mistakes, and the four women would be held accountable. They had better not be late. This is something Biggles had insisted on.

'Magnificent.' Lucy clapped her hands. 'You know, we couldn't have planned it better.' She settled into a brief moment of quiet thoughtfulness, then she said excitedly 'We arrive at ten and we had better not be late.' 'The raid must be scheduled for one o'clock in the morning, perfect, pow!' She punched her left hand with her right fist. 'And I hope to God they are not late.'

Jurelene Patterson watched her room-mate with bulging eyes, totally infected by Lucy's excitement at the prospect of finally removing the shackles that the unscrupulous drug dealers had used to enslave them over the past several years.

At ten o'clock the two women would be in the lion's den accompanied by two similar fated women. Experience painted a vivid picture in Jurelene Patterson's mind. She could remember the day when Frank Biggles and Paper Bag Jones, in a fit of anger, had held the feet and arms of a young strong-willed woman who had dared to defy their instructions to accompany them to a pimps' convention in some small town in Kansas. Jurelene could almost feel the needle penetrate the skin as the poor woman struggled on the floor, the liquid in the syringe slowly pushed into her veins. Jurelene Patterson knew she would never be able to forget the satisfying look in the eyes and on the face of Frank Biggles as he slumped against the wall after administering the injection, the young woman at his feet, comatose, with a stupid grin on her face. Biggles's words rang loudly in Jurelene's mind like a church bell in a tunnel, 'When I say you are coming, you are coming.

When I say sit, you sit. You ain't nothing but my dog, dig?'

In the end, the young woman did not come, neither did she sit. She had died in hospital about a month later. As far as Jurelene Patterson knew no one was charged with her death - another useless drug addict had pumped herself full of some solution and said goodbye to sunshine. That was that.

'Shall I telephone Mr Lazarus?' Lucy Sharpe was next to her room-mate. Apparently it was the third time she had asked the question.

Jurelene Patterson wanted to know the time.

'Six fifteen, and time for us to find some food', replied Lucy Sharpe.

'Okay, I'll call Stumpy, you raid the kitchen.' Jurelene began to dial the number.

* * *

Jennifer Singleton was totally engrossed in her conversation with Maureen Carter. The two women had staked their claim at the kitchen table and somehow managed to erect what seemed to be a force field across the entrance to the kitchen. They had excluded the rest of the population from their little domain without a word, and in the enclave Broxy Singleton listened to her friend's every word and occasionally sipped from the cup of coffee in front of her.

Above them, in John Carter's bedroom, Katherine Carter was chairing a much more important meeting of her own. She was sitting on the floor, cross-legged with a pad of ruled paper on her right knee and opposite her, arms folded and cross-legged on the floor were pyjama-clad John Carter and Kazeem Kazi.

This was not their first meeting. Over the course of the year Kathrine Carter had held several such meetings with her younger brother. The pad on her knee contained details of every such meeting - dates, agendas, conclusions and finally the summary of the meetings. Today's meeting was slightly different from previous meetings because the number of participants had increased by one, in the shape of Kazeem Kazi.

Katherine had already opened the meeting with a brief account of the significant events that had taken place in the city. Not surprisingly, the east side of the city seemed to feature in the headlines for all the wrong reasons. With incredible detail, Katherine summarized the events of the past week, the deaths, the community hall meeting, the occupation of the Pepperdine and finally a little-known fact about the near expulsion of a brilliant young pupil from their school for non-payment of fees.

'Near expulsion, what's that?' asked John Carter.

'Well, they were going to kick her out, but they decided against it because her grades are so good, so the head decided to place her on a scholarship.'

'Who?' asked John Carter eagerly.

'You know we never get personal in our meetings,' Katherine replied, 'and besides, it would be wrong to tell.' She moved seamlessly into the day's agenda and opened the floor to debate. 'I know there is not much we can do as children, but if we could, what would you suggest as the best way to help the poor people of the east side to get the best out of life?' She paused thoughtfully. 'Like we do?'

'I have told you the answer to that on many occasions', replied John Carter. 'Stop people from taking drugs and stop crime', he said confidently.

'And I have always asked you how do you stop people from taking drugs and stop crime?' She turned her attention to Kazeem Kazi who was leaning forward with his chin resting in his hands. 'This is an open debate you know.'

'Teach them that drugs are bad for the body, and for the crime part,' John Carter reflected, 'give them money, but they should do something to earn it.'

'So education and jobs', Katherine summarized, writing on her pad.

'My father says education costs money', said Kazeem Kazi.

'He is right.' Katherine was twirling the pen in her hand. 'And so does health, job creation, travel, food, in fact everything. Do we agree?'

They looked at one another and nodded their heads in unison. Katherine Carter continued to write on her pad.

'What about voluntary work, that does not cost any money', John Carter argued.

'Okay, suggest what voluntary work you'd like to do to help the poor people of the east side', said Katherine.

'Teach some of the children maths and stuff', John Carter replied eagerly. 'And I am sure I could do that very well too', he concluded proudly.

'I am sure you could, but think of what you said before. Do you think that would stop drug abuse and crime?'

'I guess not.'

'So then we are back to money again.' Katherine scribbled on her pad.

'I can tell you how we could get money to help.' Kazeem Kazi was rubbing the cast on his right arm and pretending to read the names inscribed on the cast.

'How Kaz?' asked John Carter.

Katherine Carter was curious and just as eager to learn the answer as her brother. She watched Kazeem, who was intently rubbing the white cast on his arm, and waited patiently for the answer.

'Well?' she said.

'Shamka!' Kazeem Kazi shouted the name with such conviction and certainty that it resonated through the room.

'Shamka?' Katherine echoed the name, only this time it was a question.

'Come on Kaz, how?' John Carter looked like a fourteen-year-old man, not a boy. The meetings were a regular occurrence between himself and his sister. Sure they had taken it seriously enough whenever they had met and thrashed out the city's problems in the past. But this was different. There was a different feel to this day's meeting. Kazeem Kazi knew and understood horses and John Carter respected that. There is no way Kazeem would have suggested Shamka as a possible solution to the problem confronting them in their little meeting if he were not convinced that the horse could be the key to solving their little puzzle.

'Okay Kazeem, so it's Shamka.' Katherine Carter's chest was heaving visibly as she focused all her attention on the gypsy. 'What are you saying?'

'Race her', said the gypsy boy simply.

'No!' Katherine Carter said emphatically.

'Why not?' asked John Carter.

'I don't want her hurt, and besides, I didn't want my Shamka for that purpose.'

'What purpose do you mean?' enquired Kazeem.

'Racing her for money.'

206

'If you love Shamka, and I am sure you do, you would race her. If you don't want to race her for money, don't, but you must race her because she needs racing, she wants racing. Katherine, she is a thoroughbred.'

'Let's get back to the topic', said Katherine.

'We are on the topic.' John Carter could see possibilities in Kaz's suggestion.

'Thoroughbreds love to race. It's their nature. So all I am saying is that you let your Shamka enjoy herself.' The gypsy boy concluded with a reassuring smile.

'And if, while Shamka enjoys herself, we collect some money to help the children of the east side...' John Carter let his voice trail away with a shrug of his shoulder.

'Are you sure that racing would not harm Shamka in any way?' Katherine Carter's concern showed on her face.

'Why don't you ask my father?' suggested the gypsy.

'I will,' said Katherine, 'and after I have done that we shall meet again to discuss how we can help our friends on the other side.' With that, she concluded the meeting, thanked the two boys for their time and marched off to her room with her notepad under her arm.

* * *

Stumpy Lazarus poured the glass of white wine and passed it to Rosalynn Brando. He felt honored that Mickey Steiner had decided to bring her along this evening. The tension in the flat was unmistakable and the unease was justified as the lives of Jurelene Patterson and Lucy Sharpe and possibly others depended on the raid going according to plan. Steiner and Stumpy Lazarus had done their utmost to coordinate the raid that they hoped would bring the killer of the two youths to justice and free the women from their tormentors. If they were lucky, one or two drug pushers would be arrested as an added bonus. Failure could result in the summary assassination of the two women. There was therefore reason for concern. Quietly they waited for the final telephone call.

It came at fifteen minutes past six, the loud ringing tones screaming with urgency. Stumpy Lazarus crossed the room to lift the receiver.

'Lazarus', he said into the telephone.

'Hi,' it was Jurelene Patterson, 'could we have breakfast at one? You know the place.'

'Table for two?' asked Stumpy.

'No, four.'

'Okay.' Stumpy Lazarus replaced the receiver and turned to face Steiner and Rosalynn Brando.

'The raid is on for one o'clock this morning, there'll be at least four girls in the house.'

'That means there'll be at least four men,' Steiner deduced, 'most likely four to six men.' He picked up the receiver and dialled. Rosalynn Brando watched him in silence, the tension draped around her shoulders like a cloak. There were innocent lives at stake. Two lives had been taken needlessly, a few more would not make any difference to those who had already smelt blood in pursuit of drug wealth. This was a test of wills, good versus evil. The silent majority had been silent for too long and frankly the east side of this beautiful city had been under siege long enough. It was time for brave men to stand up to the faceless evil men. Rosalynn felt pride as she continued to watch Mickey Steiner. The night would be long but the wait would be worth it, Rosalynn hoped.

* * *

Shamon Kazi was happy and totally settled in mind and spirit. With Simon Carter's help he had once again found the means to shelter his family. He walked slowly around the tent, his temporary home for the past few days, and sprinkled the mixture of salt water and lemon juice. Kazi held the large plastic bowl containing the solution in the crook of his left arm - like one would cradle a baby - and dipped in the bowl from time to time with his right hand as he walked around the tent.

In his world, as taught to him by his grandfather and then by his father, communication formed the center of one's being. Shamon Kazi walked around his tent with his grandfather's words ringing in his ears. He could actually remember the words clearly, as if the withered old man was beside him; stride for stride, pace by pace. In those days, the communion was with family members.

Kazi had never had the privilege of meeting them because they had long preceded his entrance into this world. The old man had the most simple ways of putting forward his arguments and ideas. Kazi walked, sprinkled his mixture and once again listened to the old man:

'*Your father is my son and you his son; someday there will be your son and your father to him will be like I am to you. Then there will be his son and you to him like I am to you. It was like this long before and it will be like this long after. Who and what you do not see, does not mean they never existed, do not exist or will never exist. If I could explain the mysteries of the world to you I would be called "God". I know there are mysteries beyond my ability to understand and to explain to you my grandchild, so I pray to my ancestors and to the "God" that understands what they did not understand, to protect those of my family that I have had the good fortune to share my mortal life with. I may not see your son during my lifetime but if you should have a son, remember that the thread ran through me before it got to him so if he ever wants to speak to me he can do so.*'

Shamon Kazi continued to walk around the tent. As he sprinkled the mixture, he thought of Kazeem Kazi. His boy had not had the opportunity to sit on his great grandfather's lap. To Kazeem, Shamon Kazi's grandfather may have been the wind; it blows past us, it is a part of our consciousness but we don't dwell on it until there is reason to focus on it briefly, only to be forgotten when it's blown away.

When Shamon Kazi finished his long and private dialogue with his ancestors, he placed the empty bowl at his feet, raised his hands to the heavens and said thanks for sparing his wife's life. He could see the whispers of light that streaked through the heavens and exploded on the puffy cotton wool clouds. Kazi admired the great work of art in the skies, the same unbelievable scenes that Lucy Sharpe had experienced from her window in her east side flat. Two separate, totally unconnected souls had witnessed an experience of incredible beauty but each from a different perspective. Lucy Sharpe's gloom and doom surroundings were contrasted by Shamon Kazi's experience of the five beautiful horses, evenly spaced and spread across the field, trotting gracefully towards him.

It was then that Shamon Kazi, having finished his prayers and communion with his ancestors, made his wish. It was a simple wish, a kind gesture that may have saved innocent lives. Kazi spoke quietly under his breath. This time he spoke Hungarian but his words were:

'To the person or persons with whom I have shared the experience of these wondrous skies, may obstacles be removed from their path and long life and happiness prevail.'

He did not know why he said it. Kazi picked up his empty bowl, placed it inside the entrance to the tent, gathered his four beautiful horses and Katherine Carter's Shamka and merged himself into the world of the horse.

* * *

Frank Biggles was showing off to his guests. These were men of power and influence as far as he was concerned. It was not his intention to be stuck in a town such as this, operating on a small-time basis for somebody else who gave him instructions from Detroit, Chicago or New York. In his trade, kids in Los Angeles made more money in a week than he made in two or three months. He had plans and they would work, because he would use this community as a springboard to the big leagues and then... for the moment all he had to do was to show the boys from the big city that he was made of the right stuff.

'More drinks, gentlemen.' He made his rounds and filled the glasses. 'Ain't nothing cheap here so enjoy yourselves,' he winked at Sam Dingles. 'The girls will give you better service when they arrive.' He glanced at the expensively flamboyant gold watch on his wrist. 'Won't be long, fifteen minutes, that's when the party begins.'

There were six men in the house, two from the big city of whom one was the well-known ex-convict and drug king Julian Moses. Moses had been accompanied on this journey by a baby-face-man of thirty-two called Trinkets. The odd thing was, everybody knew Trinkets was thirty-two but no one knew anything about his background or even his other names, that is, if there were any. Sam Dingles had settled himself in a deep, comfortable armchair next to the window. Opposite Dingles, Big Joe Kelly and Paperbag Jones shared the two seater.

There was an ugly look in Kelly's eye and he did not care if everybody saw his anger. Not for the first time since the arrival of Moses and Trinkets, Big Joe Kelly showed his disdain for the baby face, with an ugly, piercing stare that spat blood and, like a snake's tongue, flicked darts of threats. Joe Kelly did not like 'fairies', his word for men of a different persuasion. The word was Trinkets was gay and for that reason Big Joe Kelly showed inclinations of wanting to throttle him. Kelly was still shooting poisoned visual darts at Trinkets when the door bell rang.

'Ladies, ladies, ladies.' Frank Biggles had opened the door to four beautiful women; well, three and a half - if one considered the fact that Lucy Sharpe was only half beautiful. 'Right on taaaa'm.' Biggles, still showing off, exaggerated the last word.

They had come to conquer, literally, in every sense of the word. They spread themselves around the room with the expertise that comes from years of practice. Jurelene Patterson knew that the next three hours meant more to her than her twenty-four and a half years and however many more hours that preceded that. She discarded the expensive-looking, black, mink shawl to show the full effects of the low-cut black dress that hugged her like the proverbial glove.

Suddenly, Julian Moses uttered an excruciatingly painful scream. Trinkets had stuck a toothpick in his side for showing lascivious interest in the lady in black. He had administered the punishment to remind Julian Moses of his rightful place as his partner for this evening. Lucy Sharpe felt extremely good tonight. There was no particular reason for her to feel as she did and, in fact, for obvious reasons, she should have been feeling the exact opposite. She selected the music, turned the lights down low and watched contentedly as the three girls selected their dancing partners; the party had begun.

* * *

It was unusual for Jack Maldini to hold business meetings in his home. He preferred such meetings to take place in his private offices in the Hood Acre, or as the mood took him, in one of the Red Rooms. Tonight, he had summoned Jack Dawson to his home for a meeting.

The message had come in the form of a note penned by Dawson's woman friend with whom he had a long-standing, convenient arrangement. It would not have been wrong for the non-understanding bystander to assume the woman to be Dawson's wife. Anyhow, she had taken the urgent telephone message from Jack Maldini, written the note, and via a taxi driver, a hotel front-desk clerk and a bellman, the note had finally landed in Dawson's hand at the bar of the Cisco

River Hotel.

It was unusual.

For all the years that Jack Dawson had worked for Jack Maldini, he had never been summoned to meet the man at short notice. They had always worked according to strict timetables, specific locations and advanced preparations. This was totally out of character.

Jack Dawson wheeled the black Chevrolet into the massive driveway of the Maldini Mansions, took in the massive white pillars of the main building visually and blew a long, soft whistle under his breath. He parked the car next to the Cadillac and started to walk uncertainly towards the massive front doors of the building.

Vivian Maldini received her guest graciously and led the way through the house to the patio where her husband was tending what looked like a tropical plant in a porcelain plant holder.

'Ah! Jack.' Maldini seemed pleased to see him.

'Mr Maldini', Jack Dawson said timidly, unconsciously crushing his hat in his hands.

Jack Maldini had finished with the plant. He stepped off the patio and slowly walked the length of the massive garden where in two days' time the marquee people would erect the three large tents in preparation for the anniversary celebrations. Jack Dawson followed.

'How much do you know about horses, Jack?' Maldini asked suddenly.

'If you mean betting on them, I do a little of that,' replied Dawson, 'but I haven't had a bet for over six months,' he added quickly, in the manner that a schoolboy would try to convince the headmaster.

'Do you know anybody who knows about horses, I mean really knows about horses?' Maldini had stopped in the middle of his expansive back yard, the two men facing each other.

'Peter Thrushle at the race track is good. I believe he was a trainer once, could talk to him I guess.'

'Remember the doctor, the sixty-seven grand man, what was his name?'

'Doctor Ben Swinton.' Jack Dawson fished the name from the back of his mind. 'But the guarantor was Doctor Simon Carter, a shmuck.'

'Get Thrushle to my office at eight tomorrow morning. Find the two doctors and send them to me at ten. And Jack, bring the dossier on those two.'

Chapter Sixteen

Jack Dawson had no idea of Peter Thrushle's whereabouts, and as for the doctors, they could easily be in surgery with their hands in some unfortunate patient's stomach or heart. He knew he had been set a difficult task but he dared not question Jack Maldini, so he did the next best thing.

'Yes sir, Mr Maldini, tomorrow morning at eight and then ten', he confirmed.

Jack Maldini walked Dawson as far as the front door and watched the man scuttle to his car. It didn't matter if Dawson found Thrushle and the doctors for tomorrow, Maldini knew Dawson would have found and delivered all three by Friday. He had two full days, that's what was important.

* * *

The door came crashing in with an almighty bang.

'What the...' Frank Biggles choked on his words, blinded by the powerful white lights which illuminated the room.

They were all darkly clad, weapons at the ready and noisy. They were methodical in the tactics they employed to surprise, control and subdue the ten occupants of Frank Biggles's front room. The four women were manhandled roughly and pushed along the walls with the six men; in this desperate instance, Trinkets was considered or at least presumed to be a man.

The commotion fizzled out as quickly as it had erupted. The room - now overcrowded with darkly clad, menacing-looking law enforcement officers and manacled men and women - succumbed to the melodious tones of '*Fly me to the moon*', to which Sam Dingles had been smooching with the gorgeous blonde. The moon fell silent again as soon as Lieutenant Carpichi's boot smashed into the record player.

'When we are through with you guys,' Carpichi chewed the end of his cigar violently, 'we won't just fly you to the moon, we'll plant you on the dark side of it so you never see daylight again.'

'Do you know who I am?' Julian Moses was recovering from the surprise.

'Shut up, Moses!' Carpichi pushed him against the wall. 'We'll read you your rights soon enough.'

'I want to speak to my lawyer, you can't come busting in here without a warrant.' Biggles was still trying to impress somebody. He was about to make some more noise when Carpichi shoved the piece of paper under his nose.

'This is a warrant to search these premises, signed by Judge James Colman.' Carpichi pulled Frank Biggles away from the wall. 'Now, lead the way', he said as he escorted him into the other rooms.

Lucy Sharpe should have chosen a different profession. It was an Oscar-winning performance. She went berserk, screamed her head off and attempted to bite Sam Dingles who was rescued and shoved to the far side of the room by a large policeman.

'You set us up for this', Lucy wailed, her fiery eyes glaring at Big Joe Kelly.

She could see Jurelene Patterson and the other two girls cowering against the wall and sobbing quietly. A few paces away from her, Paperbag Jones, his hands manacled behind him, was making a futile attempt to reach into his right trouser pocket to remove something incriminating. Lucy watched him. She could feel the excitement welling up from her stomach to her chest. Laughter would have been the most appropriate reward, but she dared not laugh so she wailed loudly instead, with feigned anger.

'Bring them in here.' It was Carpichi's voice from another room.

Jurelene Patterson knew exactly where they would be led, but she fell in line with the others quite naturally and allowed herself to be pushed along into the bedroom.

The bed had been turned on its side, causing the mattress and sheets to slide awkwardly in front of the bedroom door. They all had to step over the obstruction, and eventually gathered around Carpichi and Biggles. The brown carpet had been folded over, and against the wall stood two small, wooden boards. The gaping hole revealed three rectangular plastic containers, lined side by side, unopened.

'Biggles tells me these are yours.' Carpichi had his left hand behind the head of Paperbag Jones, pressing his head slightly forward to allow him a better view of the plastic containers.

'He is lying!' screamed Paperbag.

'Biggles?' Carpichi turned to Frank Biggles, his eyes questioning, as if to say, 'Look you bums, you know we are going to get the truth sooner or later so you might as well save us the time.'

The gloved hand of the kneeling officer pulled the containers out one by one, and held long enough for the clear adhesive to be sealed around each container before it disappeared immediately into a large, black plastic bag. After the containers followed boxes of cartridges and a shotgun.

'That's the lot.' The officer stood back from the hole.

'Read them their rights.' Carpichi had found the murder weapon. 'If I were you, I'd call my lawyer.' He was already on his way out of the bedroom, the rest of the crowd trailing in his wake.

* * *

It was two thirty-five in the morning when the telephone message finally came. Mickey Steiner squeezed Rosalynn Brando against his body and watched her rub the sleep from her eyes. He looked across the room to Stumpy Lazarus and released his hold on Rosalynn long enough to give Stumpy the thumbs up.

'They have got the gun and the girls are safe', Steiner said, replacing the receiver.

'What now?' Rosalynn Brando was relieved, but also concerned about Lucy Sharpe and Jurelene Patterson.

'The girls are safe', Stumpy Lazarus assured her. 'They'll be kept overnight to convince the others. The plan is to arraign them with the others tomorrow and then,' Stumpy began to smile broadly, 'guess who is coming to dinner?'

'I saw the movie too.' Rosalynn Brando threw her arms around Mickey Steiner's neck. 'We'll celebrate when the girls come home.'

CHAPTER SEVENTEEN

The large red and white banner fluttered defiantly over the entrance to the east side community hall as they trooped in. There were whispers about how the banner got to be put up, but they were merely whispers, rumour, nobody really knew. The large red letters over white, proclaimed, *Community Spirit*.

Something had moved them, the whole damn lot of them. Usually, they would be congregated around the barbershop, joking, laughing, teasing and generally watching the community fall down around their ears. Today, they were streaming through the community hall gates with the rest of them - the whole damn lot - from the barbershop.

'I ain't never known this community to supply no spirits before.' The shoeshine man nudged John Dempsey as they walked under the banner and entered the hall. 'Me, I aim to stick to the bourbon, thataway I gits to walk outa here standing up.'

'Fool, ain't nobody talking drinking.' Dempsey glared at the man.

'It says "community spirit", don't it?'

'Look here now Payton.' Joe Logan was getting tired of the shoeshine man's jokes, and whenever that happened he referred to him by his surname. That was usually the shot across the bow to straighten the man out. One more crack from the shoeshine man and Logan would resort to calling him by his full given name, Samuel Kinkidine Payton. The man hated the name, so usually the use of the last name drew a line under any tomfoolery.

They sat right in front; John Dempsey, the barbershop owner, sandwiched himself between Bob Taylor and Joe Logan, with Kinkidine next to Logan. The hall filled quickly, forcing the latecomers, who in fact had arrived before the officially announced time of seven o'clock, to spill into the corridors and finally onto the steps outside.

Braxton Walker made his second appearance onto the community hall stage, Christina Coomes by his side. They waited for the murmuring to die down.

'Brothers and sisters,' Christina was at the microphone, 'who said there is no community spirit in the east side?'

216

'Ooooh yeah!' someone shouted from amongst the crowd, followed by enthusiastic applause.

'We got some good news for you.' She held the microphone in her right hand and swept the room with a pastoral look which covered the entire flock.

Word always got around quickly in the east side. The standing joke in the community was that the east side telegraphic system for passing information was much faster and much more effective than Ma Bell's telephone network. The telegraphic system had worked so well that, by ten o'clock Wednesday morning, almost the whole community knew about the arrests that had taken place in the middle of the night. The news had coincided with the community hall meeting that had been called by Braxton Walker and the community leaders for this Wednesday. So the hall was full to bursting. The community indeed had spirit and they sat in anticipation of the details of the good news which the telegraphic system had sacrificed for speed.

'Doctor Braxton Walker will now speak to you', Christina said simply and handed the microphone to Braxton Walker before seating herself behind him.

'Friends, neighbours, my community folk', he began, his left hand holding the microphone close to his mouth, the right hand pointing and waving like a music conductor's baton. 'Saturday night we lost two beautiful flowers in this community,' he paused, 'flowers that had not yet bloomed, but still trampled upon by the heavy boot of the drug menace.' He stamped his heel on the stage, bringing the boot effect vividly to his audience. Christina Coomes watched the doctor and juggled her thoughts. She was seeing a politician at work, a politician called a doctor who should have been a preacher saving souls instead of lives. Braxton Walker was in full flow. He had produced his list, the very list which he had held in his hand on Sunday. 'Last Sunday, and that's only four days ago,' he chuckled, threw his head up in the air to stare momentarily at the ceiling, 'seems like a lifetime don't it?' He spoke deliberately in the colloquial for their benefit. 'We met here to try to do something about this community of ours which some evil people tried to take away from us; remember?' He stabbed his fore-finger at the left of the room, 'Remember?' He was now stabbing center. 'I know you remember.' He had just stabbed everybody to the right of the room and sure enough they all remembered, the whole room nodding remembrance as if under a magician's wand. Behind him, Christina Coomes was in remembrance mood too, as she murmured, '*I do, I do*'.

Damn it, the doctor was single and she was no longer beholden to the no-good bum who had fathered her two sons and disappeared from the face of the earth.

Braxton was strong, intelligent, charismatic, powerful and good-looking and oh yes! 'I do!' Christina was on her feet, 'I do!' she shouted again together with the rest of the crowd who were now on their feet.

Braxton Walker waved them gently to resume their seats. 'Brothers and sisters,' the paper was unfolded, the hall now deathly silent, 'last Sunday I named eight people who we want to remove from this community. Today I can happily say that four of those are now in custody, arrested last night by our community police force which has promised me their cooperation in the cleansing of this community.'

'Names, Doc! Names!' some were shouting.

He did not hesitate. Braxton Walker rattled the four names off in quick succession, 'Big Joe Kelly, Frank Biggles, Sam 'Pretty Boy' Dingles and Paperbag Jones.' The hall soaked up the hum of approval and quickly gave way again to silence when Doctor Walker began again.

'Folks, this is only the beginning, we have four more fish to fry. He rattled those names off as well, 'Smokey 'White Shoes' Peters, Shoeshine Joe, Mo Franks and Joseph 'Tiny Bags' Moses. We made them a promise last Sunday and we aim to keep it.' He produced a letter from the inside pocket of his jacket. 'The mayor wrote to me yesterday, a letter which is actually to you but passed through me. I'd like to read it to you.'

He knew he had their complete attention, the hall so silent that the slightest cough reverberated, creating waves of sound that rippled along and escaped through windows and doors and crevices, only to leave a cemetery-like silence over the crowd once more.

They waited in anticipation, heads turned slightly upwards like statues towards the stage upon which Braxton Walker stood with the mayor's letter in his hand.

The telegraphic system had buzzed through the community all morning. The news was transmitted before dawn, first to the

218

Shackleton Bakery and then to the Leggy Joint Butcher Shop. The attendant at the Texaco petrol station received it at five fifteen in the morning. By six, Sister Palmer - everybody called her Ma - the sixty-nine-year-old woman in charge of the Prim and Proper Laundry, had heard the news and sat on her bench to say a quiet prayer of thanks. From the Shackleton Barbershop, the news sprouted wings later in the morning, so by three in the afternoon practically the whole east side community was aware that some of the most notorious drug activists in the community had been arrested in the middle of the night.

The combination of the heavy canvassing by Christina Coomes and other community leaders to spread the word about this Wednesday's meeting and the arrests in the middle of the night, in conjunction with the telegraphic service, had compelled them to find their way into the community hall. And now, like eager schoolchildren in an assembly hall, they sat with their heads upturned towards the headmaster on stage, waiting to hear some important news.

Braxton Walker had them in the palms of his hands. He knew the mayor's letter was something special. After all, since when had any mayor of this city taken the trouble to recognize the existence of the east side community; except when the riots broke out back in sixty-nine. That was the time of Mayor Kruger. Kruger was one hell of a mean man, some say a racist. He had wasted no time in sending the masses of police to quell the riots and in the end three members of the community and one policeman had lost their lives. The governor of the State had had to step in to restore peace. Since then, other mayors had come and gone but they had managed to run the important part of the city and ignore the east side.

'You all know my business', Braxton Walker was going to tease them just a little longer, political hat removed and the surgeon's cap firmly on his head. 'My business is to patch you people up after you've had too much to drink and busted your heads. Sometimes I've had to cut pieces of your bodies when things ain't working too well,' he looked at them, smiling and they looked back at him with respect and appreciation, 'small pieces mind you.' Now they were roaring with laughter.

'What we want is simple.' Walker was now very serious. 'We want a community that allows our children to go to school in the morning without fear, a community within which every adult is an automatic parent and guardian and protector of every child. A community where we protect one another's interests, and I mean black, white, Spanish American, American Indian, Chinese American, Japanese American, a community where we respect and protect our women, because they are our sisters and mothers, a community in which we can all work hard for our families with pride and a sense of purpose.' He could see Christina Coomes from the corner of his eye. She had moved a small table next to the doctor and she was now filling a glass with clear bottled water.

'Thank you Miss Coomes.' She backed away quietly and resumed her seat behind him on the stage; did he have to be so formal, she was thinking. To have called her Christina would have sounded much more romantic, sort of special, you know, a little more intimate than the distant sounding Miss Coomes. Anyway, she just sat there and looked at him, head slightly cocked, and wished her two boys could have him for their father.

'We need good schools, good hospitals, safe playgrounds for our children and money to build these things. But you know, before we can begin to have all of these things we need most importantly to rid ourselves of the menace of drugs. We can do that, indeed we can, with a two-pronged attack. And that means we've got to fight like hell to get rid of the dealer and educate our children,' he sipped some of the water and looked over the crowd, 'and some of the adults too, about the terrible things this poison can do to the body and the mind. We can do this with community spirit, your spirit,' the forefinger was out again, pointing, stabbing and sweeping over the crowd, 'my spirit,' he was stabbing his chest with his thumb and turning slowly, 'and your spirit.' Both hands outstretched, the mayor's letter still in his left hand, he was now facing Christina Coomes, whose spirit had long since left her body and was on a magical stroll with his spirit on some faraway tropical beach.

When he turned to face the crowd again, the mayor's letter was open in his hand. He began to read:

'*To the members of the east side community of this wonderful city, I wish to express my sincere appreciation for the initiative you have taken to try to eradicate the evil menace of drugs from our midst.*

I pledge to you my support and the support of our police force in a joint effort

to banish this evil from our society once and for all. I commend you.'
Signed Mayor Culhane

'We have waited a long time for this', Braxton Walker said after a long pause. 'The mayor's commendation is a tribute to all of us. If this is the sort of reward that community spirit brings, along with a pledge of support from the mayor of a city that for a long time has shut its eyes to a community that existed but was never seen, then I say to you my friends, we are on our way.'

'Yeah!' someone shouted loudly from the audience as the applause began. Braxton Walker extended his hand to Christina Coomes, whose spirit had since returned from her romantic journey. He wrapped his powerful arms around the woman's small frame, and together they bowed to show their gratitude for the standing ovation - community spirit indeed.

* * *

The task seemed simple enough, get *Thrushle to my office at eight tomorrow*, Maldini had said. The question was, where was Thrushle? Jack Dawson drove out of the city racecourse clerk's home. He had spent a pleasant fifteen minutes with the man but he had failed to gain any useful information about Thrushle's whereabouts. Dawson drove north-east, towards the Hood Acre. Surely there would be connections there to point him in the right direction. The trouble was he had not been in contact with Thrushle for so long he was not sure if the man was still in the city or whether he was still alive. If Thrushle was alive, he, Jack Dawson, would find him.

There it was, the Hood Acre, still gleaming, bathed in lights and offering the best in entertainment, the best of the very best of nightlife that money could buy. Dawson wheeled the Chevrolet into the parking lot and thought of the meeting he had had with Jack Maldini, Sam Templeton and Jake Watson last Friday morning in this very building. He marvelled at the transformation. In the cold light of day, the building looked like any ordinary big building surrounded by a large parking area, but at night the Hood Acre seemed to dress up, opened its arms to all-comers and soaked away their sorrows for a relatively small fee. Dawson sat in the car, the engine still running, and thought about Maldini's instructions.

Whatever it was, it had to be big. Dawson's mind was now in overdrive. He had known and worked for Jack Maldini for many years and he also knew that for Maldini to have called him to his home at night to ask about what he, Dawson, knew about horses meant that Jack Maldini had discovered something of great importance and was keen to act on it as quickly as possible. Jack Dawson suddenly became aware that the engine of the Chevrolet was still idling. He switched the engine off, removed the key from the ignition and tapped the key in his left hand as he sat in the car thinking. *How much do you know about horses, Jack?* Maldini had asked, *and get Thrushle to my office at eight tomorrow morning. Find the two doctors and send them to me at ten. And Jack, bring the dossier on those two.* What was the connection between horses and the doctors? Jack Maldini certainly knew something, something very important.

Dawson stepped out of the Chevrolet, slammed the door with some force, an indication of his frustrations this evening, and strolled into the Hood Acre. He entered the building and climbed the spiral staircase. He would first take a look in the Green Room, then, depending on what turned up, he would try the other rooms with his enquiries. He entered the Green Room just as the thought occurred to him. Dawson looked at his watch; forty minutes past two. Why was he sweating this assignment alone? The boys were good, they could trace anybody to the four corners of the country if necessary, particularly if there was a collection to be made. They had their system, an effective system honed to perfection over several years of practice. He finished dialling the number and held the receiver loosely in his hand.

'Yeah.' It was Steiner's voice. Dawson had expected Stumpy Lazarus. He issued his instructions quickly.

Jack Dawson was aware of the late hour but he made no attempt to apologize for having intruded in his private life in the middle of the night.

'Meet me in the Green Room.'

'Now?' Steiner was incredulous.

'Now.' Jack Dawson had a job to do and he needed his two most trusted associates. 'This is important, I'll explain when you two get here. I am going to circulate some, but I'll look for you in the Green Room.' Dawson had replaced the receiver and walked away from the phone before Steiner could say another word.

'Something's come up.' Steiner was addressing Rosalynn Brando. 'Stumpy and I have to leave, a meeting with Jack Dawson at the Hood.' It was not an explanation, neither was it an excuse, just a statement of fact about what he and his partner had to do. 'I suggest you stay here for the night.'

Her eyes told him that she understood. He had been honest with her on Saturday night. She knew what he did for a living and if he had to leave at two thirty in the morning to do a job then so be it. The kiss lingered for a moment or two before Steiner followed his partner out of the flat.

In the Hood Acre, Jack Dawson was putting himself about, asking, probing. He moved from the Green Room to the Yellow Room, hardly anybody there, then to the Blue Room. The Blue Room was also almost empty, and Dawson could not see any familiar faces. He would try the Fantasia, he thought, and walked out of the Blue Room to climb the stairs to the floor above. It was at this point that Lady Luck threw him a crumb.

'Jack!' The shrill voice shot through his spine. 'Jack Dawson', the man repeated, stepping gingerly down the stairs, his black bow tie undone and hanging loosely around his neck. The effort required to negotiate the next few steps seemed to be too taxing for the man, so he sat on the stairs, clasped his fingers together and stared drunkenly at Jack Dawson. 'I can tell you can't remember me.' The man wagged his finger at Dawson and slapped the empty space on the stairs next to where he was sitting, an invitation for Jack Dawson to join him.

It hit him like a bullet. Jack Dawson suddenly remembered the man.

'Isaac Pascalis, am I right?' The man nodded sleepily. 'Is your brother still working security for us? What's his name,' Dawson searched the memory banks. 'That's it, Robert, Rob Pascalis.' The drunk nodded again, making gurgling apologetic sounds.

This wasn't much more than a crumb, but it could be worth something so Jack Dawson sat next to the man and began to speak slowly, bearing in mind the man was drunk and might not be able to comprehend the questions being put to him.

'Isaac, are you still at the racecourse?'

The man nodded. Isaac Pascalis was a bookmaker. He often worked the racecourse and the boxing circuit so it was possible, just possible that he might have some idea about Thrushle's whereabouts. 'I am looking for Peter Thrushle... private matter, nothing negative', he added quickly to assure Isaac Pascalis of his good intentions. 'Do you have any idea where I might find him?' The man nodded in the affirmative.

'Where?' Dawson was now eager, anxious. He moved aside to allow passage for the two couples coming down the stairs, presumably from the Fantasia, and sat next to Isaac Pascalis again. 'Where, Isaac?' Dawson shook the man who was now falling asleep.

'Where, where?' the bookmaker repeated, spreading his arms before returning his chin to his chest, and proceeded to fall asleep.

'Damn you!' Dawson looked at his watch, it was three thirty in the morning. He wanted to satisfy Jack Maldini, *get Thrushle to my office at eight the following morning.* If this drunk knew where Peter Thrushle was, he'd damn well better speak up now. Dawson began to shake the drunk again, this time with slightly more vigour.

That's how they found him, still sitting next to Isaac Pascalis and vigorously shaking him. Mickey Steiner and Stumpy Lazarus had arrived. They expected to find Dawson in the Green Room. Instead, there he was on the stairs to the floor above, shaking and occasionally slapping the gentleman with the loose bow tie.

'What's up?' Steiner leaned forward, his left foot on the floor leading to the Blue Room and his right foot on the second step, next to Pascalis.

'Get Security,' Dawson instructed and watched as Stumpy disappeared from sight. 'Sorry to drag you two out here in the middle of the night, but this is important'. Jack Dawson said to Steiner and continued to shake the drunk.

Two security men came running up the stairs from the ground floor, Stumpy Lazarus just behind them.

'You all know me', Dawson spoke quickly to the security men. 'Take this gentleman and sober him up as best as you can. Don't let him out of your sight, understand,' he was serious about that, 'and bring him back to me in the Green Room when you think he is sober enough to talk to me.' Dawson was about to tell them one more thing, 'His name is...'

'We know,' the security men spoke at the same time, 'Rob Pascalis's brother.' Of course, thought Dawson, these were security men who worked with Rob.

'Okay, take good care of him and bring him back to me', said Dawson.

When the drunk and his escort were gone, Dawson ushered his two boys into the Green Room and offered to buy the drinks.

'Something seems pretty urgent.' Steiner was looking over the beer glass at Jack Dawson. 'I take it, it couldn't wait till tomorrow.'

'I am looking for a man by the name of Thrushle, works at the racecourse, I brought you here to help find him, but in the meantime I bumped into that guy they just escorted out of here. He knows where Thrushle is so when he is sober we'll find the answer. Now, about the two doctors, remember them, Swinton and Carter. I want them here at the Hood tomorrow at a quarter to ten, in the lobby. I don't care how you get them here, just bring them.'

They looked at each other but in silence. 'It depends on where Thrushle turns out to be but if he is in this city, I want him here at a quarter to eight in the morning.' The determination showed on Dawson's face and Mickey Steiner knew something very important was happening. Jack Dawson held his lips together, the muscles in his temple pulsating steadily.

'And by the way, the doctor's debt is now seventy grand, the usual four and a half per cent per week. Tell them that when you pick them up in the morning.'

'Suppose the money is given to us in the morning,' Stumpy had a valid question, 'what should we do, take it or bring them in?'

'Take it and bring them in', Dawson said tersely.

'No Jack,' Steiner interrupted, 'that'll be kidnapping.'

'Okay,' Dawson thought better of it, 'refuse it and bring them in. Tell them it's our standard procedure when debts are late. I don't care how you manage it, just bring them here in the morning.'

'Jack, tell us a bit more about Thrushle', said Steiner. 'What sort of a man are we dealing with?'

Jack Dawson took his time to inform his two associates. He told them as much as he knew, concluding with, 'They finally pulled his license as a trainer when he was found guilty of doping his horses.'

'So what's the connection.' Steiner looked Dawson directly in the eye. 'I mean what's the sudden connection between Thrushle and the doctors?'

'That I don't know. Honest.' Dawson was telling the truth. He wished he knew.

The security men brought Isaac Pascalis back to the Green Room just before five. The man had undergone some kind of transformation. He looked refreshed, sober and, although he had removed the bow tie and now wore his shirt open at the collar, he seemed in complete control of himself and behaved impeccably. He offered his outstretched hand to Jack Dawson, which was shaken vigorously before Dawson asked him to sit down.

'May I offer you some coffee?' Dawson eyed him curiously.

'No, those boys,' this was in reference to the security men, 'pumped me full of coffee, I think I've had enough.'

Dawson had no time; he went straight to the point. 'Isaac, I need your help and I need it now.' He bent forward. 'I asked you earlier if you knew where Peter Thrushle is. Do you?'

'Yeah Jack,' he replied confidently, 'over at the cemetery, he died about five months ago, stomach cancer, poor soul.'

Jack Dawson sat back in the chair, his face red, showing the rush of blood which suddenly flooded his face from the shock of the information he had just received. What was he going to tell Maldini? That the best horse man he could offer was six feet under, pushing up the daisies with the worms. His mind was swimming as he tried to work out his next possible move. He brightened up suddenly, fresh ideas coursing through his brain. He was smiling at Isaac.

'Tell me Isaac,' he said, 'as a bookie you spend a great deal of time at the racecourse, don't you?'

'It's my job.' Isaac shrugged his shoulders.

'You know jockeys, trainers, horse owners, and stable lads, don't you?'

'It's my job to know', he said, adjusting his shoulders, first one way then another, as if he were carrying all the trainers and jockeys and stable lads on his shoulders and they needed balancing to keep some sort of stability about the whole thing.

'So you know who is good, who is not and, most importantly, who is the very best, right?' Dawson was bending forward again, this time somewhat excited.

'Right', replied Isaac, looking around the table, first at Stumpy Lazarus and then a long fixed look at Mickey Steiner.

Dawson continued, 'I was looking for Thrushle because I was made to believe that he was the best when it came to knowing horses.' He was looking straight into the man's eyes, more than that, into his heart, a piercing, searching look, the kind of look that stops a liar in his tracks and brings out the truth regardless of one's will. 'So, who is the best, and I mean the very, very best?'

'The one you are looking for,' Isaac paused, his eyes still held captive by Dawson's hypnotic look, 'does not work in the horse racing business. There are many good ones, I can give you ten of those right here and now, but the one you are looking for,' he started to shake his head, 'you'll have difficulty getting.'

'Is this person, and I assume he is a person, better than Thrushle?'

'Thrushle was average. There are many better than him, but the one I have in mind is someone special.'

Jack Dawson's heart was beating faster. He could feel the excitement that Isaac's comments were creating around the table. In their silence, Stumpy Lazarus and Mickey Steiner were channelling their energies into taut muscles straining to get going. They would have to find this superhuman and bring him here before eight o'clock, so who was he?

The word was out and Jack Dawson was not wasting any more time, 'His name, Isaac, and where I can find him?' He was already peeling off one hundred dollar bills and piling them on the table. Isaac stared at the notes disinterestedly, pretending to struggle with the name that was at the very tip of his tongue. When he was satisfied with the number of notes that he deemed to be the fair price for the information he was willing to provide, he sat back in the chair.

'Shamon Kazi, a gypsy. You'll find him on his farm about half an hour from here. I can take you. And you know, I would have told you for free', he said.

Dawson had peeled off four of those sweet notes. He folded the money and stuffed it into the top shirt pocket of Isaac Pascalis, then rising from his seat and holding the man's head in both hands, kissed him on the cheek. Dawson looked at his watch; five forty, 'Half an hour from here eh?' He was calculating. 'Leave at six thirty to pick him up.' He rubbed his hands gleefully. Jack Maldini could have the very best.

CHAPTER EIGHTEEN

He had awakened with a start but for no apparent reason. William Nylander looked around the darkened room, unsure of what he was looking for and afraid of what he might find. The air conditioning unit hummed monotonously from the far corner of the bedroom, sending its own special nerve impulses to greet the warm air that infiltrated the room from the hot Saudi deserts and instantaneously forced a conversion, turning the room into a comfortable, cool haven.

Nylander was aware of the unit; its drone, ever present but not unpleasant, reminded him of the small bible under his pillow. He swung his feet from the bed and sat on the edge, still in darkness, his hands on his knees, and weighed the action he had taken the night before. The Sheikh wanted proof and, despite the fact that in the end Al Walhadi had indicated his willingness to arrange some kind of a race for the horse he refused to call a thoroughbred, Nylander was unwilling to wait for crumbs to be dropped at his table by the Arab.

He was wide awake by the time he pressed the switch to turn on the bedside lamp, a simple act which seemed to have simultaneously switched on his brain to kick the electrical impulses into motion. He could see the pad on the bedside table next to the lamp, the shining silver pen seemingly at attention, as if on guard to protect his scribbled notes of his actions the night before. He reached for the pad, gently lifted the silver pen and, with his right thumb, consciously and very deliberately did what millions of people do every day across the face of the earth without a thought. The click of the silver pen preceded the sound of the bedside telephone by milliseconds, but somehow it resonated through the cavities of his mind and then mingled with the ringing telephone.

Nylander picked up the receiver, turning at the same time to consult the radio clock.

'William.' The voice came over from a long way away, carrying a sense of urgency which gave the impression that the marathon of a distance had been hard fought but eventually the tape had been crossed. 'I am sorry to wake you but you wanted to know', the speaker panted.

'Quite all right Paul. What time is it there?'

'Just about six in the evening.' Paul Wainright paused. 'Yup, three minutes to, to be exact.' He was still panting. Nylander's Saudi clock had already made the adjustment. The numbers on the radio clock stared boldly at him, the two little dots, like a colon, blinking several times before shoving the seven out of the way and dragging the eight into view. After that, the colon began its blinking, announcing proudly 2:58 and beside that AM.

'That's central time, Paul', Nylander said with some surprise.

'You are a genius', Wainright laughed, a dry raspy sort of laugh. 'I left New York yesterday after the first pictures hit my desk. Got in touch with a guy I know down here; works for KTMZ Radio, you know, an old college friend.'

'All very discreet, I trust?'

'Of course.' Wainright flicked through the A4-size colour pictures of the magnificent horses. 'I have your original fax right here in my pocket and, like you said, hush! hush! So I decided to assign a trusted photographer. The KTMZ man and I will try to meet with the handler, some gypsy character. William, you should see these pictures. I agree with you, the chestnut filly looks something special, wow!'

'That gypsy character you refer to is Shamon Kazi. Paul, I want you to accord him all due respect and treat him kindly. He may look simple but he is a man of quality.' William Nylander was looking at his notes from the night before. The idea had entered his mind after he had returned from his visit to Al Walhadi. It was a simple plan which, if orchestrated properly, could yield the most magnificent end result and once and for all prove to the whole world that Shamka, the horse he had witnessed for the first time on the front lawn of the Carter home, was, as he believed, the most exciting thoroughbred the world of racing had ever seen.

Nylander looked at his notes and issued his instructions to Paul Wainright.

'Contact the *Echo*. Speak specifically to Kim Schuster, the sports editor, and make the best picture of Shamka available to her. She'll be expecting your call.'

'Where do I find Schuster?' asked Wainright.

'The *Echo* is the leading local newspaper, you'll find Schuster there, on the corner of Main and Watercress.'

'Okay.' Wainright noted the information on a small pad. 'Next?' he asked.

'Following the article in the *Echo* which should appear a day after your visit to Schuster, have your paper do a nationwide spread on Shamka. Use some of the material in my fax to you. Quote a mysterious source about why connections have refused to race the horse, why its pedigree has been kept a secret and, most importantly, the trainer's statement about Shamka being unbeatable.' Nylander finished reading from his notes. 'And Paul, please fax me copies of both newspaper articles.'

'You will get them both', Wainright assured him. 'Expect my call', he said and hung up.

William Nylander replaced the receiver and remained static on the edge of the bed. He wondered if he could pull it off. An article on Shamka in the prestigious *New York Times* would catch the eye of the racing world. If he was correct in his assumptions, questions would be raised, a debate would ensue and then, hopefully, the challenge would come. Nylander rubbed his eyes, turned off the light and, satisfied with the seeds he had sown, placed his head on the pillow. He was asleep within minutes.

* * *

He saw them long before they reached the tent. From the cover of the large oak tree which had managed to withstand the catastrophic events of the previous Thursday night, Shamon Kazi watched the two men as they approached.

They looked unsure of themselves, jittery, nervous even, but they came. These were men more comfortable in the city environment. Here on the farm they looked somewhat out of place in their dark suits and polished shoes, shoes which had already gathered dust.

'Mr Kazi.' He could hear the taller of the two men clearly. Shamon Kazi remained motionless. These were strange men; strange, uninvited men of whose intentions he was unsure. 'Mr Shamon Kazi', the taller man repeated himself. 'My name is Paul Wainright of the *New York Times* and my associate is Mr Steven Kramer from your local radio station KTMZ. May we speak with you for a moment, please?'

Chapter Eighteen

They had not seen him but the newspaper man spoke with the certainty of one who knew that he was addressing someone nearby. Kazi could see the two men chatting amongst themselves and waited. The day before, he had watched the stranger with the long lens taking pictures of the horses. The man with the camera had hidden in the trees at the far side of the farm near the well. Using the trees for cover, he had moved in the shadows and snap, snap, snap, before running to his car and driving off in a hurry.

He made his decision all of a sudden. Emerging from the shadows like an extension of the cover in which he had secreted himself he walked silently towards them until finally he stood directly behind them, his hands folded across his chest with the confidence of one who was comfortable in his surroundings.

'I am Shamon Kazi', he said.

'Good God, man!' Paul Wainright exclaimed, wheeling round at the same time with Steven Kramer to face the gypsy. 'You scared the hell out of me mister', Wainright said and, reaching for a handkerchief from his pocket with his left hand, he put out his right hand to be shaken by the gypsy.

'My name is Wainright, Paul, please call me Paul, from the *New York Times* and this here is Mr Steven Kramer from your local radio station KTMZ.'

The words were spoken so slowly and precisely that it made the radio call letters sound like kay-tee-em-zee. Wainright went straight to the point. 'Mr Kazi, we want to do a small article on Shamka, the wonder horse,' Wainright found himself saying, 'and we would like to ask you a few questions,' he paused and studied the man, 'if you don't mind.'

Why didn't they say so in the first place? If it was horses they wanted to talk about, all they had to do was come right out and say so. No need to hide in bushes and take pictures surreptitiously; Shamon Kazi was beginning to feel comfortable again. He led the two men into the tent, offered them the inevitable cups of tea and listened patiently to Wainright who had by now produced a small pad and a pen.

'Shall we start with Shamka's pedigree?' he asked the gypsy.

'What do you mean, pedigree?' asked Kazi.

'Sorry Mr Kazi, I meant Shamka's history, its parents.'

'That goes back a long, long way.'

'That's what we would like to know.' Wainright leaned forward, eager.

Shamon Kazi's face changed suddenly. His thoughts had shifted to Katherine Carter and the sudden but unusual visit the young lady had paid to the farm the day before. She had come very early in the morning, alone, just as the sun was rising, with a worrying look on her face. Katherine had walked the distance from the Carter home to the farm early that morning just to ask her question.

'Mr Kazi,' she had begun before correcting herself, 'Shamon, is it true that Shamka will not be harmed if we were to race her against other horses?' She had asked her question and waited with her eyes wide open in anticipation of the answer, an answer which Shamon Kazi knew would be taken as gospel if it came from him. In the end, the answer turned out to be more complicated than the question as Kazi patiently explained to Katherine that life was full of uncertainties.

Yes, Shamka was a thoroughbred, a racehorse bred for the purposes of racing; yes, she would enjoy the challenges that other quality horses would present and she would thrive on the experience, but to guarantee absolute safety, no harm, no injury, would be stretching the truth.

The question that followed did not surprise Shamon Kazi.

'Shamon, would you be happy to race Shamka?'

'Yes,' the gypsy replied confidently, 'she is ready.'

Katherine Carter did not explain to Shamon Kazi why she had walked to the farm so early in the morning but once she got her answer and felt satisfied in her heart that the horse she loved was in no danger of being damaged by racing, she threw her arms around the gypsy horseman she was growing to love and, after a satisfying hug, skipped through the grass on her way back home. Shamon Kazi had watched her skip until finally she had disappeared from sight.

'How did you know about Shamka?' Shamon Kazi addressed Wainright.

'A call came to my office, anonymous.' Wainright thought about the word, 'I mean the caller did not want to leave his name, but we were told to see you about a very special horse.' He had written the name of the horse on his pad. He passed the pad to the horse trainer. 'Is that the proper name of the horse?' Wainright sought confirmation and watched as the gypsy horseman nodded his head.

Shamon Kazi began his story with pride and enthusiasm. No one had ever asked him to talk in detail about his horses before, so he relished this opportunity to let the world know that in his horses and, particularly in Shamka, there was something special. He kept his eyes on the flickering candle in the center of the tent and told his story. Opposite him, the newspaperman scribbled on his pad.

* * *

Kim Schuster was climbing the corporate ladder steadily. She was the first female sports editor for the *Echo*, an opportunity she had grasped with both hands on her twenty-seventh birthday. That was two years ago. She sat at her desk in her small office tonight and gazed intently at the pictures that were spread all over the desk. She had found Wainright pleasant and direct, an attribute she cherished. The *Times* man had since left her office with a promise to keep in touch so she adjusted the table lamp, picked up several of the photographs and examined them closely. One by one she discarded them until finally she held the two A4-size colour photographs of the most magnificent horse she had ever seen.

Katherine Carter had described the horse to her mother during their conspiratorial discussion on the previous Thursday night as 'a two-year-old Chestnut with a white face'. In a way she was right, but to one who knew and had studied horses, Kim Schuster was looking at a Chestnut (Sorrel), with a blaze (a broad white mark down the face, extending from the eyes to the muzzle) and stocking (white on the leg from coronet to knee). She knew that she could not judge the quality of this horse by its appearance alone because according to true breeding criteria she would need additional information such as the horse's performance, its pedigree and progeny. She looked closely at the sleek ginger coat of the horse in the pictures - turned, twisted, away from the light and close to the light - and decided to stake her reputation on the article.

Kim Schuster wrote the article herself. It covered the whole of the second and third pages of the sport section of the *Echo*. The two magnificent colour pictures were shown side by side at the bottom of the article. The issue would be on the street by morning.

* * *

He knew why they had come and frankly he was getting tired of the sudden interest everybody seemed to be showing in him and his horses. They had given him time enough to prepare for the journey and, although they had not threatened him, he knew it would be unwise to resist their demands. Shamon Kazi sat in the back of the Buick and resigned himself to be taken to wherever they chose to take him. Occasionally, he stole quick glances at the man who sat next to the driver of the car and wondered how the man had come by the ugly scar that ran along one side of his face. He hoped they would be finished with him by tomorrow morning, the day on which his wife would be released from the hospital.

They arrived at the Hood Acre at exactly seven forty-five and were met in the lobby by Jack Dawson.

'Jack,' Isaac Pascalis beamed with some satisfaction, 'meet the best horse trainer in this town - heck! - in the whole USA as far as I am concerned.'

Shamon Kazi had recorded the face of the man in the black Chevrolet who had soaked him so timely on the road. He was now face to face with Jack Dawson. It had occurred almost a week ago but the gypsy had recorded the face and he had not forgotten. Kazi could tell from the way Jack Dawson looked at him that the man had no recollection of the incident. He waited.

'Are you sure?' Jack Dawson was addressing Isaac Pascalis, while at the same time he looked disdainfully at the gypsy who, so far, had not uttered a word.

'I tell you he is the best Jack. Now you can take my word or ignore it but I tell you, you are looking at the best horse trainer in the business.'

'A gypsy bum, the best in the business.' Dawson shook his head and motioned Kazi to follow him. 'Bring the other two for the ten o'clock meeting,' he instructed Steiner and Lazarus and walked up the stairs with Shamon Kazi behind him.

'That man is worth ten of you', Isaac Pascalis mumbled and walked away.

Unlike Jack Dawson, Jack Maldini got up from behind his large desk when Dawson entered his office with the horseman and walked around to meet the gypsy. He extended his hand to Shamon Kazi. 'It's a great pleasure to meet you Thrushle.' Maldini shook the gypsy's hand and offered him a seat.

'I am Kazi, Shamon Kazi', the gypsy horseman said proudly and sat in the chair.

Jack Maldini looked across the room at Dawson, his expression confused. He saw Dawson's attempts to draw him away from the stranger in the room and walked towards the far side of the office where the private consultation began.

'Mr Maldini, Thrushle is dead, died five months ago. The man you are looking at is the best in the business, named Shamon Kazi.'

Maldini looked coldly at Dawson. 'You said Thrushle was the best, now all of a sudden he is the best.' Maldini jerked his head in Shamon Kazi's direction. 'What am I to believe?'

'I've been made to understand that the gypsy is even better than Thrushle. Besides, Thrushle is dead and of no use to you now.'

'Get out!' Jack Maldini hissed and watched as Jack Dawson almost ran out of the office.

Maldini had composed himself by the time he rejoined the gypsy. 'Mr Kazi, they tell me you are the best horse trainer in this city, possibly the whole damn country.' He offered the gypsy a cigar, lit it, and lit one for himself. 'Shall I believe what they tell me or is everybody just talking?'

This was not the way Jack Maldini had planned it. He had been told of Shamon Kazi by his informants at the radio station as soon as Nylander's fax had been made available to them and he knew full well that the gypsy was the trainer of the horse which had been brought to his attention. He had hoped to learn as much as possible about horses from Thrushle or whoever the best trainer in the city was prior to meeting the man who now sat across from him. Under the circumstances he would do the best he could.

Jack Maldini found himself completely relaxed in the company of the gypsy; the tension, which usually accompanied him when he met people for the first time, seemed to have dissipated in the presence of this quiet stranger. There was no doubt that they were worlds apart in their possession of material wealth but, in spite of that, the quiet gypsy exuded a powerful, pleasant aura which seemed to cast a shadow over Maldini's ostentatious display of acquisitions.

'I know my horses', said the gypsy finally in response to Maldini's question.

The statement was significant. There was something specific about what the man had said. He did not say he knew horses, which no doubt he probably did. Instead, he had said, 'I know my horses.'

'Shamon,' Jack Maldini had moved around the table and was now sitting on the edge of the table next to Shamon Kazi's chair, 'there is nothing I like better than a man who knows his worth, a man who believes in his own abilities and knows his strengths. That's how I see you', Jack Maldini was being truthful. 'Let me be honest with you.' Maldini went on and told the gypsy everything: what he had been told about Shamka, why he had brought him here early this morning, his everlasting dream of wanting to own a horse or at least to be part owner of a horse which would be internationally famous. It was as if he could not help himself. The room was shrouded in a pale haze of smoke created by their own cigars but, as far as Maldini was concerned, he was in a bubble of smoke, floating along with a childhood friend and sharing his deepest thoughts. He felt lighter and lighter as he continued to tell the gypsy about his plans, the inner conflict he experienced at times for possessing so much but wanting more. Finally, for no apparent reason, he held the gypsy's hand and began to plead with him, his words unintelligible.

'Stay Shamon, please stay until they've come and gone', he kept repeating over and over.

The knock on the door was faint but clearly audible. In an instant Jack Maldini was back to his usual authoritative self, absolutely composed and in complete control of himself. 'Come in', he said, barely raising his voice. The door opened slightly, the security man showing his head around just enough to announce the two men who stood directly behind him.

'Mr Dawson said to bring them up, sir, Doctors Swinton and Carter.'

'Show them in', Maldini said and walked around the table to resume his seat. He had not expected them so soon and glanced at his watch. It was exactly ten o'clock; once again Jack Dawson had delivered.

The security man placed the dossier on the table directly in front of Jack Maldini and pulled two chairs for the doctors to seat themselves. He then looked at Maldini and took the nod of the head as his cue to exit. The security man pulled the door behind him and left the four men staring at one another around the table.

'Gentlemen, I am sure you think you know why you are here this morning. Whatever you think, my reasons for bringing you here are entirely selfish and self-serving.' He opened the folder the security man had left on the table and looked down at the pictures.

'You had no right.' It was Ben Swinton who spoke first, his eyes blazing with anger as he reached into his jacket pocket for the check book. 'The figure is now seventy, right?' He began to write the amount. 'You can accept this and redeem it tomorrow or wait for the full amount in cash by morning.

Maldini watched him patiently, a shadow of a smile on the corners of his mouth. He took the check when Swinton passed it to him, read the figure out loud and tore up the check into small pieces before placing it in the waste basket next to his desk. 'Consider the debt paid,' he addressed Swinton, 'and Doctor Carter, your obligation as the guarantor is now fully satisfied. Here is the receipt to prove it.' He pushed the small piece of paper towards the doctors.

They read it together without picking it up. It was a bone fide receipt clearing the debt of sixty-seven thousand dollars plus an additional four and a half per cent interest. Maldini watched them as they read. At the foot of the small piece of paper in bold print they read: *Amount owed = 0* and just below that Jack Maldini's signature.

Shamon Kazi had watched the three men with detached interest, occasionally blowing a puff of smoke from the large cigar tucked between his fingers. Maldini had not introduced him to the doctors when they had entered the room and the doctors had not shown any signs of recognition of the gypsy, but this would change.

Simon Carter lifted his eyes from the piece of paper. There had to be some kind of an explanation. Jack Dawson had tormented him, threatened him, pursued him and frightened him for almost a week. He had not been able to sleep properly for all that time because he had taken responsibility for a friend's debt. On a morning that he should have been busily performing his duties at the hospital he had been dragged out of his car en route without any explanation except for the simple statement, 'Mr Maldini wants to see you.' Now he had sat and watched the man opposite him tear up the check, cancelling the debt for which he had suffered so much, without any explanation.

'Why?' Maldini had said that his reasons for bringing the two doctors to his office this morning were self-serving and entirely selfish. Carter's eyes bore into Maldini. He had to know why.

Jack Maldini opened the drawer of his desk. He did it slowly without a word and produced two large pictures, A4-size, and slowly handed the pictures to Simon Carter. 'That's why.' Jack Maldini sat back in his chair. 'I understand she belongs to you.' Ben Swinton had moved closer to his friend and was peering at the magnificent colour pictures of the horse. His thoughts were of the conversation he had had with William Nylander on the night of the party, the conversation about thoroughbreds. The doctors must have been thinking the same thoughts because they turned towards the gypsy at the same time. It was as if they had not noticed his presence since entering the room and that they were seeing the gypsy horse trainer now for the first time.

Shamon Kazi still held the cigar in his hand, his smile to Simon Carter that of affection, kindness, mischief and mystery. Once again the room seemed to undergo an inexplicable change. They were here for a purpose, a strange and incongruous group of men thrown together by some unseen force which would direct their actions and thoughts to some accomplishment, of which, for the moment they had no comprehension or appreciation.

'*Stay Shamon, please stay until they have come and gone*', Maldini had repeated over and over, but it was as if he had said the words without any awareness of what he was saying or even of his surroundings. He had stayed and they had come. Now they were together in the strange, mysterious, cocoon-like bubble and again Maldini began to speak frankly, just like he had done earlier, to the other two occupants in the room.

He began with the events that led to his imprisonment; he was young then, only twenty-four, when his world came crashing down around him because of betrayal by the one person he trusted most. He had duelled in the strangest kind of way with his business partner for abusing his trust in him; death was what he was looking for, hoping for, but he had survived the ordeal and won. That victory had cost him five years of his life in prison. The experience had shattered his belief in mankind. It was then that he had sworn to take what he could from life, trusting no one, believing in no one except in his own ability to survive in what he considered to be a jungle, a jungle of human beings no better than that of the animals, humans considered to be of the inferior kind. Prison had reinforced his new-found beliefs and hardened him. He smiled at Carter as he recollected the one incident in prison that finally sealed his beliefs and shaped his future.

'It was over a thinly rolled cigarette', Maldini said and crumpled a huge cigar on the table to demonstrate the point he was trying to make, 'This thin, possibly one fiftieth of the amount of tobacco on this table.' He had separated a small portion of the crumpled cigar from the rest of the mess on the table, arranging it in a thin line. He began to breathe heavily, just staring at the thin line of tobacco and breathing deeply. 'Old Man Slade just shoved the fork deep under the Adam's apple of the con and dug it out in one quick motion and watched the fountain of blood gushing from the man's throat.' It was as if Maldini was having his own private conversation without an audience.

'For a cigarette?' Ben Swinton asked in a strange voice which did not sound like him.

'All for a cigarette; this much tobacco.' Maldini was once again pointing at the thin line of tobacco he had separated from the crumpled cigar. 'And I'll tell you why. Because Old Man Slade had done all sorts of things and schemed for five days to earn that amount of tobacco and for him it was all he had to look forward to. A vision of enjoyment beyond all enjoyment, dreams woven in every single puff of the tobacco which he envisioned smoking at his leisure.'

'But why?' Simon Carter had forgotten all about his hospital duties. He was in a different world, a world of iron bars, prison guards, striped uniforms and minds. Minds, into which were crammed oceans and mountains and deserts and dancing girls and loved ones and wonderful activities that did not exist but in the minds behind bars.

'Earlier that morning, the con had removed the precious cigarette from behind Old Man Slade's left ear, pushed him around a bit and with great arrogance smoked the cigarette in front of several of the inmates. You see, for Old Man Slade, the cigarette meant everything, everything that meant anything in the whole wide world, his dreams, his life. The humiliation did not matter so much as the cigarette itself and for that he had taken the con's life in return, the one thing that meant more than anything to the enemy,' Maldini said and sat back in the chair.

'A human life for a cigarette?' Ben Swinton could not believe his ears.

'Doctor Swinton, in life things assume their own value at different times', Maldini said quietly as he walked across the room to fill a glass with water. He returned to his seat and placed the glass of water on the table. 'See this,' he pointed to the glass of water, 'you could spill it a thousand times over from where you are sitting and it wouldn't make a difference to you or anybody, but if you were in a desert and in need of just this one glass of water, you would give all your worldly possessions for it.' Maldini looked at all those around the table. 'I dare say you would kill for it.'

They knew he was right, although they could not quite measure in their minds the 'cigarette for life' incident that had taken place almost twenty-eight years ago. To Jack Maldini it made perfect sense, especially when he reflected on Old Man Slade's subsequent reasoning that because he was already serving a life sentence the trade-off was truly a life for the all-important cigarette.

Jack Maldini had told them a lot. They knew now that their presence in the man's office had something to do with Shamka but so far he had not made his intentions clear. What was it he wanted? And how did it relate to the cancellation of the debt which had almost caused Ben Swinton to commit suicide?

Simon Carter picked up the pictures of the horse. 'What about these?' he asked Maldini finally.

'I'd like to be a part of it', Maldini replied and turned to Shamon Kazi. 'Shamon, we could conquer the world with her.' There was a strange look in his eyes, a look which seemed to show a mixture of greed and power. 'Imagine the impact, the success this horse could have on this city, the jobs it could create, the money we could all make. Doctor Carter, imagine that. I am willing to invest in this venture to make it a success. I'd like to be a part of it.'

'The horse is not mine. I am sorry that I am not in a position to accommodate you.' Simon Carter began to rise. As far as he was concerned the conversation was finished. It was time to return to his duties.

'Doctor please sit down,' Maldini said. 'I don't think you quite understand. I need to be a part of this, I have to be a part of this and whether you own this horse or not is not going to change my mind about what I know must happen. If necessary I shall buy the horse -

240

either at a fair price that the owner is free to quote or at a fair price that I shall quote. Don't you think the owner would be happier to have my backing instead?' He was smiling. 'So who owns this magnificent filly?'

Shamon Kazi would not dream of allowing any harm to come to Katherine Carter or to Shamka. They were both imbedded deeply within his family now and in his heart. Jack Maldini's story about the cigarette and the murder of the enemy had registered in his mind. He was the one person in the room who fully understood what Maldini had implied. Like Old Man Slade's last cigarette, Jack Maldini had set his heart on being involved in some way with Shamka and for the moment it was probably more important to him than half of his empire, possibly all of his empire. To stand in the man's way would be suicidal. He wondered if his friend, the doctor, and Ben Swinton understood that; he hoped they did. All the same he would play a part in this delicate situation.

'Sir, my daughter Katherine owns the horse. Whether you become a part of it or not, whether Shamka races or not, will be decided by Katherine and not by you or me', said Simon Carter. The doctor's demonstration of strength in this situation impressed Maldini. That's what he liked about people; if it matters then defend it, protect it, kill for it if you have to. That was the Maldini way and Simon Carter was living up to it.

'Doctor, please speak to your daughter. Shamon, explain my proposal to the little girl and ask her for her terms. Of course she must decide, but let her understand the good we could do with her Shamka. When she has decided, and I hope she will do that, we can meet again and discuss it further. Doctor, you have two days.'

Ben Swinton stood first. 'Mr Maldini, thank you for writing off my debt,' he slid the receipt on the table back to Jack Maldini, 'but I would feel a whole lot better if I paid it. You will receive seventy thousand dollars in cash tomorrow.'

CHAPTER NINETEEN

The sprawling County General Hospital that was situated on the southern fringes of the east side was experiencing its quietest period for several weeks. It was as if the new community spirit which was washing over this part of the city had somehow reached out and cleansed the hospital, providing a welcome break for the overworked doctors, nurses and the ancillary staff. Even the patients seemed less distressed than normal.

Braxton Walker strode along the corridor between Pinkerton and Stranton Wards in the company of two junior doctors whose enthusiastic clinical discussions reminded him of his earlier years in medical practice, The two clinicians veered off into Stranton Ward, white coats flapping, with the inevitable stethoscope dangling around the shoulders. Doctor Walker waved them off with a smile and walked towards the newspaper vending machine. He would catch up on the latest news over lunch and after that he would honor the mental agreement he had made with himself - that was to give his body and soul as much rest as possible before returning for duty the following Monday.

The hospital staff canteen was quieter than usual. The smattering of occupants were dotted around the room as if each one had purposely selected their spot to allow as much space as possible between themselves and the closest neighbour. Walker followed the imaginary rule and strolled along the edge of the room, tray of food in one hand and the folded broadsheet of the *Echo* in the other hand. He found a place, having allowed for the unwritten territorial niceties, and settled himself at the dining table. He read as he ate, flipping through the pages of the large paper with ease. It did not take long to digest the current affairs and political events of the past day or two. The County Court seemed to be overloaded with work, according to the *Echo*, as the trial of the motorcycle gang had begun that morning. The brief about the suspected murderer of the two boys caught his eye and within minutes he had absorbed the information. He turned the page, thought better of it, and returned to the article about the suspected murderer. Using the knife with which he had been carving the steak on his plate, he cut around the article in the paper with the skill of a surgeon, folded the article and placed it in his pocket. Before long he had discarded the first section of the paper. He flipped through the business section without interest, once again discarding it without much thought.

It was the two colour pictures of the horse that first caught his eye as he turned to pages two and three of the sports section. He focused on the pictures, admiring the horse. Eventually, he noticed the title of the article as he discarded the fork and decided to give the piece his undivided attention.

Shamka
An example of the Perfect Thoroughbred,
By Kim Schuster, Sports Editor.

Braxton Walker plunged himself into the article, gobbling up the information, and from time to time returned to examine the two fascinating colour pictures. He finished reading the article, turned his attention back to the pictures and decided to read the last but one paragraph again:

'The Thoroughbred was developed as a flat-racehorse, and this remains the main reason for breeding. The largest prices were paid for the horses that had, or appeared to have, the potential to run faster than the others. The most valuable of all are the horses that are at their best as three-year-olds over one to one and three quarter miles. These are called the 'classic' distances, and the top races are called 'the classics' (such as the Kentucky and British Derby).'

There is no such thing as perfection in life. Braxton was once again reading the title and focusing on the word 'perfect'. However, he could not disagree with the writer that the pictures showed a horse that was as close to being perfect as any horse could be. For the first time, he had learned that the country of origin of the thoroughbred was Britain; that the height of a thoroughbred was about 14.2-17.2hh, about 147 to 148 centimetres, but generally around 16hh (163 centimetres) on average. He found himself wondering about the letters 'hh', not having a clue as to its meaning or symbolism. He was re-reading the second last paragraph for the third time when it suddenly came to him; 'hh'. hands high he smiled triumphantly. Why were horses measured in hands high? He gave up the thought. Some things are better left alone, like asking questions such as 'Where did God come from?' He could not explain his fascination with the horse, but he knew, in fact he felt in some strange kind of way, that this would not be his only encounter with this magnificent beast.

The staff canteen had started to fill up as more nurses and doctors descended upon it. Braxton Walker emerged from Kim Schuster's creation on the sports pages to discover a canteen full of white coats, blue starched nurses uniforms and the odd green surgical cap. The territorial advantage that the earlier occupants of the canteen seemed to have negotiated secretly for and enjoyed was no longer a viable commodity. Space was now at a premium. He watched as the four doctors and two nurses descended loudly upon his position and knew it was time to relinquish his space. He gathered the *Echo* which was now spread all over the dining table, hurriedly rearranged the pages and slid along the wall before the loud gang of six arrived at the table. He walked out of the crowded hospital canteen into the open spaces of the hospital compound. It was time to honor the mental agreement he had made with his body.

* * *

The three tents stood majestically in the spacious back yard like jolly green giants. It had been a busy Thursday. The frantic activity in the massive Maldini back yard was now finished and the workmen were gathered under one of the huge green tents they had just erected for Saturday's anniversary celebrations. Barbara Lazlo, Elizabeth Templeton and Vivian Maldini were serving soft drinks and cakes to the workmen, an expression of their appreciation for a job well done.

Vivian had meticulously sorted the list of guests who had responded to the invitation and, with the help of her two friends, she had managed to prepare the seating arrangement in such a way as to ensure compatibility and a sense of fun around each table. Everything was going according to plan and Vivian Maldini was pleased with herself. Her happiness seemed to rub off on her two closest friends as they joked happily with the workmen and dished out larger portions of cakes and poured copious amounts of liquid refreshments.

Each marquee would shelter seventy people. Under each tent, ten round tables had been arranged, each round table surrounded by seven comfortable white chairs. The women knew that by early Saturday afternoon they would have transformed the current plain setting with their colourful tablecloths, specially selected flowers and expensively decorated china and, most importantly, they would have replaced the tough muscle-bound workmen with the creme de la creme of the most powerful and influential people in the city.

At four thirty, the workmen, now stuffed to the gills with food and drink, thanked the women for their hospitality and trooped out of the back yard through the small side entrance that led past the garage and into the street. Within minutes the roar of the engines of their three pick-up trucks had dissipated in the pleasant evening breeze as silence once again blanketed the exclusive neighbourhood.

The three women were in the middle of their Bridge game when Jack Maldini walked into the house with Lazlo, Templeton and Watson. Vivian Maldini excused herself, met the men in the main living room and happily informed her husband about the marquees.

That was where the men chose to hold their evening discussion. They settled themselves under one of the large tents and looked forward to Vivian Maldini's special shaken martinis.

She left the silver tray in the middle of the table, touched Jack Maldini's hand affectionately and left them to serve themselves while she returned to join the ladies and the game of Bridge. Vivian Maldini did not have to be told that these men had chosen their location purposely to allow them the privacy they craved for whatever secrets they had intentions of sharing. Twenty-five years of experience had taught her not to meddle in her husband's affairs so she settled down to her game of Bridge with a clear conscience and hoped that Saturday's anniversary celebrations would be a success.

Jack Maldini opened the brown envelope, removed the pictures of the horse and passed them to Joe Lazlo. The pictures went from Lazlo to Watson without comment and then to Templeton who studied them carefully before returning them back to Maldini.

'She is Shamka', said Jack Maldini.

'Strange name, fantastic looking horse', Sam Templeton added.

'How old?' Lazlo was looking at Maldini.

'Three-year-old, a class act.' Maldini handed Lazlo the *Echo*.

The paper was passed from one to the other, each person taking time to read the article with interest before returning the paper to Maldini.

'Well,' Maldini looked around the table, finally fixing his look on Jake Watson who had so far not uttered a word, 'what are your thoughts Jake?'

There was no doubt about the quality of the horse, at least as far as the pictures were concerned, but Jake Watson was the most cautious man among the group and it was unlikely he would base his comments on a mere picture.

'When do we see her?'

'In a few days I hope.' Maldini did not sound convincing.

'You've never been wrong about anything important, Jake Watson said diplomatically, 'so I am with you on this. I hope, though, that we, get a chance to see her before we take the plunge.'

'You will, yes sir, you will', Jack Maldini said confidently and filled their glasses. The four of them had been in many successful business ventures together.

* * *

In the county jail, lawyers had been toing and froing all through the early hours of the morning in their attempts to post bail for the six men and four women who had been arrested in the middle of the night. All attempts at bail had been refused by the police on the grounds that the suspects might abscond. Under strict and secure guard, the six men and four women had been driven the short distance from the county jail to the courthouse in two separate police vans.

Outside the courthouse the long line of spectators who hoped to gain entrance into court number thirteen to witness the arraignment of the suspects consisted mostly of members of the east side community, most of whom had been affected in one way or another by the activities of those to be paraded in court.

They began shuffling into the courtroom at exactly ten o'clock, their progress slow as they were scanned with metal detectors for weapons and frisked by hand.

Women were ushered through door A, men through door B.

Finally, at ten thirty, the heavy wooden doors of court thirteen were shut. Those unlucky enough not to have gained entrance murmured their objections to one another before dispersing to find some other pursuit to occupy the time they had allocated to the court proceedings.

The lucky ones sat bunched up on the row of benches which faced the raised platform of the judge's bench. Court thirteen had a capacity of seventy-five. On this occasion the numbers seemed to be slightly more. The court had transgressed but no one was going to pass judgement on that. The business at hand was to wield the power of the law in court thirteen to let justice prevail.

The courtroom fell silent when the bailiff announced the entrance of Judge James C Colman. He appeared looking somber and serious at the same time, if that was possible. His black robe covered his wobbly stomach and accorded him the dignity of his high office. The judge had a busy day ahead of him. The arraignment in court thirteen was to be followed by the trial of some of the members of the Eagle motorcycle gang, also in court thirteen.

'Please be seated', he instructed the standing courtroom and, rearranging his robe, slid carefully into his high chair.

All six men and four women sat together on the front bench, flanked by the two powerful lawyers who had arrived from Detroit to represent Julian Moses and his associates. In the wings, the armed bailiffs tried to look unobtrusive.

'The case of Cromwell County versus Frank Biggles, step forward please', the bailiff announced and retreated to his corner.

Frank Biggles stood up and moved forward to join one of the lawyers who had already moved forward to defend him. Judge Colman looked down from his platform upon the accused and his lawyer and began the proceedings with the skill of one who had spent a great number of years in courtrooms. The whole thing boiled down to whether bail would be allowed by the court, how much it would be and to set the date for the trial. Of the six men, bail was set individually for all except Frank Biggles who was accused of possessing the murder weapon and therefore would have to stand trial for the murder of the two boys. The others were bailed to return to face the court for the possession of drugs or accessory to the possession of drugs. Trial date was set for 15 May, in thirty days. The four women were released without charge because, according to the police, they were said to have been invited guests, and that searches had revealed no incriminating substances either on their persons or in their coats or bags.

The plan seemed to have worked pretty much the way that Mickey Steiner and Stumpy Lazarus had planned it. Frank Biggles was out of the way and chances are he was going to be out of the way for a very long time. Sam Dingles, Paperbag Jones and Big Joe Kelly were allowed bail to reappear along with Julian Moses and Trinkets. The beauty of it was, no one suspected the women for the part they had played in Biggles's arrest. The court had apologized to the four women for their incarceration and, in the true spirit of the Colman judiciary method, Judge Colman had looked down on the four women, his glasses down on his nose, and uttered wise words which he hoped would save them from future troubles.

'As the old saying goes,' Judge Colman had begun, 'birds of a feather flock together.' He removed his glasses and rested his elbow on the table in front of him as he leaned forward. 'But as an English friend of mine once said, you birds certainly don't have to flock with certain members of our society, you know what I mean.' The courtroom erupted with laughter at Colman's final words. He slipped the glasses back on his nose and adjourned the case.

* * *

William Nylander had seen the sun long before Judge Colman adjourned the case and carried his massive frame out of the courtroom and into his private chambers in the courthouse. For Nylander, darkness had already fallen and the weekend in Saudi Arabia was fast approaching, He sat in the quiet office with all the lights off except for the green-shaded table lamp that illuminated the desk directly in front of him.

The plan was working as far as he could gather from his communication with Wainright. The newspaperman had been true to his word and on the desk in front of William Nylander were the faxes of the articles in the *Echo* and the *Times*. On the top fax sheet, the scribbled message was simple:

Schuster tells me the telephones haven't stopped ringing since the Echo hit the streets. I understand the whole of Cromwell County is buzzing with the news about your horse. We go to press late tonight so expect copies of both newspapers by courier tomorrow.
Regards, Wainright
The Times 04/15.

The statement did not go unnoticed, 'the news about your horse'. That's exactly how he felt. Nylander was in a daze, sitting in his darkened office, staring at the faxed sheets and deep in thought. He had recognized the potential of the horse, probably the only one amongst the whole group of people at the party who had, except Shamon Kazi, of course. He did indeed feel as if the horse was his. If his plan worked, and he hoped it would, he would be sure to let everyone know that he was responsible for Shamka's fame, that he was the one who first recognized the special qualities. To be fair he was not interested in financial gain, but he was obsessed enough with the horse to do whatever it took to prove his point.

He began to read the fax sheets; first the *Echo* article. The two pictures did not project the same effect on the fax sheets as they had done when Braxton Walker had studied them earlier in the hospital canteen, but the article was satisfactory. After the *Echo* came several sheets of the *Times*' version, headed:

Shamka, A Thoroughbred Ready to Conquer the World.
By Paul Wainright

Nylander was enjoying the article when the air conditioning shuddered, as if to warn him of the heat and humidity outside and to remind him that office hours had long since passed. He had reached the part of the article in the *Times* where, as instructed, Wainright had used Nylander's quotation, *'Our secret sources inform us that Shamka's connections deliberately refused to race the horse to limit exposure. Its pedigree is believed to have been kept a secret although our own investigations seem to point in the direction of Sir Galahad III or possibly the great Wajima. According to Shamka's trainer, the horse is unbeatable.'*

The soundless alarm on his wristwatch began to tweak slowly, increasing in intensity with the passing seconds as the small pin dug softly into his skin. It was time to telephone his wife and daughter. He knew they would be waiting for the call. It would be an opportunity to feel the pulse of the city about what the *Echo* had reported about Shamka. Nylander picked up the telephone and dialled.

It was Jill who answered the phone, her excitement oozing out of her voice and over the airwaves to the darkened room in which her father sat. He felt lonely all of a sudden as he listened to the young lady's chatter. It must have been the regular five-minute summary sessions of the week's activities in her English classes which enabled Jill to condense the past week, package it in a juvenile chatter box and deliver it from the States to that dark room in Jeddah on a late Thursday night. She finished the chatter with, 'Daddy, you wouldn't believe what the *Echo* printed about Katherine's horse, you remember, Shamka.' She paused to gulp several cubic liters of air. 'Everybody in town wants to see her.'

That was the information he wanted to hear. He wished he could be home again because he missed his daughter and his wife and also he wanted to be in the thick of things as the Shamka saga unfolded.

The actual copies of the two newspapers would arrive by courier the following day. Wainright would see to that.

The *Cromwell County Echo* was unlikely to appear anywhere in Saudi Arabia but the *New York Times* was freely available. If he was correct, it would not be long before CNN, the BBC and the rest of the respected world television and radio broadcasters joined the bandwagon to expound the Shamka story.

The world of guidance missile systems was far from Nylander's mind as he drove through the deserted Jeddah streets on his way home.

He drove home wondering how long it would take to receive the inevitable phone call from Sheikh Al Makhtoum Walhadi.

* * *

A few days ago Katherine Carter had promised her brother and Kazeem Kazi another meeting as soon as she had had the chance to ask the all-important question. Katherine was satisfied with the answer Shamon Kazi had given her so she sat on the floor in John Carter's bedroom, their usual venue for the important meetings. A copy of the

Echo and the inevitable notepad lay on the floor between the four of them, the newest addition to the group being her friend, Jill Nylander.

The meeting began with a briefing from Katherine Carter. She read from her notepad and for Jill's benefit she was quite thorough in the recapping of their previous meeting. She picked up the copy of the *Echo* from the floor and asked the same question that she had previously asked her father and Maureen Carter.

'Has anyone here spoken to the Press about my horse?'

The other three children looked at one another in bewilderment and then returned their attention back to Katherine. They all shook their heads.

'I didn't think so.' She seemed sure of herself. 'I had to ask, because what is printed in here,' she waved the paper in the air, 'is exactly what we will discuss tonight.'

The *Echo* article about Shamka had come as a surprise to all of them. As far as they knew, their previous meeting about raising money to assist the development of the east side was their secret. They had not mentioned their private discussions to their parents and Kazeem Kazi had not discussed their conversation with his father. The horse belonged to Katherine and the decision to race or not to race Shamka was hers to make.

The *Echo* article meant their secret was out.

'Let's take it from where we left off.' Katherine Carter had the notepad open. 'Our worry,' she corrected herself, 'my worry, was Shamka's safety.' She paused and looked at the others with concern, a look which soon changed to a bright, confident smile. 'I am convinced that Shamka can race, will race, and you know what,' the gleam in her deep blue eyes convinced the others, 'she can win against any horse in the whole wide world.'

She took her time to inform the other children about her walk to the farm to visit Shamon Kazi. She told them of her anxiety that morning, her fears and finally of her absolute relief and happiness when Shamon Kazi confirmed that Shamka was a racehorse, a thoroughbred born for racing and, most importantly, that she was ready, as Shamon Kazi had put it.

'So we can race Shamka to raise money to help the east side', John Carter's eyes shone brightly, matching the deep blue of his sister's eyes.

'Yes', replied Katherine.

'Cool.' John Carter beamed at Kazeem Kazi.

'My father seems to think she is the best, probably the best thoroughbred to have come along in a long time,' Jill Nylander said excitedly.

'Your father is right.' Kazeem Kazi's eyes were focused on the white cast on his right arm. The gypsy boy had a habit of concentrating his attention on the cast whenever he had something important to say. He had been taught a great deal about horses. There was no doubt in his mind about Shamka's ability or potential to take on other horses, but his worry now was something completely different from what Katherine Carter or any of the others had even begun to contemplate.

'Kaaz!' John Carter knew his friend, and somehow he sensed that there was something important going on in the gypsy's mind. 'You've got to trust us.' John Carter was speaking for the other people in the room, his attention focused on Kazeem Kazi. He wanted to know, wanted to share his friend's anxiety. 'Please share your thoughts with us, because we are doing this together.'

The gypsy lifted his eyes from the cast. 'Horses are like people, well, in some ways, and they must have trust, complete trust.' Kazeem Kazi made the statement and withdrew back to his cast, eyes down, left hand rubbing the cast, feeling the itch underneath but unable to reach the areas that itched.

They seemed confused, unable to comprehend the gypsy, so all three looked at him, as if he was something or someone from outer space.

'This is our meeting, our own private meeting,' Katherine Carter tried to take charge, 'so if there is something on your mind Kazeem, spill it.' It did not sound cruel, it did not sound harsh. It was a statement loaded with authority and all the sincerity of a child who wanted to reach the end line. It simply said, speak your mind.

'If you decide to race Shamka, you'll have to consider who rides her,' Kazeem paused, 'that is, if you want her to win.'

'But she is a thoroughbred', Jill Nylander intervened.

'Even thoroughbreds have to be controlled in a race.' Kazeem was back to the cast, itching to scratch but unable to do so.

'Explain yourself,' Katherine Carter demanded, her eyes swimming over the gypsy boy.

'Go on Kaaz, tell them.' John Carter believed in his friend and if the issue was about horses, as far as he was concerned there could be no better authority, except possibly Kazeem Kazi's father.

Kazeem Kazi looked up from his cast. He had to make the other three understand. He began his explanation with the sincerity and surety of one who knew what he was talking about.

They listened with interest as Kazeem Kazi enlightened them about the world of the horse, particularly the thoroughbred. He explained that all thoroughbreds possessed the qualities that Shamka exhibited so well; handsome, alert horses with a good deal of presence. He talked of their ability to move with great freedom and how they have an easy ground-covering stride at the gallop. Finally, he explained about the courage and stamina of the thoroughbred that set it apart from the other breeds.

'Excellent thoroughbreds will all possess these qualities, so in racing, more often than not, the difference in just winning or just losing will depend on the jockey.' Kazeem Kazi finished imparting his thoughts and returned his attention to the now yellowing cast on his right arm. The itch was still there but there was nothing he could do about it. Kazeem tried to shut it out of his mind.

Katherine Carter had managed to note down all the important points of the gypsy's argument. She put the pen back on the pad and turned her attention to those around her.

'Thank you Kazeem.' She was smiling at the gypsy. 'We have many things to think about and plan for; like when to race, where to race and, as Kazeem has just pointed out, who will ride. First we must arrange a meeting with mum and dad and Kazeem's dad to see what help they can give us, agreed?' She looked from one to the other, her blue eyes sweeping over them.

'Agreed', the others responded.

Little did they know that their innocent attempt at racing the horse which had become a part of their world, the horse of Katherine Carter's dreams, was to be consumed in the twisted adult world of greed, power, money and intrigue.

CHAPTER TWENTY

The flowers had been arriving almost every two hours since ten that morning. Interflora seemed to have cornered the market on flowers, the statistical evidence showing three to one in its favor.

At exactly six fifty-five another huge bunch of red roses entered the ward, the Interflora man ramming home the statistical advantage. This was the fifth and last bunch of flowers to be delivered to Juliana Kazi at St Agnes Hospital on this Thursday.

Interflora - four, competitors - one.

Juliana had made a remarkable recovery.

She was to be discharged from the hospital on Friday afternoon so Shamon Kazi had sent his bunch of flowers earlier in the afternoon after leaving the Hood Acre and he was now sitting next to his wife's bed with his son beside him.

They watched as the forest of red roses was unwrapped by the nurse. She carefully placed the flowers in a large glass vase, taking time to arrange them to her satisfaction and, with a starched smile, she handed the accompanying envelope to Juliana. 'I wish someone would send me a bunch like that one day', the nurse said jealously and swished off to carry on with her evening duties.

Juliana Kazi added the envelope to the bunch in her hand. 'I know who sent this one', she said pointing to the beautiful arrangement of chrysanthemums on the right side of the bed near her pillow, 'and they are my second favorite.' She shuffled the envelopes and passed one to her husband. Shamon Kazi handed the envelope to his son.

Kazeem Kazi fished the small white card out of the envelope and read it aloud.

'Wishing you continued good health and much love. Come and visit when you can, love, Maureen and Simon.' Shamon Kazi smiled at his wife and nodded his head.

The bunch of yellow roses to the left of Juliana's pillow had come from the nurses who had looked after her for the past week. She had been voted unanimously as the best patient of the year as pronounced by the card in Kazeem Kazi's hand.

254

Chapter Twenty

'These are my favorite.' She was referring to the bunch of a dozen red roses from her husband. Shamon Kazi leaned forward to be hugged and smiled sheepishly. 'I have no idea where the other two came from.' She handed the two small envelopes directly to her son. 'The small white envelope came with that one.' She pointed to the beautiful arrangement of red carnations.

The boy removed the card and began to read, 'We wish you health and happiness, Wainright and Kramer.' Below the names, was the inscription... *New York Times and KTMZ Radio*. She shrugged her shoulders. It was the only bunch that did not come via Interflora. Some company called Brown and Castle Flowers. Apparently, quite global, as indicated by the small print; New York, London, Paris, San Francisco & The American Midwest.

'They are the reporters who came to interview me about Shamka.'

'Nice flowers, thank them for me.'

He did not know if he would ever get the chance to thank them but he said, 'I will,' adding, 'nice fellas.'

All that remained was the forest of red roses. It must have been six dozen. Beautifully arranged, and very red petals. They waited for the boy to open the envelope. Kazeem Kazi read the inscription to himself first, then slowly he began to read it aloud: 'To Mrs. Kazi, Health first, then wealth. Happy to learn of your rapid recovery, regards, Jack Maldini, a friend of the family.'

'Who is Jack Maldini?' asked Juliana

'A businessman', Shamon Kazi replied with a smile.

'Good business or bad business?'

'Could be good, could be bad.' He was still smiling. 'But you know if I have anything to do with the business, it will be good business.'

Juliana Kazi knew that was the truth. She had never known her husband to involve himself in anything that was not completely honest. There had been times in the past when people had doubted them simply because they were gypsies. But Shamon Kazi had always triumphed in the face of such doubt. They had lost count of the numerous apologies that had come their way after doubters eventually succumbed to the truth and came to accept that Shamon Kazi was one gypsy whose word stood as strong as the word of any other honest man on the face of this earth.

'They are lovely.' She was looking at Jack Maldini's roses.

Juliana Kazi was happy to be going home on Friday. She had placed her faith in Shamon Kazi totally. She would accept whatever Friday had in store for her.

* * *

Paul Wainright was excited. He had spent most of the evening dashing from one office to another in the Times Building. His adrenaline level was so high he felt much younger than his fifty-two well-worn years, most of which had been spent on Manhattan Island.

He answered the ringing telephones from time to time but mostly he watched as others did so and gave him thumbs-up to indicate another enquiry about the Shamka article. Judging by the number of enquiries flooding in over the phone lines, the people of Manhattan, The Bronx, Brooklyn, Queens, Long Island and those across the water in New Jersey, seemed to do nothing but dream of horses.

They wanted to know everything. Where was this special horse? Could they have more details about its pedigree? When could they see it race? Did the name have any special significance? And on and on.

Each inquiry was logged and categorized according to the location of the caller and the type of questions posed.

The small package had already been dispatched by courier to Jeddah earlier in the morning. Wainright could not wait to make the call to Nylander. He looked forward to their conversation in the full knowledge that he was now involved in something special. His newspaper nose told him that they had started one of those stories that seemed to gather their own momentum and steamrolled from week to week until eventually they either exploded or imploded in on themselves. Wainright zigzagged through the Times Building, hopping from one floor to another, slapping backs, shaking hands, accepting congratulations for the article and generally beaming with satisfaction.

Eventually, he found his way back to his own office. He shut the door behind him, took in a deep breath and plonked himself into his chair behind the large desk. The wheels of the heavy chair automatically rolled him a few feet backwards as his feet shot up and came to rest, right ankle over the left, on top of the desk. He placed both hands behind his head, his fingers interlocked, and leaned comfortably back in the chair. He closed his eyes and his mind wandered off.

The journey was mostly pleasant as he floated through years past, recounting the stories that carried their own momentum: NASA projects that excited America during the space race; presidential elections that wooed even the most non-political of citizens and glued them to television sets; the Bay of Pigs fiasco; the Cuban missile Crisis; The Kennedy assassination; he lingered there for a while, feeling slightly dejected, before floating off again. He arrived in 1969 and decided to settle there.

Most of the sporting articles had been written by him. The Jets were telling the world what they were going to do and Joe 'Willie' Namath was shouting louder than most. All of New York was going mad with excitement and anticipation and the story was carrying its own momentum and steamrolled from week to week until finally it exploded with the Jets', most memorable win of the Super Bowl.

He opened his eyes slowly. Yeah, he thought, Shamka was one of those stories. It would carry itself.

The telephone on the desk beside his feet began to ring shrilly. Wainright ignored it for five rings. Irritation forced him to silence the bell.

"Okay! What is it?' he shouted into the receiver, forgetting such mundane things like etiquette and politeness.

'Paul.' It was Schuster's voice.

He quickly threw his feet off the desk and made an attempt to organize himself. 'I am sorry Miss Schuster, I thought it was internal.'

She began to laugh pleasantly over the phone. 'I am pleased to learn that even after all these years you still feel the pressure.'

'What pressure?' His voice was serious but she knew there was a smile behind it. Wainright was indeed smiling. 'They are going nuts over the article in the *Times*, just like your people are doing with the *Echo*. I think we've started something big you know.'

'That's the reason for my call', she said hurriedly. 'Didn't you say you visited a gypsy with a man called Kramer?' She paused, expecting a response which did not come. 'Steven Kramer, that's it, works for KTMZ Radio. Do you know who Kramer works for?'

'No, should I?'

'If you don't, maybe you should. Everybody around here does.' She waited again for a comment which did not come.

'Okay', he said, and waited to be surprised.

'Kramer works for a guy called Maldini, Jack Maldini', she added, as if she expected the name to shake the *Times* man from his slumber. 'Maldini is throwing a huge party on Saturday. Twenty-fifth wedding anniversary stuff, ritzy, wants me to come. I know it's short notice, but I'd like you to come with me.'

'Oh!' the *Times* man sounded surprised.

'Okay, I am asking you for a date', she said smoothly. 'What's a single girl to do?' She sounded almost apologetic.

'Wow Kim,' Wainright regretted calling her by her first name, but decided to let it go, 'it'll be my pleasure to come with you,' and he meant it. Then he added quickly, 'What triggered all of this?'

'Maldini just left my office, serious as hell but pleasant. It's got to do with my article in the *Echo*. He seems particularly interested in Shamka, extremely so. I think we are onto something.'

'What do you mean?'

'He wanted our sources for the article.'

'You make this Maldini character sound important', said Wainright.

'The man owns practically half of this city. Influential as hell, connections you wouldn't believe and an ex-con.'

'Ex-con?' Wainright could not hide his surprise.

'Yeah.' She was satisfied with the interest she had created. 'Killed his business partner many years ago, shot him and served five years for it.'

'Marvellous.'

'I thought the party might give us access to such an interesting man.'

Wainright put her on hold and called a secretary. He quickly passed his instructions for her to arrange a flight and tickets. He wanted to be with Kim Schuster by early Saturday.

'What sort of attire do I need for this party?' He was back on the phone to Schuster.

'Informal', she replied. 'Starts at two thirty. I'll pick you up from your hotel at two.' It suddenly occurred to her that she did not know where he would be staying. 'Where do I come at two?'

He put her on hold again. The secretary who had booked the flight provided the information quickly. Wainright returned to Schuster. 'The Holiday Inn on Townsend', he reported.

'Two o'clock tomorrow then, chow.' She was gone.

Chapter Twenty

Paul Wainright held the receiver in his hand for some time. He could hear the dead tone that signified her absence on the end of the line. Then, eventually, he said 'chow' and replaced the receiver.

* * *

The shiny black Mercedes Benz came to an abrupt stop in front of the complex of flats that mostly housed expatriates working for various foreign companies and the embassies. The driver rushed round to open the rear door for the tall Arab. Moments later, the intercom buzzed loudly in William Nylander's flat.

Nylander ignored the bell. He stared into the bowl of cereal and tried to decide whether he should answer the intercom. The bell rang again, this time two long blasts. Whoever it was was intent on drawing him to the door, their impatience showing through the strains of sound screaming through the flat.

'Yes', Nylander almost shouted, his thumb on the intercom button, his own impatience showing through his voice.

'William, Al', the voice came back at him. Nylander could not remember when Sheikh Al Makhtoum Walhadi had ever referred to himself as Al.

'The door is open', Nylander told the Arab as he pressed the door release. 'Al, come right up.' The Arab had never come to him unannounced. Ordinarily he would have been upset by such a surprise but on this occasion he almost looked forward to the unwelcome visit. Nylander could hear the sheikh rushing up the stairs, his footsteps pounding hard as he came. The door was already open. The Arab rushed in waving the large newspaper.

'Have you seen this?' He unfolded the paper and flicked through the pages.

Nylander looked at him calmly, unable to determine whether the Arab was angry or just excited.

'Yes', he replied. There was no surprise in his voice, no emotion. 'I received copies of the *Times* from New York earlier this morning and the *Cromwell County Echo.*' He pointed to the papers on the center table. He had already read both articles, his second time of reading them because he had digested Wainright's faxed copies at the office the night before. He had been impressed with the colour pictures of the horse. They were good, in fact excellent. The pictures reminded him of his very first encounter with the horse on the Carters' front lawn.

Al Makhtoum Walhadi took his time with Kim Schuster's article in the *Echo*. He made comparisons in his mind with the *Times* article that had brought him to Nylander's flat. Eventually, he looked up at Nylander. 'Do you really believe all of this?'

'I tried to tell you', Nylander replied.

'According to the *Times* article, the trainer believes the horse is unbeatable.'

'I told you about my gut feeling about Shamka.' Nylander was leaning against the wall, arms folded, confidence written all over his face.

'This animal looks good.' The Sheikh was examining the pictures in the *Echo* closely, 'But, you know, pictures mean nothing.'

Nylander shrugged his shoulders. 'There is only one way to find out. Besides, I don't think you would be here this early if you weren't somewhat curious about this horse.'

'I promised I would arrange a race for Shamka.' The Arab looked at Nylander quizzically. 'Could you let me know by tonight the schedule of races in Cromwell County for the next six weeks? I'll sponsor Shamka's entry in any mile distance race you choose.' Al Walhadi was going to prove his point once and for all. What did Nylander and all those newspaper people, particularly the woman, what was her name - he picked up the *Echo* and confirmed Schuster's name in his mind - what did they know about thoroughbreds? He could show them quarter horses and Arab breeds, and they wouldn't have to be very good, which would leave this so-called thoroughbred standing over a mile.

First he would test the quality of this horse in a novice race in Cromwell County. If she was lucky enough to win, and she might, he would test her a second time, using the handicapper's judgement as his guide before he would decide what to do next. He was sure that the horse would be pulverized in the space of two races and that would be that.

He made a mental note to write to Wainright and Schuster after Shamka had been defeated. It would give him great pleasure to tell them to stick to writing articles about baseball and golf and leave the business of the thoroughbred to people like himself and his Arab 'brothers' in Dubai and Abu Dhabi. He genuinely believed that in the horseracing arena there were no better horses anywhere in the world that could compare to those in Arabia.

'You can reach me at home anytime', he said with a cynical smile. 'I hope you don't mind my coming unannounced.'

'I am glad you came.' If only the Sheikh knew how glad he was. The plan was working incredibly well. Oh! How glad he was. He walked the Arab down the stairs and out of the building and shook hands with him by the shining black Mercedes.

He wondered if Wainright would be able to supply the information about the Cromwell County racing schedules. The man was resourceful, of course he could. Nylander dashed up the stairs. He had the urge to telephone Wainright but he was already expecting a call from the newspaperman so he produced a pad and concerned himself with questions he would ask him and notes about the next phase of the plan. I'll show him, he was thinking of Al Walhadi.

The telephone interrupted his thoughts. He almost pounced on it.

'I hope you've got the package, we sent it by courier.' Nylander detected a twinge of worry in the newspaperman's voice.

'Yes, excellent writeup, thanks.'

'We've been receiving calls all day and they are still coming in. This horse had better be good.' Wainright expressed the doubt that was beginning to crop up in his mind. When this whole thing started, the idea sounded good but now, well it was beginning to take flight, its wings mightier than he had envisioned.

'You sound worried Paul', Nylander noted.

'I am beginning to wonder where this thing is going. It seems to be bigger than I ever dreamt it would be.'

'Stay with me Paul, this is not the time to express doubt.'

'Okay, but you should know that powerful people are beginning to show interest. I received a call from Kim Schuster today. Apparently she had a visit from one Maldini, an ex-con, do you know him?'

'I've heard of him. Jack Maldini, one of Cromwell County's most powerful businessmen. Yes, he's been to prison but I wouldn't refer to him as an ex-con, at least not in the way that you express it.'

'Well,' Wainright still sounded cautious, 'Schuster has invited me to a party at Maldini's on Saturday. She thinks we can gain information', he sighed. 'Anyhow, I have already accepted the invitation. What do you think?'

'Great idea, Paul.' Nylander felt a shot of adrenaline through his bloodstream. 'You must go, definitely a must. You know, that Schuster is one hell of a woman and one hell of a newspaper woman at that. Of course you must go, this is a great opportunity to solidify our plan.'

'Okay.' Wainright was catching the Nylander enthusiastic bug.

'Now, listen Paul, we have sponsorship for Shamka's first race. Could you get back to me tonight with a schedule of races in Cromwell County for the next six weeks?'

'I guess so.'

'Our sponsorship is for any race over the distance of one mile, three-year-olds. Start with the novices.'

'Okay, I can arrange that.' Wainright sounded sure.

'Good man, call me as soon as you have this information.' Nylander was feeling good. 'And Paul, I am going to make you famous', he laughed.

'I am leaving for Cromwell County this evening, I'll contact you from there.'

'Fine Paul, enjoy the party, put all your expenses on my account and give my regards to Schuster. I shall await your call sometime tonight.'

By the time Wainright said goodbye, he was feeling a whole lot better. He was already looking forward to seeing Kim Schuster again. This whole thing could be fun. At fifty-two he was beginning to think of retirement but, all of a sudden, retirement seemed a long way away.

First there was a party to go to, information to gather, exciting articles to write for the paper and, you know, the woman was quite attractive. He had entered the world of Shamkamania.

* * *

Simon Carter believed in democracy. He and Maureen Carter had done their best to teach their two children about the importance of democratic practices. It was something they treasured, fundamental to a free society, a free-thinking home, in which children could express themselves and voice their opinions as much as the adults. He was therefore not surprised when he and his wife were informed of the meeting that her daughter had called.

They assembled in the living room of the Carter home not long after dinner on Thursday night. There were the four members of the Carter household and five invited guests: Jennifer 'Broxy' Singleton, Kazeem Kazi, Jill Nylander, Shamon Kazi and Doctor Ben Swinton. It was made clear from the beginning of the meeting that the five guests would be accorded equal voting rights.

Katherine Carter chaired the specially convened meeting.

'We, the children, are here to seek the advice of the adults gathered in this room', she began. 'After a full and complete discussion of the subject matter, we shall take a vote. Our actions thereafter will depend upon the vote that is cast, and the will of the majority will be respected and acted upon accordingly.'

Broxy Singleton looked across the room at Maureen Carter and smiled. She had been in many meetings before, but never with children. She had no children of her own but she felt a certain sense of pride about what was happening in the Carter front room.

'It's about my horse.' Katherine paused. 'Shamka.'

She flicked open her notepad and slowly and methodically took them through the previous meetings which had involved only the children. With complete confidence, she briefed them all, taking them through the children's concerns about the divided city within which they all lived. Her briefing encapsulated the issue of drugs that, as she put it, led to some children being deprived of their right to a decent, normal and a happy childhood. Two children had died, shot by adults over drugs. She turned to her father, her eyes moist with tears and with powerful questions.

'How would you have felt if John or I had been shot over drugs?' She turned her attention to the other adults. 'Do the children over there, the east side of this city, have the same opportunities as we do? Could some of them be hungry tonight? Don't concern yourselves with the adults, because they can make decisions for themselves. Our concern is for the children. Their health, their safety, their well-being.' The tears were now flowing freely from her eyes.

No one said a word; no one dared.

'Can you imagine the fear we would have felt if that motorcycle gang had chosen to ride through this sector of the city instead of the east side? Especially if you are a child?'

'Last week, three women were raped in the east side.' She looked at Broxy and then at her mother. 'Can you imagine how horrible it must be for any woman or girl over there when they decide to step out of their homes?'

Broxy coughed and dabbed her eyes gently. Simon Carter wrapped his arms around Maureen Carter who was doing her best to choke off the sobs.

The air was heavy, the silence unbearable, Katherine had made her point. Somebody had to come to their rescue. It was Ben Swinton who volunteered.

'Tell us your plan Katherine', said Doctor Swinton softly.

'We wish to race Shamka to raise money to help the children of the east side.'

'What a novel idea', said Broxy.

'How do we go about it? We need your help.'

They looked at one another and then Simon Carter spoke. 'Shamon.' It was an invitation to the gypsy horseman to give advice.

The meeting came to life. Shamon Kazi talked them through the procedures of entering a horse for racing. There were things in his mind he wanted to discuss privately with Simon Carter as a result of the meeting they had had with Jack Maldini, but for now he restricted his information to the basic facts:

Katherine Carter was, of course, the official owner of the horse. It was up to her to decide whether she wished to take partnerships on board. If she chose to do so, agreements and financial arrangements would have to be entered into. She had the right, as the principal owner, to select her trainer. Then came the question of the jockey. That would be decided between the owner and the trainer. For the time being, Katherine would have to spell out exactly what the children had in mind. Shamon Kazi looked at Simon Carter.

'How much money do you wish to raise?' Simon Carter's attention was on his daughter but the question was for all the children. 'And assuming you can raise it, what exactly do you plan to do with it?'

The children had already discussed what they wished to do with the money. Their problem was trying to determine how much it would cost, so Katherine made that clear. That, in fact, was the most important reason for having come to seek the advice of the adults.

'All right, tell us what you'd like to do with the money', said Simon.

'Stop people from taking drugs and stop crime', John Carter quickly responded with his stock answer, his universal solution to all of the east side community's problems. Katherine Carter gave him a look, which spoke louder than anything she could have said. Maureen Carter just giggled and self-consciously covered her mouth with her right hand.

'Go on Katherine, tell us', said Swinton.

'Okay,' Katherine Carter began, 'but please don't laugh because these are serious issues.' The adults nodded their heads while the children fidgeted momentarily, as if to harness spiritual support for their spokesperson.

'Here is our list.' Katherine flipped through the pad and began to read.

'First, we want two new schools to be built in the east side. Second, the construction of a drug rehabilitation center.' She looked up quickly, as if to ensure she had their full attention, and returned to her list. 'An adult educational facility, a public park to entice the children off the streets, two well-equipped clinics to take the strain off the only existing hospital over there.' It sounded as if the east side was on the other side of the world. 'Finally, several small day-care centers to enable mothers with young children who wish to work to do so.' She looked up from her pad. 'That's it, these are the things the four of us have agreed to do for the children of the east side.'

'We'll need millions of dollars', said Broxy. She had been impressed and touched by the children's concerns for their counterparts on the other side of the city. Already, she was juggling with the idea of contacting Ocean Pacific for a small contribution.

'This is a massive project, Katherine.' Simon Carter was impressed but unsure of how such a big project could be funded. 'How do we begin?'

'The drug rehabilitation center first', Katherine replied immediately. 'Whatever money comes in will go to start that and then the others will follow.'

'It can be done.' Shamon Kazi sounded absolutely sure of himself. 'I would like to talk to the two doctors outside, then we will come back and share the ideas', he said as he motioned Carter and Swinton to join him in the back yard.

The three men paced quietly to the far side of the back yard and came to a halt at about the point where Maureen Carter had witnessed Kazeem Kazi going through his prayer motions the day after the heavy downpour.

'The answer is Maldini', Shamon Kazi said all of a sudden.

'You can't be serious!' shouted Swinton.

'Doctor Swinton, I am very serious', the gypsy replied without hesitation.

'Why?' asked Simon Carter.

'Because I see danger', replied the gypsy. He was thinking of Maldini's veiled threats. There was no doubt that Jack Maldini was obsessed with the horse and that he would do whatever it took to own her, preferably to own her outright or, alternatively, to become a major shareholding partner. Shamon Kazi knew that if Maldini had to resort to killing to own the horse, he would. The people in most danger were Katherine Carter and John Carter, Maureen Carter and finally Simon Carter. Kazi knew that if Maldini were excluded from being a part of Shamka he would not hesitate to kidnap Katherine or John Carter for starters and then apply the necessary emotional pressure until he got his way, or some sort of tragedy ensued. On the other hand, they could invite him with open arms to become a partner. Kazi could see some excellent qualities in Maldini despite his enormous ability to resort to violence when it suited his purpose. He took his time to explain all of these things to the doctors.

'I see your point', Carter said, sighing heavily.

'I agree.' Swinton had been reviewing in his mind the meeting they had had with Jack Maldini. It would be better to put Maldini's obsession to good use rather than allow him to wreak havoc. The three men agreed to persuade Katherine Carter to bring Jack Maldini in as a partner. Ben Swinton was given the job of doing the persuading.

Back in the house, Maureen Carter passed around cups of coffee for the adults and soft drinks for the children. When they settled down again Ben Swinton presented his arguments.

Swinton began by saying that he had a friend who could help them to achieve their aims. The friend was obsessed with good horses; he was also influential and rich. It was likely he would be thrilled to join up with Katherine to support Shamka in her quest to prove her qualities and fulfil their aims. Ben Swinton would be happy to approach the friend if Katherine did not mind having a partner.

'May I suggest that the four children take some time to consider this proposal before we finally take our vote', Swinton concluded.

They were back inside ten minutes. Katherine spoke for them.

'We have discussed the matter thoroughly amongst ourselves and we are now happy to put it to the vote.'

There were two issues to consider. First, should Shamka be raced to raise money for the purposes of assisting the children of the east side? All nine people in the room voted by a show of hands that resulted in a nine-nil vote in favor of racing. The second issue was that of partnership. It was Katherine Carter's decision and hers alone to make.

'Yes', she responded positively and settled the matter once and for all.

Ben Swinton would approach his friend and preparations would be made to register the horse. The jockey issue had already been settled in Shamon Kazi's mind, so all that remained was to select a race for Shamka.

CHAPTER TWENTY-ONE

On Friday morning, Jack Maldini received an envelope by courier from Doctor Ben Swinton. Maldini signed for the envelope that contained exactly seventy thousand dollars in one thousand dollar bills and signed the separate receipt that showed the contents of the envelope. He shook his head, threw the envelope into a small safe behind his desk and spun the knob to lock it.

Not long after he had received the money, the telephone call came. It was Ben Swinton. The doctor informed Maldini that Katherine Carter had considered his offer and had agreed in principle to accept his proposal of partnership in the ownership of Shamka. Details of the agreement were being drawn up and it was hoped the terms would be satisfactory for all.

Jack Maldini rubbed his hands together and picked up the receiver to inform Lazlo, Templeton and Watson. Their names would not appear on any paperwork involving the partnership agreement, but, as always, they would be fully involved by injecting finances as required by their front man Maldini. He sat behind his desk and wondered when he might see the horse. Sunday would be good, he thought, the day after the anniversary celebrations. The thought of the party on Saturday gave Maldini an idea. He reached into the drawer of his desk for the dossier on Simon Carter and Ben Swinton and recorded the telephone numbers onto a pad on the desk. He replaced the dossier in the drawer and pulled out the newspaper clippings on Shamka. The articles in the *Times* and the *Echo* impressed Maldini even more now than when he had first read them. After staring at the pictures of the horse for some time, he placed the pictures on the newspapers and, with the recorded telephone numbers on top, he placed them in a thin, plastic file and left the file in the center of the desk.

He would telephone Swinton and Carter later in the evening.

* * *

Broxy Singleton was happy that her husband would be arriving on this Friday evening. She would be accompanying Maureen Carter to the airport later to collect him. What Robert Singleton did not know was that there would be work for him to do as soon as he arrived at the Carters'. Broxy had assured everybody at last night's meeting, after the vote had been taken, that Robert would be happy to draw up the partnership agreement and that he would be most honored to represent Katherine as her appointed legal adviser.

Since last night's meeting with the children, Broxy Singleton had toyed with the idea of doing something to assist their noble cause. She had tossed and turned all through the night, wondering why the adults of this world could not seem to see things as children did. She had always loved children and, although she had had intentions of having one or two of her own, she had given up the idea at the age of twenty-nine and settled for a career. When she turned forty-one, Robert Singleton suddenly appeared in her life. She married him a year later, toyed with the idea of bearing him a child, and eventually decided against it after consulting her doctor.

It was the pain and regret of her inability to have children of her own and her admiration for the children that kept her awake all night. She had finally managed to sleep for about two hours before dawn broke. Through her sleeplessness, she had made up her mind to do what she could to help the children. She decided to make a phone call to test the waters.

At two thirty Friday afternoon, Broxy Singleton telephoned the Ocean Pacific head office in San Francisco. It was her first opportunity since returning from Europe to speak directly to the Chairman of the company, Roy Masterson. Broxy thanked the Chairman for his congratulatory telephone call that she had received on her answering machine. Masterson hoped to see her in San Francisco after her holidays for the official celebrations that were being planned in honour of the all-female transatlantic flight.

Broxy knew that on such public occasions, the company always announced its contributions to selected charitable institutions. This was a useful public relations exercise that helped to boost the company's image. She hoped Masterson would allow her the opportunity to add a small request to the charitable list when they met in San Francisco. She would supply the details later, and no, the request was not going to make a big dent in the company's resources. The two exchanged general pleasantries before the deep tones of Masterson once again thanked her and wished her well.

When Jennifer Singleton replaced the receiver, she felt sure that she would be able to play a small part to support the children's cause. She was looking forward to Robert's arrival and after that to see the horse that everybody seemed to be talking about. Hopefully, that could be done tomorrow.

* * *

An hour after Robert Singleton was collected from the airport by Maureen Carter and Broxy, Paul Wainright disembarked the United Airlines Boeing 737-200 from New York's La Guardia airport. Wainright was in a hurry. He hailed a taxi and headed directly for the Holiday Inn on Townsend Avenue.

The briefcase on the back seat next to him contained a complete list of all of Cromwell County horseraces for the next eight weeks. Nylander had only asked for the next six weeks' races but Wainright had obtained an extra two weeks' racing schedules just for good measure. He was eager to study the schedules before communicating with Nylander. He sat back in the cab and thought of the cold glass of beer he hoped to have in the bar of the Holiday Inn. That would be after his communication with Saudi Arabia.

Wainight smiled cheerfully at the pretty girl at the front desk.

'Reservation for Paul Wainright, *New York Times*', he said to the girl, who was smiling pleasantly back at him. Almost instantaneously, the girl produced Wainright's reservation, pushed a few keys on the computer keypad and handed him the programmed disc that would give him access to room 674.

'Will you need help with your bags, sir?' the front-desk girl enquired, still smiling.

'This is all I've got', replied Wainright as he tapped the small holdall in his left hand with the black briefcase in his right hand.

'Sixth floor, turn right when you exit the elevator.' It was as if the smile had been pasted on her face. 'And enjoy your stay with us.'

'Thanks', Wainright replied mechanically and headed for the elevator.

'Oh! Mr Wainright,' the girl at the desk shouted after him, 'there's an envelope here for you, sir.' She passed the small white envelope to a bellboy who seemed to materialize out of thin air. The man handed the envelope to Wainright just as the elevator opened on the ground floor.

'Thank you.' Wainright took the envelope and disappeared into the elevator just before the doors eased shut. He was wondering where the envelope had come from and pressed the button for the sixth floor.

He entered the room, tossed both the holdall and the briefcase onto the bed and tore the small envelope open.

'Welcome to excitement. I hope you had a wonderful flight. See you at two tomorrow, Kim.'

Wainright smiled at the note, then placed it back in the envelope before tucking it into the inside pocket of his jacket. He turned his attention to the briefcase, removed the list of scheduled race meetings and studied each sheet with some care. He made an asterisk beside several races as he read through the list twice, and picked up the phone beside the bed.

Following his long telephone communication with William Nylander, Wainright showered, changed, and went in search of the bar. He entered the dimly lit bar and was surprised to find it much less crowded than he had anticipated. He stood just inside the entrance to the bar, allowed his eyes to adjust to the dim interior, and took in the melodious voice of Frank Sinatra doing it his way.

The attractive, slim waitress approached him, her short, dark hair covered with a colourful scarf, the colours of which were difficult to discern in the soft blue lights.

'What'll it be, sir?' she asked in a pleasant voice with a slight southern drawl.

'Miller', he found himself saying without thinking.

'Don't you think you'd be more comfortable sitting down?' She flashed a set of beautifully arranged teeth and, pointing at a vacant stool at the bar, led the way.

'You are not from around here', she said as she poured the bottle of beer into the tall, slim glass. It was a statement rather than a question.

'Just arrived from New York', Wainright replied. Then he spontaneously added, 'I've been invited to a party and I am looking forward to tomorrow.' He sipped the beer.

'All the way from the Big Apple to Cromwell County for a party,' she winked at him. 'You must be rich or they must be important.'

'They must be important', Wainright repeated her, raising his eyebrows.

'Lucky you.' She picked up her tray and surveyed the room. Seeing that her services were not needed by any of the few people in the bar, she placed the tray back on the bar and folded her arms. 'So, who is the important host?' she asked.

'Jack Maldini', Wainright replied, studying her face.

'My, my.' She placed her hand on her chest, somewhat flat-chested for such an attractive girl, he noticed all of a sudden. 'You are going to Jack Maldini's party tomorrow?' she asked, her eyes wide open, the southern drawl deepening.

'Uhuh.' Wainright calmly sipped his beer.

'Mister, you must be rich!' she concluded.

'Frankly, I've never met the man', he smiled at her. 'I bet you know more about my host than I do.' He hoped she would tell him something new. Like a good newspaperman, he would do most of the listening.

After two hours, five tall glasses of Miller Highlife, several spins of Frank Sinatra, Nat King Cole, Lou Rawls and all he could learn from the waitress about Jack Maldini, Paul Wainright said goodnight to Mandy Sears and shuffled his way out of the bar to the tune of Dean Martin's *You are nobody till somebody loves you*.

It was two thirty when his head hit the pillow.

* * *

It was Vivian Maldini's lucky day. The sun shone brightly and hot, not a whisper of cloud in the skies. She looked out of her bedroom window down into the huge garden and surveyed the three jolly green giants in the back yard. It looked as if the anniversary party had been given the good Lord's blessing. She counted her rosary and expressed her gratitude to God.

The verbal invitation from Jack Maldini to Ben Swinton and Simon Carter had been accepted by both men; more out of curiosity and as a result of the powers of Maldini's persuasive skills, than a real desire to be in the man's company. Simon Carter was unwilling to attend the party with Maureen because he did not wish his family to be anywhere near Maldini whom he did not trust. Simon and Ben Swinton therefore decided to attend the party together.

Despite having slept late, Paul Wainright was awake by eight in the morning. He lay in bed and recounted his conversation with Mandy Sears whom he had found pleasant and attractive. The woman had told him more about Jack Maldini than most people knew, her source of knowledge stemming from the days when she worked as a croupier in the Hood Acre. She had resigned her position at the Hood Acre when her sleazy boss began to make her life miserable by forcing his attentions on her on a regular basis. She liked and respected Jack Maldini because she had always known the man to be fair, respectful of women and kind-hearted.

Wainright could remember asking her about Maldini's past, the murder of his business partner and his incarceration. She had answered without blinking.

'If I were your wife and you found me in bed with your most trusted friend, would you shake his hand and congratulate him?' She had looked almost angry as she answered the question, 'Damn it, you would probably kill us both and that would make you a double murderer, but would you be a criminal?' She had concluded with her eyes blazing, before she resorted to her gentle southern ways with, 'Shucks, that was a crime of passion, ain't nothing wrong with Jack, the man is good.'

Schuster had told him over the phone that the man was an ex-con. Mandy Sears believed Maldini was good, he would have to find out for himself. Wainright looked forward to two thirty.

At exactly two o'clock, Kim Schuster pulled up in front of the Holiday Inn in a white Buick Wildcat convertible with red interior. Wainright had been waiting for her in the foyer.

'Let's go to a party', she said as he settled down in the seat next to her. Kim Schuster was not just going to a party, she was going to make a splash. She looked stunning in the light blue, cropped, stretch trousers, trimmed with velvet ribbons at the hem, topped with a three-quarter sleeve stretch cardigan, trimmed with beaded ribbon and velvet trim. She wore a pair of large, pale blue sunglasses. Her short, golden blonde hair glistened in the afternoon sun. To put it simply, Kim Schuster looked incredibly beautiful.

Paul Wainright sat next to her, unable to take his eyes of the woman who had invited him, and wondered why someone so beautiful chose to live without a partner. He wished he was considerably younger than his fifty-two years,

'Nylander tells me you are not sure about Shamka', she said.

'I wouldn't put it that way exactly.' Wainright shifted his attention to the surrounding scenery. 'I merely wondered if Shamka would turn out to be the wonder-horse that we are making her out to be.'

'What do we have to lose?' she said, seemingly without a care in the world. 'If Shamka turns out to be extraordinary we will take the credit for having recognized her qualities and brought her to the attention of the racing world. On the other hand, if she turns out to be a failure, we can always blame our mysterious sources for having fed us incorrect information. Either way, we would have succeeded in bringing Shamka to the public's attention.'

'I am interested in what you think, so you can tell me. What do you think of Shamka?' Wainright asked.

'Paul, I know a little about horses and I grant I don't have enough information to be conclusive, but my gut feeling is that Shamka is very, very special.'

'We'll know in a few weeks, and I hope you are right about her.'

She turned into the drive of the Maldini mansion and pulled up in front of the young parking attendant in the yellow jacket. They both stepped out of the car and Schuster handed the keys to the young man in yellow who in return gave her ticket number 139. When the car was gone, they were taken in tow by a freckle-face-sixteen-year-old girl whose job it was to usher them to their seats under one of the jolly green giants.

'This is the place to be', Schuster whispered and slid her left arm through the right arm of Wainright.

Vivian Maldini had ensured that none of those present would forget this twenty-fifth wedding anniversary party.

At exactly two thirty, the band struck up, the Master of Ceremonies stepped up to the microphone and, as the music quietened down, declared the party officially open.

'Ladies and gentlemen, Vivian and Jack Maldini have invited you here to help them celebrate their anniversary. The idea is to have fun and enjoy yourselves.'

He cleared his throat. 'If there is anything you need, but you can't find, please don't hesitate to attract the attention of one of those men and women in the special green jackets that you see around you. If they can't accommodate you, then please see me because the buck stops here. Enjoy a most wonderful afternoon.'

The band immediately struck up again.

Barbara Lazlo, Elizabeth Templeton and Vivian Maldini had managed to do it. They had provided the floral arrangements, the colourful tablecloths, the gleaming china, the crystal cut glasses and the shining silver cutlery to which mother nature had added a touch of golden sun. Everything gleamed, not to mention the faces.

Unlike the muscle-bound workmen who had erected the marquees on Thursday afternoon, most of the people wandering in the Maldini Wonderland were the rich, the powerful and the influential people of Cromwell County. Sprinkled amongst them, however, were those not so rich, powerful or influential whom Jack Maldini or Vivian had invited for personal reasons.

In the second group were Mickey Steiner, who had accompanied the famous Rosalynn Brando; Doctor Ben Swinton and Simon Carter; Kim Schuster and Paul Wainright; and Doctor Braxton Walker who had been invited along by Mayor Culhane.

The catering company had fulfilled Vivian Maldini's request by preparing a variety of menus - ten in all, spanning from exotic Mediterranean dishes to traditional English and American dishes. Those who were vegetarians were more than adequately catered for with special menus which read like names from a botanist's most exotic garden but tweaked with selected French accents in the right places.

Judge James C Colman had spread himself comfortably at the mayor's table, and was busily studying the menu which boasted of *Roast Goose with Honey and Pecan Nut Glaze*, he had already consumed two glasses of Gordon's special dry London Gin with a splash of tonic and had adjusted that wobbly stomach of his in preparation for the afternoon's intake of exotic food and drink.

Ben Swinton's eyes floated over the Judge's table and wandered along until he finally made contact with Mickey Steiner who was in conversation with Rosalynn Brando. He nudged Simon Carter. 'Do you recognize him?' Swinton said, and, without pointing, allowed Simon Carter to follow his gaze.

'That's one of the two men who carried us to Maldini yesterday. Come to think of it he is also one of the two who threatened me at the hospital. He came along with the one with the scar,' said Carter.

'Do you recognize the woman?' asked Ben Swinton.

'That's Rosalynn Brando. I remember reading about her in a fashion magazine that Maureen showed me some time ago. From what I hear, the women of this country swear by her when it comes to fashion.'

'And in the company of that man?'

'Stranger things have happened', said Simon Carter.

A mixture of anger and curiosity gripped Ben Swinton. The band began to play that song which was now at the top of the charts - *'Everybody wants to go to heaven but nobody wants to die'* - Swinton decided to satisfy his curiosity.

He stood up, excused himself from those at his table and crossed over to where Mickey Steiner and Rosalynn Brando seemed to be thoroughly enjoying the afternoon.

'May I have this dance?' Swinton stretched his hand towards Rosalynn Brando who was taken by surprise by the tall, handsome stranger. She turned to Mickey Steiner, her eyes questioning. When Steiner nodded his head gently, Rosalynn got up and followed Ben Swinton onto the dancing area.

'You seem to be enjoying yourself. I am Ben Swinton.'

'Rosalynn', she said with a smile as she danced.

Mickey Steiner felt a twinge of jealousy for the first time as he watched Rosalynn dancing quite comfortably with the tall, handsome doctor.

Vivian Maldini watched the dancing couple and appreciated the fact that Rosalynn Brando had accepted her invitation. She knew that the presence of Rosalynn at her party was enough to elevate her in social stature within Cromwell County. The doors to almost all of the society and female social clubs would now be open to her. It had taken her a long time to rebuild respectability for the Maldini name. These were Jack Maldini's home, Jack Maldini's party and Jack Maldini's guests. The mayor was here with several other politicians, Judge James Colman seemed happy enough, and the most respected fashion personality in the whole of the USA was dancing in her back yard. Vivian Maldini had satisfied her aims in her own quiet way.

Ben Swinton escorted Rosalynn Brando back to her table and

thanked her for the dance. The anger in him had waned by the time Rosalynn introduced him to Mickey Steiner. The two men shook hands without displaying a trace of familiarity. The twinge of jealousy which Mickey Steiner had felt when he watched the doctor and Rosalynn on the dance floor had not deserted him. Steiner knew then, that he was truly in love with Rosalynn Brando.

The party had livened up considerably. The initial quiet conversations at the round tables were now more lively and giggles and laughter could be heard more often. Paul Wainright watched the freckle-faced girl as she marched dutifully towards the table. 'Miss Schuster', she said when she arrived and held out the tray on which was a small pink envelope. Kim Schuster took the envelope, nodded her thanks to the girl and opened it feverishly. She read the note quickly.

'Glad you could come. Please join me with Wainright. The girl will direct you.' She slid the note to Wainright, excused herself from the others at the table and allowed herself to be guided by the girl with Paul Wainright in tow.

They found Jack Maldini standing in the middle of his large study, surrounded by a wall of well-known authors all beautifully bound in expensive leather.

'Thank you Virginia', Maldini said to the girl and directed Kim Schuster and Wainright towards the comfortable leather sofa. He waited for the girl to shut the door, smiled at the two journalists and sat on the edge of his desk.

'Stunning, absolutely stunning,' Maldini said to Kim Schuster, 'a rare combination of beauty and brains, how lucky you are Miss Schuster.'

She smiled at him uneasily, 'You have a beautiful home.'

'I must say I've been lucky too, thank you for the compliment.' He turned to Wainright. 'I've read your article in the *Times*, Mr Wainright and I am very impressed. If Shamka's pedigree points in the direction of Sir Galahad III or the great Wajima as your article pointed out, then I agree with you that we have a thoroughbred ready to conquer the world.'

They turned their attention to the door when the knock came. The waiter entered, silver tray gleaming with three champagne glasses and a large bottle of champagne. He moved effortlessly as he filled the three glasses and handed the first glass to Kim Schuster before serving

Wainright and finally Maldini. In an instant, he was gone, the door shutting soundlessly behind him.

'As you know, this is my twenty-fifth wedding anniversary.' Maldini raised his glass, the other two raised their glasses and together they drank. 'I have been lucky enough to achieve just about everything I've wanted to achieve. Some have said I should run for political office but you know, it doesn't appeal to me.' He paused. 'My interest is in horses and I've waited patiently for the dream to come true. With Shamka, I believe I can finally fulfil that dream.'

'I didn't know you owned Shamka', Wainright said with some surprise.

'I don't,' Maldini replied, 'at least not wholly. You see I've just become a part-owner. It is my intention to promote Shamka, to ensure that Cromwell County can boast of a world-class thoroughbred and, of course, to make money in the process. That's not a bad thing, is it?'

Kim Schuster looked at Maldini. She had a question of her own. 'Mr Maldini, you said that you have achieved just about everything you wanted to achieve, certainly money is no longer a problem.'

Jack Maldini looked at the journalist as if she were some lost soul in an untamed jungle. For him everything had a price and most things were priced in monetary terms. What one did with money after it had been acquired was what mattered. It allowed for choices, for freedoms and most importantly for power. The power for one to buy or manipulate as one wished. Which brought him back to freedom. The freedom for one to do as one liked, more or less.

'Money is always a problem, Miss Schuster.' The woman was going to learn about the Maldini logic. 'Ask a man who has never had money and he'll tell you the problem is not having any but wanting some.' Maldini paused and sipped his champagne. 'Then ask a man who has always had money and he'll tell you the problem is making sure that he keeps what he has got. Poor people do not often worry about writing wills, neither do they worry about mitigating against inheritance taxes. It is the rich who think and worry more about the taxman, so you see, money is always a problem, Miss Schuster.'

You do have a point', said Wainright.

'Of course I do, and I'll tell you something else, that horse is going to put money in most pockets in Cromwell County. That brings me to why I invited you here. I think you can play a very constructive part in this venture.'

'Oh.' Wainright turned to Schuster who simply spread her hands, palms upward, in an expression of don't look at me, I am as lost as you are.

'You've already done most of the good work with your articles in both the *Echo* and the *Times*. The most influential people in this city, this county, are here enjoying themselves. I'd like to introduce the two of you to them. Miss Schuster is well known to most of them and I am sure they have heard of you, Wainright, but I think a formal recognition of the two reporters in the Shamka story here today will not be bad for yourselves and for me.'

'Obviously you have your own reasons for wanting to do this', said Schuster.

'To keep the story alive in their minds, Miss Schuster, and to pave the way for a great racing future in Cromwell County. They will, of course, be informed to look forward to further articles in your great newspapers as the Shamka story unfolds.' Jack Maldimi was smiling broadly. 'There will of course be rewards for you both.' Kim Schuster seized her chance. 'Mr Maldini, the Shamka story will be more interesting if we wove you into it.' She produced the miniature tape recorder from her handbag and, without asking his permission, turned it on and placed it on the table next to Jack Maldini. 'Is it true that you served five years in prison for the murder of your business partner?' Jack Maldini looked at the device and back at the two journalists. He could hear laughter from the back yard when he cleared his throat and began to tell his story. He felt it was necessary to do so.

* * *

In a very subtle way, Vivian Maldini had managed to introduce Rosalynn Brando personally to most of the influential people at the party, making sure her focus was on the wives rather than their famous husbands. The mayor's wife had fussed and fussed but finally they had completed the circuit and Rosalynn was back in her chair beside Mickey Steiner.

'You were jealous', she said all of a sudden.

'What!'

'I could see jealousy all over your face when I danced with Mr

Swinton.'

'Doctor Swinton', Steiner corrected. The other occupants of their table were all on the dance floor so they could talk freely.

'He never said he was a doctor or I might have been a little more aggressive in my approach', she teased. 'Do you know him?'

'Not really, but I know of him', Steiner replied.

'He is handsome and from what you say, also brainy, but remember always that it is you I am in love with', she said and kissed him deeply and unashamedly.

'I am sorry', Mickey Steiner said, his jealousy having dissipated.

'Don't be, it's natural', she smiled at him.

'I love you', he whispered to her and squeezed her hand gently.

* * *

The tape recorder had run for exactly forty-three minutes when Jack Maldini finally reached out and pressed the stop button. Most people had heard a version of the story in some form but in most cases they had heard it from second-hand sources. In the quiet study, Jack Maldini had set the record straight and it was up to the reporters to write his story as accurately as he had told them.

He pulled the drawer to his study desk open and removed the envelope which had been delivered to him earlier that afternoon by Ben Swinton. He had shut the tape off because he did not want the information he was going to give to the reporters to be recorded on tape.

'This document was delivered to me this afternoon. It clearly states the terms upon which my proposal for partnership with Shamka's present owner will be accepted.' He pulled several sheets from the large brown envelope, 'By the way, did you know Shamka's current owner is only sixteen years old?'

The two reporters glared at each other, obviously surprised.

'Here are the terms', Maldini said and began to read from the legal document which had been drawn up by Robert Singleton. 'First, the entire proceeds from Shamka's first five races and sixty per cent of all proceeds from subsequent races will be donated to the east side Children's Foundation Fund, Gulver City, Cromwell County; said proceeds to be expressly earmarked for the development of the various projects as stated in appendix "A" of this document and said projects to be administered by the trustees of the fund.' He looked up at the two in the sofa who seemed stunned.

'Second, all initial expenses which will be incurred by the partnership in respect of Shamka's upkeep, racing expenses, travel and veterinary care up to the first $50,000 will be borne by the junior member of the partnership, namely Jack Sebastino Maldini.'

'This is my favorite bit', he said and read on: 'Under no circumstance must Shamka's welfare be compromised for money or any material gain and as a safeguard to this measure, the senior partner in this partnership, namely Katherine Anna Carter, reserves the right to nullify this agreement provided the sum of $1,000 is paid in full to the junior partner, namely, Jack Sabastino Maldini.'

Kim Schuster was flabbergasted. 'And you are accepting such an agreement?'

'I am.' Maldini actually looked happy.

'Why?' asked Wainright, 'your partner seems to hold all the cards.'

'I am looking forward to meeting my partner and our horse tomorrow, I am sure you'll be welcome to join us.'

The two reporters accepted the invitation.

* * *

The party was in full blaze by the time the three returned to the back yard. Judge James Colman was the happiest man alive this afternoon. He had managed to sample just about all the non-vegetarian dishes and washed them down with gin and several glasses of champagne. Despite the amount of alcohol in his bloodstream he showed no sign of drunkenness and laughed heartily as the jokes came thick and fast from the mayor and the others around the table.

The Master of Ceremonies announced him.

When Jack Maldini climbed onto the raised platform and took the microphone they were all eager to hear what he had to say.

'Ladies and gentlemen, honorable mayor, Vivian and I thank you for sparing the time to share this afternoon with us. Our anniversary party wouldn't have been a success without you and for that we thank you. I'll take this opportunity to confirm some rumours that have circulated throughout the city for the past few days. You've all read the papers

and by now we are all aware of the existence of a fantastic thoroughbred by the name of Shamka. In a moment I'd like to introduce to you
the two intrepid reporters who have risked their reputations to tell us
how great this horse is. Now, they could be right or they could be
wrong; either way they have been brave enough to inform us.'

'I am pleased to announce publicly that I have put my faith in the
articles written by these two reporters and, for that reason, I have
become a part-owner in Shamka, the horse that I am sure in time we
shall all refer to as the Great Shamka. I regret that my partner is not
here with us at the moment, however I am sure there'll be an opportunity for my partner and I to face the press together. Ladies and
gentlemen, Miss Kim Schuster of the *Cromwell County Echo* and Mr Paul
Wainright of the *New York Times*.' He waved the two to join him on the
podium as the guests applauded loudly. Maldini handed the microphone to Kim Schuster and walked off to rejoin his wife.

'Thank you Jack.' Kim had been told by Maldini to call him by his
first name. 'Ladies and gentlemen, Mr Mayor, it's been a pleasure to
spend this afternoon in your company. Like most reporters, Paul and
I have our ears to the ground and our eyes wide open, but today we
both agree that we have had an education of sorts. It is our intention
to bring you some interesting stories about our host and about this
horse that we feel sure, as Jack does, will be a sensation in the coming
months and years. Naturally, if Shamka is to be a success there'll be
others involved in her preparation towards that success, so you can
expect in-depth information about her trainer, her owner (now Jack's
partner) and as much information as possible about her preparation.'
She had their full attention so she decided to lower the boom.

'I'd like to share two important secrets with you.' She looked first at
Wainright, who winked, and then she sought out Jack Maldini with her
eyes. Maldini nodded. 'The mayor has promised that the city will
match any charitable contribution that Jack Maldini and his partner -
whose name I am afraid we have to withhold for a little while longer -
make towards the improvement of the east side of this wonderful city.'
She waited patiently for the loud applause to die down and continued,
'Our sources have revealed that top racing enthusiasts in Saudi Arabia
have their eye on Shamka. While we cannot give you names at the
moment, we believe that international interest and curiosity in Shamka
is already gaining ground because of the recent articles published in

the *Echo* and the *New York Times*.'

Paul Wainright stepped forward at this point. He took the microphone from Kim Schuster and put his arm around her shoulder. 'Ladies and gentlemen, Mr Mayor, honorable guests, I am pleased to inform you that credit for the discovery of this fantastic horse belongs to this knowledgeable woman, the superb sports editor of the *Cromwell County Echo*.' He bowed to Kim Schuster and led the applause that rang through the back yard for a very long time. 'The interest in Shamka in New York and New Jersey has been overwhelming since the New York Times published its article on this magnificent horse. It is our hope, therefore, that Shamka will live up to its billing when she gets her chance to take on some of the best milers in Cromwell County in a few weeks' time. We ask you for your support and ask you to join us in toasting our hosts. I believe Mr Maldini also has a surprise for us.'

'Ladies and gentlemen, honorable guests, our hosts.' Wainright finished, replaced the microphone in the stand and watched Mr and Mrs Maldini as they approached the podium in the company of a confident, pretty teenager in a light blue, sleeveless dress with a matching cardigan draped over her left arm. Her long auburn hair flowed freely in the light evening breeze as she walked confidently between Jack Maldini and his wife. Together they climbed onto the podium.

The band was playing again, a soft melodious tune from the early thirties.

Simon Carter watched his daughter on the podium and wondered how Jack Maldini had managed to entice Katherine Carter away from Maureen, or had she been kidnapped?

'She is safe,' Ben Swinton seemed to have read Simon's mind. 'As long as she is here with us, no harm can come to her', he said to Simon reassuringly.

'How did he do it?' asked Simon, not really expecting an answer.

The Master of Ceremonies began to speak as the music died down. He turned to face the Maldinis and Katherine, a glass of champagne in his right hand, microphone in his left hand and close to his mouth. 'Ladies and gentlemen, honorable guests, a toast', he said and raised his glass high in the air. The others joined in, with the exception of Ben Swinton and Simon Carter who stood with their arms folded across their chests.

CHAPTER TWENTY-TWO

Friday evening had been special, one of the most special days in Juliana Kazi's life. She could remember the joy she had felt on her wedding day and also on the day she had had her son. Those were special days. But Friday evening brought a peaceful inner feeling of contentment she had not experienced in a long time.

At four o'clock Friday evening, she was wheeled out of the hospital by a junior nurse surrounded by four other nurses who carried several bouquets of assorted flowers.

Outside the main gates of the hospital sat the gleaming black limousine, while the chauffeur, cap under his left arm, opened the door and assisted her into the back seat. She was joined by her husband, Kazeem Kazi and John Carter, who had come to represent the Carter family. The chauffeur arranged the assorted flowers neatly in the trunk of the long, sleek vehicle and slowly wheeled out of the hospital compound while the nurses waved and wished her well.

Juliana could not hold back the tears as the flood of emotion overcame her. She placed her head on the shoulder of Shamon Kazi and, through clouded eyes, she watched the two boys in joyful conversation as the limousine floated along comfortably towards the farm.

'How did you manage this?' Juliana finally asked her husband when she found her voice.

'Jack Maldini sent it', he said without explanation.

'Where are we going?' she asked, as flashes of her encounter with the branch in the trailer on the fateful Thursday night crisscrossed her mind.

'Home,' Shamon Kazi smiled at her, 'back to the farm.'

She had no idea what she was going back to but she had complete belief in the man she had married all those years ago, so she eased herself into the soft leather seats of the limousine and let herself be taken along.

Juliana Kazi felt the gentle taps of her son on her knee. Her eyelids fluttered as they struggled against her tiredness and finally opened to let in light. She rubbed her eyes like a child who had been given her first experience in a colourful amusement park and then opened her eyes wide to take in the beautiful trailer.

The huge Winnibago Special sat in the middle of a garden of newly planted saplings of pine and spruce. Two rows of rose bushes lined the path to the entrance of the trailer and, on the door, the banner read, 'Welcome Home Juliana'. The scenery was in complete contrast to the devastation of last Thursday. There was no sign of the broken trailer that had been her home.

She took the hand of the driver, stepped gingerly out of the limousine, allowing herself to be supported, unsure of the strength in her legs, and walked weakly into her new home with a smile on her face and tears streaming down her cheeks.

'Thank you Shamon, God bless you', she said.

She could hear the hoofs of horses as they trotted past.

'They know you are home', Shamon Kazi announced and strode into the kitchen to switch on the kettle.

Shamon Kazi had woken up at dawn on Sunday morning to put his horses through their paces. He had decided to spend most of the morning with Shamka alone and kept the other horses penned up in the constructed wooden corral in the hollows at the far end of the farm.

By sunrise he had gathered everything he needed for Shamka's special preparation. In the past he had either ridden Shamka and, for that matter, most of the other horses, bareback or he had used a general purpose saddle.

There was a purposefulness about this morning's activities.

Methodically, he selected the jointed snaffle bit. He had always preferred the use of the single-jointed, thick mouthpiece with wire rings because he knew that it acted upon the lips, the tongue and the bars of the mouth and was generally better than curb bits which acted more strongly upon the jaw of the horse.

Within moments Shamon Kazi had bridled and saddled Shamka with a comfortable racing saddle, adjusted the stirrup leathers and checked the stitching: something he did regularly. For his girths he selected the foam-padded cotton type which he knew was comfortable for the horse and, as he was opposed to bandages around the legs, he placed on the exercise boots. The boots, which were made of impact resisting material, also moulded to the shape of the horse's legs to prevent injury.

It was time to train for the challenges that were sure to come. Shamon Kazi mounted Shamka and noticed the pricked ears. The horse was ready and prepared to be put through her paces.

Shamon Kazi spoke to Shamka softly and she began to canter. Kazi followed the high line and rode along the edge of the farm past thick brush and fallen trees until finally they were in the clear; vast open spaces which dipped and rose according to the contour of the land. Shamon Kazi rubbed his hands over the mane of the horse and with his teeth together he flicked his tongue against the roof of his mouth to make faint clicking sounds.

Shamka understood his master's commands. The canter changed smoothly to a fast gallop as the wind blew cool and dry over the horse's mane and on the weathered face of the gypsy horse trainer. They kept up the fast pace for a mile before Shamon Kazi slowed her down and brought her to a slow trot. Up to now, all of their training had been in secret and Shamon Kazi was now satisfied that it was time for the world to witness a most amazing horse.

He got off the horse when they approached Bramble Creek and allowed Shamka to drink. After that he spoke to her, as he always did, in a quiet, serene voice before he remounted and walked her along the edge of the creek and back to the farm.

They approached the farm from the west. The magnificent filly showed signs of contentment and with her master proudly in the saddle they trotted freely towards the sun which was now breaking through the clouds. Kazi had declared this Sunday an open day at the farm for two reasons: first, the papers had made such a fuss over Shamka that just about every horse lover in the county wanted to see her; second, he was proud of his new trailer home and hoped that he would be able to thank those who had wished his family well during their short period of crisis. He hoped it would be a glorious day.

* * *

The party had been a great success. Vivian Maldini felt sure that she had finally managed to erase the blemish on the Maldini name. The powerful and influential people of Cromwell County would no longer see her husband as an ex-convict who happened to have made good. She hoped, indeed prayed, that the past was behind them. She was appreciative of the fact that her husband had involved himself with the magnificent horse that everybody was talking about and what better way to show the positive side of her husband than to have him play his part in the development of the godforsaken east side. She would contribute her share to make the new venture a success, because it would keep her busy and enable her to draw in other women who shared her zeal to do something for the community.

* * *

Once again the power of modern technology had made light work of the vast distance that separated Paul Wainright and William Nylander. The electronics expert had driven the short distance from his apartment to the office to collect the fax sheets of race schedules that the resourceful Wainright had sent.

Nylander planned to telephone Sheikh Al Makhtoum Walhadi later that morning. For the time being, he would make sure he had digested the information Wainright had sent.

There were eight races in all, details of each race on a separate sheet. Two sheets had been marked with an asterisk; two others bore double asterisk marks and another sheet with three bold asterisk marks in a circle.

Nylander arranged the sheets in order of importance. From the top, the three non-asterisked sheets, then one, followed by two and finally three. He placed the sheets on the coffee table, picked up the cover letter and began to read.

William,
Schuster and I met Jack Maldini today, an incredible man. Possibly a modern day Robin Hood (will explain when we meet). Cromwell County now absolutely ready for Shamka's first race. I have attached possible races but believe (***) to be the most promising. Maldini now part-owner in Shamka. Sponsorship from this end not a problem but would enjoy your presence for the making of history. PS. A Doctor Ben Swinton sends his regards. Handsome type. Carried off Schuster after party. Haven't seen her since. Let me know which race.
Best wishes, Wainright.

Nylander smiled at the cover letter, he could remember his conversation with Ben Swinton, pleasant man and lucky, he thought, because Schuster would be a perfect match.

He concentrated his attention on the race schedules, flipping through the sheets one by one. Shamka's first race could be in one of the maiden stakes or alternatively a novice race. Nylander reached for the diary and began to crosscheck the dates of the races supplied by Wainright. In time, he narrowed his selection down to three, basing his choices on the dates of the races and also, as indicated by Wainright, on the opposition and the type of race. Sponsorship would not be a problem, according to Wainright.

Nylander could guess where the money would come from. As far as he was concerned it did not matter who sponsored Shamka's races; the important thing was for the thoroughbred to be exposed on the racing circuits, from where he was sure Shamka would emerge, as he always believed, as the most spectacular racehorse in modern racing history.

William Nylander decided to pay Sheikh Al Makhtoum Walhadi a visit, but first he would call.

He dialled the number, waited for a brief moment and requested to speak to the Sheikh when a man answered.

'Mister Nylander,' the Sheikh said excitedly, 'I expected your call last night.'

I've just got the information today, Sheikh', said Nylander. 'Maybe you'd like to join me for lunch.' Nylander had decided on the spur of the moment that the Sheikh was obsessed enough about the mysterious Shamka to come to him. After all, Wainright had said that sponsorship was not a problem. Sooner or later horse lovers all over Arabia would know about Shamka, and he was sure that when they did, they would not be able to resist the temptation of the challenge.

They agreed to meet at two that afternoon at the Al Waseeb Golf Club. They would enjoy a light lunch together, play a round of eighteen and enjoy dinner at the Sheikh's home. That suited Nylander. When he replaced the phone, he returned his attention to the fax sheets.

Nylander narrowed the choice to two races:

The Cromwell County Race Course Maiden Stakes - which Paul Wainright had given a two-star rating - or the Mid Western USA

Chapter Twenty-Two

Classic Trial (A), the only three-star rated race and circled by Wainright. Nylander consulted the diary. Both races were on the same day: Saturday 20 May, in exactly four weeks. He circled the date in the diary and noted the race times in the appropriate time slots.

What next, he thought. The fact that he wanted Shamka to be entered in one of those two races meant nothing and Nylander knew it. As far as he could gather from Wainright's short cover note, Shamka had a new and powerful owner. It was obvious that Maldini would have every right to decide which races Shamka would race in. How much did the man know about horses?

Nylander closed his eyes and began analyzing all the possibilities in his mind. Shamka had never been raced before in public, which made her a novice. If Shamka was as good as he believed, she would have to be tested against the best in Cromwell County and the best three-year-olds would be featured in the Classic Trial as Wainright had correctly indicated with the three stars. The horse would have to be put in at the deep end, where she would have to sink or swim, as the saying went. He had made his decision.

The first thing to do would be to telephone Paul Wainright and again try to manipulate the situation to keep him in control of Shamka's destiny. He was about to reach for the telephone when the loud ringing tone caused him to draw his hand away nervously. Nylander had not expected that. By the third ring he had gathered himself. He picked up the receiver.

'Nylander', he spoke into the receiver and waited.

'Good morning, William.' It was Kim Schuster.

'Oh, hello Kim.' Nylander could not hide his surprise. 'I was about to give Wainright a call. I have received the information he sent to me by fax.'

'Good', she said and giggled.

'Where are you, Kim?'

''On top of the world', she replied happily and giggled again.

'Are you all right?'

'Couldn't be better', she replied. 'Paul and I met Jack Maldini, what a party.'

'Good for you', he said sarcastically. 'I hear you met Doctor Swinton at the party, interesting man?'

'And gorgeous', she added still giggling.

289

'Excellent Kim, but you didn't call to talk about him, I am sure.'

'As much as I'd like to, the answer is no.' She was serious all of a sudden. 'I'd like to write a piece in the *Echo* tomorrow. I'll tell our readers that Shamka will be entered in the Mid Western USA Classic Trial on 20 May. I know I have no authority to do that, but I thought I'd seek your opinion first.'

There must be a God, Nylander thought. Seconds before Kim Schuster's telephone call, he was about to telephone Paul Wainright to instruct him to contact Kim Schuster to place an article in the *Echo* and following that, confirmation in the *New York Times* that arrangements had been made for Shamka's first race in the Classic Trial.

'Do you think that's a good idea? I mean, shouldn't you check with Jack Maldini first?' He felt like giggling himself.

'Come on now, William, show some balls. We've come this far dictating the pace, excuse the pun, and now you are telling me to seek permission?' She let the robe slip onto the floor and stood in the middle of her apartment, stark naked. She ran her fingers through her golden blonde hair. 'Say yes, because I'll do the article anyway.' She had reached the bedroom and stood in front of the mirror, quite content with the wonderful body she had been blessed with.

'I think you are right', Nylander told her.

'I'll get Paul to send you a copy of the article.' She was about to replace the receiver. 'By the way William, stay away from those dark-robed Arab women. I hear they wear chastity belts under those robes.' She giggled again. 'Chow.' She clicked off, made a face at her reflection in the mirror and walked into the shower.

'We'll make it ten dollars a hole', Nylander said to himself, picked up his golf clubs and went to meet Sheikh Al Makhtoum Walhadi at the Golf Club.

* * *

Commodity trading in the east side had resumed again despite the police presence which had become quite visible since the trial. The difference, though, was that most of the small-time drug dealers were now being hauled in on a more frequent basis to the police station as locals resorted to telephoning the drug line that had been set up by Braxton Walker and the community leaders.

The drug line had been set up only two days ago, a free phone number which the people of the community were encouraged to call, anonymously, to report any drug activity in the east side. The line had been sponsored by the city, with the help of Mayor Culhane.

Free advertising had been negotiated with the radio and the television station, again with the help of the mayor.

Culhane was determined to reunify his city. He had entered politics because he believed he could make a difference. The dereliction of the east side and the constant crime wave had always been a blemish on his otherwise successful record of bringing jobs and wealth to the city. Politics was Culhane's passion and, while he aspired to the seat of power in the State, he was practical enough to know that a mayor of a divided city stood little chance of wining the gubernatorial race in three years' time. The people of the east side community were giving him a chance to rectify this, and so Mayor Culhane was pulling all the stops to do what previous mayors had failed to do.

It was a matter of time before the mayor's efforts and the contributions of the community leaders would begin to bear fruit.

Smokey Peters was under constant surveillance, Frank Biggles was in jail awaiting trial for the murder of the two boys and Mo Franks, Big Joe Kelly, Shoeshine Joe, Sam Dingles and Paperbag Jones had all left town suddenly as the deadline imposed by Christina Coomes approached. For some of them, a trial awaited their return according to the conditions of the bail set by Judge James C Colman. Nobody seemed to know the whereabouts of Joseph 'Tiny Bags' Moses and nobody seemed to care, so long as he was not supplying the young men of the community with his tiny bags of poison.

Things were looking up in the community.

As always, the east side telegraphic system had gone into motion once again and the news was circulating fast about Jack Maldini's promise of help to the east side community, which was to be matched by the city. There was a lot of gossip about some miraculous horse but the details were sketchy. Those who were inclined to place a few dollars on horses, in the hope that their miserable existence might all of a sudden be transformed when their accumulated selections all won, were already beginning to calculate the possibilities of what might happen if they could manage to use the miracle horse as their 'banker' in future multiple bets. To the majority of the families in the community, however, it was the future prospects of jobs and simple hope that seemed to lift their spirits.

Christina Coomes put her two sons to bed and contemplated a telephone call to Doctor Braxton Walker. She looked at the clock, paced the kitchen floor for almost a minute and debated in her mind how she would begin the conversation with Braxton. She walked to the phone and picked up the receiver, then put it down again. Go for it girl, she thought to herself; she picked up the receiver and began to dial the number. She managed six digits, stared at the inanimate plastic receiver, 'shit girl', she said aloud and gently replaced the receiver again and walked off to bed.

* * *

They had been arguing for the past fifteen minutes, an unusual occurrence in the Carter home, especially in front of guests.

'I just can't be sure about the man's sincerity', said Simon Carter.

'You said yourself that he promised to do everything possible to help the east side community. Besides I told you again and again that Katherine was in no danger.' Maureen Carter showed exasperation.

The others simply watched as Simon Carter and Maureen Carter argued about the prudence of allowing Katherine to be whisked away to the party by Jack Maldini's messengers.

'Simon, the fact is, Katherine seemed to have enjoyed the occasion and certainly no harm came to her.'

Ben Swinton intervened, 'And I must say that Maldini is beginning to fascinate me.'

'That was kidnapping', Simon Carter said angrily. 'They could have taken her anywhere, I mean anywhere, then what?'

'But they didn't', Maureen snapped back.

'Okay, so this time they didn't. Can you be sure what might happen next time?' said Simon, the worry lines showing clearly on his forehead.

'Sweetheart,' Maureen Carter tried a truce, 'we are all concerned about the children's safety, so why are we fighting one another?'

'I just can't trust him', Simon Carter said finally. 'We'll have to be more careful from now on.'

'I've never seen a horse like that in my life.' Robert Singleton tried to steer the conversation away from the heat of the argument between the doctor and his wife.

'I was thinking the same thing', Broxy joined in, nodding her head vigorously. 'Honey, we must be here for that first race when it comes, I can't wait.' She reached out to her husband excitedly.

'Well, I couldn't miss the first race even if I wanted to. I've got a date', said Doctor Ben Swinton. They all looked at him.

'It's about time too.' Maureen Carter had rejoined her husband on the sofa, the argument between the two of them now truly forgotten. 'When do we get our chance to meet this mysterious person?' She was smiling mischievously at Ben Swinton.

'Kim Schuster', Simon Carter answered for his friend.

'Kim Schuster?' Maureen Carter gawped, '*the* Kim Schuster?'

'That's the one', Simon confirmed. 'By the way, where did you two disappear to after the party?' he asked Swinton and watched the confused look on the Singletons' faces.

Ben Swinton looked sheepishly around the room, a broad grin on his face. He tapped the side of his nostril with his forefinger and sat back in the settee.

Realizing that the Singletons had no clue about what they were talking about, Maureen gave them an abridged introduction to Kim Schuster.

'You haven't heard the best part yet,' said Simon Carter, 'and I am sure this is going to make you girls really jealous. 'Ben danced with Rosalynn Brando.'

'Are we talking fashion here?' asked Broxy, leaning forward in anticipation of what she hoped would be the right answer,

'We *are* talking fashion, Madam', Simon replied and eyed the two women with an air of satisfaction.

'You didn't.' Maureen turned to Ben Swinton who was still nestled deeply in the settee.

Swinton simply looked at her, reached inside his coat pocket and produced the expensively printed menu. He handed it to Maureen Carter. 'I knew you would appreciate this', Ben Swinton said and sank even deeper into his settee.

'By Golly, he did', said Maureen as she read the inscription Rosalynn had penned on the top left-hand corner of Vivian Maldini's exquisitely designed menu: *To Maureen, be fashionable, be chic, let your clothes enhance your personality, signed, Rosalynn Brando.*

Maureen handed the menu to Broxy who snatched at it and

examined the inscription as if she were in a position to verify authenticity. She nodded her head in approval, at the same time noticing the quality of the card and print. 'Jack Maldini has a bit of class', she commented and handed the menu back to Maureen.

'You'll have to introduce me to Rosalynn someday', Maureen said to Swinton. 'I shall treasure this.' She waved the menu in the air. 'Thank you for being so thoughtful.'

'There are some papers for Katherine to sign', Robert Singleton informed them. 'I am surprised that Maldini agreed to all of Katherine's terms, I'd also like to have a word with Shamon Kazi sometime tomorrow, is that possible?'

'I'll drive you down to see him tomorrow', Simon Carter told him.

'What about Kazeem? I shall miss him when he's gone', Maureen said wistfully.

'And so will I', Simon agreed. 'We'll give him an open door policy so he can come and go as he wishes.'

Maureen Carter refilled their coffee cups.

* * *

Unlike Vivian Maldini's grand affair on Saturday, Stumpy Lazarus was content to have a get-together with friends - not that he had many.

The decision had been made by Stumpy and Mickey Steiner to invite Jurelene Patterson and the girls to celebrate their success in the capture of Frank Biggles. Stumpy was looking forward to seeing Jurelene Patterson again and hovered nervously around Rosalynn Brando, who had taken on the responsibility of making the preparations for the party.

Mickey Steiner was playing chauffeur and would return at any moment with the girls.

'I am so proud of you', Rosalynn said to Stumpy as she strained the string beans at the kitchen sink. He smiled at her, unsure of what to say because he had no idea of what she was talking about. 'I'll be happy to help you if you'd like', she added, and continued with her food preparation.

'Help?' Stumpy was now confused.

'Yes, and I mean it. When you start your adult education classes, I'll be happy to help you along', she said with great sincerity and handed him the kitchen towel. 'I want you to know that it is never too late to learn new things, because life is about learning. Just let me know when you need me.'

They could hear giggles and laughter just before the door opened and all four girls followed Mickey Steiner into Stumpy's flat.

'Guess who is coming to dinner', Steiner announced grandly and began the introductions as the door shut behind them. 'Ladies, meet your hosts; Miss Rosalynn Brando and Mr Stumpy Lazarus.'

'Oh my God it's her!' shouted Lucy Sharpe, pointing to Rosalynn like some apparition. Lucy's reaction was not uncommon and Rosalynn was used to that. She offered her hand to be shaken by the four women in turn. They may have been considered the dregs of society by those who set themselves judge and jury above others they considered inferior, but these were women, America's women, and like most other women, they appreciated fashion and thus they appreciated Rosalynn.

With the exception of Jurelene Patterson and Lucy Sharpe who were known to Stumpy Lazarus, the other two girls, Mandy Waters and Sharon Watson, were new faces. All four women were hardened, pretty women who managed to survive by living on the edge. These were women from the east side, from deep within the bowels of the mammoth beast, America's island ghettos, where day-to-day living was a combat, their ability to survive, based purely on their womanly assets. They were the 'material' upon which, like the drugs, the survival of Smokey Peters, Frank Biggles and the other vultures depended.

Biggles was in jail and the others had scattered; the chains were now unshackled, and this evening they sat in the company of one of America's finest daughters, in the person of Rosalynn Brando. So Mickey Steiner poured the wine and they celebrated the triumph of decency over ugliness. As they ate and talked, each had their own story to tell; the overall consensus was that, at some point in their lives, they had turned left instead of right, just to make ends meet in a society where the big picture had been sacrificed for the greed and selfishness of the few.

'Life could be so much better for all of us in this wonderful city of ours,' Rosalynn Brando found herself saying, adding quite positively, 'but things are changing.'

It was the one statement that no one around the table could dispute.

CHAPTER TWENTY-THREE

The four bright yellow coloured sanitation trucks descended on the east side city streets early on a Friday morning to the delight of the residents. By nine the yellow juggernauts had managed to criss-cross through the whole community, often to cheers and waves from people on their way to work, and delighted children on their way to school. To some of those children, it was their first time of seeing street sweeping vehicles in action in their community. Immediately after the yellow trucks came, four more green tankers to spray water along the swept streets.

By noon, Shackle Avenue gleamed in the sunshine and asserted its right to be on par with the Park Avenues and Fifth Avenues of much more grander cities. This was American soil and Shackle Avenue for once seemed proud enough to let everybody know.

It was exactly three weeks to the day since the *Echo* had published the information about Shamka's entry in the Mid Western USA Classic Trial. The article had induced Jack Maldini to hold an emergency meeting with Shamon Kazi and Katherine Carter, following which he had personally endorsed the date and announced publicly on radio and television that Shamka was ready to live up to expectations.

Paul Wainright had managed to stoke up interest in the impending race with a brilliant article in the *New York Times* and once again the telephones had rung and rung.

The Holiday Inn on Townsend Avenue and the Cisco River Hotel had taken all the reservations they could, and were now fully booked for the next two weeks. But the reservations kept coming from all over the world, and now even the smaller hotels and motels in the east side were receiving a fresh coat of paint.

In a small conference room in City Hall, Mayor Culhane chaired an important meeting.

Culhane was a politician but unlike his predecessors who were all old and often hardened businessmen and who simply considered the east side of Gulver City as a wasteland unworthy of consideration as a part of a prospering small American city, he had always hoped that in time, and given the opportunity, he would amalgamate the city which he had come to love so much.

A graduate of Penn State University with degrees in Politics and Economics, the mayor, now thirty-seven and married with two children, was intent to prove to America that there was a way to couple the strengths of capitalism with the best of socialist ideas to improve the lot of every person in the community he had been elected to serve.

'Ladies and gentlemen,' he beamed at the small group of people in the room, 'I know how busy you are, so I shall keep this meeting brief. But before I say anything else, I would ask you to spare a moment to watch this footage with me.' He then pointed to his young assistant at the back of the room who immediately dimmed the lights and turned on the projector.

At first they were unsure of what they were watching, as the screen brought to life various day-to-day activities of ordinary citizens. Soon, they had become aware that they were watching their own community as familiar street names and the downtown area of Gulver City was projected onto the screen. One or two of them shuddered when they heard the gunshots and watched three hooded young men scramble out of Crocker Savings Bank on Cromwell Avenue. They watched as two of the three were gunned down by uniformed police officers while the third made a dash for the entrance to the Holiday Inn where a Japanese tourist and his wife were held at gunpoint by the hooded man.

Instantaneously, the scenes changed. They watched the pristine streets and enormous homes nestled in the foothills of the Corsegrove Heights area, the haven of Judge James C Colman and the mayor himself. The scenes changed again, now at night as fabulously dressed men and women streamed into the Hood Acre, most laughing and of a very happy disposition.

The small conference room was completely silent except for the whirling sounds of the projector which now spanned the sprawling farms on the outskirts of town before returning to the city and then, as if someone had thrown a switch, the camera was racing along on top of a fire engine rushing through the city streets and heading east with loud sirens screaming to force ramshackle old cars and pick-ups out of their path.

Without prompting, the scenes had changed again, now daylight.

297

Children walked to school through filthy streets, some sidestepping drunks and drug addicts on the sidewalks of Shackle Avenue. The camera picked up the large clock in front of the east side community center. 8:45 it announced, but shadowy figures were already stumbling out of the Shackle Avenue Liquor Store with brown paper bags under their arms, no doubt containing the vodkas and the gins and the brandies which they hoped would carry them through the day. In front of the Pepperdine nightclub, pieces of paper and plastic bags floated gently in the wind as if to escape from the mounds of garbage piled along the side walk. A little further down Shackle Avenue, the east side Pentecostal Church stood in silence, its gates firmly shut to keep away the vandals who from time to time sneaked in to its hallowed interior to lift their spirits with their syringes of heroin.

Several lines flickered across the screen and then the screen went blank as the whirling sounds of the projector finally clicked and fell silent.

The light came on in the small conference room. Mayor Culhane walked slowly to the front of the room and faced his audience.

'Ladies and gentlemen,' he sighed heavily, 'as you saw, it is impossible to carve up a city into sections, one section immune to the activities of the other. Up until now we seem to have been content with containing crime on the east side. But you know, sooner or later, the drugs, the murders, the muggings, the burglaries and the rape of innocent women and little girls will find a way to cross the tracks and spread its tentacles through this whole city. This city is polarized, sitting on a powder keg waiting for the fuse to be lit. Now that's the dark side.' Mayor Culhane looked in the direction of Braxton Walker and Christina Coomes. 'Please excuse the pun.' They smiled back at him. 'The bright side is what I am interested in, what I am sure you are interested in, hence our presence here in this room. I tell you we have the greatest opportunity ever to set a bright example for this state, this nation and possibly even the world. We have already started crawling, but soon I expect us to stand and like a toddler take our first tentative steps towards our goal. In the not too distant future I expect us to be walking boldly forward, together, east side, west side, black, white and colours in between.' He folded his arms across his chest and hoped they shared his vision.

At this point, the mayor invited his young assistant, the projection-ist, to join him up front and to bring them up to date on what City Hall had managed to do so far.

'As the mayor has already alluded to,' the bespectacled young man began, somewhat overawed by his audience, all of whom were much older than his twenty-three years, 'we have made great strides in a very short time. Police presence in the east side has been increased five-fold, the Sanitation Department has been supplied with extra trucks and will now clean the community three days a week; by the way, that started today and we have received several telephone calls already from members of the community expressing their gratitude.' He seemed proud of himself as he watched heads bobbing up and down in approval. 'The Police Commissioner has confirmed our own internal figures which seems to show a sixty per cent reduction in the transaction of illicit drugs within the community. Obviously we are aiming for one hundred per cent success in this area and we hope in time, to be successful.'

'Thank you, Bob', the mayor said to his young assistant who nodded shyly and resumed his seat by the projector. 'Now, ladies and gentlemen, one of the pillars of our society, and in my view a big part of the engine that will move this city forward to where we wish to go, please welcome Mr Jack Maldini.'

Nobody clapped, and nobody was expected to. This was a serious affair, a meeting to assess where the city was going and how it was going to get there. So Jack Maldini strolled up front and shook the hands of the mayor who sat down and allowed Maldini to begin.

'Friends...' That was unusual for starters. Jack Maldini had never called anybody a friend with the exception of Lazlo, Templeton, Watson and, of course, Old Man Slade. 'Most of you know me or at least know of me', he spoke calmly, confidently. 'I have to admit that I have been a part of the problem, and I will explain. You see I have made money from the Pepperdine over the years. I own several other small businesses in the east side, but I was running so fast that I never stopped to look at the fact that there were people suffering. You know,' he paused to reflect, 'it took an exceptional sixteen-year-old girl to open my eyes.

'There is nothing wrong with capitalism and I am sure some of you in this room may disagree, but look around you and you'll see what I mean.' Jack Maldini spoke sincerely. 'The current positive attitude which is being shown by members of the east side community needs to be recognized and I can tell you why we are seeing such enthusiasm. They can see something in the future: benefits, comfort, satisfaction, something to aspire to, a decent future for the children, but, above all, they can see hope. And I'll tell you this, when there is hope, the hopelessness that drives a person to drugs and crime disappears.

'Last night I drove through the east side, and although I never gave much thought to the place, I could see great potential. Believe me, ladies and gentlemen, we are going to transform this city. I mean the whole city, but with emphasis on the east side.' That was that. He had told them what he intended to do and they knew he would deliver.

This time they applauded, rapturously. They acknowledged the fact that the city stood a much better chance of success with Maldini's millions behind the colossal project.

After Jack Maldini's brief speech came the Police Commissioner and then Braxton Walker, who was now considered by everybody as the official spokesperson for the east side.

After the meeting, they stood around in clumps of twos and threes. They chatted quietly, their faces beaming and bright. The occasional laughter erupted from one or two of them, as they talked about the impending race on the coming Saturday and the business opportunities which were now quite visible.

The sleek black limousine pulled up at the bottom of the concrete stairs in front of City Hall. Jack Maldini shook the mayor's hand and bounded down the stairs. They all watched him. Some thought of how fit he was for his age, others were envious of the man's power and wealth. Nonetheless, they watched him until he disappeared into the plush, dark interior of the limo, and they watched until eventually there was nothing to watch.

* * *

Saturday was approaching fast. The city was bursting at the seams with the masses of tourists, journalists, television and radio people and some commodity traders. The difference was, the city was changing. Commodity traders were picked up just as quickly as they came. Some were hauled away from the Greyhound Station straight to jail while others were stopped in their cars at the city limits and turned back.

The Cisco River Hotel bar was shifting more cocktail and beer than it had ever done before. The patrons were mostly from out of town, as far afield as Los Angeles, London and Sydney. Paul Wainright and Kim Schuster deserved medals. They had been instrumental, along with their scheming partner in crime, William Nylander, in fuelling the belief that Saturday's Classic Trial would unveil a horse on par with the great Wajima and Sir Galahad. There was excitement, a buzz in the air, so they drank and talked about horses and famous victories.

In the sea of people in the Cisco River Hotel bar, he sat alone. He should have been at the bar, on his usual corner stool, propped up by the long, highly polished slab, from where he consumed his whiskeys and water and when in good spirits a glass or two of Harvey Wallbanger. Tonight, he sat in the middle of the bar, the only table he was lucky to find. One small table, one chair, in a sea of humanity pre-occupied with Saturday's big race. They swam around him as he sat alone, lost on an island in his own wicked thoughts, plotting the downfall of the man he hated above all others. Jack Dawson stared into the half-empty glass of beer and wished Jack Maldini darkness.

It was a simple plan. The race was on Saturday - a week from tomorrow - which gave him enough time to contact the various banks and go liquid. Going liquid was a term he had heard Jack Maldini use on several occasions. To Dawson, going liquid simply meant drawing all of his savings from the various banks in preparation for his well, orchestrated plan. He hated Jack Maldini, no doubt about that, but he had to be careful because as he had often reminded himself that Jack Maldini had a dark side.

They were swirling around him; newspapermen being as boisterous as always, TV camera crews, now relaxed and confident in the knowledge that the heavy trucks had arrived with their cables and camera equipment in preparation for the big race. By tomorrow they would begin rigging up the racecourse and plugging Gulver City and Cromwell County into the rest of the world. This was the age of television and the TV crewmen were enjoying themselves with the famous words: *testing, testing, one-two-three.*

Dark side or not, Jack Dawson was determined to deal a heavy blow to Maldini for showing him little respect, which Dawson felt he deserved. The gall of the man. Maldini had thrown him out of his office in front of that gypsy, that bum, and all because Maldini had more money than him. Yeah, he would go liquid, he thought, and seek the help of the Arab to bring Jack Maldini's empire crashing down like the proverbial ton of bricks.

Jack Dawson awoke from his slumber and looked at his watch. He drained the half-glass of beer, reached for his hat, barged his way through the crowd, ignoring the admonition of several of the TV men, and walked out of the bar. He decided to take a stroll along the river to concentrate his mind before driving to the Holiday Inn to keep the eight o'clock appointment.

Dawson arrived in the lobby of the Holiday Inn Hotel at ten minutes to eight. Keeping time was one of his strengths. He pulled the folded sheet of plain paper from inside his coat pocket as if to confirm its presence, shoved it back into the pocket and approached the girl at the desk.

The girl looked at him, the smile on her face fading as she took in the man's wrinkled coat and pasty appearance.

'Can I help you, sir?' she asked, her tone carrying a different meaning, like, what is someone like you doing here?

'Meeting with Sheikh Al Walhadi, penthouse suite, eight o'clock', he said brusquely. 'Name is Dawson, Jack Dawson.'

'Oh, Mr Dawson,' the smile was back as she flicked through several messages, 'the Sheikh is expecting you, just a moment please.' She picked up the telephone, pressed a couple of buttons and waited. 'Mr Dawson for Sheikh Al Walhadi, she said into the phone, listened for the instruction and replaced the receiver, still smiling. 'Top floor. Someone will meet you when you exit the elevator, Mr Dawson. Have a pleasant evening, sir.'

Dawson entered the elevator, 'Fucking bitch', he mumbled to himself and floated upwards towards the penthouse.

He was met by a tall, dark Arab in a sharp suit when he stepped out of the elevator. 'Jack Dawson?' the Arab asked, and when Dawson nodded, began to frisk him expertly without another word. 'Please follow me.'

A podgy, mean-looking Arab sitting by the door to the penthouse eyed him suspiciously and opened the door for Dawson to enter.

'Ah, Mr Dawson.' Sheikh Al Walhadi stepped towards him, his hand outstretched. The two men shook hands. 'I believe you have some important news.'

'Yes your highness', Dawson said nervously, squeezing his hat tightly, the perspiration showing clearly on his forehead.

'Please.' Sheikh Al Walhadi pointed to the comfortable cream leather sofa.

Jack Dawson looked around the plush surroundings, unsure, and finally sat on the edge of the sofa.

'Well', the Sheikh said simply and took his seat in the settee opposite.

The air conditioning unit hummed quietly from somewhere in the tastefully decorated penthouse. Dawson shifted position nervously on the edge of the settee and coughed. The Sheikh looked at him, completely relaxed and waited.

'Your highness', Dawson began. Al Walhadi felt like telling him to get on with it but maintained his calm exterior, his face businesslike. 'It's about next Saturday, the Classic.' He coughed again, this time covering his mouth with his hand.

'Yes', Al Walhadi waited.

'Shamka will not win', Dawson said emphatically.

'Oh!' Al Walhadi said and waited to be informed.

'It's all a con, it's a set-up.' He reached into his coat pocket and slowly pulled out the folded plain paper.

'You are sure of this?' the Arab said, more a statement than a question.

'Yes your highness, I am absolutely sure and I have proof.' Dawson unfolded the single sheet, unsure of what to do with it.

'Why do you think I am interested in this information?' Al Walhadi feigned disinterest. 'Your telephone call sounded more important than this.'

'Yes sir, I mean your honor, eh, your highness.' He shifted again, the paper shaking visibly in his hand. 'You see, the *New York Times* and our own local newspaper have written a great deal about your opinions about Shamka. I must say first of all that I agree with your opinions one hundred per cent, yeah, one hundred per cent my highness, I mean your highness. And I know something else.' He looked at Al Walhadi directly in the eye for the first time since entering the room. 'There have been many comments, comments by some very rich people in this city. People who know nothing about horses, unlike your good self, and the word going around is that...' He paused and wiped his forehead with the back of his hand. 'Well, the word is that, and this time I quote, "If those desert boys think they know anything about horses, they can put their petrodollars where their Koran lies." sorry about that my highness. Sorry sir, your highness.'

That offended Al Walhadi. He had made up his mind when Dawson walked into the hotel that he did not like the man, but he was willing to listen to him. He was unsure of Dawson's motives. However, he believed that last statement. The man was nervous, unsure of himself, in fact pitiful. It would be impossible for such a man to make up that last bit about petrodollars and the Koran. Now, that was an insult and he would make someone pay heavily for that.

'Who are these rich people?' Al Walhadi asked calmly.

'There are quite a few sir, your highness, and I will give you every information you need.' He wiped his mouth with his right hand. 'It's just that I might ask for a small consideration for my information, a very small consideration.'

'Such as?' Al Walhadi said sternly.

'Well, your highness, I am sure that Shamka cannot win the race on Saturday. I also know that you have, with your expert knowledge and wide information network when it comes to horses and racing, a pretty good idea of which horse will most probably win the race. I was wondering if you might see your way to granting me a small favor in return for the names of these wealthy people and anything else I can tell you about Shamka.' He smiled cheerfully.

Jack Dawson had no idea about diplomacy or how to conduct himself in circles other than the criminal fraternity within which he saw himself as quite an astute individual. His brief dialogue with Al Walhadi had somehow satisfied him immensely. After all he had found the right words like 'your highness' or was it 'my highness', he felt quietly satisfied with his final sentence, in his mind, a powerfully, diplomatically worded sentence; a sentence which sounded a whole lot better than his usual rough, 'You scratch my back and I'll scrape yours.'

'Mr Dawson, in my country we take all racing very seriously. I mean all racing, and that includes camel racing, Formula One racing and of course horse racing, particularly horse racing. This Classic on Saturday is really not that important. I am sure you know that yourself. I am here out of curiosity and also because a friend wanted me to come. You may have heard of him - a Mr William Nylander of Nylander Electronics.'

Jack Dawson had not heard of Nylander and frankly he didn't care, but he nodded his head vigorously and added, 'Oh, yes, very big, very successful businessman.'

'I was at Ascot last year, and then at the Epsom Derby. Missed the Kentucky, though, but I expect to be there this year.'

Again, Dawson nodded vigorously. He had never left the United States and had never heard of Ascot or Epsom. He hoped the Sheikh would not ask him any embarrassing geographical questions.

'As I was saying,' Al Walhadi continued, 'we take our racing seriously, so even though this Classic Trial is unimportant, we have managed to enter a horse which will put Shamka to shame once and for all.'

Beautiful, Dawson thought, going liquid all the way.

'About these rich men,' Al Walhadi smiled at Dawson, 'Will they take bets on Shamka?'

'Yes Siree.' Dawson had gone liquid and forgotten diplomacy for a moment.

'I agree to your terms, Mister Dawson. Now, who are these rich people?'

Dawson began to reel off the names: 'Jack Maldini, Samuel Templeton, Jake Watson and Joe Lazlo.' He took in a deep breath and then exhaled, very slowly. He felt drained all of a sudden. 'All very rich men', he concluded.

These were the men who had sustained him for years. They had taken him from the scrapheap and given him a job. They had given him access to some of the most exclusive clubs in the city. They had paid his medical bills, allowed him four weeks' vacation a year and arranged for his taxes to be handled by their own accountants.

He felt faint all of a sudden. 'Could I trouble your highness for a glass of water', he said, having returned to his diplomatic mode. In his head, the single name bounced around: *Judas, Judas, Judas.* He accepted the glass of water from the podgy Arab when he appeared, drank it loudly and returned the glass to Podgy without a word of thanks. Al Walhadi watched him.

'Do you think these men will accept a straight bet with me?'

'A straight bet?'

'Yes, a very straight bet. Shamka wins, they win. Shamka loses, they lose', Al Walhadi said, his voice flat, without a shred of emotion.

'I guess so. How much does your highness have in mind?'

'Ten million dollars,' the Arab said, 'US of course and cash.'

'Ten million!' Dawson shouted. His eyes bulged, danced out of their sockets momentarily and returned into his head.

Sheikh Al Walhadi simply nodded.

'I'll have to come back with an answer to that your highness, say tomorrow?'

'Tomorrow is fine, Mister Dawson.'

Al Walhadi was intent on punishing anybody who had the temerity to call him an Arab boy. Did they not know that the almighty Allah himself put the oil in the desert to sustain his children? And as far as putting the petrodollars next to the Koran, did they not know that the Holy Book was the guidance for the humble Bedouin in the vast desert underneath which the rivers of oil flowed? The infidels should be punished, he would see to that.

Dawson folded the plain sheet of paper and placed it back in his coat pocket.

'Just a minute Mister Dawson, you had proof.' Al Walhadi extended his hand and waited for Dawson to fish the paper out of his pocket.

'You agreed to my terms your highness,' he said and handed the paper to the Sheikh. Al Walhadi looked at him angrily.

'Do you doubt my word?'

'Oh no your highness,' Dawson said quickly, 'never.'

Al Walhadi unfolded the plain paper and began to read. It was a photocopy of a letter addressed to Jack Maldini, from Jake Watson.

Dear Jack

You know I write about two letters a year, but I feel I must say this to you in writing. Following our meeting with Sam and Joe, and having viewed the horse on Sunday, I must, this once, go against your judgement.

Sure, Shamka looks good, a true thoroughbred and indeed wonderful to behold. However, the horse has never been exposed to racing conditions. You know full well that thoroughbred racing is a demanding and expensive business. I should like to wait a little longer before I make my final decision with regard to Shamka.

I doubt that she can win her first two or three races, but after that, who

knows. It is my opinion that Joe Lazlo and Sam Templeton agree with you,
so this short letter is to register my 'no' vote.
I shall of course accept your decision should the final vote go 3:1 against
me.
My love to Vivian.
Your ever loving friend Jake.

The Arab handed the letter that bore Jake Watson's signature back
to Dawson with a smile. 'Proof indeed, Mister Dawson, solid proof.'
   'I knew you'd be satisfied, your highness.' he was folding the letter.
   'Sword Dancer', Al Walhadi said, rose from the settee and extended
his hand to Jack Dawson.
   'And my small favor?' Jack Dawson shook Al Walhadi by the hand
and waited.
   'I just fulfilled my side of the agreement; Sword Dancer.' He
repeated the name and ushered Dawson to the door. He stepped out
of the penthouse to find Podgy and Sharp Suit having a conversation
in Arabic. They both looked at him, then turned to continue with their
conversation.
   Dawson found the elevator and floated happily to the ground floor.
He stepped out of the elevator with a spring in his step. He was going
very liquid with Sword Dancer in his mind. He could see the front-
desk girl watching him intently. He took off his hat with his left hand,
bowed slightly, waved it twice in front of his body and blew her a
massive kiss with his right hand. He glided out of the Holiday Inn,
found the car and headed towards the Cisco River Hotel.
   He hoped he would find his corner stool unoccupied.

CHAPTER TWENTY-FOUR

Mayor Culhane was keeping his word and the people of the east side of Gulver City were showing their appreciation. They lined the streets and cheered as the limousine approached the community hall, only half a mile down Shackle Avenue.

'Stop the car', the mayor said sharply to the driver. Beside the mayor sat Braxton Walker and across from them Bob, the mayor's trusty young assistant. They both looked at Culhane, unsure of the mayor's intentions. The limousine pulled to a stop in front of the Prim and Proper Laundry. Culhane jumped out and headed for the old woman who had been waving a clean white handkerchief joyfully. By the time the mayor reached the woman, he had been joined by Braxton Walker and Bob.

He extended his hand to the old woman. 'I am Mayor Culhane', he said and shook the woman by the hand. 'What's your name, madam?'

'Sister Palmer.' The old woman pumped his hand. 'They all call me Ma', she added, still pumping.

'Ma,' said Culhane, 'it's a great pleasure. How long have you lived in this community?' he asked, having managed to free his hand.

'I was born here Mister Mayor, been here for sixty-nine years', she said and laughed, showing good white teeth, all of which belonged to her and not a denture in sight. 'Been running the Prim and Proper for well nigh forty years', she said proudly, pointing to the laundry behind her.

'Well now,' the mayor turned to Braxton and Bob, noticing the crowd which had suddenly gathered, 'isn't that something?'

'You are doing a wonderful job, Mister Mayor and I want to tell you I voted for you and will do so again', she said exuberantly, her old black face gleaming in the bright sunshine, eyes engaging.

'Tis a pleasure to meet you Ma, and I give you my promise that as long as I remain mayor, we'll make your community a better place to live.' He offered his hand for more pumping, said goodbye and, to loud cheers and applause from the crowd, entered the limousine to continue his journey to the community hall.

Culhane had made Ma's day. She returned to her seat in the laundry and accepted congratulations from all those who loved her so much. That afternoon, Ma cried quietly with joy; her community was indeed changing.

* * *

It was a first. Never, in all the years that Jack Dawson had worked for Jack Maldini and his three friends and associates had a meeting been called by anyone else but them. On this occasion, they had gathered in one of the Red Rooms because Jack Dawson had some important information for them. It was extremely urgent, according to Dawson, so they sat around the polished mahogany table and faced him as they always did in their regular monthly meetings.

Dawson squeezed his hat under the table and watched the four men.

'Well Jack,' said Maldini calmly, 'we are all here.'

'Yes sir, Mister Maldini.' He cleared his throat self-consciously. 'It's about the big race on Saturday', he said and waited.

They watched him, not a word from any of them.

'There is this Arab, see, name of Sheikh Al Walhadi. Met him through some of my contacts.' He squeezed the hat some more. 'He doesn't believe your horse Shamka will win the race on Saturday and wants a big bet.' He smiled nervously.

Sam Templeton whipped out a huge cigar, clipped the end and waited instinctively for Dawson to hover around and light it. Dawson did not move. Sam Templeton struck a match and lit his own cigar, eyeing Dawson through the flame.

'Wants a big bet you say?' Joe Lazlo said and frowned.

'Yes sir, Mister Lazlo, that's what he wants.'

'Okay,' Maldini said, 'so what's a big bet?'

'Ten mill', Dawson replied instantly, and for some strange reason, added, 'US.'

Jake Watson shook his head slowly. Templeton looked at Lazlo who smiled and then turned to Jack Maldini who showed no emotion whatsoever.

'It's a straight bet', said Dawson. 'Shamka wins, you win; Shamka loses, you lose.' Lazlo thought he detected a whisper of a smile on the edges of Dawson's mouth. We should have fired this guy a long time ago, he thought and smiled.

'Do you know which horse this Al Walhadi thinks might win the race?' Maldini asked Dawson.

'No sir, Mr Maldini', Dawson lied.

'Thanks Jack', Maldini told Dawson. 'Can you wait outside for a minute while we discuss this?'

'Sure, Mr Maldini, I'll be outside.' Dawson shut the door behind him.

'Ten million, now that's a bet', said Maldini.

'We don't know anything about this horse, Jack', said Jake Watson.

'Ten million', Joe Lazlo repeated.

'Exciting', said Templeton.

'What's the maximum we could raise between the four of us?' asked Maldini.

'Thirteen tops from me', said Templeton, blowing smoke.

'Eighteen from me is possible', chipped in Lazlo.

Jack Maldini turned to Watson. 'You know my feelings about this Jack, but if we've got to go, sixteen tops from me.'

'Thanks Jake.' Maldini had always considered Jake Watson a true friend. 'And thirty-three from me', said Maldini.

He whipped out a small, dainty calculator from inside his coat pocket and began to press buttons.

'Okay, gentlemen, this is what I propose', he said after the brief calculation. 'Al wants a ten million bet, that's fine. But we all know that a man who talks ten is probably considering a tenth of what's available to him if he is on his own. In this case, I am guessing that if Al is on his own, he's worth about one hundred. Now, if he has access to funds from other associates, and I am guessing he has got three more, just like ourselves, and assuming he is the leading man amongst his group, the other three must be worth say fifty each. If Al is alone he will stick to the ten but if I am right and he has associates, based on the assumptions I've made, we'll be looking at a tenth of two hundred and fifty million.' He looked at the others and knew those sharp minds were with him all the way.

'Remember too that Al is an Arab so chances are the funds are available. Gentlemen, I propose we up the bet to forty, which is fifty per cent of our total.'

'Exciting', Templeton said again and puffed a huge blue smoke from his cigar.

'Now, we'll do this the fair way', said Maldini. 'I'll go sixteen and a half, which is fifty per cent of my total. Sam, can you go six and a half?' Maldini checked with Templeton.

'Six and a half, fifty per cent, sure', Sam Templeton agreed.

'What about you Joe, put you down for nine?'

'Nine is fine', replied Joe Lazlo.

'I know I am being foolish, Jack, but I'll stand for eight', Watson said before he was asked.

'What if Al refuses the raise?' asked Lazlo.

'Then we'll come back to ten and do two and a half each.'

'One more thing, gentlemen.' Jack Maldini replaced the calculator in his coat pocket. 'You know we have a big project going on in the city and the east side needs our help so if Al goes forty and we win, we'll take two and a half each and donate the extra thirty million to the city.'

'We've got schools to build, exciting', Templeton said.

They all shook hands. There was not a paper in sight for signatures but they had sealed their agreement. Jack Maldini pressed a button. The security man opened the door and Jack Dawson walked into the Red Room.

I hope we haven't kept you too long, Jack', Maldini told him and asked him to sit down. 'We've decided to accept a bet with Mr Al Walhadi because we believe Shamka will win the Classic Trial on Saturday', he said confidently. 'Forty million on Shamka to win, cash, US.'

Jack Dawson swallowed; the eyes bulged, rolled outside the sockets and disappeared back in. 'Forty mil', he croaked.

'Forty million, Jack,' Maldini was very calm. 'Please convey our message and inform me by Wednesday evening if he accepts.'

'Yes sir, Mr. Maldini.' Dawson shot out of the chair and made a dash for the door. 'Forty mill', he repeated and disappeared.

* * *

The most peaceful place in the whole of Cromwell County was Shamon Kazi's farm. Juliana Kazi was now on her feet again and life was back to normal. The city now had too many people and amongst them, naturally, were some undesirables. However, law and order had taken center stage in the city, both east and west.

Taxi drivers were earning bundles and they were no longer afraid of venturing into the east side, even at night. The demarcation line was fading and one particular city in the whole of America was doing everything possible to excise the cancer that made ghetto communities possible. Culver City endeavoured to become a shining beacon and the majority of its citizens were contributing their part to make it possible.

Jack Maldini was the name and Jack Maldini was the man. He was the engine that was steadfastly towing the whole locomotive along. In the engine room, though, were some serious boiler makers; Mayor Culhane, Braxton Walker, the Police Commissioner Jason Biggins and many, many more. Their activities were paying dividends, but the biggest dividend of all fell heavily on the shoulders of Shamon Kazi and his son Kazeem Kazi.

The decision had been made, once again in a meeting between Katherine Carter, Jack Maldini and Shamon Kazi. Katherine had sought the counsel of her parents and Shamon Kazi and had had the decision sanctioned by a secret vote at the children's last meeting. Kazeem Kazi had been conspicuously absent at that meeting. In the end the decision had been made and the jockey for Saturday's big race meeting had been decided.

It was now mid-week, early morning, and the two rode side by side, Shamon Kazi on Talisman, the black gelding, and Kazeem Kazi on the chestnut filly, Shamka. The boy listened as his father spoke. He spoke few words and even that, only occasionally. They trotted the horses for a while, then walked them and then galloped them. At Bramble Creek, they rested and the horses drank. It was to be their last day of serious training before the big race. There could not have been a more peaceful place on earth that morning, than the tranquillity experienced by the horses and their riders at Bramble Creek.

* * *

Paul Wainright arrived from New York on Wednesday evening and headed straight for the *Echo* offices to have a final meeting with Kim Schuster.

William Nylander shared dinner in the Holiday Inn penthouse that Wednesday evening and almost fell off his chair when the Sheikh informed him privately about the forty million dollar bet.

Chapter Twenty-Four

'My God Al, have you gone mad?' Nylander had expressed his shock in the most verbal way possible and heard the Sheikh reply, as if without a care in the world.

'If Shamka wins, it'll be worth every dollar to have seen it happen.'

It was the same Wednesday night that Jurelene Patterson and Lucy Sharpe started work in the Pepperdine. For the first time that any one could remember, the Pepperdine served drinks without the drugs on the side. In honor of its owner, the head bartender had managed to concoct a special cocktail and named it after the amazing horse that was to carry the hopes of the whole community on Saturday. The recipe for the Shamkamaldi special was displayed proudly at the bar and at a price of $2 per cocktail. Who needed drugs.

* * *

Mickey Steiner spent the Wednesday evening with Rosalynn Brando. He practically lived with her now, spending their time either at Steiner's flat or at Rosalynn's home. It was over dinner that Wednesday evening that the subject came up again.

'I've always wondered you know', she said with a wicked glint in her eye. 'I'd bet anything you two knew each other very well.'

'Which two?' He knew exactly what she was talking about but pretended as if he had no clue.

'Come on now Mickey, a woman can tell these things you know.'

'What things?'

'You've had something to do with Doctor Swinton before. I know it. It was in both of your eyes.'

There was no reason to pretend any more, so he told her the full story.

'You've got to give it to the guy, though; in the end he paid the full amount. I got it from one of the security boys. Apparently, Jack Maldini tried to write off the bet but the doctor wouldn't have any of it. The one I really felt sorry for was the other doctor, Swinton's friend, Simon Carter. He was at the party too. In fact it's his daughter who owns Shamka along with Jack Maldini.' He looked at her. 'I would like to apologize to him someday.'

'Don't be too hard on yourself. I am sure you were only doing your job', she stated trying to ease his burden.

'Yeah,' he said simply.

313

There was silence for a while as they carried on their own thoughts.

'Jack Dawson has been acting very strangely these past few days. I know he is up to something although Stumpy doesn't seem to see anything wrong,' he said.

'He is a bit of a strange character, that Dawson', she said. 'I wish Stumpy wouldn't trust him so much.'

'Stumpy is fine, really, he just never had a chance. Someday I'll tell you about his background, harsh, real harsh.'

'Did you know he went to his first evening class last night? English and maths. He was so proud he telephoned me today to tell me. By the way, I've promised to help him along.'

'That's good.' He was smiling.

'That's where he is right now, in class', she said and they both laughed, not in jest but pleased for Stumpy's efforts.

'I can't wait till Saturday, it'll be quite a race. Do you really think Shamka can win?' She sounded slightly worried.

'She'll win,' he said with certainty, 'for two reasons. One, Jack Maldini lives a charmed life, and two, there was too much good in that little girl, you know the doctor's daughter. You saw her at the party. How could her horse lose?'

'I hope you are right. I'll bet twenty dollars on her', she said excitedly.

'Make it forty', he taunted.

'I will.'

* * *

Wednesday was also the day that Jack Dawson went liquid. It was a busy day for Jack. Four different banks, scattered across town. It was not so much the distances between banks that caused him to feel frustrated and angry. It was the time he had to wait in each bank to get the closure paperwork sorted and finally for the account to be closed.

Four banks and approximately six hours later, Jack Dawson had gone completely liquid. Exactly $178,234.46 liquid. He carried every cent he owned in two sacks in the trunk of the Chevrolet and drove north.

The bookies he had selected for his 'investment' were not well known to him. They had come as recommendations from Isaac Pascalis. He had thought of using Isaac but the man drank too much

314

and talked too much. Their conversation about the best bookies in the county had been casual. Dawson had made it seem as if Jack Maldini and his associates were considering some shrewd bets and that they wanted the whole business hush, hush. Naturally, Pascalis had pointed him in two or three directions, so Dawson drove north feeling liquid and dreaming of getting much wetter by Saturday evening.

Dawson felt good. He began to whistle as he drove. In his mind he could picture the race as the horses entered the final two furlongs. Some silly horse he could not remember the name of was in the lead, followed closely by a promising grey filly. He could now hear the commentary clearly and stopped whistling. In the final furlong, he could see her now, and the commentary was much louder now, *'It's Sword Dancer, and it's Sword Dancer going clear now chased by.'*

The truck driver saved his life. He pulled the cord long and hard and the horn blasted sound waves through the foothills to bring Jack Dawson back to his senses. He swerved just in time and felt the gush of air and sand blast his face as the heavy rig swished by him with only inches of space between the two vehicles. It would have been his fault. Dawson was racing in the truck driver's lane. The truck did not stop. Dust and smoke billowed behind it and in Dawson's head the loud sound of the horn just kept bouncing around.

Jack Dawson survived the trip north and deposited his liquidity with the bookies in exchange for a slip of paper that promised to pay him 12:1 if Sword Dancer conquered all on Saturday. He did not need a calculator to tell him that he would be a millionaire twice over by Saturday evening. That excited him, so he took a piece of paper and a pencil from the glove compartment and worked out his future: exactly $2,138,808. He threw the pencil and paper on the floor of the car, brought his palms together and rubbed them gently as if afraid to squeeze the air out. 'And that's US', he said quietly, although there was not a soul in sight.

According to Dawson's calculations he would be a multimillionaire by Saturday evening. Jack Maldimi should have lost at least ten million; he figured a quarter of the forty million dollar bet to be Maldini's.

He had kept the forty-six cents from his liquid assets in his pocket, plus the fifteen dollars he had in his wallet. That was all he had in cash. For the next couple of days he would live off the credit cards, and God knows he had many of those, so he drove south and thought of Jack Maldini.

This time he did not visit the racetrack. He would leave that till Saturday.

* * *

It was difficult to explain why Wednesday 17 May had assumed such importance in the lives of many individuals in Cromwell County and Gulver City in particular. One explanation was that most people were drawing a line under whatever the past must have been for them. They could see a new dawn coming and the midweek activities were simply to be prepared long before Saturday.

For more or less the same reasons, Christina Coomes had decided to clear her slate before Saturday and this Wednesday evening was the time to do so.

In Christina's mind, the most villainous human being in Cromwell County was Smokey Peters. The man was simply vile. Unlike other commodity dealers who had taken the hint and made themselves scarce, Smokey Peters considered himself a businessman. He could still be seen from time to time on Shackle Avenue, dressed to kill, hat askew and doing the walk, you know, like his left leg was hurting and that he had to lean more on the other leg to walk comfortably.

Smokey is known to have said to a newspaper reporter the day he walked out of the Pepperdine after the Braces incident, 'What went on in there ain't none of my business. I am a businessman. I don't deal in guns. I deal in Ds, Gs and Bs.' The reporter, incidentally from the *Echo*, is reported to have pressed Smokey to explain himself further, at which time Smokey apparently translated his Ds, Gs and Bs to mean drugs, girls and booze.

He was treading a thin line lately, especially since the second warning from Stumpy Lazarus for him to avoid any kind of contact with Jurelene Patterson and Lucy Sharpe.

Smokey entered the Mousetrap Cocktail Bar on the corner of Shifton Street and Shackle Avenue just before six. He wore a pair of dark glasses and, despite the warm temperatures, he had a long cashmere coat draped over his shoulders. He took the dark glasses off because the interior was dim, the hat, as always, askew. It took him a moment or two to attune himself to his surroundings and spot the black woman in the red dress at a small table in the far corner of the cocktail lounge. She was looking directly at him.

His left shoulder dipped slightly, the left leg waggled and the strut was on, cashmere coat looking good. She smiled disarmingly when he arrived and watched him as he took great care to hang the cashmere and then the hat. Smokey was focused, the woman looked good. There was therefore no reason to pay any attention to the other couple at the table several paces away from them. He took his seat, made a motion of brushing his short hair backwards with both hands and threw his first verbal jab.

'Oh baby, where you been all my life?' That was Smokey's favorite line. 'A pretty flower like you must have a name?' he said, flashing gold teeth.

'Abigail Coomes', the young woman said shyly, giving her correct name.

'Tell me Abigail, what's your best drink?' He was already waving for service.

'Coke', she replied, leaning forward, elbows on the table, fingers interlocked under her chin and a bright, admiring smile on her face.

'Coke for the pretty lady and double gin and tonic for me', he told the waitress, all the while staring at the cleavage that Abigail chose to show him.

'You say you are from San Fransisco?'

'Yes', she replied, still showing cleavage.

'What brings you to Gulver City and who recommended me?'

Abigail took her time. She was articulate, confident and very attractive so it was easy. She told Smokey Peters that she had attended San Fransisco City College in California but she had had to drop out because of financial constraints. After that, a friend had introduced her to a wonderful young man, 'sort of like yourself', she had thrown in, who had introduced her to rich businessmen. Things were going real good until suddenly the young man died in a terrible car accident. She could no longer face being in San Fransisco alone, so she had come home to Gulver City to live with her sister for a while.

A few days ago, she had met some girls in the Pepperdine. They had talked. She needed money and did not have a job so...

'Your name came up, they gave me your number and here we sit.'

'Do you do drugs?' he asked suddenly.

'I don't even drink beer.' She picked up her glass and sipped the coke.

'Do you have your own place?'

'You must be kidding, with no money? I live with my sister and her husband.'

He showed anger for the first time. 'Damn it, girl, if you are planning on working for me, the first thing you got to learn is that none of my girls talk to me like that, understand?' He stabbed the table with his finger.

'Okay sugar', Abigail said meekly.

'Another thing, you'll dress the way I say, you'll sleep with who I say and when I want you, you come to me, understand?' She understood.

'Be back in a minute.' He got up and headed for the door marked gents.

Abigail checked the tiny microphone in the small broach on her red dress and made sure the tape was still running. She could see Lieutenant Carpichi and her sister still at the table several paces away. The job was almost complete.

'You say you don't do drugs. Did your boy in San Francisco do drugs?' asked Smokey when he returned.

'Sometimes.'

'Did you ever carry for him?'

'Carry for him?' She decided to plead ignorance.

'Yeah baby, didn't he ever send you to deliver packages?'

'Oh! that', she said knowingly.

'Well baby, Abigail, you will carry for me. You see, I only do drugs on special occasions but there are fools out there who want to do it all the time. So I sell it to them, lots of it; you name it, I sell it. I am going to have to teach you how to use coke for recreational purposes and I am pleased to say that lesson will start tonight. Tonight, you and I will do some coke and I don't mean that shit you are drinking. I mean pure, good quality, Colombian cocaine to recreate ourselves. Yeah, that sounds good don't it? Re-create ourselves.' He was flashing gold and looking at her cleavage.

'I've always wanted to do that', she smiled seductively. 'If you have any of this good stuff at home, why don't we just go and start the re-creating.' She leaned further forward, exposing a little more flesh. 'Master', she added.

They picked him up outside the doors of the Mousetrap. Christina Coomes hugged her sister Abigail tightly. She had performed beautifully, and for her contribution Smokey Peters was now in the hands of the law.

Christina felt the gentle tap on her shoulder. She turned to face the lieutenant. Carpichi hugged her, gave her a kiss on the cheek and handed her the handcuffs.

'Please do me the honor.'

'I warned you, Peters', Christina said and slapped the cuffs on Smokey's wrists. His hands were behind his back. 'You should have got out of town when you had your chance. Them old days are gone, brother.'

That was the best game of 'solution' ever. Christina Coomes had pulled off the sort of solution Maureen Carter had planned for Jack Dawson. In Maureen's case, the problem had solved itself, so she had enjoyed the company of Broxy and sent her back home with immense gratitude.

Broxy and Robert were due back on Friday, the day before the big race, the day on which Simon Carter was to remove the cast on Kazeem Kazi's arm.

CHAPTER TWENTY-FIVE

The heavens opened up without warning on Friday evening. It was a deluge. Within minutes the streets had cleared as citizens sought shelter, helter-skelter. It lasted for about an hour and, just as quickly as it had come, the rain stopped.

Vince Krakowski had been the clerk of the Cromwell County racetrack for over fifteen years. The sudden deluge had worried him. He walked the course with the course stewards to check the condition of the racetrack. All the forecasts for tomorrow's race had pronounced the 'going' to be *good to firm*. It was their duty to ensure the fit state of the course and to pass their observations to the jockey club and the newspapers and television. And so, several men walked the course and discussed Saturday's big race.

In the *Echo* offices, preparations were under way to give full coverage to the Classic in the Sunday papers. Kim Schuster had worked tirelessly for sixteen hours straight, yet she managed to look gorgeous when William Nylander and Paul Wainright walked into the office at eight this Friday night.

She smiled at the two men with whom she had become quite close during the past few weeks and led the way into her office.

Paul Wainright pulled a chair and sat opposite Schuster, who settled herself in her chair behind the desk. Nylander did not bother to sit down. He folded his arms and leaned against the wall.

'How's the doctor?' asked Nylander.

'Fantastic', she replied, smiling. 'He is coming to the race with me tomorrow.'

'I am amazed at you two', Nylander told the two reporters. 'I can't believe that Shamka will race in a Classic Trial tomorrow.'

'You'd better believe, William, because it is going to happen, tomorrow', Kim Schuster said.

'The question is, can she win?' asked Wainright.

'There is a forty million dollar bet says she won't', Nylander told them.

'What!' Wainright shouted.

'You know Al Walhadi has entered a horse in the race, don't you?' said Kim.

'Yes, Sword Dancer,' replied Nylander, 'and from what I understand, a very good racehorse. Had her brought in all the way from Kentucky.'

'What about this bet?' Wainright said.

'It's quite simple and straightforward. Al Walhadi says Shamka will not win and Jack Maldini says she will'. Nylander explained.

'For forty million?' Wainright asked.

'For forty million', confirmed Nylander.

'What if Shamka does not win the race but finishes ahead of Smoke Dancer?' Wainright wanted to know.

'You mean Sword Dancer', Nylander corrected.

'Yeah, him.'

'It's a filly,' said Nylander, 'so a she', Nylander corrected again.

'Damn it William, just answer the question', Wainright retorted.

'Shamka must win the race or Jack Maldini loses the bet, period'. Nylander informed them.

'Forty million', Wainright said and whistled. 'That Maldini has balls.'

'Paul, in one of your notes to me in Saudi, you referred to Maldini as "possibly a modern day Robin Hood", what did you mean?'

'When Kim and I interviewed Jack Maldini in his home on the day of the party, he said something I'll never forget.' Wainright fished out Maldini's statement, word for word, *'When are you gonna learn that greed drives us all. I've known men who are so greedy that, if it were possible to bottle the air that we breathe, the world would be short by about a billion human beings. Others just have much more money than they know what to do with. It is from these people that I enjoy taking money. The Red Rooms in the Hood Acre are for that purpose - to relieve the extremely wealthy of a small percentage of that wealth.'*

Kim Schuster had one elbow on her desk, her beautiful face resting in her palm. 'Do you know what he does with the money after he has taken it from those he calls the greedy ones?' She was looking coolly at Nylander who was shaking his head and no doubt curious to find the answer.

'Have you heard of the Slade Foundation?' she asked Nylander.

'Yes, who hasn't? Don't tell me Jack Maldini is involved with the Slade Foundation.'

'He is not involved with it William, he *is* the Slade Foundation.'

Kim Schuster went on to lecture William Nylander about the history of the Slade Foundation.

The Slade Foundation had been established twenty years ago, several years after Jack Maldini had come out of prison. While in prison he had managed to run his businesses with the advice and guidance of the oldest man in the prison, a man named Brad Slade. Slade had used his influence to connect Jack Maldini with the prison warden, and subsequently the prison governor, with whom Jack Maldini became very close. With the help of these men, Maldini's companies were initially given the contracts to supply just about every item that was required by the prison system in Cromwell County. In time, the contracts extended to the State and eventually throughout the whole Mid West. Some say that Jack Maldini's companies supply the needs of more than fifty per cent of America's prisons. As profits rolled in, Maldini established the Slade Foundation in honor of Old Man Slade. The Foundation offered university scholarships to bright underprivileged children; funded medical research in selected medical schools; and provided food and medical aid to several developing countries throughout the world.

'It's a billion dollar Foundation and getting bigger all the time,' Kim Schuster concluded.

'So forty million dollars is not a problem, should Jack Maldini lose', said Nylander.

'You are wrong William.' Kim Schuster's thoughts flashed back to the meeting she and Wainright had held with Jack Maldini in his study on the day of the party. 'Money is always a problem, Miss Schuster.' She had learned about the Maldini logic that Saturday afternoon and, as she thought about Maldini's words, she became absolutely convinced that Shamka and her owners would emerge triumphant in tomorrow's Classic Trials.

* * *

Saturday 20 May descended upon the city wearing a cloak of cloud. The watery sunshine had begun its battle early, and by the hour of eleven the sun had won that battle and blazed gloriously over Cromwell County.

There was an unusual serenity about Gulver City and for once both east and west of Cromwell County's most populous city embraced a day with one heart, one mind and one common purpose. They were going to the races and they were all behind the one name, the one thoroughbred about which they had read and heard so much over the past few weeks. Shamka had put Cromwell County and Gulver City on the map, so the people of Cromwell County honored the day by trooping to the races.

As promised by Mayor Culhane, the streets on both sides of the city glistened in the morning sun. The Holiday Inn and the Cisco River Hotel began to disgorge their patrons onto the west side city streets before noon. On the east side, the smaller hotels emulated their bigger, grander cousins without shame. Shackle Avenue began to fill with people. Not blacks with a sprinkling of Latinos and whites, but people.

They had come from all over the world. They had been accommodated, protected, fed and now disgorged onto Shackle Avenue, all with one purpose in mind; to find their way to the Cromwell County race course to witness the race of a lifetime as pronounced by the *Echo*'s morning headline.

Lucy Sharpe stood at her favorite window and gazed down the east side streets. She had never seen those streets so clean. It suddenly dawned on her that she had indeed never seen such a mix of people either.

'Jurelene,' Lucy shouted, 'you've got to see this.'

They stood side by side in the window and gazed down the streets, upon the whites, and the blacks and the Latinos and the other colours in between. They gazed upon the young and the old and upon men and women. For once they noticed that the eerie gloominess that constantly hung over the east side seemed to have been lifted like a cloak. The faces showed no fear nor anxiety.

'Let's go to a horse race', Jurelene Patterson, the beautiful black girl, said to her redhead room-mate as they turned to hug each other.

* * *

The Cromwell County racecourse opened its arms at exactly eleven thirty on Saturday 20 May and prepared to embrace the multitude, some of whom had travelled from afar to witness what the *New York Times* billed as 'a race which will unveil a remarkable horse the likes of which have not been seen this century'. The first scheduled race was at one o'clock. By twelve thirty, the racecourse was almost full. They had come primarily for the 3:05 race, which the programme listed as:

The Cromwell County Classic Trials
(3-Y-O: $230,000: 1m) (12 runners).
Below, followed a list of twelve horses, all thoroughbreds, along with the number of the horse, the owner of the horse, weight to be carried, the name of the jockey and the stall from which it would race.
1. **Rock Solid** Cromwell Racing Enterprises 9-0 K Bradwell (11)
2. **Shampoo** Mrs Tammy Funswell 9-0 A Alexander (3)
3. **Prickle Weed** Time Share Racing 9-0 T Nixon (9)
4. **Sword Dancer** Sheikh Al Walhadi 9-0 S Mahmood (4)
5. **Shamka** Miss K Carter/J Maldini 9-0 K. Kazi (5)
6. **Dollars & Dimes** Mr S M Boxer 9-0 J Kratski (10)
7. **Chu-Chu Train** Dr T L Samson 9-0 J Tamara (1)
8. **Flaming Arrow** R Jacobi 9-0 P Chevron (8)
9. **Pure Procedure** F Tamazi 9-0 K Tamazi (12)
10. **Krakle and Pop** Y Yazikawa 9-0 S Maru (2)
11. **Switchblade** Mr K Grundi 9-0 O Pollock (7)
12. **Chase Me Home** D S Mason 9-0 T M Appleton (6)

Two of the first three races laid the foundation for what was to come. They had turned out to be a nip and tuck affair between three horses and eventually one had ended in a dead heat and the other had been won by a beautiful gray, which the owners had for some reason, named *Moonshine*.

Jack Dawson arrived early. He watched bookmakers lay their odds for the big race and felt a quiet satisfaction when the odds on Sword Dancer were slashed from 9:1 to 7:1.

The twelve horses paraded in full view of those who had come to watch the making of history. The city had gone into a coma, all activity centered on the racecourse. Television cameras brought close-up pictures of horses and jockeys into homes, factories and shops across America. Some analysts discussed the reasons why Shamka could not win, while others swore that they had never seen a horse in such fine shape.

As three o'clock approached, Shamon Kazi checked Shamka for the last time. He would have noticed the loose stitching on the stirrup leathers but for a minor distraction.

'We've come to wish you luck', said Katherine Carter, Jack Maldini beside her. The two spoke briefly with Shamon Kazi and to Kazeem Kazi who prepared to mount Shamka for her pre-race warm-up.

'This is for luck, Kazeem.' Katherine handed the jockey a silk handkerchief on the edges of which she had stitched her name and the names of John Carter, Kazeem Kazi and Jill Nylander. 'We shall ride with you', she said and followed Jack Maldini back to the stands. The Carters did not mind.

Gulver City and Cromwell County had waited for this race for a long time. The seconds seemed to tick much more slowly now and most felt a strange sensation of excitement, apprehension, anticipation and anxiety. Those who had gone as far as placing substantial bets on Shamka to win the race even felt a certain amount of fear.

Jack Dawson had not had much sleep the night before. His eyes hurt along with his head as he meandered through the crowd. He perched himself at the railings near the finishing line, close to the exit gates. When the race was finished and he had won, he needed to be in a position to reach the car and drive north. He could hear the shouts as bookies slashed the price of Sword Dancer from 5:1 to 3:1. That did not concern him. In his pocket was a slip of paper which guaranteed 12:1. It had almost cost him his life on the highway last Wednesday. He felt the slip in his pocket and visualized the two million dollars plus, then picked up the binoculars and searched for Shamka. 'Would the stirrup stitching separate at the right time?' he wondered. That was his little insurance.

The trumpet sounded, bells rang and the crowd went wild with anticipation. The time had almost come. Gulver City, the divided city, had pinned its hopes on a chestnut filly that no one had ever seen on a racecourse.

Handlers began to load the stalls. Bookies worked frantically. Shampoo jumped from 12:1 to 16:1; Krakle and Pop showed at 6:1; some rushed to take that price having watched it drop from nines. A roar went up as Shamka was quoted at 3:1, joint favorite with the respected Sword Dancer.

Broxy Singleton squeezed her husband's hand tightly and tried to contain herself. Maureen Carter sat between her son and Jill Nylander. Behind them, Katherine Carter was sandwiched between Jack Maldini and Joe Lazlo. Five of the twelve horses had been loaded into their stalls. Rock Solid bucked and kicked but eventually settled and entered stall number eleven.

'I saw Sword Dancer when she won her first two races down south', a voice behind Dawson said. 'She is a great horse and S Mahmood is a fantastic jockey, can't see them losing.' Dawson felt much better. He turned to the 'clairvoyant' behind him and smiled - a liquid kind of smile.

Simon Carter must have been the only person on the city streets this afternoon. The emergencies at the hospital had delayed him. At one stage he had been sure he would not be able to attend the race but things had quietened down later. There was not much time but he was determined to try. The engine responded when he pressed down on the accelerator, only three miles to go. He looked at his watch, 2.58 - seven more minutes before the off. He gritted his teeth and drove. He negotiated the final bend and saw the racetrack ahead. The trumpet sounded as he pulled to a stop amongst the maze of cars and ran through the turnstile, flashing the special pass that Katherine had given him.

The stalls flew open and twelve thoroughbreds charged out, a mile the quest. Jack Dawson felt the bump and ignored the mumbled apology from the panting newcomer. The binoculars were glued to his eyes, twelve horses filling his vision as riders jockeyed for position. The horses ate up the meters and spectators cheered and willed them on.

'And here we go, half a mile gone and half a mile to go,' the course announcer's voice boomed from the loudspeakers, his running commentary crisp and informative. *'Its Rock Solid taking them along, followed closely by Switchblade and Shampoo. Prickle Weed, Chu-Chu Train and Flaming Arrow are all in a line and behind them comes Shamka, who is tracked by Sword Dancer.'*

On Shamka, Kazeem Kazi relaxed and balanced the horse. Even then, with half a mile to go, he knew the race was his for the taking. She cruised along beautifully, effortlessly.

There was no warning. The stirrup just snapped.

'I think there is trouble. The jockey on Shamka has fallen. What a tragedy.

My, my, my. The loudspeaker boomed, 'Rock Solid is joined by Shampoo. They are followed closely by Sword Dancer, who has just breezed by Dollars & Dimes. The race goes on but Shamka is dropping out of the bunch. She is in last place and fading fast. A quarter of a mile to go, it's Shampoo and Sword Dancer, these are tracked by Chu-Chu Train. Hang on, there is a jockey on Shamka. Ladies and gentlemen there is a jockey on Shamka but I see no saddle.'

Jack Dawson had lit a cigar and he blew a massive smoke ring. He placed the binoculars back to his eyes and scanned the crowd until he could count the hairs on Jack Maldini's eyebrows. He shifted his gaze to Katherine Carter and saw the tears. Just as stupid as the father, Dawson thought. Only a fool would sign as a guarantor for another man's gambling debts, a real shmuck, a loser, as he referred to Simon Carter.

His interest, this wonderful, glorious, sunny afternoon, however, was Jack Maldini. He shifted the binoculars once again onto Maldini. The man was on the verge of losing forty million dollars. Dawson hoped for some sign of distress from him, maybe a tear or even a wince to show the pain, the anguish Maldini must be feeling. He adjusted the zoom on the binoculars and drew Maldini closer to him. In his mind, he could picture it all. The demise of Jack Maldini and the rise and rise of Jack Dawson, Cromwell County's new power broker.

Kazeem Kazi had been taught an unforgettable lesson as a child. He could indeed hear his father's voice when the stirrup broke, 'You've got to learn to stay on your horse no matter what, because if your horse leaves you in snow or in the wilderness, it may cost you your life.'

The rest of the horses were ahead of him. Kazeem Kazi battled to save the saddle for he knew that if he won the race without the saddle, he would be disqualified at the weigh-in.

'Ooooh my goodness, this race is over. Sword Dancer has hit the front with just a furlong to go, but wait it's the wonder horse, it's Shamka, it's the wind, a hundred and fifty meters to go and it's Sword Dancer with Shamka in hot pursuit, and it's Sword Dancer and Shamka, it's Shamka! Oh my word, I've never seen anything like it, Shamka has won the Cromwell County Classic Trials - just!'

The racecourse erupted. Hats sailed through the air. Blacks hugged whites and whites hugged blacks. The poor rubbed shoulders with the rich and the demarcation line melted away in the liquid sunshine.

In the excitement, no one saw him struggling. At first he grabbed his chest with his right hand, then with both hands. He was gasping for air as the pain shot through him. Jack Dawson swayed; first forward, then backwards and finally, with his eyeballs rolling around in his head and eyes wide open, he fell into the hands of the panting latecomer. Simon Carter went to work immediately. He worked on just another heart attack victim.

Gulver City, Cromwell County, a quiet, divided community in America's Midwest, celebrated victory. The victory of a city reunified by the belief of those who refused to succumb to evil and greed, belief in the invincibility of a thoroughbred.

Shamka had won the Classic Trials. Could she win a Classic? The Epsom Derby? The Kentucky Derby?

What do you think?